Anne Perry is a *New York Times* bestselling author noted for her memorable charact... hist... ... ... social and ethical issues. Her ... the ... g willia... ... have been published in multiple languages. Anne Perry was selected by *The Times* as one of the twentieth century's '100 Masters of Crime'.

Death in Focus is a gripping thriller of espionage and murder introducing Anne Perry's fans to a vibrant, new heroine.

Anne Perry has written over sixty novels,
all of which are available from Headline

For a complete list of all Anne Perry's novels, visit:

www.headline.co.uk
www.anneperry.co.uk

Anne Perry

DEATH IN FOCUS

HEADLINE

First published in 2019 by
HEADLINE PUBLISHING GROUP

First published in paperback in 2019 by
HEADLINE PUBLISHING GROUP

1

Cataloguing in Publication Data is available from the British Library

ISBN 978 1 4722 5727 7

Typeset in Adobe Garamond by Palimpsest Book Production Limited,
Falkirk, Stirlingshire

Printed and bound in Great Britain by Clays Ltd, Elcograf S.p.A.

HEADLINE PUBLISHING GROUP
An Hachette UK Company
Carmelite House
50 Victoria Embankment
London EC4Y 0DZ

www.headline.co.uk
www.hachette.co.uk

To Anna Maria Palombi,
who first introduced me to Naples

List of Characters

Elena Standish – a photographer
Margot Driscoll – her older sister, a war widow
Charles Standish – Elena and Margot's father, an ambassador
Katherine Standish – Elena and Margot's mother
Ian Newton – an economic journalist
Walter Mann – an economic journalist
Lucas Standish – Elena and Margot's grandfather
Josephine – Elena and Margot's grandmother
Peter Howard – works for MI6
Pamela Howard – his wife
Roger Cordell – Cultural Attaché at the British Embassy in Berlin
Winifred Cordell – his wife
Cecily Cordell – their daughter
Winston Churchill – former politician, now out of office
Jerome Bradley – Head of MI6
Cossotto – an MI6 agent in Italy
Jacob Ritter – an American journalist
Zillah Hubermann – works to save fugitives from the Nazis
Eli – Zillah's husband, a research chemist
Marta – the Hubermanns' housekeeper

Adolf Hitler – Chancellor of Germany

Joseph Goebbels – German Minister of Public Enlightenment and Propaganda

Commandant Beimler – a Berlin policeman

Mitzi Kopleck – an old friend of Katherine's in Berlin

Kurt Weissman – Cecily Cordell's fiancé, in the Gestapo

Max – a forger

Chapter One

1933

Elena narrowed her eyes against the dazzling sunlight reflected off the sea. It was warm in the May afternoon, the light so much softer here in Amalfi than it would have been at home, on the English coast. Brilliant sprays of bougainvillaea arched against the sky, burning purples and magentas, vibrant with colour but without perfume. They covered parts of the ancient walls, old, mellow stone houses, and flights of stairs down towards the whispering sea. There were glimpses of mosaic pavement, two thousand years old, and children playing marbles. Above them seagulls hovered on the wind, looking for scraps.

Elena was staring at a woman further down the steep hill. She wore a scarlet dress and she was dancing by herself, within her own imagination, perhaps lost in time in this exquisite town on the edge of the Mediterranean, which had lured the Caesars from the wealth and intrigue of Rome to dally here.

'Do you suppose she is real?' a man's voice said gently behind her. It was on the edge between pleasure and laughter. 'Or could she be a figment of a fevered imagination?'

1

Elena turned to look at him. He was noticeably taller than she, and the sun caught the auburn lights in his thick hair. His face was in shadow, but she could see the outline of it, his strong bones.

'Oh, she's real,' she replied with a wide smile. 'Should I be sorry? Would a vision be better?'

'Only for a little while. Reality always comes back. If it didn't, you'd be considered mad.'

'Oh dear,' she said, keeping a straight face with some difficulty. 'And I thought dancing in a red dress was the ultimate sanity.'

He shrugged. 'An old woman with a bag of onions would be more interesting than most of the delegates at the economics conference I'm attending!'

Elena laughed outright. 'I will tell Margot you said that!'

'Margot? Is that her name?'

'My sister, dancing alone in a red dress? That could only be Margot!' She meant the implied praise and the exasperation, and yet fleetingly she wished for a moment that that figure could have been her.

The man looked startled, as if unsure for a moment whether to believe her or not.

She saw it and laughed again. 'Really.'

Margot was her older sister, who had come to this very tedious conference on a whim. She was bored, and she wanted to come to Amalfi anyway, so she had offered to come with Elena, who was to photograph the delegates. 'It will be more fun to go together,' Margot had insisted. 'You can't take photographs all the time,' she had added in the slightly disparaging way she always used when speaking of Elena's photography.

For Margot, Elena's photography was something to do,

and a way to make a moderate living, but she also knew it was a passion that she herself did not understand.

Elena could not argue. Margot could usually read her too well, at least in the uncomfortable things, like self-protecting lies. Perhaps it came from being those few years older.

And of course Margot knew about Aiden Strother. Not all of it. Nobody but Elena knew that, although no doubt others had guessed. Elena had started out after university in a high position in the Foreign Office, due in large part not only to her excellent academic record, but to her father's position as British Ambassador in several of the most important cities in Europe over the years: Berlin, Paris and Madrid in particular.

Elena had fallen in love with Aiden while working for him. It had been easy to do. He was charming, handsome in a wry, good-humoured way, and clever. Very clever. He fooled them all utterly, even Elena. But she was too in love to accept the signs, which in hindsight she now saw quite clearly. He had betrayed them all, and she had been stupid enough to help him, albeit unwittingly. Looking back, she burned with shame at her own stupidity. The only good thing was that nobody thought her guilty of complicity, only of being young and incredibly naïve.

All the same, she had been asked to leave, to the acute shame and embarrassment of her father, Charles. He had felt that, of his two daughters, she was the one to follow in his footsteps, perhaps rise as high as a woman could in the Foreign Office. Elena's brief enchantment with Aiden was still an obstacle between her and her father. She was guilty of gross stupidity and had not denied it. It still hurt when anyone chose to mention it, not for a lost love, or even an illusion of it, but because she had been stupid and had let everyone down, especially herself.

Charles had never quite understood his elder daughter, Margot, but he had always adored and admired her, and everyone felt the consuming grief that had smothered her life when her husband of one week had been killed in the last month of the war.

In the square alone, Margot had stopped dancing and was beginning to walk slowly up the steps towards Elena and the young man, every now and again lost to sight by a bend in the walls, or an over-exuberant bower of coloured bracts.

'Don't tell me she's an economist?' The young man spoke again, amusement still in his voice, but quieter, as if he were aware of her momentary emotional absence. Fifteen years after the war, everyone still had their griefs: loss of someone, something, a hope or an innocence, if not more. And fear of the future. It was in the air, in the music, the humour, even the exquisite, now-fading light.

'Certainly not.' Elena kept the lift in her voice with an effort. 'And please don't ask me if I am.'

'I wouldn't dream of it.' He held out his hand. 'Ian Newton. Economic journalist. Sometimes.'

She took it. It was strong and warm, holding hers firmly. 'Elena Standish. Photographer. Sometimes.'

'How do you do?' he replied, and then let go of her hand.

'And that is my sister, Margot Driscoll,' Elena said.

'Not Standish . . . she's here with her husband?'

'Margot is a widow. Her husband, Paul, was killed in the war.'

Ian Newton nodded. *Of course* . . . This was a situation everyone encountered every day, even now, fifteen years after the war had ended. He looked over to Margot, destined to dance alone in a world populated by superfluous women.

4

'Will you and Mrs Driscoll dine with me tonight?'

'I'd like that,' Elena answered for both of them. 'Thank you. We're staying at the Santa Catalina.'

'I know.'

'Do you . . .?'

'Certainly. I followed you here.'

She did not know whether to believe him, but it was a nice idea. 'Eight o'clock? In the dining room?' she suggested.

'I'll be waiting,' he replied, then turned and walked away up the hill easily, straight-backed.

The next moment, Margot appeared on the steps from the square. She was as unlike Elena as sisters could be. Margot had dark eyes and hair like black silk. She was lean and elegant, no matter what she wore. Elena was the same height, she had a certain grace, but she could not match Margot's. Her eyes were quite ordinary blue, and her hair was nearly blond. She felt insipid beside Margot's drama.

'Daydreaming again?' Margot asked, exasperation thinly veiled in her voice. She hardly ever forgot her few years' seniority. 'If you want to be a serious photographer, you'll have to take some decent pictures, which you won't do standing here.'

'I don't know,' Elena said patiently. She had been nagged many times before, and although she knew it was true, she also knew Margot said it out of frustration and affection. 'I got a couple of a woman dancing alone in the square below, in a scarlet dress. A little crazy, but a nice study.'

Temper flashed in Margot's eyes for an instant, and then vanished again. 'I'll have them, please.'

'Don't be daft!' Elena said impatiently. 'I'm not wasting film on you. I just like watching you enjoy yourself.' It was the truth.

Margot put her arm round Elena and silently they walked up the hill, towards the hotel.

After lunch, Elena went out to see if she could get any pictures that captured the beauty of Amalfi. The town was very old and had once been one of the biggest ports in the Mediterranean. There was an unfailing permanence about it that was an ironic backdrop to the frenetic happiness of the people holidaying here, escaping reality for a brief season. The clinging greyness of the Depression melted in the sun here. The American music, with its haunting tunes and its clever, bittersweet words, emanated from the bars, encapsulating the emotions perfectly. In her imagination she danced to it in the arms of the young man whose hair was almost auburn in the sun.

But what picture would show the fragility of this place, the beauty that haunted it. You knew it, even as it wrapped its warmth around you. She had seen life-changing photographs of the faces of hunger and hopelessness, figures struggling against the overwhelming, and they had moved her to tears. But what could capture this? She really needed Vesuvius in the background, the sleeping disaster that hovered over Naples and could be seen on the skyline of every picture. It was nearly two thousand years since it had buried Pompeii and Herculaneum in fire and gas and burning lava. But it was waiting!

She imagined a dragonfly in the sun. Something that lives exquisitely, for just a few days. She needed a face that would mirror that, except with a knowledge of its own briefness. There must be one, if she were imaginative enough to recognise it. How could the camera show in black and white, light and shadow, all the brilliance and nuance of colour?

That was why she had not photographed Margot dressed in red, dancing by herself. It needed the splash of colour to say what she meant. A woman dressed bravely in scarlet, dancing alone. It was the perfect image of a million women in Britain – nearly two million, actually. They were called 'surplus'. That meant 'surplus to requirements', because there were no men for them to marry. Elena was another of them.

But maybe that was better than being locked in the arms of someone who marched to a different tune.

In the slanted light of the lowering sun, Elena saw exactly the picture she wanted to take. A young woman, younger than herself, perhaps twenty, was standing half-facing the light. It was soft, almost gilded, and it touched her gently, catching her youth, the totally unlined face. She had a mane of tawny-coloured hair, and the light reflected in her pale, hazel eyes. All the lines around her were straight, angular, classical. Only the smoke from her cigarette curled up in front of her, vague and wandering, but she did not see it.

Elena had her Leica out of her camera bag and found the focus, steadied a moment, then took the picture.

The girl heard the faint click of the shutter and turned. The moment was gone.

'I hope you don't mind,' Elena apologised. 'You're lovely, and you fitted the scene so perfectly . . .'

The girl shrugged. 'I don't care.' She gave a half-smile and walked away.

Elena was still thinking about that picture when she went up to the room she shared with Margot. It was time to change for dinner. She was looking forward to dining with Ian Newton, more than she had done with anyone for quite a while. Margot was ready for the evening. She had changed the red dress for a sequined gown in purple. It clung to her outrageously, and yet it was flattering. On someone else, it might have been vulgar, but she was so slender that it suggested her shape rather than revealed it. She looked gorgeous, and she was clearly aware of it, but then Margot always was.

'Where have you been?' she asked as Elena came in. 'There can't possibly be an economist all that interesting.'

'I got a picture of a girl in the fading light, which could be really good. The shadows caught and heightened the lines of her face,' Elena replied. 'For a moment, she was really beautiful . . . and young . . . and hopeless. It was as if she could see time rushing by in front of her, disappearing even as she put her hand out to touch it.'

'And so it is,' Margot said briskly. 'We'll be late for dinner, if you don't get a move on.'

Ten minutes later, Elena was out of the bathroom, washed and changed, her hair brushed and her face lightly made up, no jewellery but the ring she always wore on her right hand.

Margot looked at her critically. 'For heaven's sake, Elena! Everything about that blue dress says "stick-in-the-mud"! "Don't challenge me," it says. "I'm a watcher, not a player. I'm safe, don't disturb me."' She walked right up to her. 'You could be buried in it, and no one would be afraid you were still alive!'

'That's unkind,' Elena protested.

'It's true. You look about twelve, if you didn't have such a bosom. Take my black dress; I haven't worn it yet. And be quick.'

'It won't fit me,' Elena protested. She did not mean that. It would fit her rather too well.

8

'Oh, shut up complaining and just do it!' Margot ordered. 'It'll wake a few people up! You might even get a decent photograph. I take it you won't be apart from your camera for the evening?'

Elena obeyed. She knew Margot was right about the blue dress. It was safe; she'd been trying to be safe ever since Aiden. It was obliquely tactful of Margot not to say that. Another few minutes and she would have.

They went downstairs and into the dining room. Elena felt self-conscious in Margot's dress, and was aware of several heads turning, but which were staring at her she was uncertain. Margot's purple was just as startling.

Ian was waiting by the door, as he said he would be. He had his back half towards them, talking to a dark-haired man about his own age, tall and pleasant-looking. It was he who saw Elena and his eyes widened.

Ian turned and, recognising her, came towards them. 'You look marvellous,' he said simply. 'And you must be Margot.' He did not mention having seen her dancing in the red dress. He held out his hand. 'Ian Newton, how do you do?'

Margot smiled. 'Margot Driscoll. How do you do, Mr Newton?'

Ian turned to the other man. 'Walter Mann, Margot Driscoll and Elena Standish.'

Walter Mann took a moment or two to regain his composure.

Elena was surprised and amused. Was the black dress so breathtaking? 'How do you do, Mr Mann?'

'Miss Standish,' he replied, scrambling to catch up with the moment. He had level brows and very dark eyes. He turned to Margot. 'Miss Driscoll.'

'Mrs Driscoll,' Margot corrected, but with a smile. Widows of Margot's age were too many to count.

Ian took Elena's arm very lightly. 'I have taken the liberty of reserving a table for four.' He looked at Elena and Margot. 'I hope that's all right?'

'Of course,' said Margot. What else could she say?

Chapter Two

Margot walked across the dining-room floor towards the far side with its exquisite view of the sea. Walter Mann was charming, and he did not attempt to hide his admiration for her. She was not overwhelmed by it; it happened quite often.

They reached their reserved table and while Ian drew out a chair for Elena, Walter Mann asked Margot whether she would rather face the sea or the room.

'Oh, the room, please,' she replied. 'I love the sea, but it doesn't change very much. The people are always changing.'

'You're a people watcher?' He smiled as she took her place, and then sat beside her.

Margot laughed. 'That's more my sister. She's a professional photographer. Half her attention is on expressions, light and shadow, and framing a picture.'

'And she's good?' He seemed interested.

Margot saw Elena and Ian Newton were deep in conversation already. 'How honest do you want me to be?'

'Ah, have I stepped into a rip tide?' Walter Mann was too polite to laugh, but it was there in his eyes.

'Yes. Actually, she's on the edge of being very good indeed,

11

if she'd just let the emotions keep up with her technical skill,' she replied. That was the truth.

Even so, when dinner was ordered, and she ate with pleasure, part of her attention was on Elena. She was lost in the moment with Ian Newton. She seemed happier and more alive than Margot could remember ever seeing her. It was the way she used to be, before Aiden's betrayal of his country and, more personal, of Elena herself. She was so afraid of being hurt again. Who wasn't? And yet, to deny it was to kill part of yourself.

Margot had thought that she would find someone else to love, after a reasonable time of mourning Paul. But how long was 'reasonable'? For her, even fifteen years after his death, nothing was more than casual to her. She had idiotically hoped that there might be another love and yet guilty at even the possibility. How could she go on, when Paul was gone? There had, however, never been anyone else who mattered. Perhaps half Europe was like that, if you could see between the wine and the laughter. But for Elena it was different. There were no perfect memories with Aiden. They were all painful and needed to be obliterated, replaced by something that was at least honest.

While paying surface attention to Walter Mann, she watched Ian Newton. Even from the little she had overheard she learned he had been at Cambridge. So many of her family had been there, too. Her grandfather, Lucas Standish, although she didn't know what he had studied, was one. It was probably history and classics, or something like that. Her father, Charles Standish, had studied languages and modern history, obvious really, for someone who was going into the Foreign Office. Mike, her brother, had been going to read classics but war had interrupted all of that.

And Elena had gone to Cambridge too, and taken classics for the love of studying. Margot could imagine her sister sitting elegantly in one of the flat-bottomed punts, with Ian standing in the back, a pole in his hand as they glided smoothly along the shining river. Maybe they knew each other, at least by sight? She must remember to ask Elena.

Margot had not gone to Cambridge, or anywhere else. She had been a bride at eighteen, and a widow a week later.

Walter Mann was watching her. Was that compassion in his eyes? Damn it, she had no need of his pity! She smiled as if she were happy, and she was good at that. She had had sufficient practice.

There was a band playing gently and the music was hypnotic, exquisitely rhythmic, American. On the small dance floor young people danced as if lost in its embrace. She could see their faces, so many of them beautiful in their own way.

Why was she watching instead of joining in? Everyone had finished dining; it was time for her to enjoy herself.

As if reading her thoughts, Walter stood up. He smiled at her, meeting her eyes. 'Will you dance with me? That gown is marvellous. It really needs grace, movement. And you are exactly what it requires to be perfect.'

Her answering smile was sudden and quite genuine. He had not said what she had expected. 'Thank you. It is a new and rather appealing thought: so little is perfect.'

'I disagree,' he said lightly. 'Everything here is perfect: the light, the music, the faint air of desperation, as if it would all slip away the moment we stop enjoying it. It is like sunshine in an English April. It's so precious because we know that, in an hour or less, it will rain again. The light must go, and suddenly it will be even colder than before.'

13

She looked at him with real interest now, searching his face.

He kept the same charming smile. 'If it were here all the time, we would take it for granted and cease even to see it any more.'

The band was about to begin again, fingering their instruments. 'I would love to dance,' Margot accepted, taking a half-step towards him.

He held her very lightly. The music began in earnest, almost as if it were a literal tide sweeping them into its current. He was an accomplished dancer and, thank heaven, he had the good taste not to talk. Margot simply let herself move with the beat, enjoying it, following him exactly.

The music changed, and the rhythm, but it did not matter. He moved as smoothly from one to the other as she did. That was part of the secret of success, not only in art, but in life – moving from one beat to the next without hesitation.

Margot gave a little laugh of pleasure at his skill.

He held her closer, just an inch or two.

She leaned back and looked up at him. He had remarkable eyes. Did she see the pain of memory in them, or imagine it, mirroring her own? He held her closer again, more gently. Perhaps he had lost someone, too. Who hadn't? They should hold each other more tightly, and dance more perfectly, drowned in the music.

Elena also was dancing now, not even thinking about it, moving as easily with Ian as if she had always known him. Like Margot, she hated to talk while dancing. All the conversation was in the movement, and the music was master of it all.

Elena looked around the room. Mostly men: civilised, intelligent and as dry as dust. Some of them had drunk a little too much, but they only looked sleepy. Good heavens, had they bored themselves to death?

The music stopped and members of the band stood, signalling the end of their playing.

Margot, Elena and the two men went back to their table, where Ian wished them all good night. 'May I walk you to your room?' he asked, offering Elena his arm.

They passed through the large doors and climbed the stairs to the first landing. Elena turned and faced him. 'Thank you for a lovely evening,' she said. It was no mere politeness. It was the happiest day she could remember in years.

'It was fun,' he said quite lightly, but his eyes were totally serious. 'I think I shall become a photographer's assistant. It's infinitely more satisfying than writing about economics.'

'It's very uncertain,' she said, playing at being serious.

'Life is very uncertain,' he replied. All humour vanished for a moment. 'Cling on to the good bits.'

Whatever he had been going to say next was interrupted by a shriek from the landing above them, shrill and edged with horror. For a moment they froze, then Ian swung round and began to run towards the screams as they came again and again.

Elena followed, taking her camera out of its case. Someone was obviously in great trouble.

Ian stopped abruptly. A young woman in a black maid's dress and white apron was standing ashen faced with one hand to her mouth. The linen cupboard was open and just inside was the crumpled body of a man. From the unnatural angle of his head and neck it was clear he could not be alive.

Ian's face had turned completely white. He put his arms around the sobbing maid gently, holding her tight, but when he spoke his voice was half-strangled in his throat. 'Come away. You can't help him. Don't look . . .' Firmly he guided her round the corner from sight.

Elena was left staring at the dead body sprawled on the floor. The closed door must have been holding him up, and when the girl opened it he fell out. He was an unremarkable middle-aged man. Dark skinned. Black hair receding a little. He was probably Italian, but he could have come from anywhere. Did Ian know him? Is that why he was so upset? He had looked totally shocked. She was shaking, yet she managed to shoot one picture before putting the camera away. She was a photographer, true, but it might seem intrusive, and perhaps it was illegal, to photograph a crime scene like this.

'Signorina . . . Miss . . . please, come and sit down . . .' A man took her tentatively by the arm.

She turned to face him. 'I'm all right, thank you, but he's . . .' she took a breath, '. . . clearly dead. Who is he?'

'I have no idea.' The man was an assistant manager. She knew him by sight from the last few days. 'Please . . . I wish to call the authorities. It cannot be an accident. Where he is . . .'

'No, of course not.' At least he had not tried to soothe her with lies. 'I'll go to my room.'

'Are you all right? Do you need someone?'

'No, thank you. I am with my sister.' She thanked him again and went back along the corridor to where Ian was speaking gently to the maid in fluent Italian, but he was still very pale, and the hand on her arm, where he was still supporting the maid, was white-knuckled, almost as if she were holding him up as much as he was holding her. An older maid appeared along the passageway and took control, thanking Ian and firmly dismissing him.

Two uniformed police officers went past the woman and spoke to Ian in English.

'Now, sir, if you will tell me what happened?' one of them began.

Ian told them honestly, in English.

'And this young lady was with you?' He looked at Elena.

'Yes,' Elena agreed.

'And do you know this poor man?' He indicated the body lying on the floor.

'No, sir,' Ian replied, his jaw muscles tight, his voice shaking a little.

Elena was almost certain he was lying.

Chapter Three

Lucas Standish sat in the armchair in his study and stared out of the windows into the garden. The pattern of leaves against the sky always pleased him. Even the bare winter branches had a unique delicacy. Now the trees were at the height of their spring perfection.

The study looked like the room of an ordinary elderly man in pleasant retirement, except perhaps for the remarkable number of books that lined the walls. Lucas was a quiet man who read about life. That was what he was to others, even his own family.

But he had been head of Military Intelligence – MI6, as it was known – for a good part of the war. In his thoughts, he would say 'the last war' because he feared that there would be another. He was in his early seventies, and not officially part of the service any more, but his interest had never slackened, and he knew a great deal of what was happening now. He had many sources, quite apart from piecing things together with his own intelligence: what was written in the newspapers and, at times, what was not written, the half-truths that concealed the greater lie.

Winston Churchill was the only politician whose judgement

he trusted. He knew and liked the man personally and thought his opinions sound. But Churchill had been out of power for some time, and what mattered now, he was likely to be for the foreseeable future. No one in office listened to him because they did not want to believe that what he said was true.

Lucas could understand that, dear heaven, too easily. He longed to be able to believe that the meteoric rise of Adolf Hitler was no danger to Europe, certainly not to England. But every sense in him, every instinct, told him that it was, and that the danger was increasing by the week. Only at the end of this January, four months ago, Hitler had assumed complete power with an almost unanimous approval of his people.

New ideologies were surging up all over Europe in the wake of the devastating losses of war. Since the assassination of the Tsar of Russia, fear of Communism had sent power to the right-wing ideologues everywhere else. In Italy, Benito Mussolini had created much change for the good, but his total control was already tightening, becoming oppressive, creating the bedrock for the madness of dictatorship. Some of the stories Lucas had heard bordered on the ludicrous, and yet he knew they were true, and the present laughter would be short lived.

In Spain, various political factions were vying for power. Who knew where that would lead?

But it was still Germany that was the source of his deepest concern. The treaty after the war had been too harsh. Millions of people who were not to blame for any part of the Kaiser's glory-seeking had suffered. Blame was pointless. Probably no one was free of it, even if it were for complacency; not for action, but for inaction.

19

Lucas's thoughts were interrupted by a light knock on the door. 'Come in,' he said quickly. He knew it would be his wife, Josephine, to remind him that their son, Charles, and daughter-in-law, Katherine, were coming to dinner, and he should get himself ready, physically with a clean shirt, and emotionally for the differences of opinion that would inevitably arise. They always did, no matter how much he swore to himself not to be drawn in.

Josephine entered the room. She was the same age as Lucas. They had been married for over half a century, and yet he still found pleasure in looking at her. More than pleasure, a warmth, and gratitude for all they had shared. Many men might not have found her beautiful, but he still did. It was in her eyes, and her quick smile, the vitality in her, even when she sat unmoving. He knew her candour frightened some people, but he liked it. He found it a touchstone of honesty, a cleanness of mind, even of soul. His granddaughter Elena had some of that quality. It had skipped a generation. There was nothing of it in Charles.

'I know,' he said, before she could speak. 'They will be here in half an hour. He's always on time.' He was not sure if that was praise or complaint. If he were honest, he was not looking forward to the visit. Recently he and his son always seemed to be disagreeing about politics. Of course, Charles did not know Lucas's part in the secret services. One did not tell even family about such things. As far as they knew, he was a civil servant with a job too boring to discuss. The very existence of MI6 was not generally acknowledged.

Charles had gone into the diplomatic service and excelled. He had held high posts in many of the European capitals and, briefly, in Washington. His charming and intelligent American wife had always been an asset. All that information was public. When Lucas had first entered the service, he had found it difficult to keep total silence about his work, but over time it had become habit. Apart from anything else, he did not want to burden any of his family with the nature and secrecy of what he did, the kind of decisions he had had to make. The higher he rose in the service, the more discreet he had to be. Everyone knew that 'Loose lips sink ships' and no one talked about troop movements, what was done in which factories, or any such subjects.

Josephine seemed to have grown tired of waiting for his reply. 'Supper time, Toby!' she called cheerfully, and the dog sitting beside Lucas shot to his feet and pattered after her eagerly. He knew quite a large vocabulary of human words, and 'supper' was prime among them. He followed so closely behind her that, had she stopped, he would have bumped into her.

Lucas smiled and rose to his feet also. He walked out slowly, past the bookcase that held all his favourites, the books he had read and reread. There was plenty of poetry, especially the more recent ones like Housman, Sassoon and Chesterton. The ones that stayed in the heart. There was a very worn Shakespeare, which if left to itself fell open either at *Hamlet* or *Julius Caesar*, and a Dante similarly well used, particularly *Inferno*. It was so appropriate. If a man could only learn that you are punished not for the sin, but by it, and you thus became less than you could have been, how much that would change you.

What was also there, and he could not always bring himself to look, was a photograph of Mike, his only grandson. It was one Elena had taken, practising her portraiture. He was nineteen, in army uniform, smiling out at the room. It was one of the last he had had taken, and it had caught his warmth and his optimism so well. It was hard to believe he would not ever come home.

Lucas went out this time without looking at the photograph, although that made no difference, he could see it in his mind, even with his eyes closed. He could remember Mike's last leave. How he had enjoyed it so much, made the most of every hour, almost as if he knew he would not come back. But all men in wartime feel that. Everyone had lost friends, people they had grown up with, and new friends made in the horror and loneliness of war. It was a comradeship like no other. Mike had always made wild, silly jokes. He had been so intensely alive that Lucas found it hard to believe when the telegram had come.

Did everybody feel this? The denial? The bewilderment? Then the long, slow pain of grief eating away at you? Eating away at the heart? The soul?

Margot had lost her husband in the same week, on the same battle front. He could remember her face as if it were yesterday. That look came back again sometimes, when she thought no one was looking. Poor Margot, she was still lost in so many ways. There was nothing Lucas, or anyone else, could do. Elena had tried, and Josephine. Even Charles, who had been so close to her. Every family he knew had lost someone.

He reminded himself of that as he went across the hall and up the stairs, because he needed to be patient with Charles, and with his son's determination that there should never be another war like the last one. Other men should not mourn their children as he did. That was the only decent thing the war could give the next generation: the conviction that it should never happen again.

Lucas knew thousands of men who felt the same. There

had to be another way, no matter what it cost. Those who had fought and returned felt it so deeply, one had only to look in their faces, in their eyes, for any argument to die.

Charles had lost his only son. Lucas still had his, and whatever their differences, he must not quarrel.

He must not for Josephine's sake. She knew enough about war to think of it with reality. She had spent a lot of the time during those years working at a decoding centre outside London. Lucas knew something of her work, even though he could not share his with her.

Peter Howard was one of those with whom he could speak openly, and they were still friends. Howard was his one liaison with MI6 and the secrets he still knew, the actions he still contributed to. Technology had advanced, codes were mostly different, but human nature was the same, in its weaknesses and its strengths.

As Lucas prepared himself for the evening ahead he looked at his own face in the mirror, lean, aquiline, and at first glance, ascetic. Only with a closer examination did one see the humour and a certain gentleness about the eyes.

Charles and Katherine arrived exactly on time, as Lucas had known they would. Katherine was a uniquely elegant woman, not quite beautiful but, better than that, full of character. She was a little taller than average, and very lean. She managed to make it graceful, and to dress with individuality. Tonight, Katherine wore a long charcoal-grey silk dress that was all soft lines, very flattering to her angularity. It looked completely effortless, but that, too, was one of her gifts.

She came in now with the cool evening breeze behind her. With a friendly greeting about the promise of an enjoyable evening she smiled at Lucas and gave him a quick kiss on the cheek. He returned it, lightly, realising that, as always, he had no idea what she was thinking, in spite of her words.

Charles was straight behind her. 'Evening, Father,' he said with a smile. He looked every bit the diplomat: graceful, immaculate, neat black moustache adding a dash to his face.

Lucas held the door wider. 'Come in. How are you?'

Charles came into the hall, the men shook hands warmly, and Charles hugged Josephine. She hugged him back with sudden warmth, as if it surprised her how much she cared.

They went into the drawing room. The deep red and blue Turkish carpet had withstood a generation; the Dutch painting of a harbour scene, all in muted shades of blues and greys, had hung there longer than any of them could remember, almost like a window whose view never changed. There was an inner peace to it, a timelessness that governed everything else. The curtained French windows looked on to the garden, but even though it was May, they were closed now, islanding the room from the rest of the world, at least visually. Emotionally, it could not be done.

They had barely sat down when Charles began to speak of the most current news. 'I know he's a bit eccentric in his manner,' he said, referring, as they all knew, to Oswald Mosley. 'But he's the only one so far to grasp the nettle. We can't go on spending like this. Hasn't the Depression taught us anything? This is the last time in the world that we should think of re-arming, let alone building more ships! We simply can't afford it!'

'It would give employment to men desperately needing it,' Josephine pointed out. 'The shipyards, in particular.'

'We don't need warships, Mother,' Charles replied patiently. 'The war is long over, and we have all realised that such a world disaster cannot ever be allowed to happen again.' His

24

face was pinched. He could not even mention the word 'war' without remembering the loss it had brought, not only to him personally, but to almost every man with whom he had been at school, or university, every friend of his entire life.

Lucas ached for him. He understood it with a recollection of grief that was bone deep, but he simply did not agree. He kept silent with difficulty. They would have one family dinner without the anger that lay barely below the surface of all their political disagreements.

Josephine regarded her son patiently. 'It will be a little late to build them when we do need them,' she pointed out. 'Shipbuilding takes a long time, and a lot of men.'

'And a lot of iron, steel and other materials that could be far better used for houses, trains or, if you must build ships, for the Merchant Navy,' Charles responded. Without looking at Lucas, he went on, 'You're listening to Father, and he's listening to Churchill.' He lowered his voice and took the sharp edge off it with an obvious effort. 'Churchill is finished, Mother. He's yesterday's man, with yesterday's ideas. I know Mosley is a bit . . . vulgar, at times, but a lot of what he says is true. And look at what Mussolini has done for Italy! When you get the infrastructure right, the roads, trains, draining the marshes and building houses and factories, you get the people united and self-disciplined, you can achieve miracles.'

'It might work well for Italians—' Josephine began.

'It does work for them!' Charles insisted. 'There's no "might" about it. Ask Margot when she gets back. She'll tell you.'

'Or Elena . . .' Katherine suggested.

Charles smiled at her briefly. 'Darling, Elena won't even notice, she'll be far too interested looking for faces to make pictures of. She's hellbent now on being a great photographer. She won't consider a new factory or the trains running on time to be interesting, much less a work of art. I'm just glad she's found something harmless to do . . .' It was an oblique reference to her disaster at the Foreign Office, and a reminder to Lucas that Charles had not forgotten it, or forgiven the embarrassment it had caused him.

'Has anyone heard from her?' Josephine asked before Lucas could speak. 'Or from Margot?'

'It's a little soon,' Katherine shrugged. 'A wire from Margot to say they've arrived, but that was three days ago. I expect they're having fun. Amalfi is a gorgeous place, and very fashionable this time of year. Everybody who's anyone at all goes to Capri.'

'Then Margot will be there,' Charles said with a smile. References to Margot's spirit and glamour always pleased him. She understood loss as much as he did.

'There's no reason why she shouldn't have fun.' Katherine was instant in her defence, misunderstanding. Charles had meant no criticism. She longed for Margot's happiness. She was a woman very aware of her children's pain. It was simply a side of herself she seldom allowed to show.

'Of course she's having fun,' Josephine agreed, referring back to Margot. 'It's part of survival. And the little dash of wit or glamour serves others as well. They can aspire to it too, if they see it's possible.'

Charles drew in his breath as if to argue, and then seemed to change his mind. For the moment the discussion was over.

Quite willing to turn the conversation along a different course, even if her tactic was obvious, Josephine asked if anyone had seen any motion pictures recently, and if so, what they thought of it.

'*Dr. Jekyll and Mr. Hyde*,' Katherine said, immediately picking up the thread. 'Fredric March was brilliant.' She went on to describe the actor's skill, and how thoroughly she thought he had deserved the Oscar that he had won for it.

Lucas smiled. He tried to make it look like interest, but it was as much amusement. He admired her diplomatic skill as much as her good humour. Did Charles realise what an asset she was in his career? Probably. Lucas looked at him now and saw the total attention in his son's face as he watched his wife. His regard for her was unmistakable. He was surely aware that she was deliberately keeping the peace, for all their sakes. No one could heal the differences, but she could ignore them. Perhaps that was what diplomacy was really about? Finding the meeting grounds you could, and choosing to ignore those that could never blend, because to force them to mix required a winner and a loser. In a good agreement, there were no losers.

They went into the dining room shortly after and Josephine left briefly for the kitchen. Katherine offered to help, as she always did, and it was declined, also as always. Now that there were only Lucas and herself at home, Josephine preferred to do all the cooking, which she was good at and which interested her, though she had other domestic help.

They had saved the best for entertaining, as one always did, and they ate an excellent roast saddle of mutton with the very first of the spring vegetables from the garden.

It was Katherine who touched back on *Dr. Jekyll and Mr. Hyde*. 'It's extraordinarily clever acting,' she said with admiration. 'No special effects or make-up. You could watch him almost changing shape in front of you. He begins as a gentle, benign person, then the darker side of him gradually takes over, and within seconds, less than a minute, he becomes

27

brutish, all humanity gone out of him and something vile is in its place. Something completely out of his control.'

'It was in the writing,' Charles observed, 'but it was certainly clever. I wonder how long it took him to get that effect?'

Lucas did not answer. It suddenly seemed to him far deeper than the skill of an actor or even the imagination of a fine writer. 'Did he fear it in himself, do you suppose?' he said to Charles.

'What?' Charles asked, interested but slightly puzzled.

'Stevenson,' Lucas replied. 'Did Jekyll know there was a monster inside him over whom he had no control? Was that what Stevenson was showing us? Knowledge, and at the same time, helplessness.'

'What on earth made you think of that?' There was a set in Charles's face that showed his determination. He had scented a real meaning, something deeper than polite discussion over the dinner table. Was that what he himself had intended?

'All sorts of things can spark off the emotions we can't control,' Lucas replied. 'A good artist knows that, and so does a good politician – or a good demagogue.'

'A contradiction in terms.' Josephine shook her head. 'Demagoguery is not good, by definition. The only civilised rule is by consent.'

'That wasn't what I meant,' Lucas corrected. 'Not good as regards morality. Perhaps I should have said skilled, effective, achieving its aim.'

'There's a lot to be said for that, at certain times.' Charles looked at him steadily. 'Now would be one of them. Feed the hungry, house the homeless, create jobs to bring honour and a sense of purpose to those who have none. Is that demagoguery?' There was challenge in his voice, and in his eyes.

The temperature in the room had dropped, or perhaps it was the light that had changed. Everyone was watching Lucas. Josephine still held her dessert fork in her hand, but she had forgotten the pastry on her plate. She was watching Lucas, knowing him too well to imagine he could be stopped from answering.

Lucas chose his words very carefully, looking only at Charles. 'It isn't what you do with power, certainly not to begin with. It is whether those who give it to you have any chance of curbing it once you have it, when and if you abuse it, and one day you will.'

Charles sidestepped the issue. 'Would they rather be cold and hungry? There's not much point in worrying about a problematical tomorrow if you don't survive tonight. Any woman with hungry children pulling at her skirts will tell you that, Father. Sometimes I think you live in such an ivory tower that you have no idea of the realities of war and Depression, and what it has done.' There was pain in his voice, as well as anger. 'If you back people into a corner and leave them no dignity, and no hope, sooner or later they'll fight . . . and to the death, if you take it that far! You've left them nothing to lose. Always leave people a way out, to save face. That's the essence of diplomacy. You live in your safe Civil Service castle and don't even see the realities, never mind taste them.'

Josephine drew in her breath sharply, as if to speak, and then looked down at the table and said nothing.

Of course, Charles had no idea what Lucas had done during the war, the sleepless nights worrying about the men he had sent on crazy, too often hopeless, errands behind

29

enemy lines. And the women! Never knowing if they'd come back. Too many of them didn't. Charles didn't know of the secret meetings, the waiting, the judgements that could win or lose, save lives, or cost them. He did not know how many times Lucas had taken a small boat across the Channel in the dark and landed secretly on the shores behind the fighting, in German-occupied Belgium, or Holland, for secret meetings, dealing with misinformation, betrayals of every sort. Was it harder than in the daylight, when you could see the enemy? Or at least see your friends? What could Lucas say that would not break the secrets he had kept all these years, and must still keep? The one he hid even from himself was that he missed it, missed the passion of purpose, the knowledge that he was part of the battle, not a bystander. He saw the anger, and a degree of contempt, in his son's eyes. It was the contempt that hurt.

Josephine spoke softly, reproach in her voice. 'You have no idea what your father did or did not do in the war, Charles, and your assumption that you have the right to judge has no place at this table. Perhaps if the diplomats had been a little more skilled at their jobs, and a little more diligent, we wouldn't have had a war. Had you considered that?'

Charles stared at her. It was a blow he had not expected, especially from her, and Lucas saw the idea cross his face and fill him with surprise. He turned to Josephine, but she was not looking at him.

The point Lucas had been going to make was about fear, and how people can use it to manipulate others. Frighten a man enough, not only for himself, but for his family, and he will believe anything if you promise safety. 'I know many people are cold and hungry,' he said, breaking the hot

30

silence, but trying to keep the anger out of his voice. 'And the homeless have no hope of jobs. A man who isn't frightened of the future has no idea what the hell's going on. Hitler offers them hope and, I suppose in his way, Mosley does too. We're all afraid of war, because, dear God, we know what it is. We're a long way from over the last one. We're hideously vulnerable to being frightened out of our senses, or values, the better parts of ourselves that saved us before. I know that, Charles. I saw the war too. And I know what hunger there is in Germany, and here. And I know how easy it is to believe someone is responsible for all the misery, and if we just get rid of them, it will all come right.'

'Do you?' Charles looked at him steadily, his head a little on one side. 'Do you really? Pardon me, Father, I'm sure you do in theory, but I don't think you have the slightest idea of the reality.'

Lucas must be careful. It was so easy to let your vanity, your need for the respect of those you love, provoke you into saying more than you meant to. Very deliberately, he eased himself back into his chair. 'Don't imagine you are the only one who knows anything, Charles. That is a dangerous position. I don't want another war any more than you do. But I am a little less certain as to the best way to prevent it, or what price I am willing to pay . . .'

'Do you think it will come to that?' Katherine asked, sitting very still. She looked perfectly composed, but a ragged edge was audible in her voice. Lucas knew her well enough to recognise it. He had known her through the loss of her only son, and then in her own grief, her attempt with immense fortitude to comfort her daughter for the loss of not only her brother, but her husband. He never underestimated

31

her courage, and he could see the fear in her now, for all its disguise and sophistication.

'No, my dear, I don't,' he said. Please God that were true. 'But we must still be careful. This time we are forewarned. We must keep fear in its place, not let it make us act in panic, or with disregard for others. The easy path is sometimes right, but more often it isn't.'

Charles straightened his shoulders. 'Of course,' he agreed. He too must have heard the edge in Katherine's voice, or even seen the momentary flicker of fear in her eyes. 'I spent quite a lot of time in our Berlin Embassy. The Germans are strong people. They are finding their way again.' He smiled at her, then turned to Josephine. 'Mother, may I help you get the coffee?'

Josephine accepted, and the tension seeped away. By the time Charles and Katherine left an hour and a half later, the atmosphere was easy again, at least on the surface. That's all it ever was.

As Lucas closed the door and locked it for the night, Josephine was still standing in the hall.

'You meant that about fear, didn't you?' she said softly.

He had kept many things from her, necessary things about his work, but he had never lied to her. That would have broken something between them that he did not ever want to live without. 'Yes. Fear begets violence, and hatred,' he answered. 'It's the easy answer. Blame someone else. Blame the gypsies, the Jews, the Communists, anyone but ourselves. Get rid of them, and it will all be fine. It's as old as sin, and about as useful!' Then he smiled and put his arm around her. 'Sorry. I don't learn. I always let him get under my skin.'

She put her arm around his waist and moved a little closer

to him. 'Yes, you do,' she agreed. 'If you didn't, then I suppose you just wouldn't care, and I never want you to stop caring.'

Chapter Four

The following day, Lucas received a telephone call early in the morning, before he had started breakfast. It was from one of the other close suburbs of London, and very brief. All the voice said was, 'Meet me as usual, ten o'clock.' He knew it was Peter Howard, so Lucas had no need to add anything but his agreement.

Josephine did not question where he was going when, at half past nine, he said he was taking the dog for a walk.

Toby did not question either. Lucas had the lead in his hand, Toby saw it and stood up, scrambling out of his basket and pattering across the floor, tail wagging. It was late spring, sharp sunlight and a chill to the breeze, perfect for a walk in the nearby bluebell wood. There was no more heartachingly beautiful place on earth, and for Lucas, there could not be in heaven either.

It was a twenty-minute walk and he set out briskly, though taking care not to overwork his ankle with a twisted ligament, an old injury that would never heal now. 'No dawdling,' he said to Toby. 'You can run where you please when we get there. Come on, now!'

Toby was always happy to be talked to. This was a usual

pattern and he pulled at his lead for interesting smells only once, then accepted that they were partners in something and had a job to do. It was enough for him just to be along.

After Lucas had left MI6, Peter Howard was the one man with whom he had kept in touch. For Howard to send a message for an immediate meeting, it must be important.

They arrived at the gate. Lucas opened it, closed it carefully behind him and let Toby off the lead. 'Not far!' he warned. 'Come on!'

Toby wagged his tail and circled round, enjoying every scent in the damp earth.

The beech trees towered above them. They had always been Lucas's favourite. Their long, clean limbs reminded him of the legs of dancers, naturally beautiful, exulting in their strength, their infinite grace. The sky was dappled with cloud, alternately light and shadow, but the ground was so covered with bluebells that he had to stay on the narrow path to avoid standing on them. He hated to crush a living thing, especially one that offered such utter loveliness. They had only the faintest, cool scent, but he imagined he could smell it. The city was actually a short underground rail journey away to the east, but here he could forget it even existed.

He found Peter Howard standing near the oak about twenty yards from the small stream, exactly where he had expected him to be. He was an ordinary-seeming man and could disappear in a crowd any time he wished to, and yet to Lucas he was unmistakable. He was a little above average height, fair brown hair, blue eyes, and regular features. You could probably have said that of roughly half the men in England. As he stood there, it was his perfect stillness that was unusual, the angle at which he held his head. There was a humour in his expression, and when he thought himself unobserved, a sensitivity.

But all this knowledge was built on twenty years of working together, since that innocent, ignorant golden time just before the war. From here, 1913 seemed like another century.

Howard straightened up and walked a few steps forward, meeting Lucas where the path turned and wound through the trees along the bank, then back into the woods again.

They did not bother with 'good morning', comment on the weather, the usual 'how are you?' All that would be taken as said. They were deep friends, too much already understood between them to bother with such things. Howard had called for this meeting, therefore he had something to say that he judged important. From the gravity in his eyes, it was not good.

'What do you know about Roger Cordell?' he asked, his voice clipped and very English, yet it was still light, as if he spoke of some trivial acquaintance.

'British Embassy in Berlin?' Lucas wanted to make certain he was thinking of the right man. 'Oxford, I think. Good degree in classics and modern languages, if I remember rightly.'

A brief smile crossed Howard's face, and vanished.

'Modern history might have been of more use, if less ornamental,' Lucas added drily. 'Why?'

Howard looked straight ahead of them at the carpet of flowers. 'Got a nasty feeling he might be playing both sides, or . . .'

Lucas waited, and Howard continued walking slowly, watching where he trod to avoid the flowers.

'Or what?' Lucas asked. There was too much uncertainty.

36

The slow tide of fear was rising inside him and he could feel it like the chill breath of a wind that heralded rain.

Was Howard running from shadows? Military Intelligence was a war of ideas as much as of armaments or factory sabotage, explosions, and derailments. It was the fear of an enemy you could not see, of betrayal by those you had thought your friends.

Toby, off the lead, ran around in happy circles, chasing the scent of something, startling birds far out of his reach. They sat high in the branches, calling out alarms to each other. It was so beautiful, so sane, Lucas looked at it with something close to pain. It should always be here, and he knew it would not be. The flowers would only last like this for a few weeks, then begin to fade, go back into the earth until next spring. Other flowers would come, and leaves, but not like this.

Of course, there would soon be hawthorn blossom thick in the hedges, almost like snow. It was already beginning. And in June the wild dog roses would tangle these paths with pink and red.

Poetry crowded his mind, the love of the land from the minds of young men who would not see it again. Too many of them. They had called it 'the Poets' War' not without reason. He could understand people who would pay any price not ever to have another like it. He could not walk these woods without thinking of Mike. But then he could not listen to good music, watch a decent game of cricket on a village green, with all the young men in whites, or share a joke, without memory intruding. There were times when he could allow Charles any latitude at all because he understood the grief he hardly ever spoke of. Some feelings were too intense to share in anything but a glance, and silence.

'Are you sure about Cordell?' he asked.

'No,' Howard replied quietly. 'But I fear it. Usually by the time you're sure, it's too late. It's only small things. The things not said, rather than the ones said.'

Lucas knew exactly what he meant. He had felt it himself: a silence where he would have expected a response, a disagreement, a reaction other than the one he saw. Sometimes it was simply carefulness, or even an anger one did not express because one knew it would do no good, only hurt pointlessly.

They walked in silence for another hundred yards or so. Toby returned, eager for attention. Lucas bent and picked up a stick. He threw it as far as he could, and Toby went charging after it, sending startled birds off in a sweep of movement through the branches.

A small copse of silver birches stood in the sunlight, like a charcoal sketch on white paper, motionless in the lack of breeze. Both men stopped and gazed at it, perhaps moved by the same impulse.

'I can't afford to let it go,' Howard said at last. 'I don't expect you to do anything.' Was that an edge of disappointment? Several times he had said how much Lucas was missed. Sometimes it was direct, at others oblique. 'I just let you know in case you trusted him,' he went on. 'Every report I get from Berlin is worse than the one before. I knew the Weimar Republic couldn't last. It was all built on hope and dreams, and damn all else. But this new order scares the hell out of me. There's a cruelty in it that's growing like some fungus on a wet wall. If we rip the paper off I think we're going to find the rot is all over the place.'

'People are afraid,' Lucas replied, although he knew Howard was as aware of that as he was. 'The peace treaty was much too hard. We sowed the seeds of another war then, we were just too blind, too deeply hurt to see it. God knows how many Germans have died since then of hunger or despair. Hitler's giving them self-respect again, and most people will do almost anything for that.'

Howard pushed his hands deeper into his pockets. 'I know. And I suppose if they'd won and we had been subjected to humiliation and slow death of who we used to be, I'd hate too. None of that is solved by the sort of internal violence the Nazis are preaching, and I think you know that as well as I do. It isn't the Germans who believe in it that scare me, Lucas, it's the Englishmen! I worry about any support for appeasement.'

'Yes, so do I. Peace at any price,' Lucas said. 'A lot of us who've seen war, the real thing, the blood and the pain, the death, the utter drenching loss of it, think that nothing on earth could be worse. I understand them. Especially Charles's generation, who were part of the reality of it. He thinks I don't know what it's like to send men who trust you to their deaths. They know what you are ordering them to do, and they do it anyway.'

'And *can* anything be worse than that?' Howard looked at him, the bright sunlight showing every line and angle of his face. For that moment he looked infinitely vulnerable. Then a shred of cloud passed over the sun, softening the probing harshness, and it was gone. 'We still need the right men to give the orders, Lucas. You were one of the best. Come back. Help us to do it right!'

'I can't,' Lucas replied. 'I'm too old. You've got new people—'

'Who haven't fought a real war,' Howard interrupted him. 'They don't know when to cling on to the impossible, and when to let it go.'

'And they certainly won't ask me in to tell them. They have new ideas,' Lucas agreed.

'The basics are as old as mankind,' Howard said with a sideways glance at him. 'Queen Elizabeth had master spies who could teach us a thing or two.'

Lucas did not answer.

They walked fifty yards or so, reached the cherry tree they often passed. Its blossom was already overblown and beginning to drop, but still a glory. It always reminded Lucas of sadness, beauty that could not last, young love lost. Then he remembered why, in the lines of Housman:

> And since to look at things in bloom
> Fifty springs are little room . . .

Written at twenty, with the imagination of a long life. Who, at twenty, believes they have only another year to live?

He was aware that Howard was watching him. Did he have the same lines in mind: *To see the cherry hung with snow*? Or were his thoughts somewhere else entirely? He turned a little and met Howard's eyes. He was certain his thoughts were the same.

'Wishing doesn't make it so,' Howard said. 'I have to know about Cordell. Just don't trust him in the meantime.' There was a gentleness in him, even a kind of pity, and Lucas realised that for all that he knew Peter in so many ways, he did not know who he had lost in the last war. He was married. Lucas had met his wife, a cool, fair-haired woman whom Howard hardly ever mentioned. They were polite to each other, but there seemed to be no laughter between them. They had no children. Was that another wound?

In Lucas's mind, in the emotions he seldom acknowledged,

Peter was the son he wished Charles could be. Lucas understood him so much better. There was a kind of comfort, never intrusive, a sense of what mattered and did not need to be explained. And yet Lucas was aware that those silences also held some kind of pain.

Lucas loved Charles – of course he did – but it was not a comfortable love. They had grown apart over the years. He had told himself it was a generational thing, but Charles was five years older than Howard, the same generation. He and Howard had experienced the same loneliness, the same guilt at failure, and the thrill at victory.

And Elena was twenty-eight, Lucas's granddaughter, and yet except for Josephine, he loved her more deeply than anyone else. In a way, Elena was the most comfortable, the easiest to be with. He had never known what to do with babies, but as soon as she could talk they had become friends. She adored him. She asked questions incessantly, all of them beginning with 'Why?' or 'How?' Margot was less curious. She had experimented for herself, refusing his help.

Now he watched Howard throwing sticks for Toby. Howard had told Lucas what he needed to. It was time they went home. An absence that took long enough to need explaining was an error. When Howard turned towards him, he nodded, and they started walking back through the bluebells towards the oak tree, and the place where their paths divided.

The following afternoon, Lucas kept an appointment that he had made on returning home from meeting Peter Howard. He enjoyed driving. He had an old Armstrong Siddeley cabriolet, with its long, sweeping lines, and its top that took a bit of manoeuvring to open, but on a day like this it was a pure joy.

As the crow flies, it would have been simpler to go through part of the city, but he never did that. The country routes were far quieter, and the extra miles flew by. He sang as he went, very often one of the patter songs from the Gilbert and Sullivan operas. It brought back memories of a holiday he had taken with Elena a few years ago. They had driven up to the Highlands of Scotland, just meandering around, going wherever they pleased. The trip had included Fountains Abbey and Rievaulx Abbey, in Yorkshire, on the way. Somehow the scarred and topless towers reaching up into the sky were more impressive, more emotionally moving, than had they been complete. The imagination created more than reality could.

They had bought fresh, crusty bread, local cheeses and fruit, and had found picnic places in deep grasses by a river, or under trees, always hearing the whisper of the leaves, and once in the heather, loud with bees. They had talked about hundreds of things, from the distance between the stars, to what kind of apple was best. They had quoted Shakespeare and Lewis Carroll and told endless jokes and invented limericks with impossible rhymes.

Lucas wondered if she had thought of it since, as often as he had, and with as much pleasure.

He had silently thanked God that she was a girl, not a boy, and too young for the war anyway. Her loss was a thought he could not bear even to imagine.

Today was a sunny day. The countryside was richly green, some fields hazed over with sheets of buttercups, but he hardly noticed them. His thoughts were occupied with the political situation and the future that he feared.

Although he liked Churchill, he was also afraid for him. The years out of meaningful office were taking a toll. Lucas dreaded finding him in a dark mood today. He felt helpless to offer anything to hope for, and platitudes were beneath either of them.

He rounded the last curve on the road and saw the house ahead of him, surrounded by its garden, and even from here he could see the brick walls that Churchill found it so soothing to build.

Fifteen minutes later he was standing next to Churchill by a tub of mortar and the stack of bricks. He was a stocky man, several inches shorter than Lucas, and today he looked old and tired. If Churchill weakened and lost the fight he had pursued all his life so far, Lucas did not know to whom else he could turn.

'Looks good,' he said, regarding the wall.

'I can build a hell of a good wall,' Churchill replied without pleasure. 'But what am I keeping in? Or out? I have no idea. I do it because I don't have anything else to do.'

'You will have,' Lucas said instantly, then wondered if he meant it, or more important at the moment, what Churchill would make of his remark. He already had the familiar 'black dog' on his shoulder. Could one die from lack of hope? Perhaps.

Churchill turned and gave him a dark look. 'Did you hear Mosley the day before yesterday?'

'Yes,' Lucas answered, recalling the sharp and ugly memory. Mosley was an admirer of Hitler and all that he stood for. Some people said Hitler's Brownshirts had modelled their uniforms on Mosley's black-shirted army. There had been too many eager faces at the rally in the West End, bright with conviction. They believed what they wanted to believe, what they needed to, as an alternative to the horror behind them.

Churchill waited for him to go on. 'Yes' was not enough.

What could Lucas say that was honest? 'I'm afraid of him,' Lucas admitted. 'But with just a little more rope, I believe Mosley will hang himself.'

'Do you!' Churchill glared at him. It was a challenge, not a question.

'We've got to make damn sure it happens,' Lucas said firmly, as if he had no doubt. 'I'm still getting news from Germany,' he added.

Churchill was now listening, curiosity piqued.

'The facts are very bad. Opposition is being got rid of, either by Hitler assuming more power himself, or appointing bloody awful men to do it for him. Himmler, for example. Used to be a chicken farmer, now he's strutting around in uniform like the only rooster on the dung heap, and exercising all the power he has.'

'I suppose every culture has them: men in bondage to their own inadequacies, who will never be satisfied because the emptiness is inside them.'

'Yes,' Lucas replied. 'They're always there, the misfits. It's the measure of a leader, which men he picks for the next tier of command . . . With Hitler it's the men who were failures in their own eyes before and have a chance to take their revenge on society now.'

'Bitter . . .' Churchill responded.

Lucas half turned, looking around him, then back at Churchill. 'Where does it stop, this tide of . . . violence? How long do we wait before we start doing something? When it's only Germany? When it's only Germany and Belgium, or Austria, or part of Poland? When it gets into France as well? A bit late by the time it gets to the cliffs of Dover.'

'Think it'll come to that?' Churchill's voice was quiet, almost expressionless, his face like that of a benign bulldog.

'What's to stop it?' Lucas asked.

'The damn British Navy!' Churchill snarled. 'If we get the Government to start building ships again. Dear God, I've tried!'

'But not as it is,' Lucas agreed.

'You've still got people of your own in Germany?' Churchill asked. 'Ones you can trust?' He looked sceptical. He knew exactly what part Lucas had played in the war, and how long he had been out of any office in MI6. Lucas had not told him how many people still passed him information; what Churchill wanted to know was the weight of it. 'What's happening, Lucas? What's really happening?'

'Hitler's gaining more power all the time. He's riding a wave of popularity, and it will get worse.'

Churchill grunted.

Lucas hesitated only a moment. 'It's going to be the hardest battle we've ever fought, and only God knows if we'll win.'

Churchill glared at him. 'Are you trying to manipulate me, Lucas?'

Lucas smiled at him. 'Yes. Is it working? So help me God, I think it's the truth.'

Churchill grunted again. He looked Lucas up and down, regarding his old shoes, well-worn and comfortable, the rather rumpled corduroy trousers, faded to no particular colour at all, then lastly his leather-elbow-patched jacket, sagging a little at the pockets.

'Like to help me build my wall?' he offered.

'Delighted,' Lucas accepted, finding himself surprisingly emotional.

'Well, get on with it, then!' Churchill snapped. 'There's the brick and there's the mortar.'

'I'll need your brick in my wall, in time,' Lucas replied.

'You'll have it. Now get on with the job.'

Lucas placed the mortar carefully, catching the dollop that slid down the side and replacing it where it should be. Then he carefully placed the brick, edged it a half-inch back, then straightened it.

'Not bad,' Churchill granted with a nod.

Lucas looked at him. He was standing a little straighter than before. 'The violence in the street is getting worse, especially against minorities: trade unionists, gypsies, Jews, homosexuals, when they know them. There's going to be a lot of suffering.'

Churchill's eyebrows rose. 'And you think that's going to change minds here? Men like Mosley and his followers? Ditherers like Chamberlain? Bloody right-wing fanatics in the highest of places? Idealists like Eden. He was a damn good officer, you know? Broke his heart to see so many of his own men blown to pieces.' His voice was bitter, almost as if he were on the edge of tears, but there was challenge in his eyes. 'Is that what you came to tell me?'

'No . . . not exactly.' Lucas gave a very slight smile. 'Although I suppose it's close.'

'So, what then?'

'To warn you that I think we have a turncoat in the British Embassy in Berlin. Be careful what you might hear from the Ambassador, or tell him.'

'I think that unlikely,' Churchill said slowly. 'But the warning is timely. Although I imagine you came to tell me just to let me know the battle is real . . . and it's already well started.'

'More or less,' Lucas agreed.

'What the devil can I do about it?'

46

'Today, nothing. But tomorrow or the day after . . .' He shrugged. 'God knows. Be ready . . .'

Churchill grunted again. 'Come inside and have a decent whisky.'

'Thank you,' Lucas accepted, and fell into step with him.

Chapter Five

Elena slept, but it had been far too tumultuous a day for her to rest easily. Her emotions were slipping out of control. After Aiden's disgrace and the pain and humiliation that it brought her, she had been determined never to fall in love again . . . at least not to the point where her judgement was impaired. She would love, certainly. To deny the possibility of loving was like choosing to freeze to death.

And she had loved Aiden, hadn't she? Or was she only in love with what she thought he was? He had fooled many people, most of all the Foreign Office! Everyone who worked with him had trusted him.

But trusting someone and being in love with them are quite different things. When you are in love, instinct tells you to be careful, to listen to the odd discordant notes, the things that shouldn't need explaining, but do. When there are things that go against your taste, instead of seeing them as a warning, you blame yourself for being narrow, intolerant, and continue lying to yourself as long as you can. You deliberately don't ask the questions to which you would rather not know the answers. You call it trust. You know too late that it is cowardice. Handsome, charming, deceitful Aiden had taken them all in. Elena was at fault because she had known him better.

Elena now shuddered and huddled her body into itself, drawing her knees up, as if closing herself off for a defence against memory.

She was hot with shame, and then shivering cold. It had all been there for her to see, if she had not been so dazzled by his gentleness, his good humour, his sophistication, and yes, she had been flattered, too. Of all the smart young women, well educated, ambitious and clever, why had he chosen her? Had he really liked her at all? Or was she just the most gullible?

No, she was the best placed to get him the information he wanted. She was Charles Standish's daughter. How that stung! Her father had not forgiven her yet.

So why was she falling in love now with Ian Newton, whom she knew so briefly, and who had been so shaken yesterday by the death of a man he claimed not to know? Certainly he was good-looking. He was also charming, clever and amusing, besides being a good dancer and a good listener. And he had tuned in to what interested Elena about Amalfi so that their dining together yesterday evening had felt easy and natural even on so short an acquaintance. There were a score of reasons for his reaction to seeing the dead man, perfectly innocent explanations she had no right to ask for. It might be as simple as a resemblance to someone else. She had called out to a man in the street once, he looked so like her grandfather. But when he had turned round, he was nothing like him at all. Tall, with grey hair, that's all. She was doing it again! Silencing the voice of fear with cool reason, because she liked Ian enormously already. She should quiet her mind with explanations and go back to sleep.

She woke early when the first light came in through her curtainless windows. They had wooden shutters on them, and she had deliberately left them open to let in the soft night air and the smell of the sea. Now it was pale, faint light filling the room, though not yet dawn.

She got up, washed and dressed quickly and silently, without disturbing Margot. She crept out and closed the door behind her. She would go for a walk. They were facing more or less east; she could watch the sun rising over the land, the light suddenly bursting above the horizon and flooding the sky, picking out every east-facing window to mirror itself, every dome, every wall in soft peach or blush pink.

The air was cool, and Elena was only on the first flight of steps down from the hotel when she saw Ian standing by the railing. He heard the slight sound of sandals on the steps and turned. His face lit with pleasure when he recognised her. 'Come and watch,' he said quietly, indicating further along the terrace where there was a view of the town rising up behind the hotel. 'This is a perfect place to see the victory of light over darkness.' He held out his arm.

She fought against all the old anxieties and went to join him.

The light was spreading rapidly now, and even as they stood there, it tipped above the town and leaped across the sky. It spread a silver path over the distant water, white walls in the town before where they stood, touched the burning reds and purples of bougainvillaea. What a photograph this would make, if the camera could catch the colour! Or the silence, or the smell of the sea.

All sorts of ideas tumbled through Elena's mind about light and darkness, but she said nothing. This was a time when those things did not need words. As if in tacit understanding, Ian did not speak either.

Half an hour later, in full daylight, they found a café serving crusty bread still hot from the oven, butter, home-made apricot jam, and hot coffee. Words were still unnecessary, an intrusion, and even a misunderstanding.

After they had finished the last fresh roll, and each had a second cup of coffee, they walked out on to the street and deliberately turned in the opposite direction from the hotel. They ought to return and work, but without needing to glance at each other, they knew they did not mean to. They walked instead towards the old city, sometimes in companionable silence, sometimes sharing their thoughts. Elena told him that, after the conference ended the following day, she planned to go to Paris before returning to London. The air was warm, with a light wind. The weather was infinitely changeable along Italy's western coast, and the locals discussed it exhaustively, and could forecast it with skill built up over generations. It would be fine all day today, the café waitress had told them.

They looked at mosaics in the pavement, endless statues of Madonnas smiling with benevolent patience on the visitors, admiring churches whose tiled floors were smoothed by the feet of over a thousand years of the faithful, the grieving, the penitent, and those seeking refuge from day-to-day turmoil.

'Did you know,' Ian asked suddenly, 'that there is a saying here that when the people born in this place die, if they go to heaven, it's just a day like any other day?'

Elena looked at him to see if he had really heard it, or was making it up. She knew from his eyes – the laughter, the softness, almost wistfulness – that they really said it . . .

51

or at least someone did. 'No,' she answered, 'but I believe it.'

They continued, stopping occasionally to consider a painting, a dome seen against a perfect sky, the grace of a statue. She could feel his arm around her, and sometimes his hand in hers, and that was all that was necessary.

When they arrived back at the hotel, the police were still there asking questions about the man whose body had been found in the linen cupboard.

Elena glanced at Ian, saw him hesitate, and a shadow cross his face. 'Did you know him?' she asked quietly.

Ian's silence stretched out to half a minute. 'No. When I first saw him, he reminded me sharply of someone I knew. It was foolish of me, because the man I knew is dead. I saw him when he was dead . . . and seeing this man reminded me of it. I'm sorry, I should have—'

'Don't be sorry,' she interrupted. 'We shouldn't be feeling guilty because we can't forget the people we've known, or even the ones we haven't. It's not . . . it's not a fault to grieve over the dead, just to make it about ourselves when it isn't; it's about them.'

He smiled at her with sudden sweetness, a warmth in his eyes that made Elena catch her breath.

The next moment, one of the police spoke to him. 'Signor Newton? I believe you were the one to find the body of the dead man late yesterday evening? That is so, yes?'

'Not quite,' Ian answered. 'The housemaid found him and let out a cry. I was very close, on the way to my room, and I heard her. She had opened the linen cupboard and the body fell out.'

'You recognised this man? You were disturbed at his death?

Perhaps you can tell us something about him.' The man was courteous, but his face was solemn, even stern.

Looking at him, Elena could see the suspicion in his eyes.

'I was distressed, yes,' Ian replied, his tone equally serious. 'He was clearly dead—'

'Clearly?' the policeman interrupted. 'That much was plain to you? You have experience in such things, yes?'

'No,' Ian replied steadily. 'But what live man is ashen-faced, and goes into a linen cupboard in a hotel, shuts the door on himself, and then falls so unconscious that even when the door is opened and he pitches out with his head at an impossible angle—'

'Yes. Yes, I see. You knew he was dead from the angle of his head, you are saying?'

'Yes. And the place he was found,' Ian added.

'But you recognised him?'

'No, I am not aware of having seen him before. But I may have, of course. If he is a local vendor. Works on the street, or behind a counter . . .' He let the sentence remain unfinished, as if the rest was obvious.

Standing beside him, Elena wanted to tuck her arm in his, and to let him know that she was with him, maybe let the policeman know it. But it would be too obviously for that reason. Better not to speak unless she were asked. Over-eagerness would raise his suspicions – at least, it ought to. Did the policeman sense that somewhere in there, there was a lie? Maybe an important one? But since the man had clearly been murdered – you don't fall down and break your own neck in a linen cupboard – who was to know what mattered and what did not?

The policeman turned his attention to Elena. 'And you, Signorina . . . Standish, is it not?'

'Yes.'

'Have you seen this man before? Did he trouble you? Was he perhaps overfamiliar? A nuisance? Did he pester you to buy something?'

She had had time to think. She gave a sad little smile. 'No, I am certain, because nobody pestered me. Unless he was a waiter somewhere, I have never seen him before.'

'You think he may have been a waiter?'

'I'm saying I don't remember seeing him, but I don't remember everyone's faces. I have been at an economic conference taking photographs, and I can definitely say he is not one of the delegates.'

'Why do you take pictures of economists?'

'It's my job.'

'I see. Thank you, signorina, signore.' He waved his hand in a gesture inviting them to leave.

They did so, Elena at least with an air of relief, and she sensed that it was for Ian also, although he said nothing.

They each went to their own room and met again fifteen minutes later in the dining room and found a table. Everyone seemed to be lunching late, and the room was crowded, filled with laughter and even a few people dancing, although it was only two in the afternoon. Elena looked around, but she did not see Margot. Perhaps she had gone along the coast to Sorrento? She had mentioned the possibility once or twice.

Elena took her seat, requested a light salad and fresh seafood, a mixture of shellfish and crustaceans, and warm, crusty rolls again. She couldn't face the frenetic laughter, the desperation to taste every bit of flavour, of sunlight, and a world of pleasure without the help of the sparkling wine. She looked at Ian and saw his rueful smile. He felt it, too. The room was full of people who did not live here. This was a dream from which they would all be awakened too soon. It was like the hour before a dawn that would show the reality of a harsher world. Maybe they did not see this as it truly was, but they did not need to. If it disappeared when they left, they would not know.

There was a small drama going on in one corner of the dance floor. The man was a little drunk and over-amorous, the woman was slender, but with an impressive embonpoint. She was swaying to the music with her arms above her golden head, and a woven garland of flowers low around her neck. Several people were too tipsy to see that it was becoming no longer amusing.

Beside Elena, Ian was watching in appalled fascination. The veneer of glamour was beginning to crack. He half rose in his seat.

'Sit down.' She leaned over and pulled on his arm. 'You can't help. You don't know who they are or how they are together.'

Ian looked at her, and the tension eased out of him.

The girl with the yellow hair was laughing a little too loudly, her bosom swaying.

A man called out something about her figure.

'It is a bit much,' Ian agreed.

'Hanging Gardens of Babylon.' Elena voiced the thought that came into her head.

Ian stared at her, and then almost choked with laughter. This side of her was new to him, but she felt no need to conceal it.

Suddenly there was a waiter beside Ian. 'Mr Newton, sir,' he said quietly. When Ian did not hear him, he repeated it with a light touch on the shoulder.

'Yes?' Ian turned to him. 'What is it?'

'A telegram for you, sir. It has "Urgent" on it.' He held out a tray with a single printed envelope. 'It's just arrived, sir.'

'Thank you.' Ian picked it up and tore it open. Suddenly, all the joy died in his face. When he looked up at Elena, his eyes were hollow, as if he had been robbed of something precious.

Fear rose inside her, catching her heart, her breath. 'What is it?'

'I have to leave. Immediately. I'm . . . sorry . . . I can't explain to you. It would be a breach of trust. Come with me! As far as Paris, at least.' He stopped, perhaps aware of what he was asking of her.

The music and the laughter went on around them, as if nothing had happened.

She thought of Margot, but only for a moment. 'As far as Paris?'

'Yes, I have to go on after that. But if you're going to Paris, and then on to London . . . please?'

Her answer was instant. 'Yes. Of course I will.'

Chapter Six

Elena went upstairs and packed, then left a note on Margot's bed to say that she had decided to leave a day early and travel with Ian as far as Paris, before going to Calais and taking a ferry home. She added that she hoped Margot enjoyed the rest of her stay, and then signed it.

Next, she went downstairs and settled her account at the front desk. Ian was tactful enough to wait for her outside, but he was already there, and standing at the door of a car, the driver at the wheel.

He put her case in the boot, beside his own, then held the door open while she got in the back seat. A moment later he was beside her and giving the driver instructions to drive to the railway station in Naples.

As if by mutual agreement, they now spoke of all kinds of things, except the reason he had been called away. The only mention of Margot was from Elena: how she had left a note on her sister's bed. No other explanations, just enough for Margot to know there was no cause to worry. Whether she would be angry was a different matter.

They spoke of the history of Amalfi, the history of the whole coast, especially of Naples, and of course Vesuvius, one of the most dangerous volcanoes in the world, because it lay dormant with only the occasional rumble or belch of fire and smoke, a giant grumbling in his sleep. But no one had forgotten that when it did erupt, it had destroyed cities in minutes, immortalising people and animals at their moment of death. It had darkened the sky and sent rivers of burning lava as far as the sea, taking whole villages with it. It was two thousand years ago, but no one had forgotten. The Neapolitans sang more lyrical music than other people, and danced a little faster, because they knew life could end without warning.

But still they did not speak of why he was leaving.

They reached Naples, paid the driver, and had only a short time to wait for the next express train to Rome, where they would change and connect for Milan, and from there to Paris. They did not plan beyond that. Elena did her best not to think of it. It was not here yet.

The train was barely out of the station, and already she missed Naples. She had begun the journey back to reality. The regret for having left Margot with only a note on her pillow was not deep enough to spoil the warmth of this sense of hope. She liked Ian more than she could recall liking any other man. The more they talked, the more gentleness she found to his character, and it filled her with interest and a sense almost of familiarity, as if the jokes were happy times revisited.

He was looking out of the window, leaning forward in his seat to catch that part of the skyline where the volcano was. Finally he sat back.

'The very precariousness of it heightens everything?' Elena said, picking up the thread of their earlier conversation, as if it had been only a moment ago. 'Yes, I do think so.' She smiled at him.

There was a sudden shadow of memory across his face. Was he thinking of the same things that she was? Young people dancing too close, too fast, intricate steps in perfect time with the music, wishing the song would never end, and knowing it had to?

In her mind, the picture faded and was replaced by Mike on his last leave, tasting every minute, making desperate jokes, laughing too quickly, one minute catching her eyes, the next avoiding them. He could not have known he would never come home again, but like all young men going to war, he must have understood the possibility. He had seen too many of his friends die ever to avoid it.

'Elena . . .?' Ian's voice cut into her reverie.

She looked up. 'Sorry . . .' She blinked hard, aware of the tears in her eyes. 'I was . . .' She did not want to tell him. He would have his own griefs; everyone did.

'It isn't only Vesuvius, is it?' he said quietly. 'It's everything . . .'

She looked at him and saw the amazing gentleness in his face. 'You would have liked my brother.' She had not meant to say that, but it was too late to take it back. 'And I wish I'd been a bit nicer to Margot before I left. She lost her husband the same day Mike died. They'd been married only a week. I think that's why she . . . drinks too much and plays too hard . . . sometimes. If that had happened to me, I might, too.'

'Does she do it often?' he asked. There was tenderness in his voice, not criticism.

Her voice should not have been so sharp or defensive.

'Yes, but you can't blame her for it. The pain doesn't go away just because time is passing and you're getting older, and it seems as if all life is bright and pretty . . . and meaningless. You don't—'

'Elena!' He cut her off firmly. 'If she does it often, and you've forgiven her before, then she knows you'll forgive her this time. You understand, and she knows that.'

Suddenly she saw his meaning. 'Oh. Yes. I'm sorry.'

'Stop it!' he said quickly.

'What?'

'Stop being sorry. Those who are gone loved us. The last thing they would want is for us to spend our time grieving for them instead of living!'

She knew that was true, but it too easily sounded like an excuse.

'What was he like, your brother?' he went on.

Memory flooded back with overwhelming pain. 'Mike was good at sharing things – he told the best jokes – and I think he got that from Grandfather. He would start off with, "Have I told you the one about . . .?" and then go on into some long, crazy story. He could do all the accents, from wherever you could think of. He loved music. He played pretty well, classical and lighter stuff. He used to invent it as he went along. He was only a year older than Margot, but five years older than me. He was nineteen when he was killed.'

'That's terrible . . .'

'You must have lost people too. Everyone did.'

'My father, but not for quite a long time afterwards. He was pretty badly wounded, but more than that, he was shell-shocked. He was never like himself again, and I can't really remember much of how he was before that. There was an acute sorrow in his eyes, as if he felt guilty for having come home, and leaving so many of his comrades behind.'

She reached out and put her hand over his, where it lay on his knee. He turned his hand upwards and clasped hers. They sat together for several minutes as the countryside slipped past them and the rattle of the train was oddly soothing.

'You don't have any brothers?' she asked eventually, withdrawing her hand and sitting up a little straighter.

'Only sisters. Three of them, and they are all older than I am. They spoiled me totally, but they did teach me considerable respect for girls. They are all clever, and none of them would take any cheek from little boys.' He gave a rueful smile. 'I know about older sisters.'

'Tell me about them . . . if you don't mind?'

He did, for about an hour. The stories were funny and intimate, and above all, kind. Elena felt as if she had known them by the time he finally stopped.

They went along to the dining car for dinner and found a table near the back.

'The Italians know how to make food such a pleasure,' Ian said, taking a piece of sweet melon on his fork and wrapping the wafer-thin Parma ham around it.

Elena agreed, but added, 'So do the French. It is an art we would be so much happier if we learned.'

'Do you know French food well?' he asked.

'Yes, to eat. I couldn't cook it to save myself. But my father was British Ambassador in Paris for a while. It was wonderful, even though it was after the war and everything was pretty grim. Nothing like Germany, of course. Whatever your losses, there is all the difference on earth between winning and losing.'

He was silent for several moments and she was afraid she had offended him in some way. She had no idea why it would bother him. Did he feel himself a loser in something, and the pain of it still hurt?

His voice was different when he spoke again, and she saw what looked like a profound sadness in his eyes.

'You say that as if it were observed personally, and not an overall political comment. Do you mean it?' he asked.

She frowned. 'Yes, of course I do. If you won you have the confidence of victory to sustain you, whatever the cost, and it was terrible. We lost people we loved, and we'll never know for certain what happened to some of them, or how, where they're buried, or even if they are. Some are still alive, but so different from what they would have been had they never seen a horror they can't even find words for, faced every physical fear and pain and loss, and seen half their friends killed. They can't tell us, and they can't ever let it go. It would seem like a betrayal of the dead.' She shook her head. Perhaps she was talking too much, but she wanted him to understand that she grasped something of the reality. 'I don't know, not with my heart and my skin and my bones, only with my imagination . . .'

He reached across the narrow table and touched her hand, very gently, and only for a moment. 'And the losers?' he asked. 'They have all of that too . . .'

'Yes. But they also have guilt and confusion . . .'

'Do they accept they started it?' He looked surprised, and perhaps doubtful.

'I've no idea. I wasn't thinking of that. But they have to accept that they lost! Even if some of them think it was a betrayal by their politicians rather than that their army was beaten.'

'You know a lot about it. Most Brits that I know don't.'

'I lived in Germany in the twenties, when my father was with the Embassy there. I had friends. It wasn't so long ago.' She had forced out all the memories she could, but a few, deeply personal, refused to be banished. People were hungry and frightened, proud of what they remembered, and confused and ashamed by what they had become: shabby and always poor. She shook her head. 'Losing is terrible,' she said, finding the words difficult. 'I'm glad they're getting up on their feet again, even if Adolf Hitler is something of a joke with his waving arms and his absurd little moustache. At least they've got their spirit back, and some sense of self-respect.'

Ian seemed lost for an answer. There was patience in his eyes, as if he were looking at a child. 'Hope,' he said after a moment, 'and a direction to turn their anger? That's not quite the same thing.' He smiled, but it struck her as a matter of intent, not with any real pleasure. 'It's pretty destructive to blame yourself for everything, but it's no better to blame other people, especially a particular group of other people.'

'You have to know the cause, in order to stop it happening again,' she pointed out. 'History repeats itself, if you let it.'

'I know it does,' he agreed. 'But not exactly the same way. There are always differences. The war wasn't the gypsies' fault; in fact, they had nothing to do with it.'

She was stunned. 'Who's blaming the gypsies?' she said incredulously.

'Or the trade unionists, or the homosexuals . . . or the Jews,' he went on, his face totally serious. 'It's what people do that's good or bad, not who they are.'

She realised that they had left talking about themselves,

or remembering. They were now speaking of their most intense beliefs, the issues they were prepared to fight for.

'How big a difference is there?' she asked. It was not a challenge, she wanted to know. It was surprising to her – frightening – how much it mattered to her what he thought.

He weighed his words before he spoke. 'Well, for some, very little. We can only answer for what we know . . . or would know if we cared enough. There's a terrible temptation to look at only what you want to, and carefully avoid seeing anything else. "I didn't know!" is the oldest excuse in the world.'

'Is it?' she challenged. 'Really an excuse?'

He smiled again. 'Am I my brother's keeper? Didn't Cain ask that about Abel? Well, the answer is, *Yes, you are!* You are responsible for what you could have done, but chose to look the other way.' There was anger in his voice, and distress.

Elena sat silent for several moments.

People passed by them, walking carefully along the narrow way between the tables, swaying a little to adjust their bodies to the movement of the carriage.

He spoke apologetically. 'With due deference to Milton, "They also sin who only stand and watch."' Then he sat back. 'Would you like a liqueur with your coffee? Something terribly Italian?'

'We should be on the night train from Rome to Milan later this evening. Let's have a liqueur then.'

He agreed, pleased she was looking forward to it, and they made their way as gracefully as possible back to their carriage.

They arrived in Rome and changed trains with just enough time to catch the night train to Milan. Normally, Elena would have found it tedious, but with Ian there it was entirely different: so much to talk about – funny things, memories from long ago, sadness, surprising discoveries. They had much to share, even more to discover about each other that was interesting, or that explained something they could never have understood otherwise. She was surprised at how much she told him about herself involved her grandfather. Perhaps it was because he had taught her the things she cared about most. Their minds seemed to have followed the same paths, and they did not have to explain themselves. Who did not love the songs of Gilbert and Sullivan? Or know exactly how far Earth was from the moon, or admire the French painters of before the war?

Ian told her more about his sisters and made her laugh. He clearly cared for them very much and was slightly self-conscious about how deeply they cared for him. They were all glimpses into the life of the heart, small pictures like the illuminated letters of a manuscript.

From Milan, they needed to catch the next train to Paris. They had to wait about two hours and took the opportunity to walk a little and take a good meal at one of the railway restaurants. Elena was surprised to notice at a table, about ten feet away, a face she recognised from Amalfi. It took her a moment to remember his name, and then it came to her: Walter Mann.

He was looking at her briefly, and then away again as he tried to attract the attention of a waiter. He must have recognised her because he smiled. It was remarkable how that lit his rather grave face. She smiled back, then a waiter crossed between them and she returned her attention to Ian. They were sharing adventures and misadventures, laughing at memories that formed the high points of childhood.

'I remember once, when Mike and I were in the front window watching the thunder and lightning,' she continued. 'We had two dogs then, and they started howling. We joined in.' She began to laugh as she thought of it. They had kneeled on the window seat, shoulder to shoulder, the dogs beside them, all matching each other in making a wonderful noise. 'Mother came in to see what on earth was the matter,' she told him. 'We must have sounded terrible, but we couldn't explain, we were laughing so hard. Even the dogs were too happy to be alarmed. Mother wanted to be furious, said we'd wakened the entire neighbourhood, but then she started to laugh, too. Silly things you remember, isn't it?'

'It's the good things,' he replied. 'The things that matter most are sometimes very small, but they're like portmanteau words: they carry all kind of meaning you can't explain.'

They walked towards their Paris-bound train and found their seats. Maybe they could each take a short nap, but perhaps it would be time wasted. Why waste such precious time when there was so much to talk about? One could sleep later.

'Have you ever been to America?' Ian asked as the train raced across the west of Italy towards the mountains and the border of France.

'Not yet,' Elena replied. 'But I certainly mean to. I have grandparents I've only met when they came to see us. The second visit was lovely because they stayed for nearly a month, and took us all sorts of places we probably wouldn't have seen without them. You know how it is – you could go to Kew Gardens any time, so you put it off. The Tower of London has stood there since William the Conqueror built it. What's the hurry? But I was so proud to show them around.'

'Were you?' He wanted to hear, and as she remembered it, the emotions came back. She found herself earing very much that he wanted to share her feelings at that time, because it was part of who she was now.

They talked until long after midnight. There was no one else in the carriage to keep awake – then they dozed a little for a couple of hours.

Elena woke up with a start to see Ian standing up. She smiled at him. It was comfortable to find him there.

'Like a cup of tea, if I can get one?' he asked.

She realised suddenly that there was nothing she would like more. 'I'd love one. Do you want me to come with you and see what there is?'

'No, it's fine' he replied, looking down at where she was curled up, with her shoes off, her feet up on the seat.

'Thank you,' she accepted. She was still half asleep.

She must have drifted off again into a doze. She woke up with a start to see that he was not back yet, but the carriage door was open and Walter Mann was standing there, looking troubled. His dark hair was fallen forward over his brow and what she could see of his shirt was rumpled under his jacket.

'I'm sorry to disturb you, Miss Standish,' he said.

'That's all right,' she said, shaking her head a little and pushing her hair back off her brow. So he was destined for Paris, too. 'What is it? You look upset. Is there something wrong?'

He came in and closed the compartment door. 'I was looking for Newton.' He remained standing, awkwardly. 'I saw him a few moments ago, and now I can't find him. I thought he was coming back this way. I . . . I expected to find him here. He had tea, or something . . .'

Elena stood up, putting her shoes on. He held out his

hand to steady her. His grip was surprisingly strong. 'Perhaps he's in the corridor?' she suggested, pulling the door open and looking out. She turned both ways, but saw only an elderly woman going a little unsteadily in the opposite direction from the dining car.

'I'm sure he came this way,' Walter said again.

'Then he must be . . .' She made up her mind. He would not go to the cloakroom after he had procured the tea, one would go before. 'He can't be far.'

'I'll wait here,' Walter said. 'But what if—'

'I'll go and look for him,' she said a little impatiently. 'He might have stopped to talk to someone.' She smiled briefly at him, then pulled the door closed and started down the corridor, looking in through the glass windows to see if Ian were inside any one of the compartments, perhaps in conversation. All she saw were people reading, or more often asleep with newspapers or books on their laps.

She stopped at the last compartment before the door closing off the gangway to the next carriage. She glanced through the window and saw someone lying crumpled on the seat. He must have fallen asleep very heavily.

It was several seconds before she recognised Ian's jacket, and then saw him move awkwardly.

She flung the door open, jerking at it, stepped swiftly in and slammed it shut behind her, going instantly to him. He was lying on the seat, doubled over, and there was blood on the floor.

'Ian!' She choked on his name, panic rising inside her.

He moved stiffly, only a few inches, but enough for her to see that there was a lot of blood covering the whole of his chest and all down his trousers to his thighs. It was still pumping. What could she do to stop it? *Anything*. The horror inside her was fogging her mind. She put her hand to his chest instinctively to try to stop the flow, but it was futile.

'Elena . . .' he said in little more than a whisper. 'Don't! There's nothing you can do . . . except listen to me . . .'

'I have to stop the bleeding!' she said desperately.

'No! Listen . . .' His face was white, covered in sweat and he was hanging on to consciousness only with an effort. 'Elena . . .'

'I'm listening.' She refused to believe she could not help, and yet already she knew. It was as if a darkness were closing in on her as well.

'You were right. I knew the man killed in the hotel. I'm Military Intelligence. He was my contact in Amalfi. The telegram I got was to tell me to go immediately to Berlin. I couldn't check its authenticity with him . . . all I could do was go,' he said hoarsely. She had to lean closer to hear him. 'To get a message to the British . . .' He struggled for breath. The blood seemed to be everywhere. '. . . Embassy. To Roger Cordell. He's MI6 . . . like me.' He tried to smile, but the strength was gushing out of him. 'To stop the assassination of Friedrich Scharnhorst . . . at a rally on Tuesday morning, where he's speaking. He's Hitler's man, and he's vile. But if he's killed, we'll be blamed for it.'

'We?' She leaned closer, cradling him in her arms. She knew the tears were running down her face, but it hardly mattered. She knew Roger Cordell from years ago but there was no time to say that.

'The Brits,' he said so quietly she could only read his lips. 'MI6. Please . . . you must get to Berlin and tell Cordell. He'll . . . he'll know what to . . . do . . .' He grasped Elena's hand and pushed a folded piece of paper into it.

'Ian!' she said fiercely. 'No! Please . . .' But she knew it was too late. His eyes were closed, there was blood thick on his body, and his face was ashen. There was not even a flutter of breath.

Elena held him closer, as if she could force her own strength of life into him. She knew there was no point, but she could not let go. 'I will,' she whispered. 'I will . . . I promise.'

Then she could not hold back the agony. She clung to him and sobbed uncontrollably.

Chapter Seven

Elena kneeled on the floor, holding Ian's body as closely as she could, unaware of time. It could have been minutes, or only seconds, before she heard the sound behind her, and even then she did not turn.

'Oh God! What happened?' A man's voice.

She heard the compartment door shut and felt a strong grip on her shoulder. Gently, but very firmly, someone took her hands, first one, then the other, and pulled them away from Ian, then slowly and with great effort, drew her to her feet.

Nearly blind with tears, she turned and saw Walter Mann. His face was white and he looked shattered, although he was more composed than she was. But then he had not loved Ian, and she knew now that she had.

He looked her up and down, and she realised for the first time that she was covered in blood: her hands were scarlet and it was all down the front of her dress. Ian's blood.

She swayed, dizzy and sick.

Walter looked past her to the body on the floor, then back at her. 'What happened?' he said again, his voice scratchy, as if he could not control it.

'He's . . .' She, too, found words too difficult. Her mind was numb, out of control.

'We must get out of here,' he insisted with more strength. 'There's nothing you can do to help him now, and you don't want to get caught by the railway police. They could keep you for hours, maybe more. I suppose you don't know who did this?'

Her thoughts were confused. 'Did this? No . . . no . . . who would . . .?' She had no idea what else to say. Her mind would not function.

'Then they'll blame you,' he pointed out. 'You were with him. They'll think you have to know.' He looked at her blood-soaked dress. 'When the corridor's clear, we'll get you to the lavatory. You must wash as much of that blood off as you can. You'll be freezing cold, I know, but no one will stop you. Take your whole dress off and put it in the basin. Get all the blood out, or as much as you possibly can. There'll be soap in there. Then wring it out and put the dress back on. Where's your coat?'

'What?' she was confused. What did it matter?

'Where's your coat? Is it in the baggage rack in your own compartment?'

'No . . . I . . . no, it's on the seat next to me. There was no one else in the compartment.'

'Good. I'll go and get it. I'll be in the corridor by the lavatory. We must get out of here, pull the blind down and close the door. It's not far to the next station. We'll get off there and catch another train. Just . . . just get rid of that blood. And don't speak to anyone. Do you understand?'

She stared at him.

'Elena! Do you understand? There's nothing you can do to help him now. And there's someone on this train who did that to him! You've got to escape, or you could be next! You're a witness.'

His voice was insistent. It helped her to be calmer now, rational. She must keep her promise to Ian. That was the only thing left. She must get control of herself, stop behaving like a child. Her legs felt shaky and she was cold all the way through, but that was of no consequence. All that mattered was she had made a promise to Ian to finish for him what he could not.

'Elena!'

Walter's voice was sharper. She could hear the fear in it now too. 'Yes,' she said quickly. 'Yes, I'll go and wash. Please see if the lavatory is vacant so I can use it. I can hardly stand in the corridor waiting for someone to come out.'

He gave a tight, painful little smile. 'No,' he agreed. 'Wait here. Close the door behind me and don't answer it to anyone else. Do you understand?'

'Yes . . . yes, of course. Be quick.' It was a plea, not an order.

He touched her on the arm gently, but he did not speak again. He went out and closed the door hard behind him, so she heard the latch click. Then she was alone. The paper was still clutched in her hand. She opened it and found the name and room number of a hotel in Berlin.

She could not bear to look at Ian's body. She was horrified by it, and yet she still wanted to hold him in her arms, as if he could feel her there and know he was not alone.

Were the dead any more alone than the living? Her parents went to church most Sundays. But then her father was a British diplomat, a very senior one. It was expected of him. They had never discussed what he really believed; it was one of the many things they did not talk about. Was that because he was so sure? Or because he had no belief at all? Or was religion just something proper Englishmen did not speak about? Too private? Too important?

Or of no importance at all?

Her mother was different. But then Americans were more open about such things, even well-bred New Englanders like Katherine. But what did that mean, beyond that she wanted to believe? Perhaps 'needed to' would be more accurate.

Her grandfather did not believe in a life after death. Elena knew that. Any kind of organised religion met with his quiet anger for all the judgement it exercised, and, he believed, without right, and far too often without kindness. Kindness was what he believed in. She knew that from observing him. Kindness, and tolerance of difference, understanding that so many acts of bad behaviour were caused by ignorance and pain rather than a decision to be wicked. But what comfort was that when you were torn apart by the anguish of loss, and all you needed to believe was that it was not for ever? That there was a God who would take care of those who had slipped beyond your grasp, beyond your heart. Like Mike? And now like Ian?

There was a sharp rap on the compartment door. She reached out to open it, then froze. What if it was not Walter? What if it was another passenger looking for a space to sit? Or a ticket inspector?

She had to clear her throat to make her voice audible. 'Who is it?'

'Walter. Open the door, it's all clear.'

She undid the latch and threw it back so hard it wrenched her shoulder. Walter was standing in the corridor, the darkness in the windows beyond reflecting him like a mirror.

'Come on,' he said urgently. 'It's vacant now. We must be

quick.' He had her coat across his arm and her smallest case in his hand. 'Come on!' he said again, even more sharply.

She slipped out and slammed the door behind her. There was no time for goodbyes or looking back. She went past Walter, along the corridor and into the lavatory and locked the door. It was a tiny cubicle barely large enough for its purpose, and it was awkward to undo her dress and take it off over her head, but there was no alternative. Thank goodness, the hot tap actually did run hot water, but there was no soap. First, she washed herself. There was blood on her hands and arms, and it had soaked through her dress in places on to her body. She used a handkerchief to scrub it off the best she could. It took three bowlsful of water, then a fourth to wash her dress beyond the first deep, wet stains. It would not all come out. Perhaps it never would. But then she would never want to wear it again anyway, once she had another! She should have asked Walter to open her case and find her a different one, but he couldn't be caught doing it, or that would be the end of both of them. They could hardly explain!

She started scrubbing hard and her mind wandered. The bloodstains were coming out, but it was not good enough yet.

She must be quick. Someone else might want the lavatory. And when they reached the station they must get off. She could already feel the train slowing down.

She wrung out her dress, then, shaking with cold, slid the wet fabric over her shoulders. It stuck to her like icy fingers and she almost tore it, pulling it down. It must look dreadful, but anything was better than the blood.

For a moment, panic almost suffocated her. She took a few slow, deep breaths and opened the door. She saw Walter only a yard or two away. He had her coat over his arm, and as soon as she was out of the door, he held it up and she slipped her arms into it, then fastened it in front. Fortunately, it was a full-length coat, falling a few inches past her knees, like her dress, as it was when dry, and not clinging to her like a freezing shroud.

The train was slowing down very noticeably now. She had her handbag with her – she would not have left the compartment without it – but what about her other cases? Above all, her camera!

'I must—' she started, turning to go back.

He caught her arm, holding it hard. 'No! We can't go back there. As soon as the train stops we must go – quickly.'

'I've got to get my cases,' she insisted.

He did not ease his grip. 'Elena! We can't carry more than one each. We will have to hurry. Maybe run.'

'But my camera. I can't leave it!'

'I know. The Leica. I put it into this case, and some clothes back into the big one. I'm sorry, but we can't worry about what's lost now. You've got your camera and your passport, and some money. Above all, you've got your life. So far, the police don't know anything about you, but they will. People will remember you, and that you were with Newton. You're a noticeable woman.' He kept his voice low, and perhaps trying to keep the anger out of it, but the fear was unmistakable.

'I'm sorry . . .' She was. After all, he did not have to have done anything to help her. He did not have to believe that she had not somehow killed Ian herself! He did not ask for gratitude, but he deserved at least compliance, and some sense of preservation for herself because she was now implicating him, too. Who knew what the police might make of

76

her with Ian, and now with Walter? And who could blame them?

She would have waited and explained, even if it had taken days, if she did not have a far more important promise to keep. And she could not help the police. She had no idea who had killed Ian, and she realised now she had not even searched to see if he had been robbed. Maybe the murderer was the same person who had killed the man in the hotel cupboard?

'Come on,' Walter said more gently. 'We need to be the first off the train, and be as far away from it as possible, before anyone discovers there's been a death. Just take your handbag. I'll carry the cases. Keep your head down, don't look at anyone. Behave as if we're hurrying to get the next train to . . . wherever. We need to know, so we make for the right platform. There won't be a lot of choice. God knows where we are, but we can't stay on this train.'

'Berlin,' she said without hesitation. 'I need to get to Berlin. I've . . . I've got some work to do there. It's important.' Did that sound cold-blooded? Work? When Ian had just died? But she could not explain.

'It's even more important that we get off the platform and away from this train,' he reminded her. 'But don't worry. I've done a lot of travelling in this area. We'll find a train, but it would be better if we got the very first one out of here, even if we only go one stop, then change. It's—'

'I know,' she said quickly. 'I understand.'

The train jolted and slowed once more.

Elena nearly lost her balance and was grateful for Walter's arm around her. She would draw attention to herself if she collapsed in the doorway. She wanted to be invisible. In fact, she wanted to wake up and discover this had all been some frightful nightmare, and she was so cold only because she had lost the cover in bed. Finding Ian bleeding to death, the horror, the grief, and now the wet clothing sticking to her, and the fear, would all vanish.

But of course it wouldn't: it was real. It must be faced, and dealt with, like Mike's death, and Paul, Margot's husband's. Life goes on, with or without you, and that would never change.

A woman bumped into her and apologised in Italian. Elena could not react quickly enough to reply. Walter said something, but she did not hear the words.

She was behaving badly. Ian deserved better than this. She forced herself to straighten up. No one else knew her dress was cold, sodden wet, still stained with Ian's lifeblood. She must not make anyone suspicious.

The train jolted again. They were at the end of a platform, she saw the name of the station, but it went by too rapidly to read it. They were somewhere east of Paris, that was all she knew. They had to be, because Paris was the terminus.

The corridor was filling with people. At least half a dozen seemed to want to get off here. Why? Where were they? Please God, no one would open the door to where Ian was. She felt such a traitor leaving him there alone, on the floor, as if nobody cared. She must force it out of her mind, though it was unbearable, a pain that tore her apart.

Was it any worse, or more anonymous than a battlefield?

Yes. It was the floor of a railway carriage – alone – and yet his death was intensely personal: someone had murdered him.

There was nothing she could do about it, except pull herself together and fulfil the promise she had made him.

The train jerked to a stop. Immediately, Walter opened

the door and stepped out on to the platform, then he put down the cases, swung round and held out his arm to take Elena's hand and steady her. It was a steep drop, but he took her weight for a moment, then as she straightened her shoulders and picked up her bag, he picked up the cases and started forward along the platform. It was still the night. She had very little idea of the time, but there were sufficient lights to see where they were going, and that there were a dozen or so other people getting on or off the train. Far ahead of them, the engine blew steam into the air, catching the light in a silver pale fog.

Walter moved quickly, crossing to the far side of the platform, away from the carriage doors and anyone else getting off.

Elena ran a couple of steps to keep level with him, and walked to his left, so he sheltered her from sight. She was more noticeable than he, with his coat collar turned up and hat brim down a little. It was May, very nearly summer, but still at this hour most men would have a coat, especially travelling north, and it made sense to wear it rather than carry it. He could have been anyone. She, with her well-cut green coat, whose shade was visible when she passed the lights, and her hair, with its heavy wave, and fair shade from the sun, would be far more easily recalled.

He had said she was memorable – her face. Was it? Was it a compliment, normally? Right now, she would rather be one of those English girls of no particular colouring or feature that one saw and instantly forgot, just like ten thousand others.

'I'm going to the other platform,' he said, 'where the light's blinking. Looks as if there's a train due in any moment.'

'Where to?' she asked.

'Doesn't matter. Right now, anywhere will do.'

'I've got to get to Berlin!'

'We've got to get anywhere that's away from here,' he corrected her bleakly. 'We can get off at the next stop.' He did not ask why she was going to Berlin, when they had been on a train to Paris. He probably did not care. Why should he?

She ought to thank him properly. She would do, later, when she had more breath to spare, and was not so busy hurrying along the ill-kept platform with its cracked asphalt and occasional broken lights. At least hurrying like this made her a little warmer, although the wet skirt of her dress flapped around her legs like ice.

They came to the steps and went up them as fast as they could. It was a rickety bridge over the track, the surface rough and uncertain. Behind them the whistle blew on the train they had left. Doors clanged shut. Was it possible no one had found Ian yet?

Elena was relieved, but at the same time felt an ache of loneliness tightening around her. It was frightening that anyone could die so terribly, and nobody even notice. She felt an overwhelming sense of betrayal at having to leave him!

Walter was going faster than she was able to keep up. He must have realised it, because he slowed a little. There was hardly anyone around, no one else on the flight of steps going down.

At the bottom, the sign was lit, but there was no train. Why were railway platforms so windy? Was hell like this? A cold railway platform in the dark, with a train that never came? The station suddenly seemed terribly silent.

On the far side of the track, she could see an official of some sort. The one functioning light cast a gleam on the rim of his cap. He was smoking a cigarette, the thin trail wafted upwards and occasionally the end glowed as he drew the nicotine into his lungs.

Walter went to look at a timetable posted up on a board, then returned to wait beside Elena.

Elena stood still, silent and growing colder. She lost track of time. Perhaps it was really only minutes, but then there was a movement at the far, northern end of the track, a distant clatter, and the man on the further platform dropped his cigarette and stood on the butt.

'Are we on the right side?' Elena said urgently.

'It's single track,' Walter replied reassuringly. 'It's just a local train. We'll get off at the next big station. It's the second one along. We might have to wait half an hour or so, but from there we can catch a train to Munich, and from Munich to Berlin will be no difficulty.'

'We? Are you coming?' She realised how much she wanted him to. Her mind was not capable of thinking clearly. Grief engulfed her.

'We'll have to stop this side of the German border,' he answered, 'and do something about our papers. The Italian border guards will know you were travelling with Newton. When his body is discovered it won't take them long to realise you've disappeared. Whatever they think – that you killed him, or that you were abducted – they'll want to find you. If they catch you crossing into Germany alone, they'll have to conclude you killed him . . . I know you didn't.' He smiled, as if he felt the absurd horror of such an idea. 'But do you want to take that risk?'

'No!' She had not even thought of that, but he was right. And she had to go to Berlin, immediately. All she could do for Ian now. It was little enough.

81

Walter smiled. She could see only the outline of his face here on the platform, where they had deliberately chosen not to wait near the lights. There was a momentary flash of white teeth, and the crown of his hat against the mist as the train lights came closer.

'I know people,' he said. 'We can get you other papers. You can come as my wife – or fiancée, if you prefer. They won't stop me. I have German citizenship.'

She started to question why he should do this for her, but anything else they might have said was lost in the noise as the train headlights swept them all with brilliant light, then darkness again, and the clatter of wheels on steel tracks drowned out everything.

The train finally stopped. Walter opened the nearest door and helped her up, going up the step after her. He did not say anything, but led the way along the aisle to find seats for them.

'Thank you,' she said quietly when they were sitting, and the train pulled out of the station.

He smiled suddenly. 'I could hardly do less! What a bloody awful thing . . .' His voice trembled as he spoke.

She tried to smile back, but tears streamed down her face, and she leaned into the high corner upholstery of the seat and wept silently.

Chapter Eight

Peter Howard knocked lightly on Jerome Bradley's door, and as soon as he heard Bradley's slightly impatient voice, he walked in, closing the door behind him.

Bradley's official smile weakened, leaving the same expression on his good-looking face, but the light had vanished from it. 'Good morning, Howard,' he said. 'What can I do for you?'

Peter Howard knew that this was Bradley's usual tactic: leave the other man to set the tone, and thereby commit himself first. He very seldom asked for a report, allowing the other man to offer it. Only if it was overdue did he assert his authority and demand it. This tactic succeeded in making his juniors seek his approval more diligently than if they had known precisely what he wanted.

It was a form of game-playing, and Howard despised it. 'Good morning, sir,' he replied. To anyone else he would have apologised, as a matter of courtesy, for bringing bad news. It was habit to do so. To Jerome Bradley, he came straight to the point. 'I have enough news from Berlin now to raise serious concerns about Roger Cordell.' As Bradley drew in breath to argue, Howard went on, 'One or two things have gone wrong there recently, and the explanations don't entirely fit together. Only small—'

'—discrepancies,' Bradley finished for him. This was not the first time Howard had come with this uncertainty. 'And you'd be just as suspicious if there were none.' He gave a bleak smile. 'I remember you coming to me with a complaint that Feltham was too perfectly consistent. You said it looked as if he were tailoring his reports to fit the circumstances. You're a complainer, Howard. Frankly, I think you're doing a good bit of tailoring yourself, looking for something to make trouble about. And where there isn't any, you manufacture it!' At last it was an open accusation. It had been lying just under the surface for a long time, three or four years at least.

Howard waited several seconds before he replied. There was some justice in it, but not a lot. He resented Bradley because he was not Lucas Standish. Lucas had been his friend, his colleague, as close as he had to family. He had not been dismissed; he had retired because of his age. But he might well have been released anyway. His methods did not fit well with the new ideas, at least the ideas of most of the men in power, especially in the Foreign Office, that there must never be another war like the last. It had to live up to its legendary name: the war to end all wars.

Howard had never been a regular soldier. He had come straight from university into MI6. Did it make any difference that his war had been covert? He had lost as many friends, certainly he had seen as much violence and grief as anyone in uniform. But he was a realist. The prospect of war does not vanish, no matter how passionately anyone wishes it.

'Don't just stand there pretending to be stupid!' Bradley snapped. 'What is it you think you know? What is it you think Cordell has done? Is his information false? Any of it? Ever?'

'I didn't suggest he was a fool,' Howard said tartly. 'He's a highly intelligent man. But he's an idealist . . .'

'I'm well aware that you like to think of yourself as a realist, Howard,' Bradley said bitterly. 'Sometimes I wonder if you half want another war, so you'll be necessary again, and having adventures with other people's lives. I know how you admired Standish. He was a man who lived in his head, if ever a man did! God knows how many died in idiotic missions because of his fancies.'

Howard's patience snapped. 'God knows, and so do I!' he said between clenched teeth. 'We're anxious about another war and so should you be. You should add yourself to us . . .'

'Us?' Bradley was suddenly rigid in his chair. This was a quarrel that had long lain beneath the surface, simmering, increasing in heat. 'Who the hell is "us"? This is not a "we" and "them" situation, Howard. Can't you get that into your head? The war is over! Over!' He sliced his hand sideways in the air. 'Finished! We won . . . if you remember? Were you AWOL at the time?' That was pure sarcasm. They had shared in the victory celebrations, watched the parade down Whitehall together. And of course, Lucas had been there, quietly, in the background, as always.

'God and me,' Howard repeated. 'And, of course, Lucas. He always knew. It haunted him.'

Bradley was lost for a moment, then his face filled with disgust. 'You put yourself and Lucas Standish on a level with God? Your arrogance is beyond my mind to grasp.'

'All men are on a level with God in understanding their own guilt,' Howard replied quietly. 'Even you.'

'Don't be so damned pompous! Putting yourself on a level with God in anything! You're . . . absurd!'

'To think of God?' Howard raised his eyebrows. 'You talk about God enough, but for you He's only really to be wheeled out on Sundays! Lucas lost more men than you did and saved a hundred times more. Well, you had better be prepared to add a few more to your losses if you don't watch Cordell. Some people see the best in others, but it's our job to see the worst also.' He stood up a little straighter, almost to attention. 'It's not what he's saying, it's what he's not saying—'

'If he's not saying it,' Bradley interrupted, 'how do you know it exists? You've contradicted yourself!'

'Do you think Cordell is the only source I've got?' Howard said incredulously. 'You'd call him out for inconsistencies quickly enough, and rightly, if I didn't check and triple-check when I can.'

For long seconds Bradley did not answer. His dislike of Howard was palpable in the air, but underneath it he had a certain respect for him, and he trusted his loyalty, if not his personal judgement.

Perhaps, if he were honest, he acknowledged, Howard could say the same of him.

'What, exactly, do you suspect him of?' Bradley said at last.

'A slightly skewed judgement,' Howard answered. 'An over-looking of some aspects of Hitler's admirers. Goebbels, in particular. Maybe Cordell wants peace so badly he can't see the warning in the building of these camps for gypsies, Jews . . . whoever doesn't fit the classic Aryan mould. It's the oldest trick in the book of a demagogue to blame all your troubles on an identifiable group, turn people's attention to something

86

they can hate, and they'll leave you alone, especially if you make them feel justified in killing them.'

'And isn't it all the fault of the Communists?' Bradley asked, this time there was no aggression in his voice. 'Aren't they a disruptive, almost nihilistic force?'

'Yes,' Howard answered. 'But sinking to their level of violence is joining them, not beating them . . .' He knew as he spoke that it was not really an answer.

Bradley knew it too. 'And isn't that irrational anyway?'

'At the moment,' Howard agreed. 'But I think it won't always be. Hitler's gaining power every week. He's building up an enormous head of steam, of energy, violence, hatred there. He'll have to direct it somewhere else, in another few years.'

Bradley sat thinking that over for several moments. Then he sighed. 'I don't much like you, Howard. And I know you don't like me, primarily because I'm not Lucas Standish, but I think you're right, in this at least. And I dare say in the long run, if Hitler continues the way he's going, I shall lose as many men as Standish. I'll be glad if I save as many! And get the same kind of loyalty!' He looked directly at Howard.

Howard felt the heat burn up his face, but he did not look away. 'You'll get it from me, sir. Not the regard, but certainly the loyalty. And before I go, I have to tell you our man in Amalfi, Cossotto, was murdered. Don't know by whom, or why. It's possible it had nothing to do with us, but it would be dangerous to assume it.'

Bradley lost a little colour in his face. 'What's happening in Amalfi, for God's sake?'

'Nothing that I know of.'

'Who told you? Not the Italian police?'

'No, of course not. One of our own. Maybe there's no connection. He was found in a hotel linen cupboard. Perhaps a jealous husband . . . or a thief.'

'Do you think so?'

'No.'

Bradley's voice was sharp with exasperation. 'Then who, for God's sake?'

'I don't know . . .'

'Then what are you doing to find out?'

'Very little I can do, without tipping my hand,' Howard replied. There was a degree of apology in his tone. 'I am more concerned with damage control regarding what Newton is working on. And also, how anyone knew the connections. I want to find out as discreetly as possible for a lot of reasons, starting with not betraying our interest in him, in case his death had nothing to do with us. Or even if it was a test to see if we would own it either intentionally, or accidentally by becoming involved.'

'A trap?' Bradley said quietly.

'It's possible. Our relationship with the Italian authorities is . . . a trifle uncertain. Mussolini is with us in some things, and very definitely against us in others.'

'The Italians were with us in the war,' Bradley pointed out. 'Half Britain has been having a love affair with Italy for centuries!'

'Love affairs and politics frequently cross,' Howard replied with a slightly twisted smile. 'They are interchangeable, and highly volatile. And often end in one sort of war, or another.'

Bradley looked at him steadily, and Howard knew that, for a moment or two at least, they had an understanding.

He took his leave while he was still winning, as much as he ever would with Bradley.

Howard thought about Cordell on his way home. He was late, as usual, but not sufficiently for Pamela to make an issue about it. They did not often quarrel these days. They both knew that nobody was going to win.

He arrived at the gate, opened it, and walked up the path. It was a handsome house and the garden was full of flowers. The middle of May was the best time for gardens, although Pamela had chosen the plants so there was always something to give it colour. There was a yellow rose in full bloom over the door. He presumed it must have a perfume, but he could not smell it.

He opened the door and went in. Should he apologise for being late? He did it regularly.

She came out of the sitting room. She was wearing a green dress. With her fair, smooth hair and perfect skin, it suited her.

'Sorry to be late,' he said.

'No later than usual,' she replied, a sadness in her face that pricked him with guilt.

He sat down in his usual chair, well-worn leather and infinitely comfortable. He dreaded the day when it would have to be replaced. Was there a lot in his life like that? Well worn, familiar, irreplaceable. He didn't feel like that. They were only the outer things. Inside, his mind, his imagination, even sometimes his emotions, were sharper, more alive, than ever.

Pamela brought him a small glass of sherry, very dry, the way he liked it. She knew all his habits; he never had to ask. The glass was crystal, purposely made for sherry. Waterford.

They had six. A wedding present from what seemed like another age. They had been in love then, or thought they were. Was it part of the definition of love that it should last? Or not.

'Thank you,' he said quietly. He wanted to add something, but they had long ago run out of conversation. Some forced observation, for the sake of saying something, would make the silence heavier. She used to ask about his day, his week, or at least if it was going well. He could not claim the victories, and found it awkward telling her half of it, and then stopping just before the parts that made sense of it. She was an intelligent woman, well educated, albeit in subjects of pleasure rather than use, such as European art history. He had found them interesting, when they had had time to talk.

But he felt as if he were always shutting her out of the things that mattered to him. He had no choice. Not speaking of subjects, even to your own family, was a rule never to be broken. It was a greater consideration to their feelings. Sharing anxiety over what he could not control was exhausting and purposeless. Sooner or later his tongue would slip, and he would say something that led to something else, and finally she would put it together. His silence was a shield for not even suspecting her of accidental error, or intentional betrayal. But failure to explain that ended in making it worse.

Now he had shut her out for too long, it was like an old door that had rusted shut. He had even considered saying how sorry he was, but it would only make the loss more obvious. It would be like taking the plaster off an old wound to see if it had healed, when it still hurt from time to time, and you knew perfectly well it had not knitted.

Roger Cordell was still on his mind. He sipped his sherry. 'Are you still in touch with Winifred Cordell?' he asked suddenly.

Pamela was startled. 'What?' She had plainly been off in her own thoughts.

He repeated his question. She looked surprised. It gave a sudden spark of life to the picture perfection of her face. He used to think it beautiful, everything was in proportion, her skin flawless, as if there were not a fallible woman behind it, someone who could be hurt just as deeply as he could.

'Why?' she asked. 'Has something happened?'

Peter felt self-conscious. He should not have tried to be oblique with her. There were parts of him – large, closed-off, vulnerable parts – she did not know existed, but the ordinary, everyday things she knew far better than he knew her. She thought he was a civil servant, something to do with the Foreign Office, too boring to talk about.

'Peter! Has something happened?' she repeated, a sharp edge of anxiety audible in her voice.

'Sorry. Not that I know of.' He must give a believable reason for asking. If she really was in touch with Winifred Cordell, she might know something of Cordell's mind. He had to ask, not only to satisfy Pamela, but to answer the nagging worry at the back of his own. He realised now just how sharp it was. It was easy to dismiss the murder in Amalfi as unconnected. He knew better than to make that sort of lazy mistake.

She did not believe him. It was clear in her eyes.

'There's a problem I think Roger could give me advice about.' He must be careful what he told her. She remembered far too much of what he said.

'Advise you?' she said, looking at him more closely.

'A diplomatic matter,' he had the answer ready now. 'He's been in Berlin quite a long time. Speaks German very well indeed. Catches the cultural references, the light and shade of a conversation, as well as just the words . . .'

'I've never heard you speak so well of him.'

There was a wealth of feeling behind that observation. In so many things she did not know him at all, not his dreams, the things he struggled with alone at night, not the clamour of memories in his head. But she knew the emotions he gave away in his speech, and his silences. Too late to go back and attempt to start now. He had needed his solitude to deal with all the pain of war, of command and decision, of being safe when he was sending men into occupied territory, possibly to die. The only one who understood that was Lucas. And anyway, he did not want Pamela's pity. He had seen it before, for other men. It too quickly grew into impatience, resentment for having to bear the second-hand pain of an experience she had been excluded from sharing at the time.

'Berlin's a tough posting,' he replied.

'It has been for years,' she pointed out.

'It's getting harder.'

'Since Adolf Hitler came to the top?' she asked. There was interest in her voice.

Suddenly he wanted to share it with her, speak honestly for once. But you cannot start off being plain, open, and then stop. She was far too clever, and it was important to her, so she would be unable to let it go, even if she wanted to.

She was watching him, waiting for his answer.

'I think so. There's more open violence, and he can't help knowing it.'

'Isn't it necessary? After all the disorganisation, the hunger, the despair, people need order. You can't get that without a pretty heavy hand.'

'I think it's a little worse than that. But I wondered how Roger was. And Winifred. She lost a lot of her family in the war. She must be finding this difficult.'

Pamela smiled, bleakly in the lips, but then with a sudden warming in the eyes. 'Yes. Poor Winifred lost her father, both her brothers, and a cousin – at least one. I don't think that she can get over that.' She stopped, uncertain whether to go on. Her face was full of pity, and a search for a way to understand it.

'Is Roger helping her?' he asked.

She spent a moment or two hunting for a way to put her thoughts into words. 'He lost people in the war, too,' she began. 'Not as many family as she did, but people he knew, and cared about. Men who served with him. He was a pretty good officer, you know . . .'

Her face was almost unreadable. Almost, not quite. He saw in it the one reason she could not understand or defend him to his friends, or more importantly, to himself. She was used to circling around the subject. Was she going to break twenty years of hurt now? He would not blame her.

'I know,' he replied. 'And perhaps it's easier for him because he feels he is doing something about it.'

'What?' she frowned, still trying to understand.

He must choose his words carefully. 'Cultural Attaché? I thought he was working pretty hard for understanding between Britain and Germany, the new leadership. They had one war with us; they don't want another war, not with anyone.'

She smiled and her shoulders relaxed. 'Yes. That's pretty

much what she said. And it is a great comfort to her, as much as anything can be. He'll do pretty well anything to prevent there ever being another war . . . in our lifetime.'

He knew she was telling the truth. It was what he had feared. He smiled back at her and said nothing.

Chapter Nine

This time when Lucas met Peter Howard it was not in the woods, much as they both enjoyed the peace and the beauty of them. If you wanted to keep secrets, habits were dangerous. There was a walk in the fields that Toby liked just as much. In fact, any situation at all in which he could be talked to, fussed over, then conveniently ignored to wander off on his own after any wonderful smell was perfect to him. He never went very far. He was Lucas's dog, and he liked to know where Lucas was. It was his job to look after him.

So, when Lucas received a telephone call just two days after their previous meeting, he put on his jacket and told Toby to fetch his lead, something which he never had to be told twice.

'Just going to take the dog for a walk,' Lucas called to Josephine, who was busy writing letters. She was a good correspondent. She kept in touch with many of the women she had worked with during the war. Some of these relationships had been friendships of forced circumstances, and after the war were packed up, like other hardships of the time, and forgotten. Others lasted, in some cases because the women had victories and losses they could share with no one else. For many it had been the least lonely time in their lives when the usual barriers of background did not matter. They had belonged in a way that seldom happened in peacetime.

Josephine had begun to explain this to Lucas one day, and then seen from his face that he already knew. She did not question his friendship with Howard, and Lucas had no idea whether she knew that they still kept the old relationship by meeting up. It was something he could not share and she had never asked him to, or pushed for explanation of exactly what he did during those dark and hectic days. She had her own secrets to keep and respected his. He loved her the more for it.

As he parked the car at the field entrance, he thought again how much he admired his wife. Despite the length of their marriage she still managed to surprise him, not so much with new ideas as with interpretations of old ones that he had never perceived. She was so often completely original. He knew that it was her unusual imagination that had caused her to be chosen for her position, and he was proud of that.

It puzzled him how she could possibly have given birth to a man like Charles, who seemed to be so desperately orthodox in everything. Was it the times he lived in? The need for conformity to preserve the old, with its values and its remembered safety? Or had the diplomatic service and the war done that to him? He had risen high and rapidly. He had married a perfect wife. Katherine was intelligent, charming, always elegant and, above all, intensely loyal. Margot had taken after her in that. She also had the same flair for style that Katherine had, and originality.

Lucas opened the field gate and went in, closing it carefully behind him, then he let Toby off the lead and watched him run joyously after a scent, nose to the ground, tail in the air.

Lucas could understand why Charles, like uncountable others – for instance, like Roger Cordell – had sworn that they would never fight another war, no matter what Hitler did. Mike had been Charles's only son, and Lucas's only grandson. But more than that, he had been a unique and beloved person. Lucas could still hear Mike's voice in his mind, his laughter, his ridiculous jokes, his endless optimism. He had been so very young, on the brink of life.

Katherine had seldom spoken of the death of her son, but it had numbed her too, as it did any mother. Too much grief.

Little wonder Margot went wild now and then, or that she had one romance after another. Lucas did not know how far she took them, nor did he want to know. But she never settled for anyone. Who could match Paul? He had not lived long enough to be anything other than perfect. Did she feel it would be a betrayal to marry anyone else? He could understand that, too, irrational as it was.

Elena had always been the one he understood best. He had missed her when she moved into her own flat in London. Her mind was so quick, so tireless. She understood him yet she was in other ways totally different from him, all emotion and imagination, full of pictures in the mind.

He had not liked the little he knew of Aiden Strother, but he would have forgiven him anything if he had made Elena happy. But he had betrayed her, as he had betrayed his country. Somehow the personal hurt more!

She would get over it. Of course she would. Most people were hurt in love, some time or other. Maybe she would find herself in her photography? She might discover her real talent at last. She was so often trying to experiment with light and shadow, with showing something in a different way from usual, so you saw a new dimension to it.

She should be home from Amalfi soon. At the thought, his heart lifted.

Toby had stopped and was barking. Then suddenly he recognised whoever or whatever it was he had seen and set off at a gallop. Please heaven it was not a cow or a sheep loose!

Lucas strode forwards up the slight slope, limping slightly with his bad ankle, and at the top he saw that it was Peter Howard, who must have come in at the far side of the field. Lucas saw him kneel down as Toby charged up and threw himself at him, all but knocking him over.

Lucas reached him just as he regained his balance, spoke first to Toby, then smiled at Lucas, a bleak, very measured gesture, looking over the dog's head. He moved quietly, stroking the animal's ears, his attention still on the comfort and the affection of touch.

'You should get a dog,' Lucas said quickly. An animal would offer Peter a companionship, an outlet for unspoken affection, perhaps a trust he would find nowhere else. It did not need explanations. Dogs only wanted feeding, exercise, to be talked to, and love, endless love. They never criticised.

Howard did not look up. 'Pamela doesn't like animals,' he said quietly.

Lucas saw the pain in his face, and was angry with himself for having spoken without thought. He had met Pamela Howard only a dozen or so times in all the years he had known Peter. The deep friendship between Peter and Lucas had grown, first through trust and intellectual respect, then wry jokes in times of tension or defeat, and an enormous love of certain music, especially Beethoven and Liszt. They had also shared a peace in the company of animals, plus a score of small things over the years that told almost too much about the inner man.

Lucas should have known that Pamela Howard would find dogs untidy, intrusive, and too demanding of her time. And also, perhaps, that Peter would show the animal a tenderness she had never awoken in him. Or maybe they had hurt each other once too often? Dogs forgive, and will come back again and again. Children will, sometimes, and get hurt again. They learned only slowly to understand that some people never need the reality of love, because it always carried the possibility of pain.

Lucas did not know what the hurt was between Peter and his wife. He did not want to. Anyone was due a degree of privacy. Some wounds healed in the light, some could be borne only because they were hidden.

It would be impractical for Peter to have a dog because he travelled too often. He would not leave an animal in the care of someone who did not love it, talk to it, touch it.

They started to walk along the edge of the field. The grass was tall already. Four months of decent weather and it would be ripe, and in this particular field it would be grazed with scarlet poppies, casually, like a spray of blood across the gold. Vivid, beautiful, and tearing at the memory, as poppies always did, since Flanders.

Lucas knew what Howard had come for, apart from the pleasure of the walk. 'Got a plan for Cordell?' he asked after fifty yards or so.

Howard continued walking slowly, hands in his pockets. The sun was bright and high. Six weeks, and it would be the longest day.

Lucas did not ask what the plan was. Howard would tell him if he wished.

They walked in silence a little further. A long way off they heard lambs bleating. Other than that, there was only the slight whisper of wind in the grass.

'That's only part of why I came . . .' Howard began.

Lucas did not say anything. Somewhere at the back of his mind he had known that the plan regarding Cordell was not the reason.

'I had a message from young Newton, from the railway station in Rome. I've mentioned him to you before. Just a telegram. He's on his way to Berlin. He got intelligence that there's a plan to assassinate Scharnhorst and blame it on the British. MI6, specifically . . . He's a good man; he's got it all in hand.'

Lucas stopped walking, and Howard stopped also, facing him now.

'You didn't say that before,' Lucas said softly. 'Why not? Are you saying you didn't know? Scharnhorst is a pretty big fish. Maybe one of the worst close to Hitler . . .'

'The worst,' Howard agreed.

'No. Goebbels is the worst. If you can't see that, you soon will. But if there was a plot against Scharnhorst, why didn't we have any word of it?'

'I don't know. But we do now . . .'

'And I suppose he'll contact Cordell,' Lucas said.

'Bound to . . .' Howard replied. 'Unless Newton's information included the possibility that Cordell knew, and didn't tell him?'

'Or is behind it?' Lucas was compelled to say it.

Howard's jaw muscles tightened and suddenly all the pleasure left his expression. 'I thought of that too. If I don't hear, I may go out there myself,' he said at last. 'I hate going to Germany, it's such a bloody tragedy, but if Cordell is a traitor, we'll have to get rid of him fast, or else use him. It's a decision that'll have to be made instantly.'

'I haven't been there for a long time,' Lucas said thoughtfully. 'I hear stories, but they're always bits and pieces. I don't see the fabric beneath. Churchill's afraid it's all got to end in war again, or else a kind of defeat for us that's worse than war.'

Howard turned sharply and looked at him, the question in his face.

'We become them . . .' Lucas answered. 'We retreat and retreat, morally, until there is no meaningful difference left between us. What you see, and allow without a fight, is what you become yourself. What is the moral difference between the man who burns his neighbour to death, and the man who stands by and watches him do it?'

Howard's face for once showed his emotion. 'None,' he replied. 'Or none that I could defend. But the Germans are starving; decent men are willing to work, yet there is nothing for them. Or there wasn't. Re-arming offers work, Lucas. And God knows, they are certainly doing that! We would know, if we wanted to look, but we don't!' He hesitated a moment.

Lucas did not interrupt him. He needed to say this.

'The violence is increasing, and the oppression. They're building camps to put prisoners in, not people who've committed crimes, but people who are born guilty of being gypsies or Jews or, God help us, homosexuals. Why the hell do we care what people do in their own bedrooms? I know, I know . . .' He made a small gesture of dismissal, chopping the air with his hand. 'They're an instinctive target, vulnerable, and we don't understand, so we are afraid. How many unhappy people are branded just because they look or sound different, and don't fit in with what we feel comfortable with?'

Lucas did not bother to respond.

'Somebody to lash out at,' Howard answered himself. 'They're frightened, and fear makes people angry because they are ashamed that they can't do anything about it. It's easier if it's someone's fault. Blame the Communists, or the Jews. Get rid of them, and everything will be all right.'

'Is it really that bad?' It was a rhetorical question, but Lucas asked it anyway.

Howard glanced at him with a rueful smile. 'Sorry. Have you seen Churchill recently?'

'Yesterday. He's in one of his "black dog" moods. Nobody wants to listen to him. We've got too many Nazi admirers in the Government, and other places of influence, and they're gaining ground. We have an infinite capacity for believing whatever we need to in order to keep our world the way we need it to be, for our own sanity. We want to believe that Hitler's fine, and as soon as he's got Germany back on its feet he'll direct his anger eastwards at the Communists, and we'll all be better off for it.'

Howard swore under his breath.

'Peter, nobody wants another war,' Lucas said quietly. 'We believe what we need to. We can't go through that again. It takes a kind of courage to hope. The more reality is against you, the more courage it takes.'

'Hope . . .' Howard turned the thought over in his mind. 'What about reality? I know! I know . . . you're going to say "whose reality?" And what is faith worth, if it's in the impossible?'

102

Lucas smiled. 'Actually, I would have said faith is only of value if it seems impossible. At least that's what Josephine would say.'

Howard gave him one of his rare, beautiful smiles, shadowless, like a burst of pure sunlight. Then it was gone again. 'Who am I to argue with Josephine?' he said.

'Nobody,' Lucas agreed. 'Certainly not me. Even Elena doesn't argue with her grandmother.'

'I must meet your Elena one day. She sounds formidable.'

'She is,' Lucas agreed. 'Argue the leg off an iron pot!'

'And you adore her,' Howard added.

'I always have. Too late to abandon the habit now.' He gave a quick shrug. 'What are you going to do about Cordell?'

'I suppose he might be useful,' Howard said unhappily. 'Feed him enough false information, although that's a risky business. It'll be even harder keeping real information from him. He's pretty high up. May have to pull him out. Then what the hell do we do with him? It's not wartime.'

'You'll have to be very careful . . .' Lucas warned.

'I'm always careful,' Howard replied. 'Well . . . almost always.' He added that because Lucas knew very well some of the wilder things he had done during the war.

Toby went chasing off after what might have been a rabbit, more likely a ripple of wind through the corn.

They both stopped and stared across the land, dappled with cloud and sunshine, but all of it basking in utter peace, like a cat in the sun.

They did not need to finish the conversation. They both knew how all the rest of it played out. Everyone was weary of war, bruised by loss, bewildered by the vast poverty and fear that covered just about everywhere. Fear of hunger, fear of chaos, change, fear of the unknown political thinking from Russia and the east, fear of more violence and loss that would begin all over again. Please God, Churchill was not right.

And yet Lucas believed he was. But right or not, you could not, must not ever persecute people because they disagreed. If you descended to that, you created a greater destruction than they could. And possibly unlike them, you knew what you were doing, and that it was wrong.

He turned to look at Howard's face as he watched the corn shaking where Toby ploughed through it, returning happily, his tail high. He had not caught anything – he never did – but he was the last one to care. He slid to a halt in front of Howard, who bent down and gave him a sudden hug, to Toby's wriggling delight. Lucas saw in his friend a wave of emotion he had not witnessed before, a complete and unselfconscious love that he seldom dared reveal. He said nothing.

Howard rose to his feet and they walked back in companionable silence along the hedgerow.

Lucas arrived home, ready to enjoy a little quiet time at the piano, perhaps have another attempt at playing one of his favourite Chopin pieces.

Josephine greeted him, shaking her head. 'You've forgotten, haven't you?' It was more a statement than a question.

'Forgotten what?' he asked. He had no idea what she was referring to. 'Was I supposed to have fetched something?'

Toby sat patiently, waiting to have his lead removed.

'Forgotten what?' he repeated, undoing the clip so Toby could go and find his dinner. He knew exactly where it was, and that it was time.

Josephine shook her head. She regarded him with

weary affection. 'We are having dinner with Charles and Katherine . . .'

'Again?' he said with surprise. 'But we saw them only the other day. Are you sure?' He was prevaricating. Of course she was sure. Josephine did not make mistakes like that. More to the point, she would not be going were there no arrangement to do so. She looked very elegant. She had kept her poise, and her beautiful hair, no less lovely because it was now completely silver. She was dressed in a dark blue gown that fell well below the knee, but clung to her because of the way it was cut. Normally he was very unobservant about clothes, but he could see that this was special.

'It's Katherine's birthday,' she reminded him.

'Oh! Oh dear. I forgot. We should have chosen something for her . . .'

'A bit late now,' she said drily, but she could not keep the smile from giving her away.

'You have something for her?' he said with the assurance of long habit.

'Of course I have! Elena's birthday is the only one you never forget!'

'Well, she was born on the fifth of November!' he said reasonably. 'Guy Fawkes' Day. If anyone else had been born on Christmas Day, or St George's Day, or something, then I would remember them,' he excused himself.

'When is St George's Day?' she asked innocently.

He drew in breath to tell her, then realised she was teasing him.

'What did you get for her? I ought not to look surprised when she opens it,' he said instead.

'A long rope of pink pearls that I know she has been wanting,' she replied. 'Actually, I rather like them myself,

although I should prefer white ones. I think pink is a little
. . . I don't know . . . anyway, it is what she asked for.'

'Naked-looking,' he supplied. But he made an instant
mental note to write down 'white pearls, long necklace' and
went upstairs to change. He was always pleased to get some
guidance in what to give people as gifts. He really had no
idea, especially women. Mike had been easy: anything
mechanical. He remembered vividly the first Meccano set,
and the time they had spent together building things.

Suddenly, he missed Mike with a terrible sense of loss. It
was all so long ago. The Meccano had been Mike's present
twenty-five years ago, a quarter of a century. He walked
along the landing to the bedroom. He must behave as if he
were pleased to spend the evening with Charles. How difficult that would be was completely irrelevant.

They arrived exactly on time, and were greeted warmly.
Katherine was an excellent cook, and not only that, but she
always managed to make it appear as if it had been no
trouble. She had help in the house, but, like Josephine, the
art of cooking was hers, the dashes of colour that added
beauty.

She was delighted with the pearls, and thanked them both
with enthusiasm. She knew perfectly well that Josephine had
chosen the necklace, but nothing in her warmth fell short
for Lucas either.

They were seated at the table and well into the first course
of cold lettuce soup, which was, to Lucas's surprise, delicious,
when Charles looked across at him, frowning.

'I thought Elena would have been home by now. Have
you heard from her?' he asked.

'No, actually I haven't,' Lucas replied. 'But she might have stayed a little longer in Amalfi. It's an extraordinarily beautiful place.'

'She didn't,' Charles said quickly. 'I heard from Margot, and she said Elena had left before she did. Went off to Rome with a new young man.'

Katherine smiled. 'Then perhaps Elena has found someone she likes and is staying on in Rome.' She looked at Charles. 'Don't worry, my dear, she'll be perfectly all right. And if she has a little fun, for a change, it's a good thing. He might even care for her. I would far rather she settled down with a decent man and forgot about trying to make a career.' She did not add, *and especially after the disaster at the Foreign Office*, but it was implicit. 'And so would you!' She touched his arm lightly, and he quickly put his hand over hers.

'Yes, of course,' he agreed. 'It's just . . . not like her.'

'People change,' she answered him. 'You always say Margot is too easy to please, and Elena is not easy enough. According to Margot, she really liked this young man, and he seemed both charming and sound.'

'Was he Italian?' Charles asked a little nervously.

'No, he was English, and a Cambridge graduate, so Margot said. In fact, she rather liked him herself.'

'Well, she could let Elena have this one,' he said a little tartly. 'And Elena could have had the courtesy to let us know she was staying in Rome for a few extra days.' He looked across at Lucas, and there was a slight edge to his voice. 'I don't suppose she told you?'

'No,' Lucas said with surprise. Although it should not actually have surprised him. He knew Elena was closer to him than she was to her father.

They spoke about Rome for a little while, and about Paris. They had all spent time in both cities, during the war, and afterwards. Charles and Katherine had lived in the Embassy in Paris for two and a half years. It was a city that enchanted, whether you wanted it to or not.

Katherine declined help in clearing away the soup plates and allowed Charles only to carry in the baked ham with peaches, though he was not permitted to carve it.

Lucas did not care for the idea of peaches with ham, but he was well-mannered enough not to say so, and was pleasantly surprised to find the mixture totally excellent. He said so, to Katherine's distinct pleasure.

With some skill, Josephine managed to keep the conversation away from politics until dessert, the best chocolate mousse Lucas could ever remember, and again he said so. Charles gave him a swift, rather critical glance, but both women knew Lucas well enough to be certain that he meant it.

Somehow or other the conversation slid to luxury, and then Communism. Perhaps it was the chocolate. It did seem to be the ultimate indulgence, at least when served this way.

'I think Communism is the greatest danger,' Charles said with some feeling. 'In fact, there is no doubt of it.'

'Here?' Katherine said with surprise.

'Perhaps not. I think Herr Hitler and his people will stop it before it gets this far. And that is something to be thankful for. They're pretty much barbarians.'

'Hitler's men?' Josephine asked politely, but with little disbelief.

'No, Mother,' Charles said patiently. 'The Communists! Hitler's only doing what he has to. If you remember Germany after the war, instead of refusing to see it – really see it – you'd realise that he's finally pulling the country together, getting people working again, and up off their knees and back to some self-respect. Everybody deserves that, German or anyone else. I said at the time that the treaty in 1918 was far too harsh, and would only create trouble for everyone later on. I have no satisfaction in being proved right. But no one would listen, at least no one with the power to change it.'

For once Lucas did not disagree, at least with the part about the harshness of the treaty. The subject of Hitler and the Communists was another matter, and better left alone.

He felt Josephine kick him fairly sharply under the table.

'Do you get any news from the Embassy in Berlin?' he asked, trying to keep both his voice and his face free from anything except mild interest.

'I am still in touch with Cordell,' Charles replied. 'He's a good man. Sees both sides of the picture, which can't be said of all of them.'

'All of whom?' Lucas asked. 'Diplomats in general, or in Berlin specifically?'

Charles's smile was a little tight. 'Of diplomats I know.' He was used to Lucas's exactness and was getting caught by it fewer times of late.

Lucas smiled at him, hoping to ease the sudden tension. But the view of Cordell could not be ignored. It reaffirmed what Peter Howard had said.

'So, Cordell is pretty fair, looking at both sides?' he asked.

'Yes,' Charles replied. 'He's one of the few who can see where the real, long-lasting enemy is, if we don't do something about it now. And the Communists are very good at misdirection. Look, Father, just keep out of things you know nothing about. I know you lean far more to the left than to the right, and you like Churchill, but you don't know what's at stake! If you listened to Cordell, you'd see what's going on in Europe . . .'

Lucas drew in his breath, and let it out again. Charles had been a good ambassador, even at times an excellent one. He knew how to mediate in the most awkward situations, and often ones that mattered very much. Lucas had had occasion, professionally, to know more about him than Charles was aware.

And Charles had no idea of Lucas's job then, or still, even if it was now unofficial.

No wonder Peter Howard was also lonely. That was the pain Lucas had seen in his face. What did Pamela Howard know, or guess? Perhaps no more than that her husband's mind was full of things he did not share with her. Maybe to her the reason was important.

Josephine had never asked. Was that because in some way she knew? He looked at her across the table. She smiled back, and he had no idea what she was thinking, only that she would not ask him. And he was grateful for that.

Chapter Ten

Elena sat on the train, still shaking with cold and staring out of the window into the night. She could have been anywhere. She could see nothing beyond the dark glass. She strained her eyes to make out the name of the station as the train slid in and stopped, but she was not in sight of anything she could read.

Rain streaked the windows and blurred everything. But it was a small place, few lights. She thought she heard the doors open and close, but no one came into her compartment. Walter was sitting opposite her, but he seemed to be asleep. Why did anyone run trains for so few people? Probably to get them to the place where they could pick up commuters in the morning. She envied them the sheer ordinariness of it, just for a moment. But perhaps they were tired and worried as well? France had suffered appallingly in the war. They would be no more recovered than England. Soon she would be going north again, towards Flanders and the battlefields whose names lay heavy on the heart: Verdun, Ypres, the Somme, the Marne, Passchendaele.

Did poppies grow there again, come July and August? Was that a reminder of life, and the infinite value of it? Or of death?

She stared out of the window as the train started to move again, knowing that she must stay awake because at the next station they had to get off and find a train going north, into Germany, preferably to Berlin itself. They still had to buy tickets. She had to reach the British Embassy by the end of the day. In fact, by the end of the afternoon, because she could give the message only to Cordell. Ian had specified it had to be Cordell. There was no time to stop at an hotel, have a hot bath and change into something better than the crumpled dress she had on, indelibly stained with Ian's blood.

He had died to try to prevent the assassination of this man Scharnhorst from happening. The least she could do was stop snivelling in self-pity and get on with the job! Being tired, shaking with cold, and stunned with grief were unimportant. She could hear Mike's voice in her head. *Come on, kiddo! There's a job to be done. You can't let the side down.* Soldiers were probably cold, wet and exhausted most of the time, and certainly overwhelmed with grief, if they would allow themselves to be. Every day they would see friends killed. Towards the end, the average life expectancy was about ten to fourteen days! What kind of a gutless woman was she to complain? She was alive and well, and she had a job to do.

Thank God Walter had stepped in to help her. Without him, would she have been any use at all?

He stirred uncomfortably, then opened his eyes. He seemed to take a moment or two to remember where he was, then he smiled at her, concern in his face. 'Are you all right?' he asked, only just loudly enough to be heard over the rattle of the wheels, although there was no one else with them in the carriage.

'Yes. Thank you. Why are you doing all this? Where were you going . . . without . . .?' She shrugged very slightly.

'To a job in Hamburg. But there's no hurry,' he answered.

'Where do you live?'

'London. But I move around quite a lot.'

'I'm sorry . . .'

'Don't be ridiculous!' He smiled again. It lit his face, making him look far younger. 'What did you expect me to do? Leave you there, alone and in trouble? It could as easily have been me! We'll get out of this. Just don't draw attention to yourself.'

She nodded and tried to smile back.

The next station came quickly. Elena got up, collected her remaining small case with the precious camera inside.

They climbed off the train and stood on the almost-deserted platform together. The sky was lightening in the east already.

There were very few people around, and they all seemed to be hurrying somewhere. Elena and Walter approached a man in working clothes. He looked weary and half asleep. Walter asked him, in French, if he could direct them to the right platform for the next train north.

The man considered it for several moments, then asked where they wanted to end up.

'Berlin,' Walter said without hesitation. The man might hate Germans, he might have lost family in the war . . . who in France had not? It was a chance they had to take that he'd mistake them for Germans.

The man grunted and looked at Walter with disfavour.

'Please?' Elena said quietly. 'We need to get to the British Embassy there. We have a friend who's in trouble.' Something of a distortion of the truth, but it hardly mattered now, and it could do the man no harm.

'You English?' he asked.

'Yes.'

'In a hurry?'

'Yes . . . please.'

'If you are quick, you'll get the first train off platform four. It'll get you to Hamburg. It's a long journey, but there should be lots of trains from Hamburg to Berlin.'

'Thank you very much,' Elena said, looking where his finger pointed to the bridge over the track.

'You'd best hurry!' he called after her.

'Thank you,' she said over her shoulder, as Walter led the way. Her legs were stiff and she felt as if there was no strength left in them. She was exhausted. Twice she nearly missed her step, stumbling, and only Walter's grip on her arm prevented her from falling. Her bag was not really heavy, but it weighed like lead right now.

She hung on to him on the way down the far side. If she fell, that would be the end of her whole purpose. She could imagine slipping and breaking an ankle, when it would cripple not only her leg, but the whole mission of stopping the assassination, and all that could follow in blaming the British.

From the little she had read of Scharnhorst, the world would be a great deal better off without him. Whoever made that choice, she sympathised with them. Normally she would have cheered them on! But if Britain was going to be blamed and an international incident would ensue, that was different.

She reached the bottom of the steps and could see the light of the oncoming train far along the track.

'Come on!' Walter urged, and ran half dragging her over the platform and through the arch of platform four. She looked one way for the sign to tell her what was the next train. There was nothing. She turned and could see nothing the other way either, except the single light of the oncoming train growing rapidly larger until it came to a grinding halt.

Where was there someone they could ask? There were no porters, no stationmaster. Panic welled up inside her. They had to catch it! But what if it were going somewhere else entirely? What if she ended up in Switzerland? Or Austria?

Walter opened the nearest carriage door just as an elderly man filled the opening carrying a small case in his hand. '*Pardon!*' he said with surprise.

'Sorry, Monsieur,' Walter said. 'Is this train going north? I can't see anything that says so.'

'To Hamburg, Monsieur. And will you please stand aside and allow me off? I have no wish to be in Hamburg.'

'Of course. *Pardon!*' Walter stood aside for him. As soon as the man was on the platform, Walter climbed up the steep steps, holding tightly on to his case with one hand, and Elena with the other. At the top they turned and went into the corridor and walked along, looking for an empty compartment. They found one near the end, and were inside, putting their cases on the rack above them, when the whistle blew and Elena nearly lost her balance as the train jerked sharply into movement again.

Walter caught her and eased her into the seat, his face filled with concern.

'I'm all right,' she said quickly, annoyed with herself. *Have some guts, woman*, she told herself.

'Are you sure?'

'Yes. Really. Thank you.' She would make it true.

He stared at her for a moment and then sat down beside her.

She was obliged to keep her coat on, and fastened, to hide

the blood still on her dress. At least it was only damp now, not really sodden. Her head ached and her eyes felt as if they were full of grit. Perhaps they were? Railway stations could make anyone dirty in a matter of minutes, and cold. She had been on one train or another for so long that Amalfi, its warmth and sunshine, the wonderful time she'd had there, seemed like a distant world she had dreamed about.

If only this were a dream, and she would waken and find herself warm and dry, Ian opposite her, laughing at her awkwardness, but kindly, perhaps even with a cup of tea in his hand. She had fallen asleep while he was fetching it, and they were still in the rich, sunlit Italian countryside.

But it was still very early morning, France, and she was heading north in the pallid, pre-sunrise light. She was chilled, and shivering. Ian was dead. It was Walter Mann sitting beside her in an otherwise empty carriage.

'Are you sure about this, Elena?' he asked gently.

She gave him her attention. 'About what?'

'Going to Berlin? Everything's changed since you made that decision.'

She drew in breath to tell him that actually the opposite was true. It was because of Ian's death that she was going to Germany, instead of home. But Ian had said he was MI6, the military intelligence service. Secret. He had trusted her to fulfil his mission that he could not. Someone had killed him so that he could not.

'Thank you. That is considerate of you. But I shall be perfectly all right. And I definitely intend to go to Berlin.' She forced herself to smile very slightly.

He looked worried. 'Are you sure? You could very easily send a message to whoever is expecting you . . .'

'Yes, I know. But no thank you. Perhaps I can sleep a bit

on the next part of the journey. We've got a . . . a lot of time yet . . .'

'You need a hot bath and a bed, not falling asleep sideways on a railway seat.' His smile was rueful now. 'And we left so many of your personal things on the other train. No choice. You haven't even got a change of clothes . . .'

'I know. But I have enough money to buy such things. Please don't try to argue me out of it. I must. That's all there is to it.'

He must have heard the determination in her voice. He was silent for several minutes, but she felt him still looking at her.

'It's a promise to Newton, isn't it?' he said at last.

How did he know? Then it was obvious. She had left early with Ian. She had changed her earlier plans because of him. Now he was dead and she was changing them again. You didn't have to be very clever to work that out. She had a ticket to Paris, not Berlin. She didn't even have a connection to Berlin. It had to be because of Ian.

'He's dead,' she said, and even in those two words her voice shook a little.

'And you made a promise of some sort to him?' he asked, but went on before she could answer, or lie to him, 'And because he's dead, you have to keep it?'

'A lot of people are dead, and a lot of promises have been broken,' she replied. 'Especially by people who didn't have to keep them.'

'Like the man in the hotel linen cupboard?' he asked.

She felt suddenly even colder, but before she could answer he went on: 'Ian knew him, you know that, don't you?'

Should she lie? Walter was asking questions she did not want to think of. 'I don't know . . .' She wasn't going to deny it. It would be awkward and very obviously defensive. 'Why?'

'He was murdered, you know?'

'Yes, of course I know. You don't fall over and break your neck in a hotel linen cupboard. What has that got to do with it? Are you saying that whoever killed him, killed Ian too?' Now she was getting angry enough to look at him squarely. 'And you think my going to Berlin has anything to do with that?'

'I have no idea.' He put his hand on her wrist. It was gentle, not at all intrusive, as touching her hand might have been. 'But two people were murdered. I want you to be safe, and not only from the police, but from whomever is doing this. It has to matter a lot for this much violence, in a hotel, and then in a train full of passengers.'

It was true. And Ian had lied about the man in the cupboard at first. 'Ian couldn't have killed the man in the cupboard, because he was with me all afternoon. And he certainly didn't kill himself!' She nearly choked on the words. Then she wondered why she had said them. Walter had not suggested he had!

'Of course he didn't kill himself,' Walter said firmly, tightening his hold on her arm a little. 'And do you know when the man in the cupboard was killed?'

She realised her mistake. 'No . . . I suppose he could have been there since the morning . . . since the last time anyone had used the cupboard. I know there's something unpleasant—'

'Unpleasant! Yes, very unpleasant, and dangerous. Elena, you don't know what you're putting yourself into! No one has a right to ask this of you. You don't even know what it is, do you?'

Yes, she did. All she had to do was deliver a message to

Cordell in Berlin. It wasn't as if she didn't know him, or any of the Embassy staff. She had lived there, for heaven's sake! 'It is a very small thing, and I'm going to do it,' she said perfectly steadily. 'Please don't treat me as if I were a child, or . . . or incompetent. I was very upset when Ian was killed. But I am perfectly capable of carrying on.' She took a long, a steady breath. 'But I am grateful for your help.'

He sighed and leaned back in his seat, a look of resignation on his face, and a wry smile, as if he might even admire her.

Elena drifted off to sleep, then woke with a start when the carriage door opened with a loud clang, and she looked up and saw a tall guard staring at her.

She had slipped sideways and as she straightened up her coat parted at the front. Was it her legs, too much exposed, that the guard was staring at? Or at the bloodstain indelible in the fabric of her dress? She felt the colour hot in his face and reached to pull the coat closed.

The guard asked to see her and Walter's passports. He looked at them carefully, then slowly raised his eyes to her face.

'Fräulein Standish?' he said, frowning.

'Yes.' He could not know of Ian's death yet. Or suspect her!

'Why are you travelling to Germany, Fräulein?' He looked at her steadily, challengingly. She was very conscious of the bloodstains over the rest of her dress. Would he demand to see under her coat?

'She's my fiancée,' Walter said smoothly. 'She will meet some members of my family for the first time. It is a little . . . nerve-racking, you understand?'

The guard smiled. 'Oh, yes! I remember that!' He gave a

119

slight shrug. 'Good luck, Fräulein. I'm sure they will be delighted.' He gave the passports back and continued along the train.

'Thank you,' Elena whispered, her throat tight. She was shaking so the passport almost slid out of her hand.

'See? It wasn't so difficult. Just don't forget, when you get to Berlin. Will you be all right there?'

'Yes. Thank you. They'll help me at the Embassy.'

'Get you a new passport? It would be wise. When they find Newton's body, which they will have by now, there will be a search for the woman who was with him. Bound to be.'

'Yes, I know. And the guards at the Italian border might remember me. But the Embassy will help me. My father used to be the Ambassador there. I'll be all right. Thank you.'

She should sleep again, if she possibly could. It was not an express train, or it would hardly have stopped at the small station just behind them, but Hamburg was the end of the line, so she would have to get off there. And she needed to be awake then, strong and clear-minded. At least she had money, and she knew Berlin well enough to find the Embassy easily. She just needed to be there before Cordell left for the day. That was about eleven hours from now.

She curled up on the seat, using her handbag to rest her head on and her coat as a blanket. Walter straightened it and tucked it in for her. The rhythm of the wheels over the track was soothing, almost like a live thing keeping her company.

She did sleep – exhaustion forced it on her – but it could not keep the dreams at bay. She woke many times, trying to find a more comfortable position, but lying along three seats was a luxury she was grateful for. Sleep where you can. Mike had told her that often. Actually, he had also told her about what it was like at the front, told her more than he had anyone else. Partly it was a matter of not burdening them. And he did not want to think it was in their minds every time they looked at him. Then he would not be able to forget, when he needed to.

'But why me?' she had asked.

She could remember the wry, funny look in his face, as if it had been only hours ago. 'Because I need to have somebody understand me,' he had said. 'When it's all over, people will want to forget. But those of us who were there never will, not completely. I need someone to forgive me when I do daft things.' Then he had laughed. 'Never mind, kiddo, just be there, eh?'

She had promised she would.

It was Mike who was gone.

She woke up with a start to find the train not moving, and Walter standing in front of her, shaking her shoulder gently.

'Oh! Thank you.' She scrambled to her feet, put her coat on, and looked out of the window. The large sign said 'HAMBURG', and she grasped her case and handbag and went to the door, Walter on her heels. It was crowded with other people getting off.

She heard the familiar sounds of German being spoken around her and easily fell into the pattern herself. It did not take Walter long to make the appropriate enquiries for the fastest train to Berlin, and to change some money into German currency.

They caught the train and found seats with only a few minutes to spare. Were the trains scheduled to coincide, or

121

was it just good luck? She had heard rumours that Adolf Hitler managed to get many things improved, and there had always been a natural pride in order. Perhaps it was design. When things worked as they should, it created ease. Trust. Even hope.

The train drew into Berlin a few minutes early. If the taxis were still in the same place, she would have no trouble finding one, and every driver had to know where the main embassies were.

The whole station seemed to be as she remembered it. There was no time now to look for small changes, new restaurants or shops. She had an hour, or a little less, to get to the Embassy before five o'clock. It should be easy, but one always had to allow for traffic jams, a queue somewhere, an official who needed to be persuaded, or was in too much of a hurry to listen.

She turned to Walter. 'I can never thank you enough for all that you have done, but I need to go alone from here.'

'I understand, at least . . . I don't . . . but I believe you. Take care of yourself, Elena Standish!' He smiled and bent forward, kissing her lightly on the forehead, then he turned and walked away, elegantly, easily.

Within minutes he was lost in the crowd, but she had no time to miss him.

She was both hungry and thirsty, but refreshments would have to wait. If she got to the Embassy in time there would be a cloakroom where she could try to tidy her appearance a bit more.

There were half a dozen people waiting for taxis when she reached the stand. There were only four taxis in sight. How long might she have to wait? Did it matter if she asked

122

anyone if they were going near the British Embassy? She could wait here long enough to be late! The big rally where Scharnhorst would appear was tomorrow at midday. If she missed Cordell tonight, she might not catch him at all. Tomorrow was Tuesday; he could be anywhere then. But should she draw attention to herself? At the head of the queue was a man in a drab business suit. Everyone looked tired, more than ready to go home. What on earth did embarrassment matter?

'Excuse me, ladies and gentlemen,' she said very clearly. 'I have an appointment for which I am late, at the British Embassy. Is anyone going in that direction? I will be happy to pay the whole fare, I just dare not miss my . . . meeting, please?'

They all looked a little startled. There was panic in her voice. She had heard it herself, and she sounded distraught. Please heaven, one of them must find money more important than time?

The silence seemed to stretch endlessly, but it was probably less than a minute. Then one of the women, the third in the queue, nodded her head.

'I'm going that way. If you take me there, and pay the taxi, you can get the driver to take you the rest of the way in a few minutes.'

'Thank you!' Elena was flooded with gratitude. 'Thank you,' she said again, adding the German courtesy of 'gnädige Frau'.

The taxi ride seemed long, although in fact it was less than twenty-five minutes. Elena remembered the streets well enough. The driver followed exactly the same route she would have expected, first to the address the woman had given him, then from there to the British Embassy.

There were lots of people out, shoppers, talking to each other, many on foot and moving quickly. Many walked with heads down, as if not wanting to catch anyone's attention. One old man, white-bearded, stepped aside into the gutter to allow a group of brown-shirted men in semi-uniform to go past. He kept his face averted, but moved even further into the street to avoid being bumped by them. They took no notice of him at all.

Two women stopped talking to each other and moved quickly in the opposite direction.

The taxi driver muttered something under his breath, but assuming he might be speaking to her, Elena asked him to repeat it. He shook his head and drove faster.

Outside the Embassy, he stopped. She paid him what he asked and added the usual tip.

'Thank you,' she said, and alighted quickly.

He drove off without answering, leaving her on the pavement in her blood-stained dress, her one small suitcase containing her camera at her feet.

Chapter Eleven

Roger Cordell sat alone in his office in the British Embassy in Berlin. It was a handsome room, old and spacious. Perhaps it was a little shabby, but the proportions were perfect, and it spoke of elegance and good taste. He did not want it decorated or, indeed, new furniture. He was comfortable here, and so were the visitors he cared about, men with assurance and who had no need of outer display.

Did he need to attend the rally the following afternoon? Scharnhorst was an important figure in Germany, and unfortunately, likely to become more so. As Hitler increased in power, so did Scharnhorst. The man affected a sort of hysteria, winding himself up into a paroxysm of Hitler worship, and the corresponding hatred of all his perceived enemies. If it was genuine, he was a lunatic, but if it were a calculated display, then he was far more dangerous. He was not out of control, but instead very much in it.

Cordell had met Hitler several times in the course of his own duties as a cultural attaché. Almost everything about British culture was both familiar and pleasing to Cordell and he had no difficulty in promoting it. He was also an admirer of German culture: the greatest music in the world, the poetry, philosophy and drama. They had a lot in common. No one else had ever created music like Beethoven. It was truly sublime. But no one else had drama and poetry like Shakespeare. He was so often quoted that even his least known works seemed somehow familiar.

Some German nationalism was bombastic and offensive. But after the ruinous demands of the Versailles Treaty, what else would anyone expect? Cordell had been too young at the time to grasp the full enormity of it. Fresh out of the army after four years of seeing hell brought to reality, of losing more friends than he could count, he had not had time or emotion to insist futilely on something over which he had no control.

When he looked back at that time, all he could remember was the final effort to get and keep a good job at the Embassy, his introduction to MI6 and his agreement to serve. It was a patriotic duty, and of some immediate concern to him then. Apart from anything else, it assured him of his position in the Embassy, and that if he was good at it, he would not be moved around from place to place too often, and he would have his contacts. Intelligence of the sort he needed was a long job, cultivated slowly, like an Old English rose.

Above all, it gave him the chance to provide a stable living for himself, and even more for Winifred. They needed time to get to know each other again. They had been so newly married in 1914, still learning the intimacies of each other's day-to-day life. That had all been swept away from them, as it had for countless others. Somehow, they had never re-established it again. War changed everyone. Sometimes it was physical, scars everyone could see. In others, the wounds were hidden. They came in nightmares, sudden loss of self-control. Cordell had seen them in people he knew, and the shame and confusion that came afterwards. There were parts of the war that would never be over. That was why it must never happen again.

Winifred was emotionally bruised by the loneliness, the grief she saw around her and shared with others, that she could not forget it. And, of course, he had not shared with her the horrors he had seen.

A new start seemed the best thing, in a new place.

As with so many surviving couples, it had not worked. They were familiar strangers now, playing at being husband and wife, honouring, pitying, but not sharing.

There was a knock on the door.

'Come!' he called.

One of his assistants came in, a young man who loved German poetry.

'What is it?' Cordell asked.

'There is a Miss Standish to see you, sir. She seems quite distraught . . . says it is extremely urgent. A message from someone called Newton. Do you want me to—'

'Standish?' Cordell asked.

'Yes, sir. She said her father was Ambassador here just after the war.'

'Yes. Send her in. I know Charles Standish well. Very decent chap. He lost his son in the last week of the war, but he had two daughters. Bring her in.'

At first, Cordell did not recognise the young woman who came into the room. She was quite tall and she carried herself well. Her face was a curious mixture of strength and vulnerability; there was even a hint of beauty. But now she looked hollow-eyed, crumpled, and she was very pale.

It had been several years since he had last seen her. He had kept in touch with Charles, but not the family. He remembered the elder daughter, a dark, very striking-looking young woman, not unlike her father, but with her mother's panache, and definitely her glamour.

This young woman had no glamour at all. She looked exhausted. She had none of the energy that her sister had always radiated.

'Please sit down, Miss Standish,' he invited. 'What may I do for you?'

She remained standing. 'I apologise for my appearance. Since I had no appointment, I was afraid I might miss you if I stopped to tidy up.'

Had she noticed his surprise? That was clumsy of him.

'I came as rapidly as I could,' she went on. 'From Amalfi . . .'

'Amalfi? Near Naples?' Had he heard her correctly?

'Yes . . .'

He started to express concern, but she continued talking over him.

'I was travelling from an economic conference in Amalfi, in the company of Ian Newton, whom I met there. We dined together and became friends . . .'

He was about to make a polite remark. He remembered Newton and knew that he was MI6. But how did Elena Standish know that?

'Ian went to get a cup of tea,' she continued. 'Somewhere along the way between Milan and Paris. I wasn't paying attention to where. We were both going to Paris. He . . .' Again, she had to stop and fight for her composure. Her voice was low, and at another time might have been pleasing. 'He did not return, and I went looking for him.' She said the words as if they were meaningless. 'I found him in one of the other carriages. He had been stabbed and was bleeding

128

. . . to death. I was there only just in time. I could not save him.' She blinked rapidly. 'He told me he was with MI6, which of course I had not known. He had an urgent message to bring to you – he named you. He made me promise to deliver it.'

Cordell was stunned. He stood motionless, staring at her face.

Very slowly, with stiff fingers, she undid her coat, showing the creased and blood-stained dress. The brownish stains still lay there in huge, ugly marks, unmistakable, once you knew what they were.

'God in heaven!' Cordell said in horror. 'Are you all right?'

She stiffened. 'Yes . . . I'm not hurt . . . just tired.' Her voice was shaking now. 'I've been in trains for two days and nights . . . I think.' She straightened up a little, clearly fighting for self-control. 'He told me . . . Ian told me that he was given a message to give to you. There is to be a large rally here tomorrow morning, and Friedrich Scharnhorst is to be the main speaker. There will be an assassination attempt.' She met his eyes steadily now, with confidence. 'I know. He is a complete pig. A pretty natural person for lots of people to want dead. The point is that we are to be blamed for it.'

'We?' he said incredulously. 'Who do you mean, *we*?'

'The British. More specifically, MI6. Please, I know you have very little time, but Ian only found out the afternoon that we left Amalfi. We planned to get the fastest connecting trains from Naples to Berlin. There is still time to stop it, isn't there? You have to. There was no way of getting to you any sooner, and still be totally secret about it.' She was talking quickly now, struggling over her words. 'He didn't know how to send you any sort of telegram, or other message, that would reach you, and only you, and say all that was necessary. But it has to be true, or why would he have been killed? And before you say anything, he wasn't robbed. I came to do this in his place. Please . . .'

Cordell put both his hands over hers. She was ice cold and beginning to shake uncontrollably. 'This is very serious indeed. Even if it is a false alarm, we must be totally prepared. You are quite right. The situation is delicate. If Scharnhorst is assassinated, there will be panic, and if we are blamed, for any reason at all, it will cause an international incident that could be terrible. I will send my assistant for a cup of tea. And perhaps a few sandwiches for you. You look exhausted. Then a car to take you to a hotel. You must excuse me. I have a very great deal to do before tomorrow. Thank you, Miss Standish. Thank you very much indeed.'

He gave his assistant brief instructions to look after her, and as she walked away from him, Cordell's mind was in a whirl. He should not have been surprised. Scharnhorst was the perfect candidate for an assassination. But by whom? Those who abhorred him for his violence, and growing power? His apparent influence with Hitler? A rival? Or even Hitler himself, because Scharnhorst was going too far, too quickly for public opinion? Hitler was careful to take the people with him – always! And how much did this girl know about MI6, a branch of the secret service not even acknowledged by Parliament?

No time to think of that now. It would be easy enough to pass the word along and see that security would be increased. Or the rally cancelled, or perhaps someone else put in Scharnhorst's place? Cordell had all the necessary connections to do that. Hitler admired many things about the English. He had made it no secret that he saw them as potential future allies in the war against Communism. Cordell knew that there were influential people in London who returned that regard. To see order and stability back in Germany again was a high sign of hope in Europe. It would be a bastion against the far greater threat of Communism, which was growing larger, and closer, even as they watched it, bringing violence and nihilism with it.

But how strange that it should be Charles Standish's daughter doing all this? Coincidence? Possibly.

He remembered vividly the last time he had seen Charles for any length of time. It had been about eight years ago, in Paris, that queen of cities. Some diplomatic party or other. They were both bored with it and had gone outside for a breath of air, a quick cigarette and a break from the meaningless, polite chatter. It had been somewhere overlooking the river. He remembered the lights on the water, the smooth arch of the bridge, and the shadows underneath. A boat had come silently out of it, seeming to materialise in front of them, achingly beautiful in its suggestion of magic.

They had both needed to experience that beautiful image, and understood that in each other. Charles had lost his only son in the last week of the war. Cordell had lost two brothers and, to all effect, his wife. He had lost all that she once was, and was helpless to change that. She had lost her father, both her brothers, and a cousin and, in a way, herself.

Charles seemed to have understood. *Never again* did not even need to be spoken. It was there in the companionable silence, and later in the trivial words about everything but reality. Roger Cordell owed it to Charles to look after this strange daughter of his, if it were possible, consistent with his own beliefs in the tangled lunacy of this Europe they had created.

Should he try to save Scharnhorst? The man needed to be shot. Damn Ian Newton for learning about it, and then getting himself killed! How had that happened? He must have been incredibly careless. That is, if Elena Standish was even right about what had really happened?

He must think some more. Whatever he was going to do, it must be done this evening. He had important contacts he must not jeopardise. They were far more important than one incident. A lot might hang on this decision.

Chapter Twelve

Lucas was working in his study, or at least that was what he had intended to do. Actually, he was sitting in his most comfortable armchair in the book-lined room, and staring out through the wide, deep windows towards the garden. This May the weather seemed to be particularly lovely. The light was sharp and clear, as if every leaf and every flower were to be etched on the memory. He had put seed out for the birds, even though he knew perfectly well that they did not need it. It just pleased him to have them come almost up to the window.

The first yellow climbing roses were in full bloom around this side of the house. They were called Maigold. He remembered the name because it described them so clearly. Probably they should have been pruned back a bit, but he liked their profusion. Each year he said he would do it, then could not bring himself to do more than the bare necessity. Perhaps when they actually blocked the windows, he would.

His thoughts were interrupted by a light knock on the door. It could only be Josephine. Why was she knocking? She usually just tapped and then came in.

He stood up and went to open it. She was just outside,

in the hall, and behind her was a man, several inches taller than she. Lucas could see his face over her shoulder. It was Peter Howard.

Before Lucas could react, Josephine spoke. 'Lucas, Mr Howard says he is a friend of yours and needs to see you rather urgently.' She looked solemn and puzzled, anxiety in her eyes as well as her voice.

'Thank you,' Lucas said a little awkwardly. Howard had never called at his house before. What on earth would bring him now?

Josephine gave a brief smile, and stepped aside to allow Howard to pass her. She did not offer to bring tea, as she would have done for anyone else. That alone told him she knew it was business.

Howard came in, thanked her, then closed the door as she turned to leave.

'What the hell are you doing here?' Lucas said very quietly, once he had heard Josephine's footsteps go down the hall and away. 'What's happened that we couldn't have met somewhere . . .?' He stopped. The look on Howard's face sent a twinge of fear into his mind. His muscles tightened.

'I'm sorry,' Howard's voice dropped even lower. 'Ian Newton's been murdered. Knifed to death on a train from Milan to Paris. His wallet was not taken. I don't know any more than that yet. We may never do.'

'It could have waited . . .' Lucas said impulsively, although even as the words passed his lips, he knew it was the death of Newton he was denying rather than the fact that Howard had broken all protocol to come to Lucas's home to tell him. Howard looked as if he were deeply hurt by it, although no emotion excused carelessness. In fact, the more important the event, the more it mattered to be even more than usually

134

careful. He would have to think of some way to explain Peter's visit to Josephine later. He hated being devious with her, but he had done it for nearly a quarter of a century. It was never that he lied, in so many words; it was the omissions, the evasions. He and Josephine were so honest in everything else.

'It really doesn't matter,' Howard said grimly.

'Josephine . . .' Lucas began.

'What?'

'. . . has no idea,' Lucas finished.

Howard gave a very tiny, twisted smile. 'She probably doesn't want to know, but she is aware of who you are. She was a decoder during the war, remember? Josephine doesn't ask because she knows you can't discuss it, but she also knows why.'

'Yes . . . yes, I suppose she must.' Looking at it as Howard was doing, it was pretty plain. Lucas considered whether he had taken her silence for granted instead of wondering why she had never questioned him, and apparently never resented his secrecy. It seemed their worlds were nothing like as separate as he had allowed himself to believe. As a decoder she had kept her secrets and now she was keeping his. He was rather relieved. And proud of her! Her intelligence and her discretion. She had never given the slightest hint.

Who else knew? Certainly not Charles. And there was no one else.

He turned his attention back to Ian Newton. He had joined the service after Lucas had left, but Howard had spoken of him often, repeated instances of his light, wry humour, and his insights. In ways, Ian had reminded Lucas of Mike. Mike would have been Newton's age now, or perhaps a little older, but the same generation. And now Ian, too, was dead. Not on the battlefield, but on the floor of a railway carriage somewhere in France.

Would Howard be the one who had to tell his family? That was the worst job of all, worse even than identifying the body. He would never forget hearing about Mike. None of them would. Nobody all over England, all over Europe, in America, would ever forget receiving that kind of news. It was one of the many things that were entirely universal. There was far more that united a German mother who had lost her son, and an English mother who'd lost hers, than ever divided them. Did those who talked about war so easily even think about that?

Howard was waiting for him to respond.

'Thank you for telling me personally about Newton. I'm very sorry indeed,' Lucas said quietly.

'There's a lot more to it than that.' Howard sat down at last, in one of the old comfortable chairs, and Lucas did the same.

'What? What was he doing in France? Do you know? Was he there for you?'

Howard looked bleak. 'No. That's the part that has me most concerned. Someone apparently gave him orders, and he assumed it was me, so he started to obey them. I told you he wired to let me know he was on his way to Berlin to prevent the assassination of Friedrich Scharnhorst. I had no notion that he thought I had given him those instructions but none of our other men instructed him either.'

'Started to obey?' Lucas sat a little further forward in his chair. 'How far?' he asked, when Howard did not answer.

'He'd left Amalfi and started on a journey to Berlin,' Howard answered. 'He must have changed trains at Rome and Milan, I assume, because his body was found on the train from Milan to Paris, rather more than halfway.'

'And do you want to prevent this assassination?' Lucas asked. 'Scharnhorst's a monster, deformed in mind, if not in body.'

'On principle, I'd love to see the man got rid of, but not in public, and with MI6 blamed for it. I dare say the rest of the world would be delighted, but it would give the Germans a first-class excuse to make a martyr of him and cause an extremely unpleasant international incident. Everyone would have to pretend to be shocked, whatever they actually felt. We would look not only to be interfering in the internal affairs of another country, but being damned incompetent at it.' Howard's face was pale, lines of tension visible in the sharp May sunlight. He looked older than his forty-three years.

'I see,' Lucas said slowly. 'Yes. There are a few people who would seize the chance to "take offence" and make a meal of it. I can think of a few here in England! I suppose we have no idea who's behind it?'

'Not precisely, though there are many cells of anti-Government factions where we have useful contacts. But I didn't contact Newton, and no one from my command did.'

Lucas's mind raced, trying to work out what could have happened, to think of all the possibilities. None of them was good.

'We can't trust Cordell with any of this,' Howard reminded him quietly.

'Or anyone else,' Lucas added. 'They'd take it to him, eventually. Is he involved in the assassination plot, do you know?'

'It's possible, I suppose. But I have no proof. I'm still

working on a plan to test him. If I move too fast, it will be obvious.'

'Then I think the best we can do is damage limitation,' Lucas replied grimly. 'We haven't time to prevent the plot. I assume we've no idea who's going to do it, or how, or you would have mentioned it.'

'Sniper, probably,' Howard said, his face tight. 'But at a rally it could be anyone from anywhere. If we interfere, we could be playing into their hands, making it easier for them.'

'There will be security.' Lucas was following another thread. 'Whoever it is could well be one part of that . . .'

'But that would be suicide.' Howard looked at him. 'Someone who's so desperate he's prepared to sacrifice himself?'

'Possibly. Who's planning it, that's the key? And who gave Newton the information, and why?' Lucas asked.

'And is it even true?' Howard raised his eyebrows. 'Is there a plot at all, or is it a plan to make us react, and provoke a reaction we can't contain? There are all sorts of possibilities, none of them good.'

Lucas's mind raced over all the facts they knew. What had they missed? Was the planned assassination real, and if so, was it the act of someone inexperienced, with an agenda of their own, even an agent provocateur? More than one disaster had been triggered by an error of judgement, a reaction ill-thought through. 'What exactly did Newton say when he contacted you?' he pressed.

Howard was sitting perfectly still, as if his muscles were locked. 'He wired me from Rome,' he replied. 'It was definitely him, no possibility of error there. He responded obliquely, in code. He explained little because he assumed the message to him had come from me.'

'And there was no mistaking the meaning? Definitely an assassination attempt on Scharnhorst, to be blamed on us?'

'Yes. He could have been going directly to Cordell, to have him act to stop it. Ironic when he's the man we can't entirely trust.' Howard's face was touched by a bitter amusement. His dry sense of humour was at its best in the worst difficulties. It was a peculiarly English trait of character, and one that Lucas both liked and admired. But it was also a sign that Howard could see the bitterness of the situation. It was a defence against helplessness.

'Given that we can't prevent it,' Lucas said quietly, 'what can we do to limit the damage – without Cordell's assistance?'

'It had better be without his knowledge as well,' Howard pointed out. 'I'm not yet ready to give him the slightest idea we don't trust him. In fact, I won't ever be ready.' Laughter came and went in his face, all in an instant. 'If he's innocent, I don't want him to know we suspected him. And if he's guilty, I'm going to use the bastard in every way I can. He'll be the perfect source of misinformation, if we do it well enough!' He gave a brief grunt of laughter. 'I'd never make a comedian – my timing is ghastly!'

'Have you considered that Cordell could be involved, if there is a plan to assassinate Scharnhorst?' Lucas asked. 'If MI6 is blamed, that could well be his intention!' He hated saying it, but it weighed on him like a collar of lead, hurting with its pressure.

'I suppose,' Howard agreed, although from the look in his eyes that thought had only just come to him. 'It follows. I don't know who to trust in Berlin. If they blame MI6, he'll have to respond and may make the situation a lot worse.' He gave a tiny downward smile, no more than a curve of his lips. 'The interesting question is, is it MI6 under his direction who'll be responding? Or could he possibly be acting in a German plot to produce an incident to start a quarrel as a way of breaking some diplomatic agreement?'

'Or both,' Lucas added.

Howard frowned, looked down for a moment, then up again, 'I took it to Bradley. At least part of it. I . . .' He looked worried and slightly embarrassed, which Lucas knew was an unusual experience for him.

Lucas asked the question he had to. 'Don't you trust him?' Until he knew that, there was nowhere else to proceed.

'Trust Bradley to be honest?' Howard smiled. 'As honest as we ever are when we're afraid. And who, with any sense, isn't afraid of something?'

'What is he afraid of?' Lucas asked. He knew Howard would understand the complexity of the question and not merely slide over the surface. They had never done that with each other.

'I suppose he's afraid of betraying the past, the war to end all wars. All the numberless dead. Or just plain being wrong. Of telling people he cares about something they don't want to hear or can't bear to hear. Of waking up one morning and finding he missed something desperately important . . .'

'We're all afraid of that,' Lucas said, suddenly crushed with memories he had forced out of his mind. It had been a way of life . . . once. 'The only way you can excuse it is to leave the whole damn job to someone else.'

Lucas had thought Peter was going to say something, but he didn't, he just sat looking at Lucas.

'I'm not coming back,' Lucas answered the silence. 'I'm only going to say what you're saying. You'll have to deal with

Cordell yourself. And if someone kills Scharnhorst, hope that the Germans get the right person for it . . . poor devil.'

'Perhaps I should go there myself?'

'No!' Lucas sat forward in his chair. 'No, that would be exactly what they want, to lure out one of our best men, high up in the order of command and a person very much worth capturing. Don't be a fool, Peter! Command requires more responsibility than that! You can't go haring off just because you want to feel as if you're doing something. You've got plenty of good men in the field. Trust them. That's what they're there for.'

The heat came up in Howard's face, but it died down again almost immediately. Lucas was right, and Howard knew it, however much he did not want to. Lucas knew what a hard discipline it was to sit in London and tell other men what to do. But Howard had too much knowledge now to risk his own life without absolute necessity. Calm was needed, courage and intelligence, not bravery on the line. It seemed like leading from the back, from safety, which they both deplored. Lucas understood all that, and had felt the same.

'You'll have to send someone you trust,' Lucas said, 'to keep separate from Cordell at all times, and he'll have to know why, without doing anything to give it away. And about the best he can do is see if he can get Scharnhorst's assassination – should it go ahead – blamed without a doubt on the Germans themselves. Scharnhorst will have many enemies. Look among those whose jobs he has cost, one way or another. Or better still, someone whose family he has ruined. There are enough to go around. Although I hate blaming someone innocent . . . It may be that you don't have to.'

Howard rose to his feet. 'I know, yes. One innocent man

141

in place of another is hardly an improvement, but there are plenty of violent people who'd be happy to see the end of Scharnhorst. I'll let you know what happens regarding Cordell. Thank you for the advice.'

Lucas did not say anything; it had all been said, and understood. He walked to the front door and saw Howard on his way.

He was going back to his study when he met Josephine in the hall. He felt oddly wrong-footed by Howard's observation of her. He looked at her now in the sunlight from the garden door behind her. She was still slim, and the bones of her face, which Elena had inherited, were only slightly blurred by age. Had she really known the nature of his work all the time, or most of it?

'Are you ready for lunch?' she asked. 'It's cold bacon and egg pie, with tomato relish on the side.'

It was one of his favourites. There was nothing better than fresh, flaky pastry around the sharpness of bacon and perfectly cooked eggs. A pot of fresh tea, fragrant and slightly aromatic, would be marvellous. Earl Grey, perhaps? He must eat. He had learned long ago that no one is at their best if they do not eat and sleep. Punishing yourself just makes you a damn nuisance to everyone else.

'Yes, please,' he replied. Then he looked more closely at her face. There was anxiety in her eyes. She might try to hide it but, once seen, it was too easy to recognise. 'What is it?' he asked, but lightly, so she could deny it, or brush it away if she chose. 'Josephine?'

'It must be serious for him to have come here openly,' she replied. 'Is it something to do with Elena? And if you dare lie to me, in what you imagine is protecting me, I will not forgive you.'

He could see that she meant it, even though he had never known her not to forgive anyone, in time. But then perhaps there was a lot he had not known.

'No, it's nothing to do with Elena,' he said honestly. Well . . . almost honestly. Ian Newton was dead, on a train to Paris. All he knew of Elena was that she had left Amalfi for Rome with a young man she had met there. The route home from Rome was via Paris. *Surely not* . . . Better to keep quiet about that until he had learned more. 'It was about something that he fears will happen in Berlin,' he added.

She looked at him long and steadily, then nodded and turned away. 'Lunch will be in five minutes,' she said over her shoulder. 'When the kettle has boiled.'

Chapter Thirteen

Elena woke up on Tuesday morning, and it took several moments for her to recognise where she was . . . in a hotel room in Berlin . . . and to remember how she had got there. It was the room Ian had booked for himself, when he came here to stop the assassination of Scharnhorst.

She sat bolt upright, cold, still aching with tiredness, and above all the deep, disabling pain of loss. She had made a promise to him to act. But she had managed to tell Cordell, so it would be all right.

She lay back again, still clutching the bedcovers around herself. She must get new clothes, clean ones, not crumpled, above all, not stained with blood. It seemed awful to just throw these away, but she could hardly keep them!

She would get up and dress, have breakfast and go out and buy decent new clothes, dispose of the old ones in some street rubbish bin. A caterpillar turning into a butterfly! A flying beetle, more likely! She could go to the square where the rally was to be held and see if anyone had been arrested. There might be something worthy of a decent photograph. Maybe one she could sell to a newspaper back in London? The British press would not be likely to have a good photographer here. They did not know there was going to be an attempted assassination. That is, if there was? Cordell might have prevented it completely. But there was a good chance the authorities would want to arrest whoever was behind the plot! Hitler never wasted the chance to celebrate his victory over an enemy. A show trial! Blame the Communists. Or the Jews.

She accomplished all her shopping successfully, and returned to the hotel with her additional purchases, and looking quite different. Her hair was washed and shining. She was dressed in plain navy, quite neatly tailored. She had kept her own shoes, because this was no time to try getting used to new ones.

She left again with plenty of time to spare, but already she saw people moving towards the square along the dusty, still shabby streets. They looked little different from when she had been here before, when her father was stationed at the Embassy, ten years ago, in 1923. Broken windows were replaced. There were new storefronts, here and there new paint, but pavements were not mended. Everything looked old, patched up rather than replaced. But this was what they did in England, too!

She moved with the thickening crowd and overheard snatches of conversation. It had a brittle sound to it. People were careful of what they said, knowing they could be overheard.

'Yes, wonderful! A real new start,' she heard over and over again. It was all statements; nobody seemed to be asking any questions.

On a street corner, two old men stood talking. Both had long beards and wore dark clothes. A couple of young men in Brownshirt uniform came swaggering along, glanced at each other, then changed direction and approached the old men, who did not move.

The young men stopped in front of them. 'You are blocking the street!' one of them said loudly. 'Get out of the way!'

'There's plenty of room,' the old man with the longer beard replied. 'I am not blocking your way.'

'You're blocking my way if I say you are!' the young man raised his voice. 'Move!'

'There's plenty of room,' the old man insisted. Indeed, there was. If he were to move in the only direction left open to him, it would be into the gutter.

The Brownshirt lifted his arm to strike the old man. He was smiling. He intended to knock him over, it was plain in his face.

Movement in the crowd stopped. There was a sudden silence.

Now the old man was trapped. Which was worse? That the crowd watched his humiliation? Or that they all walked on as if it did not matter, as if it were in some way all right?

One woman of perhaps fifty stepped forward. 'You can go around him,' she said to the Brownshirt. 'You're stronger, and younger.'

He turned and glared at her.

She froze.

A woman of about twenty came forward and took the older woman by the arm, with all her strength, forcing her to step back.

'I'm sorry, sir,' she said to the young man. 'She doesn't understand. Please excuse her.' She pulled at the woman again, almost dragging her off balance, and the older woman yielded, perhaps to protect them all.

The Brownshirt looked at the old man, who stood without moving for another long three seconds, then stepped into the gutter and lowered his gaze.

Elena was so outraged that she was shaking, but she understood. You accepted your own humiliation, rather than allow someone else to be beaten while you looked on, helpless to prevent it.

The two young men in uniform walked off, smiling.

Swine, she thought. But there was nothing she could do except stand there like everyone else, and then take a moment to steady herself, and follow the increasing crowd towards the square, still trying to swallow her rage.

But as she reached the end of the street, busier now, people almost shoulder to shoulder, she knew it was not enough. She was ashamed of herself because she had watched someone else needlessly and pointlessly shamed and, like everyone else, she had done nothing. Partly she had avoided any confrontation because she wanted to protect her camera, but what else? Fear. If not the excuse of the Leica, there would have been something else, and she knew it.

The square was already tightly packed with people. There was not much noise, at least not yet. She looked around. There was a podium built for the occasion so Scharnhorst could be seen by everyone. In all directions there were brown-shirted guards. They all seemed to carry weapons: rifles and pistols, some had cudgels as well. For show? To make them feel like men, and in control? Or would they use them against the crowd if they felt threatened? She knew the answer to that! Everyone did.

And who would report it afterwards? Would the Brownshirts say that the crowd had attacked first?

She was being ridiculous; these were civilised people. This

was the country of Beethoven, Schiller, Goethe, philosophers, scientists . . . She thought with a smile of self-knowledge that she always reserved the greatest poetry and drama for England. The greatest scientists for England, too. Newton! No one, not even Einstein, had surpassed Sir Isaac Newton.

Newton. Ian. Looking at the crowd, she realised that she was still horribly shaken by Ian Newton's death.

Her mind was rambling. She was tired and she hurt deeply inside, where 'pulling oneself together' could not reach.

The square was packed now. People were jostling each other to try to make room for more. They must be jamming the streets as well. Who was Friedrich Scharnhorst that so many were turning out to listen to him?

She stared around the square. It was faced with large buildings, some pretty high, seven or eight storeys. Their windows would offer amazing views of the whole event. It was a lovely day, and many of them were open; reflections in the neighbouring glass around them made them stand out.

What had Cordell done to prevent the assassination? Had he warned the police? The Brownshirts seemed to be everywhere, and they were heavily armed. How do you stop an assassination? Without more than hours of notice, who do you trust? It would be a nice irony if the assassin were one of the Brownshirts! She almost smiled at the idea. Then her smile vanished. It could be anyone – the man standing next to her, even. Did Cordell know? Who do you warn? Do you cancel the event? Warn Scharnhorst himself? What if he simply did not turn up? Or someone else was sent in his place? Someone who was expendable, who would be killed and nothing was lost to the Government.

People were getting restless waiting. She could feel the tension in the air. Then suddenly there was silence. Someone was getting up on to the platform, a man in a dark suit with an armband, white, with a black Greek cross on it: the swastika.

He called for attention, and instantly he received it. Over a thousand faces gazed up at him. He made a few remarks, very ordinary, all about what a great man Adolf Hitler was. He was greeted by an increasing roar of applause.

Then he announced Friedrich Scharnhorst, hero of the people, and stepped back with a wide gesture of deference, arm swinging as if he should have had a cape over it, and Scharnhorst stepped forward.

He began to speak and instantly the crowd fell not only silent but motionless. His voice was not pleasing at all. It was almost rasping, and of a higher pitch than Elena had expected, almost nasal in quality. And yet it was also mesmerising.

She stood listening to him, just as everyone around her was doing. It was several moments before she even thought to look at anyone else. She saw the admiration in their faces, eyes fixed on the figure on the podium. No one shuffled their feet or pushed for a better position. Their attention was frightening in its intensity, a perfect photograph. They looked fixated, as if they were asleep with their eyes open.

She pulled the camera out of her bag and took off the lens cap. It needed only seconds to focus. She did not want to draw attention to herself. People might not wish to be photographed, even anonymously, so she must look as if her intent were to photograph Scharnhorst, and she was merely turning the camera sideways while she adjusted it.

She was careful. She wanted to catch the look of almost rapture on the faces of the crowd as they stared at him, mouths half open, eyes wide and bright.

At one point, Scharnhorst threw up his arm and shouted, *'Heil Hitler!'* and the crowd roared back at him, *'Heil Hitler!'* arms raised in perfect copy of his.

She should not have been surprised. He had been saying the same things she had read in Hitler's speeches. But somehow it was different to hear it in a voice imbued with passion, as if it were the most perfect sense, and from all around you, like a thunderous sea, the response echoing back.

She was glad she was holding the camera; it gave her a good excuse for not raising her arm in the Nazi salute. The noise of the crowd shouting the salute in unison was as powerful as a great tidal surge, carrying everything with it, destroying that which resisted it. No one could swim against it; it was enough not to be battered, to stay afloat, upright. What Scharnhorst was saying was nonsense; these people were listening to the emotion, not reason.

She took more pictures, some of Scharnhorst, some of the crowd. She was facing Scharnhorst and the buildings behind him when a single sharp crack rang out. For an instant there was silence. Even Scharnhorst stopped shouting. Then, very slowly, he crumpled and fell on to the floor of the podium . . . and lay still.

The scene was frozen.

Then it jerked into life again, men rushing forward to the body sprawled on the platform floor, bending over, trying desperately to stop the flow of blood. People were shouting. Brownshirts appeared all over the place. Then, as they realised what had happened, people sobbed, women started to scream. The crowd suddenly moved and there were cries of rage.

Elena kept her camera high, for as long a range of focus

as possible. She tried to resist losing her balance, but the crowd was carrying her along.

More shots rang out. Everyone was too hysterical to react in self-preservation. If anyone else was hit, Elena did not see it. Nor did she see if anyone was chasing the marksman. She heard people running. Was it the killer, or the uniformed Brownshirts shouting orders, trying to herd people who were in blind panic and could neither see nor hear them?

How had Cordell failed? Had he warned Scharnhorst's people and they had taken no notice? Or had they tried, and they, too, had failed? Were they betrayed by their own people as well?

Ahead of her, the crowd was parting, moved by some force to make a pathway. She was close to the divide, and more Brownshirts were walking in line. They were carrying the body of Scharnhorst! They passed within feet of her. She could see clearly for an instant, long enough to take a picture, maybe not focused, but Scharnhorst with blood on his clothes, and a cloth over his face. So he was dead. This could only be a corpse they were recovering, not a wounded man they were hurrying to hospital.

Along the pathway, the crowds fell silent, except for one woman howling in anguish, as if she had lost her own child.

There was panic. Elena was pushed and knocked, swept along, whether she wished to be or not. It took all her strength not to be pushed over and crushed, or at the very least, trodden on.

Again, Elena wondered how Cordell had not been able to do anything about this. Had it been too late to stop it? Or had he at least managed to prevent any British person being blamed? The shot had come from the high buildings on the other side of the square. She had seen the flash! Or was it only the glint of sunlight on something metallic, or glass? Lots of the windows were open. People were watching, listening.

Elena had not thought before how grateful she was to live in relative safety and peace. She had not always thought much of her own government, and certainly did not always agree with them, but compared with this, they were sane, even boring.

As long as people like Oswald Mosley did not get into control!

The crowd was thinning around her. She must get out from among them. She turned and started to push her way towards the street and back to the hotel. There was nothing else she could do here. She had seen the man shot, right in front of her. There was death everywhere: the man in the hotel in Amalfi, Ian on the train, and now Scharnhorst here in Berlin! She felt numb with dismay.

Chapter Fourteen

People were standing around in huddles, dazed and shocked. Some were weeping with fright, others with grief. Many were trying to get away from the scene, back to their homes, or anywhere different, but the streets were blocked off all around the square.

Elena walked up to two Brownshirts and found her mouth suddenly so dry she could hardly speak.

One of the men stepped across her path, holding his gun across his body, but ready to swing around and aim point-blank at her. 'Name?' he demanded.

'Elena Standish,' she replied, stammering over her surname as if she were unfamiliar with it.

He looked at her more closely. 'Where are you going?'

'To my hotel.' She decided to be honest. She must not look as if she had something to hide. 'I was in the square. It was . . . terrible.'

'Hotel? Why are you staying in a hotel? Where do you live?' His eyes narrowed and he peered at her more closely. He looked almost as frightened as she was. Perhaps he was going to be blamed because Scharnhorst was dead.

She must give him an answer that, if he bothered to check

it, could never be disproved. 'I came . . .' She swallowed. She must stop shaking. It would make him suspect her of being afraid, which in his mind he might equate with guilt. She started again. 'I am here to visit the city. It's still beautiful. I know how hard things have been, I wanted to listen to Herr Scharnhorst speak. He talked of hope, and purpose . . .' Would the words choke her? They ought to! But if she believed that, it would account to the Brownshirt for her being so shaken.

'What did you see?' he asked, still standing in her way.

'I was watching him.' She took a deep breath. 'Listening to what he said. Everyone was. Then suddenly there was a sharp sound . . . a crack . . . and he fell forward, as if he'd been . . . struck.' She looked at him, straight into his eyes, and tried to convince herself that it was someone she thought highly of who had been killed. She told herself it had been Churchill, whom Lucas admired so much. 'I can . . . hardly believe it. Just . . . seconds . . . and everything changed . . .' She did it well, the distress was choking her throat with the effort not to weep.

'Yes,' the Brownshirt agreed. 'Changed. Go back to your hotel and stay there. Right?'

'Yes, sir. Thank you.' She was overwhelmed with relief, but she waited, holding her breath while he stepped back and allowed her to pass. Why did she feel afraid? She had done nothing wrong. In fact, she had done everything she could to prevent Scharnhorst's death.

Would she have done so if she had actually heard him speak first? It would have been harder. He was everything she not only loathed, but was actually afraid of. She could easily imagine hundreds of people who would secretly rejoice at his death. No, that was wrong, it would be tens of thousands. Germany had had a bitterly hard time. People had starved to death. They had seen their children starve, and that was far worse. Misery and grief had been like a great fog over the land. But she believed that most people were basically decent, wanting only to live safely and with enough to eat and a roof over their heads, work to do and hope for the future. Like anybody else.

As she walked quickly along the street, looking forward all the time, she remembered what it had been like in Berlin when her father was with the Embassy. She had had German friends, lots of them.

Many of the people she had known must still be in Berlin. But how had they fared in the years between then and now? A decade could make all the difference imaginable. When you were hungry, in pain, afraid of every new day, it was an eternity. What jobs could men find to do in a ruined economy, and returned soldiers needed work as well? And women. Some of them would marry, many would not, because they couldn't. As in England, the men they had loved were dead, or were a shell of what they had been, and needing care more than the women.

She was still a couple of blocks from the hotel.

She kept her head down, watching where she was going. She thought again about the friends she had had when her father was here at the Embassy. Had any of them become Nazis? Did they cling to Adolf Hitler as the hope for the future? How much could she blame them if they did?

How do you live with a man who is crippled with shame because he cannot keep a roof over his family's head, or enough fuel to take the edge off the coldness? How do you answer your children when they plead for food, and you have nothing to give them?

155

She almost walked past the hotel, and only stopped when she saw the doorman helping someone with luggage.

She nodded to him and went inside, glad to be there at last. She had kept her key, and had no need to stop at the desk to ask for it. She went to the elevator and had only a moment to wait.

She put the key in the lock of her door and opened it. She went inside and saw that the bed had been made and everything was tidy. She put her bag and camera down and washed her hands and face, brushed her hair, then thought she would change into the other dress she had bought. It was a little lighter, and the day was very warm.

She went to the wardrobe and opened the door. The other dress was hanging where she had put it yesterday, but there was something else, propped up in the corner at the back, like a broom handle. She had not noticed it before. She leaned forward and took hold of it. It was metal. She closed her grip around it and found it was heavy at the lower end. She pulled, and suddenly, with a tide of horror inside her, she knew what it was: a rifle!

She looked at it more closely. It was unusual. Not an ordinary army rifle. No bayonet, or place to fix one, but sights so the shooter could be absolutely accurate, even at a distance. A sniper's rifle. And the smell of it meant it had been recently fired.

She stood transfixed with horror. Ian had been right! They were going to blame British Intelligence for it. Him! They had been going to blame Ian himself! This was the hotel he had been going to stay in, the room whose number he had given her. They had intended that he should come back and be caught with the weapon practically in his hands, and still smelling of the shot fired.

Which must mean that whoever was going to find him, and arrest him, or perhaps shoot him on the scene, would be coming now for her. Why not? A woman could fire a rifle as well as a man. It was a distant kind of kill, not needing any strength, nor really much courage. After all, believing you could escape made it easy.

She put the rifle down as if it had burned her. Her fingerprints would be on it now, even if on the barrel, not the trigger. Still, it would prove she had touched it, and therefore knew it was there.

She must wipe them off, now! And then leave. They would be coming at any minute. What could she use? What removed fingerprints from metal? There was a soft towel in the bathroom. They might know that it had been wiped, but they could have no way of knowing by whom. Except, of course, that it was she who had occupied the room.

She must be quick, and then leave. Hurry! She went into the bathroom and seized the hand towel. It was old and well worn. Ideal. She took it straight back to the bedroom and wiped the barrel of the rifle where she had picked it up. She rubbed it hard, then when she was satisfied, covered her hand with the towel to put the rifle back in the wardrobe, hanging the dress she had worn in front of it, then washing out the towel.

She heard footsteps in the passageway outside the door. Could they be here already? Stupid question! Of course they could! She had walked back from the square. They could certainly walk as quickly, at least.

She glanced at the window. The room was three storeys up. She went across and stared out, her heart beating so wildly her breath caught in her throat. She could hardly hope to climb down the drainpipe, apart from the fact that it was yards away. She had never been quite that athletic, nor had any need whatever for such an action. She was a rebel in many ways, but it all had to do with the mind, not physical daring. If she tried anything rash, she would not only run a serious risk of breaking her neck, or at least a leg, but she would confirm her guilt. What sane and innocent woman climbs out of a third-floor hotel room because someone knocks on her door?

But could she brazen it out, with that rifle in the wardrobe?

There was a firm, loud knock on the door.

Her first instinct was to back away. Then she realised she would learn nothing that way. She stepped forward, took the key out of the lock, careful not to make a sound, then bent down to look through it. She could see nothing.

She could feel the sweat on her skin, clammy one minute, ice the next.

She heard footsteps. What if the person also thought to look through the keyhole? And saw her staring back? She straightened up and silently replaced the key. Her whole body was shaking. She must think clearly!

What if she went up, not down? Where would she finish? On the roof? Hardly. It was not flat. An attic fire escape? There must be one. Would it be from a room? No, too many would be needed: too expensive. One fire escape would serve several rooms, therefore available through a window everyone could reach. Her heart was pounding. She could be caught, trapped, executed. No time to say goodbye to her family, to Lucas. Was there an afterlife, as the Bible said? Would Mike be waiting for her, or Ian? Or were those fairy stories to comfort the frightened child facing the unknown, and really there was only darkness, eternal solitude?

As soon as it was quiet outside she would have to go. She

could hardly carry a case with clothes. Her handbag with her papers, money and her camera would be about all she could carry down a possibly rickety and seldom-used stair. If it was some kind of retracting ladder, perhaps it had never been used? It could even be eaten by rust! How far could she jump without breaking a leg?

She gathered her things and went to the door, listening for any step. She must compose herself. Stand upright. Smile. Walk as if she were about some perfectly innocent purpose. What, for heaven's sake? Going up to the attic with her handbag in her hands!

There was no sound in the corridor. Were they there, just waiting?

She opened the door. She could see no one. She went out quickly and closed the door behind her. She stood up very straight and, carrying the bag as if it weighed nothing, she walked quickly and silently along the corridor, towards the stairs that led up to the next floor, and then the roof.

She met no one. The people on the ground floor would use the elevator.

She went quickly up to the top floor. No one was there. Perhaps they were all in the dining room, or out! Which way would the fire escape be? Towards the back? Think clearly! No one puts a metal fire escape at the front of a building. They were always rather ugly, strictly utilitarian. But she had turned with the bend in the stairs. Or were there two bends? Which way was back now?

She went along one corridor, and ended up at a blank wall. There had to be a fire escape.

She heard footsteps. What possible explanation could she give for being up here? She should have thought of that before she left her room. She was being stupid!

She had had nightmares like this: running to escape something terrible, always getting higher, further, completely lost, and the thing chasing her always a little closer.

Only this was real. She had seen the Brownshirts: they were no fairy-tale monsters. She had looked into their faces and seen real people, frightened and angry, people who had the power of death in their hands, and an endless hunger for revenge on anyone they could find an excuse to hurt. They had to fight back at something. Prove they were alive.

She turned round and faced the other way, just as a man came out of the elevator and started towards her. He looked in his mid-fifties, ordinary.

She smiled at him and murmured in German, 'Good morning, sir.' He said something in return. Please heaven, he thought she occupied one of the rooms just behind her. He must occupy one. Thank goodness there were two more.

She turned the corner and increased her pace. This corridor was lighter. Was there a window at the end, around the slight elbow ahead? More importantly, did it have a fire escape? Once she was on it, she would obviously be trying to escape. What woman wearing a dress would be on the fire escape, with a case, in the early afternoon, and the building not on fire? How could she possibly explain herself? She should have just gone down to the lobby, and gone out through the front door, like any sane person.

She must stop dithering. It was not one good choice or another. There was no 'good' choice. There was getting caught, or escaping.

She turned the dog leg and saw the window ahead. It was about two and a half feet above the floor, easy enough to climb out of. If it did not open, she was prepared to smash it.

She walked forward quickly, took hold of the ring-shaped handles and heaved. After an instant's hesitation, it opened upward on its sash, and seemed to wedge there. The fire escape beyond was rusted, but looked firm enough. Anyway, there was no alternative now.

What if they were waiting for her one floor down? Or two floors? Or at the bottom? She leaned out and looked, but she could see nobody. Looking very far down, there was a shed with a slightly sloping roof, several cans for rubbish, some bins of coal and coke, and a concrete yard perhaps fifteen feet square.

Then she heard heavy footsteps behind her. A man shouted.

There was no time. She climbed through the window on to the fire escape, scratching her leg, slammed the window shut, and set off downwards, clinging with one hand to the rusty railing.

She was down one floor. She dared not look at the window to see if there was anyone waiting for her. She had nowhere else to go, even if there were.

Third floor. Down again.

Second floor. On down.

Next floor and the shed roof. Was that all there was? From there you were supposed to jump? Perhaps if the building were on fire, you would be happy enough to do that?

She heard a shout of anger from above her. The next moment there was a shot and a bullet whined past her and ricocheted off the tin roof only a few feet away. She scrambled across the corner of the roof on to the top of the ash can, and then on to the ground between the rubbish and the coke bins, sliding through as rapidly as she could.

There was another shot, but it was nowhere near her. They

had lost sight of her, for a moment. But they knew where she was. She must get into the street as soon as she could, or she would be cornered here like a rat! And the very fact that she was running would brand her guilty. An innocent woman would have waited in the bedroom to be caught and questioned, and then what? Arrested, and maybe never seen again? Or more likely shot while attempting to escape the consequences of her terrible crime.

She crossed the yard and, without even looking, went out into the alley. Which way would they search for her? In the quiet street at the back of the hotel, where they could corner her and shoot her without anyone knowing.

If she went towards the busy street at the front, they might see her, but they would not shoot her in the crowd.

But for a moment her legs would not move. They would barely hold her up. She could imagine the bullet tearing into her. She could feel the weight of Ian's body, see his face as if it had been minutes ago instead of what, yesterday? The day before?

She put the bag's handle over her shoulder and walked a little stiffly, as if she had no care, no fear and certainly no guilt. She went straight out on to the front street where the hotel lobby opened on to the pavement.

She saw the Brownshirts milling outside almost immediately, and a small crowd gathered around, waiting for something to happen. The Brownshirts kept trying to shoo them away, but they only stepped back a yard or two. They were all curious to see what was going on, to witness the arrest of whoever had assassinated The Hyena.

Elena turned, as if it was always what she had intended to do, and walked briskly away from the hotel towards . . . what? She had no idea where that route led, but any crowd would be good enough to get lost in, until she could be at least half a mile away. Then she needed to think where she was, and find her way to the British Embassy. There, at least, she would be safe.

Why on earth had Cordell failed to save Scharnhorst? Or had he not believed that MI6 would really be blamed? Well, he was wrong! Totally wrong! If whoever had shot him had not intended a British person to be blamed, and hanged for it, why would they have left the rifle in her hotel room? And how would the Brownshirts have known so very quickly where to come for her?

Then the understanding hit her like a wave of nausea. Maybe that was why she had had no difficulty getting out of the square and to her hotel room? It all fitted together. They meant to shoot her. They meant her to be blamed. And if they had stopped her and searched her before she got to the hotel, she would very definitely not have had the gun with her.

For the moment, her chest was so tight she could barely breathe. But it was not only fear, it was rage as well. She must get to the Embassy. As quickly as possible. She could not do anything at all if she did not survive!

Chapter Fifteen

It took Elena almost three-quarters of an hour to make her way through the choked streets full of frightened people, trying to avoid every group of Brownshirts that she saw. She dare not try to find any shortcuts; she must not find herself alone in an alley where, if she were cornered, she could be attacked, and no one would even see, let alone help her.

Was that what it had come to? Was the surface of sanity so fragile that a woman could be attacked in the street, beaten, even killed, if the men who did it were in uniform, and no one would dare stop them? Perhaps.

She was not sure that it was safe for her to take even the slightest risk. She found herself following groups, families, any people who seemed to belong together, and trying to look as if she were one of them.

She was no longer part of the establishment that she was used to. She was the enemy, the outsider everyone was looking for. It was only because word had not yet got around giving her description that no one had recognised her. How long would it be before they did? Not long. Before dark she would be run to ground. The only place where she could be safe would be the Embassy.

She kept walking, her eyes on the pavement, looking at no one. Why had Cordell not been able to stop the assassination? Had they somehow got rid of him, too? Surely not! He was a senior British diplomat. That would be more than an unpleasant incident between Britain and Germany, it would be a warning to every country that had an embassy in Germany: Hitler's Government were savages! And in return no German embassy would be safe anywhere, at least in the civilised world. Anyway, Hitler quite liked England, Elena's father said. Germany and England were cousins. Their royal families had been, quite literally.

She was being ridiculous. Letting her imagination run away with her. It was terrible how fear could rob you of sense . . . and courage.

The Embassy was only a hundred yards ahead of her, but she could see now that it was surrounded by Brownshirts. They looked as if they were guarding it, for its safety, against some expected attack. But whatever its purpose, there was no way she could force herself through the guard and go in. They would demand identification. Of course they would. They ought to. And then when they saw her face, or even her general description, they would say she was a danger to the Embassy. For the protection of the British officials, as guests here in Berlin, they would prevent her from entering.

She froze for seconds, her mind in a storm of disintegrating plans and potential disasters. They knew she was British. They were waiting for her, hoping she might run here for safety, for help. She should have thought of that. She must go away now, as unobtrusively as possible, as if she too had been drawn here only as part of the crowd.

She turned aside, trying to look as if they had merely

blocked her path. Her mother was American. She should try the American Embassy. They would surely help her, even if only to contact the British and find her some way out. All embassies were the soil of the country they represented. The Germans would certainly not push their way into the US Embassy. That would make an international incident they most assuredly could not afford.

No one seemed to notice her moving away. She kept her head down and carefully avoided catching anyone's eye. She did not want to be remembered. For the first time in her life, she wanted to be so ordinary as to be virtually invisible.

It was not far to the American Embassy and she walked as quickly as possible without seeming to run.

Even before she reached the building, she could see Brownshirts on all the corners and gathering crowds in the street outside. There was really no better chance of getting in there without being stopped, questioned, and possibly searched than there had been at the British Embassy. Her passport could identify her and she was sure that, by now, the militia had the description of the woman they were looking for. Could they have learned her name? Could she also be tied to having been travelling with Ian? The border police might remember her. Don't be ridiculous! They would have a record!

She stood on the pavement, frozen with indecision, and mounting panic.

'Excuse me, are you lost?' a man's voice asked in German.

She spun round and saw a young man a yard or so away from her. He was tall and dark. At first glance he seemed quite ordinary, but there was intelligence in his eyes, and humour.

'I . . .' she began, also in German. She had no idea what to say to him. He had spoken to her in German, but she detected a different accent. What could she tell him? She must look like a fool.

'What's wrong?' he asked. 'You aren't lost, are you.' That was a statement. 'You just didn't expect the Embassy to be surrounded, and by Brownshirts . . .'

With a flood of horror, she realised how obvious she must look, standing here in the street, like a rabbit paralysed in the headlights of a car. She must be drawing other people's attention too, not just this young man's.

'Where do you come from?' she asked. It was abrupt, almost rude, but she had to know if he was German, or if he were here at the Embassy because perhaps he was a foreigner, too.

'Chicago,' he replied with a bleak smile. 'Or fairly near there. Why?'

She breathed out with a sigh. He was American. 'I need to get to the Embassy,' she explained. 'I tried the British, but it's even more tightly surrounded than this. I thought of here, because my mother is American, but this looks hopeless, too . . .'

'You could try, if you have business,' he said doubtfully. 'They're looking for the woman they think shot Scharnhorst. You must have heard about it.'

'Yes,' she said quietly, 'I know. I must look like her . . .' Was that a stupid thing to say? Or would it be even more obvious if she pretended she did not know? Indecisive! She had fallen straight into the very hole she was trying to avoid.

'You do,' he agreed, looking at her more intently. 'They might stop you if you go any closer. I think you should leave, rather quietly.'

'I've nowhere to go!' she said more sharply than she had intended. She could hear the edge in her voice. 'I can't go back to the hotel. I only just managed to get away. They were actually shooting at me.' She steadied her voice. She sounded almost hysterical.

'I don't suppose you did shoot him?' he asked with a twisted half-smile. 'I'd quite like to meet a hero of that order.'

'Well, you're out of luck now, because I didn't. But when I got back to my hotel room there was a rifle in my wardrobe, and with those special sights they have for shooting accurately at long distances. I left . . .'

He took her arm and she jumped at his grip, trying to pull away.

'Stop it,' he said quietly. 'They're looking for someone alone. Whether you actually shot him or not, you'll do just as well, for their purposes, to make them look good. We've got to get away from here. Don't make a scene.' He moved so that she had to turn to go with him, slowly, casually, like a couple coming from the Embassy. Who was he? Why would he help her? Or was he taking her captive to hand her over, and take the credit himself? He was holding her arm very tightly. His fingers pinched.

'Who are you?' she said sharply, trying to pull her arm away, and failing. 'Let go of me!' She wanted to be angry; it was so much easier than being frightened.

'Or what?' he asked, this time his smile was rich with amusement, and he spoke in English. 'You'll scream? Don't be so damn silly! I'm going to get you out of here, away from the Brownshirts. I'll take you to friends of mine that you can stay with. They'll look after you.'

'Why should they?' she demanded. 'I'm a danger . . .' Again, she tried to pull away.

'My name is Jacob,' he told her. 'Jacob Ritter. I'm from Chicago, but actually I'm working out of New York at the moment. I'm a journalist. And you're English. Anyone can tell that from your speech. Although your German's pretty good.'

'It's very good. My father was with the British Embassy here a few years ago,' she snapped.

'Keep walking. What's your name?'

'Elena Standish. And I didn't shoot Friedrich Scharnhorst. I don't know who did, but I do know why.'

'Really? Do you also know why the rifle was in your bedroom wardrobe?' He kept the firm grip on her arm as they crossed the street, walking a little stiffly because his natural stride was longer than hers.

'I think so, but it doesn't matter now. Where are we going?' She ran a couple of steps to keep up with him, then tried pulling her arm free and again failed.

'We're going into a predominantly Jewish quarter,' he replied. 'I've got friends there we can stay with. At least, you can. I have my own rooms. They'll look after you. And they won't turn you in, even if you did shoot Scharnhorst.'

'I didn't! I don't know one end of a gun from the other!'

'You don't look half-witted,' he said with a smile. It wasn't friendliness, it was laughter.

If she laughed now, she would too easily lose control. She tried again to pull away.

'I said you don't look like it, so don't act like it. Walk as if you are an adult, going wherever you want.'

She straightened up and walked close beside him.

'Thank you,' he said drily.

'I didn't shoot Scharnhorst,' she said again. 'In fact, I was trying to prevent it!'

'Do you think that will bother them, if they decide to blame you?' There was considerable bitterness in his voice. 'How long have you been here in Germany – this time?'

'Only since . . .' She realised she had just met this man, and trusting him with more than she had to was stupid.

'Since . . . what?' he asked, slowing up as they came to a crossroads again.

Perhaps not trusting him, or more to the point, letting him see that she did not, was foolish. She could not go to the British Embassy, or the American. Where else was there for her to try? She certainly could not get out of Berlin. She had no friends she could turn to, not to trust now. People changed. My God! Didn't they? And could she blame them if they did it to survive? Or for their families to survive! This man was the only chance she had. Perhaps it was better to trust him. He could find out the truth in time anyway and by then she would have lost her chance to have him return her trust.

'I got here yesterday. I hadn't planned to come, but circumstances . . .' What a ridiculous word to use! She bit it back. 'I came to try to stop the assassination, because I knew the British were going to be blamed. But obviously I didn't succeed. I think perhaps it was a futile idea from the beginning.'

They were in quieter streets now. Jacob slowed his pace a little and gave her a sideways glance, his dark eyes unreadable. 'You aren't making much sense. How did you know anything about it? Where did you come from?'

She hesitated a moment. Was she walking straight into a trap? But to trust him was her only chance.

Briefly she told him about Amalfi, and Ian's murder on the train, and how she had promised him she would get the message to the British Embassy. She found her voice thick with unshed tears as she did so.

He slowed to a stop, for the first time completely letting go of her arm. 'I'm sorry,' he said gravely, his face full of pity. 'But you did everything you could. Either this man Cordell tried to stop it and failed, or I'm afraid he didn't try, for whatever reason. It's probably a damn good thing you didn't get into the Embassy. He could have made a gesture of goodwill and handed you over to the Germans.'

For a moment the quiet street swam around her, then she forced herself to focus. 'I hadn't thought of that,' she admitted. 'Damn! I'm behaving like a fool!'

'You couldn't help it to begin with,' he agreed, smiling very slightly. 'But you can now! Forget Cordell. Perhaps he did everything he could. He couldn't warn you, because it probably never occurred to him that you would go to the rally. Why did you?'

'To get photographs of Scharnhorst, of course!' she replied, as if it were obvious. 'And if there had been someone arrested for trying to attack him, it could have been a dramatic moment. I'm a photographer,' she added, almost as an after-thought.

'And I'm a journalist, but I'm no good to anyone if I'm dead!' he responded.

'I thought Cordell would have prevented the assassination!'

'Then you had more faith in him than you should have.'

'It wasn't blind faith!' Elena protested. 'I know him; I have done for years.'

'Really? How long ago?' Jacob looked slightly surprised.

'From when my father was Ambassador here.'

'I thought you said that was a long time ago.'

'Long time is . . . relative, I suppose.'

'Meaning that people change?' he asked more gently.

'Not that much. He used to be . . . fun . . .' Memory rushed back of Cordell years ago, perhaps ten years. It was five years after the war. Some people were still giddy with peace. 'He really made us laugh,' she went on. 'Teaching us about the etiquette necessary to be a good ambassador. How to take any situation whatever with aplomb.'

'Stiff upper lip?' Jacob asked lightly.

'It's more than that, it's . . .'

He stood listening, eyebrows slightly raised. Then she realised he was gently making fun of her. She answered as her memory slipped back easily. 'For instance, how do you carry it off gracefully at dinner when the duchess's false teeth slip into her soup?'

His eyes widened. 'And what do you do?'

'Well, if it's broth, you can distract attention while she fishes them out again, and replaces them,' she replied, feeling her grip on herself slipping out of control. 'But if it's tomato soup, you haven't a chance.'

'And what was Cordell's answer to that?' Jacob asked incredulously.

'You have the butler remove the plate, serve her another, very discreetly, and take the soup away to fish more effectively. Without comment, of course. The real style is to keep the conversation going without a hiccup.'

'And did he? If it ever happened?'

She remembered vividly. 'Yes. But I had to leave the room.'

'Because you were diplomatic?'

'I'm afraid not. I was bursting with laughter.'

Suddenly all the lightness vanished out of his face, even

172

from his eyes. 'You'll have to be more diplomatic now. Your life depends on it. Really! And not only yours, the lives of the people who help you.' He searched her face carefully. 'If you're telling me the truth, two men are dead already.'

'Three,' she corrected, her voice catching in her throat so it was barely a discernible word. 'There was a man in Amalfi, too.'

He looked at her. 'You didn't mention that. Didn't your friend in the train know about it?'

'Yes. I know! I know!' She could hear her own voice higher and sharper. She controlled it with difficulty. 'He was dying when he told me. It didn't seem to be terribly important at the time. Nothing else did!'

He put his hands on her shoulders, very gently. 'I'm sorry. I'm sorrier than I can say. But now we've got to do all we can to keep you safe. He would want that, wouldn't he?'

She was too near tears to speak. She nodded, meeting his eyes for a moment. Then turning away, she began to walk forward again.

He caught up in a couple of steps. 'We shouldn't be out in the street longer than we have to be. You can trust most people here, but not everyone. Fear . . .' He stopped, his face touched with pain. He looked about Elena's own age, perhaps a year or two older, but already there were deeply etched lines around his eyes and mouth. He was not handsome, but there was too much wit and understanding in him not to be attractive.

'Fear changes things,' he said, this time not looking at her, and continuing to walk. 'Most of us think we know what we believe, and what we value, who we'll defend, whether we like them or not. But when the Brownshirts come to your door, sometimes your courage disappears, your guts turn to water, and you tell them what they want to know. The best of us will lie to them and take the consequences on ourselves. But it's altogether another thing when it's your mother, or your child that they'll hurt. And they will. We know that from experience. You can see the guilt in some people's eyes. They didn't believe it because they didn't want to. But they should have. I say that as fact, not as blame. I don't know what I would do, if it were someone I love who would be made to pay. Or anyone else at all, for that matter.'

She said nothing. It was not something to which any reply made sense. The thought was too overwhelming.

They walked two more blocks in silence, all the time Elena's mind struggling to think honestly what she would do. If there were nothing that mattered more than herself, that was a terrible thought, in a way the final defeat.

Jacob turned left, left again, then finally right, and stopped in front of a handsome family home. He ignored the front door and went along the narrow stone path to the back door, where he knocked.

It was opened after a moment by a middle-aged woman wearing a crisp white apron. As soon as she saw Jacob, she smiled. 'Good afternoon, Mr Jacob,' she said cheerfully. 'Come in. Come in, Miss . . .'

'Miss Standish,' he introduced her. 'Marta is a good friend,' he added to Elena, standing back to allow her in ahead of him.

Elena went inside and found herself in a large, warm kitchen with pleasant but unfamiliar smells. She could not help staring around. It was comfortable, domestic, as if it were someone's home, made to be used, even lived in. There was china all along the dresser shelves, pots and pans hanging from hooks on the wall, and clean laundry in a pile on a side table near another door. Washed vegetables stood on a bench near the sink, and there were bunches of dried herbs hanging from hooks above.

'Is Zillah at home?' Jacob asked, as soon as the outer door was closed.

'Yes. In the sitting room,' Marta replied. She glanced at Elena, a question in her eyes, but concern also. Did they have fugitives here often enough to recognise one on sight? Or did she emanate fear as profoundly as she felt it, and anyone could pick it up?

'Come,' Jacob told Elena, then said something to Marta very quickly, in a dialect she did not understand. It was a little like German, but unfamiliar.

She followed him across the hallway, and after a brief knock, into another comfortable room, at the moment lit by the afternoon sun.

A tall woman, dark haired and a little thin, stood by the window. She turned as she heard Jacob. There was no fear in her face, only a quiet confidence, almost a serenity. She was not in the least fashionable – her clothes were dark and conservative – but there was a gentleness, a symmetry in her face that some might even have found beautiful.

'I'm sorry to catch you without warning,' Jacob said a little ruefully, 'but I have a genuine fugitive. Elena, this is Zillah, Frau Hubermann. Elena Standish. She is English. She did not shoot Friedrich Scharnhorst, but some of the Brownshirts think she did. Or they want to think so. Could be they shot him themselves, but the truth will make no difference. She can't go to the British Embassy, because they are likely the ones who made her look guilty. They were the only ones who even knew she was here. And she can't go to the American Embassy, even though her mother is American, because that's the next place they'd look.'

'Oh dear,' Zillah said with a rueful smile. She looked at Elena gently. 'Are you all alone?'

'Yes. My . . . my friend who was going to warn the British Embassy about the assassination was murdered . . . on the train from Milan to Paris.' She said it as quickly as she could, to keep her voice very nearly steady. 'He worked for British Intelligence. He told me before he died that Scharnhorst would be assassinated, and they would try to blame us, the British, to create an international incident. I suppose if he had got here, they would have blamed him. The rifle is now in my hotel room. Which would have been his room, I think.' She stopped. She was talking too much. Did it all make any sense to this quiet woman standing in the sunlight?

'Scharnhorst's death is probably the only good thing about it,' Jacob said bleakly. 'Can hardly blame anyone for wanting that bastard dead. Although I would have done it more slowly.'

Zillah looked him up and down. 'I suppose you didn't, did you?' For an instant it was impossible to tell from her face if there were any seriousness behind the question.

'I've left a few odd things in other people's bedrooms,' Jacob smiled with real amusement. 'But no rifles.'

Zillah looked towards the ceiling for a moment, rolling her eyes, then turned to Elena. 'You are welcome to stay here, until you decide what would be best for you,' she said quietly. She looked at Elena. 'Perhaps a darker dress, something more like . . .'

'A housemaid,' Jacob supplied. 'That will not cause any comment.'

Elena nodded. Everything was happening too quickly, but even in her dazed state, and the exhaustion that had overtaken her, she could see the sense in that. 'I will be happy to do whatever I can. I don't know where to go . . . yet. I should get out of Berlin, perhaps to Paris, and then home.'

'They'll be looking for you.' Jacob shook his head. 'One day at a time. There'll be a way.'

'You'll have to say that you have no idea who I am.' She looked from one to the other of them, suddenly aware that she was putting them in danger. 'Jacob—'

'We're used to it,' he said with sudden bitterness. 'Eli, Zillah's husband, thinks there's really nothing wrong, and it will all pass over.'

Zillah drew in her breath to caution him, or perhaps to contradict. Elena was not sure, but it seemed that Zillah changed her mind, as if she would not speak of her husband with disrespect, even if she disagreed with his opinion.

Zillah smiled, but only with her lips. In her eyes there was a dark fear. 'He thinks that we are Germans first, and Jews only by chance,' she said softly. 'We are necessary. He is a research chemist. They cannot do without people like him. He credits them with more sense than I do.' Her voice wavered very slightly. 'I don't think they care what we do, how long our forebears have been here, or anything else.' She straightened her shoulder. 'But you must be hungry! When did you last eat? Breakfast, I imagine? You can do nothing well on an empty stomach. I'll find a good plain dress for you, and Marta will get you something to eat.' She turned from Elena to Jacob. 'Don't stand there, my dear! Do something useful!'

177

He shot a quick smile at Elena, then looked back at Zillah. 'Would you like me to attend to the dress, or the lunch?'

Zillah did not bother to answer him, but she smiled. 'Come,' she said to Elena. 'We must be quick, and quiet about this.' She led the way out of the room, and Elena followed her.

Chapter Sixteen

Margot was really annoyed with Elena. It was nearly three days now, and she had not bothered to send any message at all as to where she was. If she had stopped off in Paris and decided to stay there with Ian, or alone, she could at least have said so! It took very little effort to send a telegram and say something, even if it was only an apology for tearing off like that without a word. Not that Margot blamed her entirely for that, if she were honest. She might well have done the same thing. Indeed, she had, more than once. But she had had the decency to let people know, and apologise, more or less.

Margot had wired her parents, and they had heard nothing at all either. She had not thought it possible to become bored with Amalfi, but she had done. There was no choice but to see if Elena was sitting in a heap in Paris, miserable that the affair had gone no further, too proud to tell anyone, and unable to go home until she had pulled herself together. Katherine had always expected Margot to look after her younger sister. Now she was going to have to do it again! Actually, Elena was perfectly capable of looking after herself! She just wouldn't do the expected things. And to be honest, she had made an awful mess of the Aiden Strother business. She took everything so deeply! She had been loyal to him far longer than had been realistic. But Elena was not a realist!

Margot checked out of the hotel and took the long, rather tedious train journey to Rome, Milan, and then Paris. The first place to look, of course, was the small Hôtel de l'Abbaye, on Rue Cassette, where they usually stayed. She went there and asked, but the staff had seen nothing of Elena. Margot booked herself in anyway, then set out to walk in the usual places, among the people and to the cafés where she and Elena had gone together in the past. Damn it, they had lived in Paris long enough, when their father was British Ambassador here. There must be some old friends still around.

She walked along the street with a swing in her step, although she had no particular care where she was going. She was wearing a black and white silk dress, and she felt the swirl of it with pleasure. They might not know if they had seen Elena or not, but they would remember her!

Three hours and many questions later, she was fed up with this and decided she would go home, whether she found Elena or not. She had memories of looking for her as a little girl. She was rather sweet then. Always asking questions. 'How does this work?' 'What does it do?' And more than anything else, 'Why?' She supposed that they had grown apart while Margot fell in love with Paul. There had been no room for anyone else then. How could there be? Who wanted a little sister along on the few short times they had together? So short . . . Elena had never fallen in love, not really, deeply in love, as far as Margot knew. She did not court Aiden Strother. That was infatuation. She never even saw the real man behind the façade. If anybody was there!

And she would know. Now there were hardly any real men left to fall for, and Elena was far too serious for most of them, and yet not domestic enough for someone who wanted a traditional wife.

Margot was sitting in the shade of the Luxembourg Gardens. It was beautiful, an island of enormous trees, sudden statues, whispering leaves above.

Where in hell had she got to? Why couldn't she at least have the decency to let people know? She was so bland on the surface, people might not remember her, even if she had walked by them some time ago! She wore too much blue. Blue and empty, like the sea, or the sky.

Margot was all fire and ice. Nobody forgot her.

She went out through the gates into the street and passed a newsstand with the morning's front pages displayed.

Margot slowed her pace. The woman staring at her from the newspaper bore a striking resemblance to Elena. But it could also be any one of a half-million other young women. She pushed the thought away, passed the newsstand . . . and then turned back.

That really could be Elena. It looked like her . . . a lot. Margot took a couple of steps towards the newsstand.

It was the woman suspected of having assassinated Friedrich Scharnhorst! Not that he didn't need assassinating; he was a monster, well-nicknamed The Hyena! Apparently it had happened in Berlin a day ago.

She really did look like Elena. Odd. Wonder what her name was? She was probably German.

Margot leaned forward and looked at the picture more closely. Then the coldness seized her with a grip like iron. It was Elena. The slightly winged eyebrows, the high cheek-bones, the unexpectedly sensuous mouth.

Margot read the caption underneath. 'Englishwoman wanted for the murder of Friedrich Scharnhorst. Possibly Elena Standish, daughter of a previous British Ambassador to Berlin.' And it gave the dates.

Margot stood frozen. That couldn't be true! Not Elena, of all people. What the hell had happened? Had that apparently harmless-looking young man, Ian what's-his-name, done it and left Elena to carry the blame? Was that what he wanted all along? God, he was convincing! Margot would never have guessed, and she was pretty skilled at judging character, especially in men. First Aiden Strother, and now this! But this was infinitely worse.

'Madame?'

She realised the newspaper seller was speaking to her. Reaching into her bag, she pulled out a few coins, and gave them to the man. Snatching up the paper, she turned and walked away quickly. What on earth had Elena got herself into this time? How could Margot help?

Obvious! First thing was to go to Berlin, to the British Embassy. Roger Cordell was still there. He had been a good friend to their father, and he had liked Margot. He had always made that clear, though he had never overstepped the mark and been overfamiliar. His own wife had never recovered from the losses of the war. In Margot's opinion, she didn't seem to have tried very hard. She had retreated from caring enough ever to be hurt again. Perhaps Margot judged that harshly because she needed to believe that grief could be overcome, because she was so deeply afraid of it herself!

Of course, Cordell was loyal to Winifred. He understood, and in some ways perhaps he had not recovered either? People who lose themselves in grief do not realise how they suck others down into the depths with them, like exhausted swimmers drowning their would-be rescuers?

Had Margot done that to anybody? She didn't think so. She hurt almost unbearably inside, but she tried very hard to look all right to everyone else. She kept hoping, trying to fall in love again. But the lightness she had felt with Paul made everything else seem dull, second rate, a pretend thing rather than a real one.

Was she remembering him as he had been? Or had she seen him always in that first flush of dizzying happiness? She would never know. It did not matter now. She must go back to Rue Cassette, get her things from the Hôtel de l'Abbaye and catch the next train to Berlin. What on earth she was going to do when she got there, she did not know. Except find Roger Cordell, of course, and ask his help. She did entertain the idea, for a very short time, of wiring her father and asking his advice, but that might only make matters worse. The Germans might well dig in even further, make a bigger incident of it, impossible to draw back from. She thought of her grandfather. He had always loved Elena the most, but what could he do to help? He was seventy now, a retired civil servant. He could achieve nothing.

No, Roger Cordell was the best. He could send for Charles Standish if there was any point. It was probably all some idiotic mistake.

Margot told herself that all the way to Berlin. It was late in the afternoon when the train pulled into the station, but there was still time to get a taxi as far as the British Embassy.

Berlin was just as grey as she remembered it, but the young men in brown uniform, standing around everywhere, with guns, were new. Everything seemed very orderly, very brisk and military. That was Herr Hitler, getting the trains to run on time! A good thing, no doubt, especially for those who had to rely on them, but a cold, mechanical thing all the same.

She found a taxi immediately and fifteen minutes later was at the Embassy gates. She had thought to have to make her way through a cordon of Brownshirts, as described in the Parisian newspaper, but they must have dispersed since the previous day, with just two or three on street corners. She told them who she was and found a guard who remembered her. She had no trouble in being shown to Roger Cordell's office.

He was waiting for her, standing in front of his desk. It was at least five years since she had seen him last, and he looked older, even a little grey at the temples. He was too young for that! Younger than her father. Then she remembered Winifred, and the grief she carried with her like a fog.

She smiled at him, with all the charm of someone who remembered him with only pleasure, from a younger and, in some ways happier, time. They had both known loss and had some idea how to bear it with grace, at least in public. She was still wearing the black and white silk dress, and she knew it looked good. She did not need to see the recognition of it in his face.

'Margot!' he exclaimed. 'You look marvellous, but then you always do.' He held out his hands and she laid hers in them. He gripped her tightly, met her eyes for a moment, then kissed her cheek lightly. 'I think I know why you are here,' he ventured, looking grave.

'I imagine you do,' she replied, stepping back. She had forgotten how direct he could be, unlike her father. But perhaps that was why Charles was an ambassador, and Cordell only a cultural attaché. 'I saw Elena's picture in a newspaper in Paris. Is it true? Are the German police, the Gestapo, or whatever they are called, looking for her? It's ridiculous! Not only wouldn't she do anything like that, she couldn't! You know Elena. She isn't competent to do that, even if she wanted to. She couldn't hit the broad side of a barn with a machine gun, let alone kill a man a hundred yards away with a sniper rifle!'

His face looked suddenly bleak. 'I knew she couldn't before, my dear, and I assume she still couldn't, although people learn . . .'

'Not Elena!' Margot said impatiently. 'And for heaven's sake, why? I know she made a bit of an ass of herself over Strother, but he took everyone in. And he was a traitor, not an assassin. I'd be willing to bet she'd never even heard of Scharnhorst when she left Amalfi. She may have been in love with Ian Newton, but she hadn't lost her wits!' She made a little gesture. 'She's a bit naïve, but not stupid. Do you know anything about it? I mean *really* know, not just believe whatever you're told?' She stared at him, searching his eyes. For all his dark good looks, he had grey eyes. At another time, she would've been fascinated by them. Perhaps in the past, a few times she had been. 'Roger! Please . . . I've got to know if she is all right. She just swept out of the hotel in Amalfi and left me standing. Now she's in the papers suspected of shooting someone! What has Newton done to her? And where on earth is he, anyway?'

Something in him yielded. There was sorrow in his eyes. 'She came to see me the evening before. Ian Newton was murdered on the train.'

She must have misheard him. 'You said . . . "murdered"! You don't really mean that?' Now, in spite of the pleasantness

185

of the room, she was cold to the bone. She knew from his face that he had made no error.

'Yes. I'm sorry. Margot, do you want to sit down?'

'I want you to tell me what the hell is going on!' she said hotly. 'What did you do to help Elena? What did you tell her? Why did you let this happen?'

He took a deep breath. There was a faint flush on his cheeks. 'I told her I would warn the authorities,' he said levelly. 'Which I did. They either made a series of errors, or more likely they simply ignored the warning.'

'Ignored it?' she demanded. 'And let one of their own get shot to death in a public rally?' Her voice dripped sarcasm.

'Margot,' he said patiently, 'what do you know about Scharnhorst?'

She sensed a change in his tone, and it frightened her. 'What does that matter?' she demanded. 'He's a monster! And Elena is being blamed for killing him.' She could hear the rising panic in her voice. She was getting out of control. 'Roger . . . please . . .'

'I'll do whatever I can, but it is at least a possibility that the best thing they could have is an Englishwoman to blame for getting rid of one of their most dangerous extremists. They can bury him with ceremony, as a martyr, and at the same time blame us for it. And be rid of the lunatic who was, frankly, becoming an embarrassment to them.'

'Doesn't he represent all they want, but only half dare to say?' she accused.

'No! Not at all.' He looked startled. She had seen exactly the same look in her father's face at some of her remarks. 'Hitler uses the extremists sometimes, but they can get out of hand. Scharnhorst had done exactly that. Hitler may be profoundly grateful to whomever killed him, but the worst element of the crowd, catering to the most gullible, would never stand for it. Now Hitler can claim to be entirely innocent and blame it on a hysterical Englishwoman. Somebody has presented him with precisely what he wants.'

'Somebody?' Margot made it only half a question. She looked at Cordell's face and saw the exasperation in it. 'All right! Elena is a fool, or gullible. We all know that. Aiden Strother proved it, the bastard. And somebody certainly used her this time, too. But she doesn't have either the skill or the nerve to have shot anyone. Especially not at a distance. And quite honestly, she wouldn't anyway. She would see it as wrong. She's . . .' She looked for the right word to use. Elena felt things deeply, but she was very traditional, like Lucas. 'She wouldn't go out on a limb . . . morally,' she finished. 'Somebody took advantage of her. Set it up to look as if she did it. You've got to . . . I mean, will you please help her?' She was no good at looking pathetic, and she knew it. No woman ever looked less pathetic than Margot Standish – or Margot Driscoll, as she now was. The Widow Driscoll. God, how she hated that word. 'Roger, please.'

He looked at her steadily. It was only seconds, and yet it seemed ages. 'Yes, of course. But you must stay out of it, Margot. You are very easily recognisable. You will lead them to her, no matter how much you don't mean to.'

'Well, what are you going to do?' Now was not the time to argue recognisability, although she had to admit that, though she had not thought of it before, what he said was true.

'Tell me the names and addresses of friends either of you still have in Berlin, the ones you know,' he replied. 'Elena will in all probability seek at least one of them. She's alone with limited money. She'll need help. Think about who she would trust, who has the means and the nerve to help, who has hostages to fortune, that you know of, and therefore could be forced to hand her over. Think like Elena and give me them in order of likelihood. If I can find her, I can probably get her out of Germany.'

Margot felt a twinge of guilt. He would be endangering his career at least, possibly his life. But Elena was her sister. Damn her for being impossibly stupid! Didn't she learn by experience? It looked as if she had trusted the wrong man – again!

'Thank you,' she said quite humbly. She had some idea what she was asking, and she really was grateful. 'I'll give it a few moments' thought, try to see it from her point of view, then I'll make the list.'

'Good. Would you like a cup of tea while you're thinking? We have some pretty decent biscuits here. Get them sent over, of course.'

'Yes, please. I seem to have forgotten to eat.'

He smiled, but she guessed he was wise enough not to make any promises he could not keep.

She respected that.

Chapter Seventeen

When Margot had gone, Cordell stood for several moments wondering what to do. He had her list. He had asked for it automatically, always seeking knowledge. And he had wanted Margot to believe that he would be all the help he could.

Tragedy had touched her deeply. There was, perhaps, a little bitterness, but he did not find it repellent. He could understand it only too well. She was angry, and she had not lost her capacity to hope, and to feel, or to be hurt by memory, or failure. There was still a hunger for life in her. He felt certain that if she had ever given up, it had been for a few moments in the loneliness of the night, but in the morning, when the light came back, she would be ready to fight again.

If you struck Margot, she would strike you back! Not like Winifred, who would do nothing, as if she did not feel it. As if she were essentially alone, and you did not exist, except peripherally, seen and heard but never felt. Was that his fault? He had tried, hard, though perhaps in the wrong ways? One way or another, he had failed.

He remembered Margot from her time in Berlin. She was like her father in that she was clever, angry, but a realist. She had more hunger for life than her father, but the same ability to see and acknowledge the truth. She had her mother's elegance, not a traditional beauty, but alluring . . . that was the word. And never a bore. There was nothing about her at all that was tedious, or cold. At least that was what she seemed from the outside. She might be hiding a coldness inside, but then so might anyone.

He looked at the paper in his hand. What was he going to do with a list of Elena's friends? If he called them and asked if they had seen Elena, that would warn her, and she would be gone almost immediately. Running from one place to another. She had been nearly hysterical when she turned up at his office two days ago – what must she be like now?

She would believe he had not warned the authorities, but he had. Though perhaps not the right ones. Perhaps he could have done more to prevent the assassination of Scharnhorst. The man was an abomination! Hitler might be quite happy to have had him killed and the blame fall on someone else.

But that was Cordell's risk to take, not Charles Standish's daughter's. He owed Charles more than that. Charles was at least ten years older than Cordell, but they had been good friends. Comfortable in conversation or silence. They had enjoyed doing the same things. They remembered and cared about the same values of honesty, stoicism, oblique humour, walking the quieter, older parts of the city. He remembered vividly searching antique shops and seeing old meerschaum pipes and wondering who had carved them, the lives of those who had smoked them! Going to the theatre and seeing small productions of classic plays, young actors, perhaps on the way to greatness.

He understood Charles's deep pain at the loss of his only son, and why he couldn't speak about it. It belittled the grief.

There are some wounds you don't touch. To say it would pass in time was offensive. One spoke of other things, shared values, and the bone-deep resolve that such a war would never happen again. It was the only decent legacy they would leave behind from all the years of work, their living in marvellous cities that were not home, and would never be.

He straightened up and put the list in his pocket. He would make a copy of it and give it to the police. She might actually be safer if she were caught and put in a prison. The Embassy would provide first-rate legal counsel for her. Possibly there was some deal that could be made to return her to England, although the German Government would ask a high price, and very possibly make a humiliating show of it.

But then maybe she would not be at any of her friends' houses.

And what the devil had happened to Ian Newton? Had he gone completely rogue? Cordell had thought him the standard, idealistic, young, upper-class Englishman with little imagination for the lives of anyone totally different from himself. Cambridge scholar in classics, or something of the sort, and modern political history. Had he taken a swift turn to the left . . . Communism, or something of the sort? God knows, there were those who had! They would wake up one day, when it was too late.

Had Elena fallen in love with him too, and even been turned herself? A young woman – she must be, what, twenty-eight? – not married, leading a fairly boring life without much hope of anything else? A handsome young man, the Amalfi coast, a lot of idealistic nonsense talked about the future. Change! The dreams of those who had not yet tasted life, except the froth on the surface.

Poor Charles. He did not deserve that; neither did Margot. She cared for her sister, as she naturally would. Perhaps he should send one of his men to look discreetly for Elena's friends. If he found her, there might be a way of getting her back to England with no one seeing her.

He pressed the bell on his desk for his assistant to return.

Chapter Eighteen

'What?' Lucas demanded, sitting in his study and staring at Peter Howard, who stood in front of the bookcase, too tense to stop shifting his weight from one foot to the other.

Howard repeated what he had said. 'Elena was at the British Embassy the day before yesterday. She saw Cordell.'

'In Berlin?' Lucas said. 'Why, for God's sake? She was on her way from Amalfi to Paris, then home with some young man she'd made friends with.' He stopped. Saying a thing over and over did not make it true, or untrue. Nor did it ease the coldness inside him of a sudden real fear. 'What did she see Cordell about?' he asked. 'For heaven's sake, Peter, give me this in some sort of order. How do you know Elena was there? Who recognised her? Are they sure? What did they say, exactly?'

Howard's face was bleak. 'That Elena Standish came to the British Embassy in Berlin, the day before the shooting. She asked to see Roger Cordell. Identified herself, unmistakably. She said it was both urgent and extremely important. It was late in the afternoon, but she insisted, and was allowed in. Lucas, the young man Elena was with was Ian Newton.' Howard went on quickly. 'She is unhurt, except emotionally. She finished Newton's intended journey, to see Cordell . . .'

Lucas could feel the ache of fear inside him tighten into a hard knot. 'Ian Newton? The man murdered on a train? How do you know she's unhurt?' he demanded. 'If she was there she can't be all right.' He felt the fear twisting inside him. 'And what do we know about Cordell now?'

'Wherever Cordell's deepest loyalties lie,' Howard responded, 'he isn't a fool. She made her way from the Paris train all the way to Berlin, eluding detection at the border, and got to the Embassy in time to give the warning, in spite of the way she must have felt.'

Lucas ought to apologise. Of course she would be all right. Cordell would betray himself if he did not look after her. And clearly, he was not ready to do that yet, if at all. 'What do we know about Cordell, for certain?' he asked more levelly.

'Nothing indisputable,' Howard replied, his face grave, the usual light of humour gone. 'It's a bad situation. Three men are dead, all by violence, and apparently connected. Cossotto, our man in Amalfi, was found with a broken neck in the hotel linen cupboard where Newton was staying. As was Elena. Then Newton was knifed to death in the train from Milan to Paris. Finally, Scharnhorst was shot by a sniper at the rally in Berlin.'

'Indisputably connected?' Lucas asked.

'It seems so. As I told you, Newton was given a message, purportedly from MI6, to go to Berlin and prevent the assassination. But he couldn't check with Cossotto, because he was dead. Newton got on the train with Elena and was killed on the way to carry out his instructions. As he was dying he passed on the instructions to Elena—'

'Is that true? *All* of it?' Lucas interrupted him. He could feel his whole body tighten with horror at the thought of how she must have felt.

'Cordell says that's what she told him, and it's the only thing that makes sense,' Howard said. 'She was shocked, and grieving, but she carried out the mission to warn him.'

'But he failed?' Lucas shifted his position slightly. 'Is he telling the truth?'

'I don't know. But it's possible. Scharnhorst was a rabid animal. Obsessed with blood and slaughter. Purifying the Aryan race, and all that poisonous rubbish.'

Lucas frowned, worried by a new thought. He looked at Howard and saw the rigidity of his body, for all the surface calm. Did the man not ever relax his guard? He used not to be so tightly strung. Had Lucas himself been like that when he was in the service? When a mistake could cost so much! He remembered it now. Yes, perhaps he had. He had escaped it, for a while. He did not want it back again. And yet what was he worth if he could watch it all unravel again, and do nothing? A man who watched was as guilty as those who took part. If he could have stopped it, even a small amount of it . . . if he had tried. Perhaps that was what he had implicitly taught Elena. He would have told Howard that, if their roles had been reversed. 'Peter! Is Cordell lying to himself, or to us? Or daren't he even look at it?' he said.

A wisp of a smile crossed Howard's face, and perhaps of pity also. 'I don't think he's faced it yet,' he answered. 'He may have tried, sincerely. The other thought is that Cordell may know more about Scharnhorst than he let us know, and it could be the Germans are only too pleased to see the bastard shot, whoever did it! What could be better?'

'Shot Scharnhorst? Really?'

'If you were back with us, you'd know enough not to be surprised,' Howard said bleakly. 'Hitler's quite capable of having done it himself. Scharnhorst was a liability.'

'I thought Hitler was for the pure Aryan race, by whatever means necessary. That's the subtext I keep hearing.'

'He's clumsy, Lucas. Raving mad under the surface, but clever. He won't take the people faster than they're willing to go. Scharnhorst was moving too quickly, and I think Hitler might well have seen that. And there were rumours he had his sights on Hitler's job. You do know that Hitler got about ninety-four per cent of the vote in the election at the turn of the year? If he knows anything, he knows his power . . . and his people. That's what scares the hell out of me. He could have been informed by Cordell, or whoever else, and let the assassination go ahead. A good, clean way of getting rid of the man, this rival. And blaming us at the same time!'

'And you really think Cordell would have been complicit in this?' Lucas asked.

'Like most of us, if not all, he passionately wants to believe there will never be another war like the last one,' Howard answered.

'From the outside?' Lucas said quietly, forcing the words, like walking into darkness.

Howard blinked, puzzled.

'Or the inside?' Lucas elaborated. 'Do you want your enemy wearing a German uniform, or a British one? A brown shirt or a black one.' He was exaggerating, and he knew it, but not by very far. The possibility was closer than they thought . . . far too close.

'We're not—' Howard began, and then stopped. 'Cordell's

not stupid, and I believe he'll see them for what they are: but whether it will be soon enough to save himself . . . I'm sorry.'

'I can't leave Elena there,' Lucas said immediately. 'I wanted to know about Cordell because I would like to have been able to trust him.'

Howard's body stiffened. Before he could interrupt, Lucas went on.

'I want to go there and find her.' Had it been anyone but Elena, he would have accepted the facts and futility of his own actions immediately. Was he getting old, losing his touch? Or was it just that this was family, a child he had known since the day of her birth, a tiny scrap of life wrapped up in a dress like something a doll would wear, and staring at him with wide, blue eyes that looked as if they had just opened on the world? She had not changed so much. 'Where was she last seen?' he asked.

'I don't know,' Howard replied. 'And neither do any of my sources. She was staying in a hotel we often use. It seems that, too, is now compromised, because the Storm Troopers went there for her almost immediately, but she escaped. Apparently, she went up the stairs to the top floor, then down the ancient fire escape into an alley, and there they lost her.'

'In an alley?' Lucas was filled with alarm. Surely that must mean they had captured her, but were now denying it. Why? Proof of British guilt was surely the purpose of it all, at least on the face of it? Ignoring what darker political purpose Hitler might have. 'Peter—'

'No,' Howard said quickly. 'They don't have her. She must have gone forward into the crowd instead of running for cover. Clever. They lost her among the people in the street, and now there is a full-scale manhunt going on for her.'

Lucas could not remember anything that had shaken him so badly. Except the news of Mike's death. In a way this was worse. There was no finality to it. He had not known Elena was in any danger. He was seared by the terror she must be feeling, alone and hunted in a city that toppled on the edge of depravity, teeming with Brownshirts, everyone afraid of them, and they becoming more and more drunk with power. He could not even allow into his imagination what they would do to a woman they believed guilty of killing a man they adored, hysterically, fanatically, as they had Scharnhorst.

Howard leaned forward and grasped Lucas's hand. For seconds he held it as hard as he could, then he let go and resumed his position in his chair. This was real. It must be faced.

'I'll go and look for her,' he said firmly. 'I have a better chance of disappearing in a crowd than you do. And I am a damn sight more up to date. But first I need to go and tell Newton's family. I owe him to do that myself. He was . . .' He did not finish the sentence. It was only words, and they both knew them too well to need to say them aloud. More than anything else, it brought back the past in its savage, bruising pain.

Slowly, Howard stood up, looking more than his forty-three years. It was all the more noticeable because usually he looked less. There was youth in the humour and intelligence in his face. Now he seemed beaten, just not yet completely aware of it. 'I'll tell you anything I learn about Elena, and I'll get my best people to do whatever I can to find her and get her out of Berlin.'

Reluctantly, Lucas conceded. He was too old to be the best man for this. For all his passion, and willingness to sacrifice himself if necessary, he had not the physical stamina, and perhaps not the mental agility any longer, to succeed. He rose to his feet also. 'I know.'

Howard went out of the French door and across the garden to the back entrance.

Lucas found Josephine waiting in the hallway. She looked angry, but there was fear in her eyes.

'What is it?' she said without preamble.

'Howard? Oh, he's—'

'Lucas, don't lie to me!' she said sharply, real anger in her voice. 'I know it's bad. I can see it.'

'It's . . .' he began, then stopped again. Up until a day or two ago, he had believed she knew only that his job during the war, and for a while after, had been secret, as her wartime job had been. She had never spoken of her work as a decoder and in turn had allowed him to think that he had his secrets still, when all the time it was her knowledge of him that was the real secret.

He was flooded with an overwhelming gratitude for her generosity of silence. The emotion robbed him of words.

But she was frightened now, and her fear was increasing with his refusal to tell her what was the matter. Perhaps just as deep a pain was her perception that he might not trust her.

'Elena,' he said. 'One of the vilest of Adolf Hitler's admirers has been assassinated. The man they nicknamed The Hyena because of his habit of mauling the already wounded, the vulnerable.' He spoke with a venom that surprised even him.

She was waiting, knowing that this was not the point.

'They are blaming British Intelligence for it, specifically Elena.'

'What? Lucas, is she in Berlin? She's supposed to be in Paris!' She was not arguing with him. He saw that she believed him, that she was looking for an explanation and trying to understand.

'Yes, she went to Berlin. I know that because she went to the Embassy and tried to warn them about the assassination.'

'Warn them? How did she know? What are you not telling me?' There was the beginning of accusation in her voice.

In as few words as possible, he told her about Ian Newton and his death.

'Then why are they blaming her?' Josephine's face was white now, her eyes glittering with rage and fear. 'Who knew of Ian Newton's instructions to go to Berlin, and who killed him on the train? It cannot possibly have been Elena. She's obviously just got caught up in all this.'

'I know,' he agreed. 'I fear we have a traitor and I think I know who it is. I have every intention of using him to feed his handlers with false information. Right now, all I care about it getting Elena back home.'

'Where is she? Do you know?' Even against her iron will, Josephine could not keep the slight tremor from her voice.

'No, except that she must be well hidden, because the German militia can't find her either. So perhaps we have a little time.'

'Until what?' she asked.

He knew the answer, as she did, but he did not want to put it into words.

'Until it's too late,' she answered herself. She seemed about to add something, then changed her mind.

He knew what it was, and why she had bitten it back.

He was far too original a thinker for obedience. People in the secret intelligence services were never known to the public. He had thought it a protection for her, at least from some of the fears, and the guilt for the disasters that happened every now and then, the deaths. How gentle of her, how discreet not to have told him. Now she deserved the openness of his trusting her with the information she would probably have worked out for herself. The trust now mattered the most, the certain knowledge that he was not lying or concealing anything from her. 'I have no idea where she is, but I still have contacts in Berlin. People I trust, and who owe me. I'll go and look for her.' He did not mention Howard. He, Lucas, would go, too, in spite of what he had said.

She took a deep breath, blinking her eyes to dispel tears. 'No, you won't, my dear. You are far too old for such things, and you have a twisted ligament in your ankle. Don't argue with me, Lucas! You'll get exposed if you're caught, and worse.'

'But Elena, Josephine! Do you have any idea what they could do to her?'

'Yes.' She did not elaborate. Perhaps she had her own nightmares. 'Has it not occurred to you that as well as old friends in Berlin, you might also have old enemies? And their memories can be even longer.'

'I know that,' he said, although it had not been at the front of his mind. His ankle he had become used to, but it certainly ached towards the end of the day. He could not run on it, but then he was long past his running days anyway. 'But I can't leave her there.'

'Send Peter Howard,' she said without hesitation. 'He's a man in his prime.'

'He's already said he'll go, but . . .' He hesitated. This was not about himself.

'I know,' she said firmly. 'High up in MI6 and shouldn't really do rescues of young women who get into tight situations. But don't argue with me. Let Peter Howard go alone or I'll go and make sure he does, myself!'

'You won't. You don't even know where to find him.'

'Don't be absurd! Of course I do!' There was a blazing certainty in her eyes, as well as a fear that was very deep indeed. She had one son, Charles, to whom she was not particularly close, no matter how much she loved him. Their natures were utterly different. But she had two granddaughters, and Elena was as dear to her as anyone in her life, perhaps even as dear as Lucas himself.

'All right. I'll go and tell him I definitely won't be going. I know where he'll be this evening.'

'Thank you,' she said simply. 'And make sure you give him some photographs of Elena. He'll need to know what she looks like.'

The moment the front door closed behind Lucas, she picked up the phone and called Charles.

Lucas took Toby with him. A man with a dog drew far less attention than a man alone. Toby was delighted, he loved riding in the car. In his experience, it went to the most wonderful places: woods, fields, sometimes even beaches, and the homes of people who fed him treats.

It was a good thirty minutes' drive in the May dusk, and they passed through one brief shower of rain. Lucas parked a distance from Howard's house, put Toby on his lead, and set out to walk. Caution was a lifetime habit.

He had met Pamela Howard a few times, but he could

not easily remember what she looked like. Fairer than Josephine, he thought, but not a paler colour so much as a lack of it. She had a beautiful skin, blemishless. He rather hoped she would not remember him well either.

He checked the numbers on the gates, opened the right one and walked up the path to the door. The light was on in the front room; he could see tiny strips of it where the curtains did not quite meet.

Toby sat obediently while Lucas rang the doorbell.

It was answered within moments by Howard, who looked startled to see Lucas again so soon, and even more so when Toby bounded forward to greet him.

'Sorry,' Lucas apologised, 'but I have to speak to you. It really can't wait.'

Howard opened the door wide and Lucas stepped inside. 'What's happened?' Howard said instantly, his voice steady, but clearly only by intense control.

'Nothing,' Lucas replied. 'I was going to go myself. I can't leave Elena alone . . .'

'You also can't go. We went over that,' Howard said between his teeth. 'I'm going to be brutal. Although you might be one of the most brilliant men I've ever known, you're also as subject to age as anyone else. You'd be a bloody liability, even without a gimpy ankle—' He broke off.

They were still standing in the hall, between the rack of coats with boots beneath them, and the very nice oak half-table on the other side with a salver for letters and small packets. It had probably been there in the past for people to leave calling cards.

The door of the sitting room was opened and Pamela Howard stood outlined against the light. She saw the dog first and took a step back.

Toby did not move. He was still on his lead anyway, and practically standing on Howard's feet.

'You seem to have got lost,' Howard said to Lucas, smiling pleasantly. 'I think you needed the last turning. Let me show you.' He glanced at Pamela. 'I'll be back in a moment. I'll just show this gentleman where he needs to be . . .' He turned back to Lucas, dismissing her from his attention. At least that was what it looked like to Lucas.

She went back into the sitting room and closed the door; her agreement needed no words and she did not acknowledge either Lucas or his dog.

Howard did not apologise, but the awkwardness of his emotion was in his face. He turned and led Lucas to the front door, and outside.

'You can't go, Lucas,' Howard insisted. 'Apart from the fact that you're not fit, has it occurred to you that that could be exactly why they'll hold her? To flush you out and get you where they can take you easily, and no one will ever know? All the diplomatic complaints in the world won't help. They'll simply say they had no idea who you were. And you know as well as I do that that will be believed, and we can hardly prove otherwise without making total asses of ourselves. We've decided, I'm going! Now, I suppose you've got a couple of decent photographs of her, and a description?' Howard held out his hand.

Lucas fished in his inside pocket and pulled out an envelope with two photographs inside. 'I want them back.'

Howard did not bother to reply.

'She's about five foot eight, or a bit less. Light brown hair, blue eyes. At first glance, I suppose she's not beautiful, but after you've looked at her for a while, you realise that she is.'

Howard stared at him, a sudden, intense gentleness in his eyes. 'We'll get her back. Now I'll take you and show you where to go. I'd better, or Pamela will think I've lied to her.'

Lucas nodded and turned to go down the path to the gate, Toby on his heels.

Chapter Nineteen

Elena woke up in the night, her heart pounding. Then she heard the noise again. It was someone moving quickly and trying to be silent. The soft sound of footsteps hurrying, then a gasp of breath.

She slid out of bed, put on the wrap that Zillah had lent her, and went to the door. She opened it quietly and looked out. The hall light was on and Zillah was standing at the top of the stairs, her hair loose round her shoulders. She was staring downwards. She had not heard Elena's door open. She was holding something, an armful of towels.

Eli's voice came from below her. 'Hurry. Maybe sheets would be better. We can replace them.'

'I've got sheets, too,' Zillah replied. 'We'll burn them if need be. It hardly matters now.' She started down the stairs awkwardly.

Without thinking, Elena went to her and took some of them from her.

Zillah swung round, startled. She was ashen pale. 'Go back to bed!'

'I can help,' Elena replied. 'Whatever it is, I can help. You don't need to slip and fall down the stairs with that lot.'

Before Zillah could argue, Eli's voice came from below. 'Let her! We need her. What will she do? She's a fugitive anyway. This can't make it worse.'

Zillah let go of half the pile of sheets and towels, and Elena followed her down carrying her share. They went after Eli into the kitchen. On the floor Jacob was kneeling with his arms around a young man covered with blood. His chest and arms were naked and all the flesh raw. Elena had never before seen anything so shocking. She stumbled as if her heart had stopped.

Zillah was looking at her. 'That's what we all look like when our skin has been taken off,' she said quietly. 'If we help him, keep it all clean, he'll be all right.'

Elena swallowed hard, trying to keep her stomach in place. The young man was conscious. The last thing he needed was hysteria. Or someone else's horror. 'What do you want me to do?'

'Antiseptic. It'll hurt like hell, but if it gets infected, it'll kill him,' Eli told her. 'Unfold the sheets and pass whatever you're told to. We've no time to waste.'

Elena obeyed. It was a nightmare of pain and blood, but the four of them worked on the young man with no words except those of direction. *Pass me this, take that. Fetch more water. Use the brandy. The pain cannot be helped. Now wash the floor. We can have no trace left.*

The young man, whose name she never learned, slipped out of consciousness, for a merciful time unaware of the pain. Zillah checked every few minutes, but he was breathing regularly, although his pulse was erratic.

Elena met Jacob's eyes once. He seemed to know what he was doing, as if he had seen it before. He worked silently, except for the requests for assistance.

Gradually, Elena realised what had happened. It was not an accident, as she had first supposed, perhaps a bad burn. It was a deliberate removal of the outer layers of the skin, a flaying. Such a thing had been outside her imagination. Dealing with the reality was a matter of trying to cope with the loss of blood, the pain, and the terrible shock to the body.

She lost all sense of time. She was taken by surprise, and then fear, when there was a quiet, triple knock on the kitchen door, and Jacob went to let in two men. He greeted one of them by name.

'Is he ready?' the first man asked.

'Almost,' Zillah replied. 'Five minutes.'

The other man glanced apprehensively at Elena.

'Wanted for shooting Scharnhorst,' Eli said simply.

One of them nodded with a bleak smile. The other stared at her for a long moment, then turned away, not unkindly, simply more concerned for the young man lying on the table. He spoke gently to him, not in German. Elena took it to be Yiddish.

Ten minutes later they were gone, carrying the young man with them, and Elena was helping Zillah clean up the kitchen and remove all signs of blood. They washed the sheets that could be saved and burned the others. The first light of dawn was breaking when Elena went back to bed, exhausted. They had not spoken. Understanding was sufficient, and no words were necessary. In fact, they had seemed to distract more than to help.

Before Elena could fall asleep, there was a light tapping on her door. 'Come in,' she said.

Zillah entered, a brown apothecary bottle in one hand,

scissors in the other. 'We need to change your appearance,' she said. 'We'll begin with your hair.'

When Elena woke in the morning, she was stiff and had a pounding headache. She had been dreaming something terrible. She did not want to make sense of it. She was in a strange room. A few cracks of light came through where she had not completely closed the curtains. She recognised nothing. There was a dressing table, and unfamiliar pictures on the walls. It was individual, nothing like the generic hotel room she could recall. What was she doing here?

Then she remembered the young man covered in blood, and the flesh beneath the raw wounds. She had been doing what she could, helping Zillah. She could remember Eli's tense face in the kitchen light, full of pity, and something else: the struggle against despair. It was not only for his own sake. He was trying to defend Zillah from what she already knew, just as she was trying in her own way to shield him.

And Jacob . . .

But she was safe, though only for the moment, because they were Jewish, which meant that if they were not hunted already, they would be soon, and underneath the brave faces, part of them knew it.

They might protest that it need not really happen. That was what Eli had said. Did he believe it now, after last night? Or was he saying it to comfort his family, because there was nothing they could do about it, whatever they knew? It wasn't practising their religion that was the problem, it was blood heritage.

What time was it? She leaned over and picked up her wristwatch from the bedside table. It was just after ten! How could she have slept for so long, leaving everybody else to . . . what . . . carry on as normal, as if nothing had happened?

Elena got out of bed quickly. She had her own small bathroom where she could wash, then get dressed in the plain dress Zillah had given her. Apart from that, she had only the clothes she had come with, and her camera. She had left her clothes on the train to Paris, and in the hotel wardrobe. She would have to buy some more again. This was getting absurd, like a repeating nightmare that became worse every time it completed the cycle and began again.

She walked into the bathroom and nearly cried out when she saw her reflection in the mirror. Her hair was very blond, short. Who was that woman staring back at her? And then she remembered Zillah, the peroxide, hair covering the bedroom floor.

She went downstairs, trying to remember the way to the kitchen. The others must have finished breakfast ages ago. She would just ask for a cup of tea and perhaps a couple of slices of toast. And apologise for having slept so long.

As far as the rest of the day was concerned, she had no idea what she was going to do. No, that was a lie. She knew. She just did not want to admit it. She must leave this house. The Brownshirts or the Gestapo . . . or someone . . . would be looking for the young man, and they would come here. If they found her, God alone knew what they would do to Zillah and Eli. And to Jacob, if he were here. Being American would not save him. Elena had no other choice that she could live with.

The kitchen door was open and she saw Zillah inside, apparently alone. She knocked on the panel, lightly.

Zillah turned from the pastry she was making and smiled. 'Good morning. I hope you slept after all that?' That was her only reference to the young man. 'Jacob hasn't arrived with the morning papers yet, but he shouldn't be long. Would you like tea? Or do you prefer coffee? And breakfast?'

The benches and the floor were clean and bright, no sign of blood, as if last night had never happened.

'I'd love tea,' Elena accepted, walking further in. The room was warm, perhaps from the sunlight, but also from the oven, and it all smelled like clean cotton and new bread. It flooded back memories of Grandma Josephine's kitchen a long time ago, when none of them even knew what war meant! It was something that happened to other people.

'Sit down,' Zillah said with a frown of concern. 'You must be terrified, although you mask it well. Sit down. And I'll get you toast. We have plenty, so eat as much as you wish.'

Of course, there would still be food restrictions in Berlin. She had not thought of that until now. How stupid of her. How self-centred.

She sat at the kitchen table. She could not help because she had no idea where anything was. 'I'm very grateful indeed for—' she began.

'All right, now you've said it,' Zillah cut across her, but with a smile. 'We know. These are hard times. Frankly, we'd help you even if you had shot that pig, Scharnhorst. But I believe you didn't. I think you would be cooler about it if you had. And perhaps you would have prepared your escape rather better.' She met Elena's glance for an instant and there was wry humour in her look.

'I would,' Elena agreed emphatically. 'For a start, I would not have gone back to the hotel where I was staying. I would have hidden the gun somewhere and gone in a different direction. Not opposite. That's too obvious. Perhaps sideways?'

Zillah looked at her, saw the harsh humour in her face, reflecting her own. 'You'll know for next time,' she said drily.

For the first time in hours, Elena laughed. 'Trouble is,' she replied, 'I would have to find another rifle. I imagine they are expensive. Perhaps I should steal one? And learn to shoot straight. I don't even know how to hold a gun properly.'

'Good idea,' Zillah agreed. 'When you are a good shot, you should aim at Herr Doktor Goebbels. He is the worst.' Her slight words had a passion of loathing behind them and a certainty deep as the bone.

Elena thought of the young man, but she understood that he would not be referred to again.

The kettle whistled and Zillah made a fresh pot of tea. A moment later she brought the toast also, a tiny portion of butter, and home-made preserve.

Elena thanked her and ate hungrily.

Zillah watched her for a few moments, standing still, as if waiting to see if it was satisfactory. Even through the pleasure of the fresh food and the warmth of the kitchen, the tension was there. They both had to be thinking of the young man who had been lying there, just a few hours ago.

Elena put down her toast and turned to Zillah. 'What Eli said last night . . . he knows it's not true, doesn't he? He has to know now . . . except it's not the first time it's happened . . . is it? You knew what to do . . .'

Zillah blinked, the tears suddenly flooding her eyes. 'No. But this time was worse. It's becoming harder to believe this persecution is just a temporary madness. Medicine, banking, art, the sciences, music – all the things that bring wealth and prestige to a nation – will not save us . . .' She tailed off, unable to finish.

Elena knew what she had been going to say. 'And Hitler

feeds people's resentment,' she finished. 'Because it is the real wealth of the nation. It's what people admire and envy. No one wants to believe the best part of their culture was contributed so much by someone else.'

'We are not someone else!' Zillah said between her teeth, but she did not look at Elena. 'We are Germans!'

Elena realised her own clumsiness. She felt the heat rise up her face. 'I'm sorry. But they need to blame someone, someone different. It doesn't matter if it makes sense or not! People are capable of believing anything they want to, if they want it enough, to justify what they feel, and what they need to be true to justify what they are doing.'

Zillah stared at her. Finally, she whispered, 'I know that. But Eli still has hope. I need to believe he's right. I *need* to.'

Elena said nothing.

'At least I need him to believe that I do,' Zillah amended.

Elena could think of nothing to say. She was choked by emotion for this proud, gentle woman who had offered her such hospitality at such great addition to her own risk. She shouldn't have said what she had, and she couldn't take it back. She ate another bite of the toast, and another.

She had just finished and was insisting on washing the plate she had used, when Jacob came in, carrying several newspapers. He wished them all good morning, looking at Elena carefully but showing no surprise at her new appearance. He put the papers on the kitchen table, then made himself a cup of coffee, glanced to see what Elena was drinking, and made coffee for Zillah as well.

Zillah broke the silence at last. 'What do the papers say?' she asked.

'A lot about Scharnhorst, of course,' he replied, setting her coffee beside her and bringing his own to the table opposite Elena. He seemed to be watching her closely. Normally it would have irritated her, but now she found it comforting.

'Anything about who shot him?' Zillah countered.

'An unknown person, believed to be English,' he replied. 'And either a woman, or someone dressed as a woman.'

'They can't tell the difference?' Elena said with a ghost of a smile.

'Covering themselves,' Jacob replied with a shrug. 'In case they catch some poor man and decide to pin it on him. They'll look like fools if they don't get anyone at all. Hardly German efficiency. They can't afford to have people think you can shoot the vermin and get away with it.'

'I am a German,' Zillah asserted grimly, then smiled at him, to show she had no ill feeling.

He looked back at her without a shred of humour. 'You are a German Jew,' he replied. 'If you don't know the difference by now, God help us.'

'Not that again, Jacob, please,' she said quietly. 'I know what people are saying, and I fear there is some truth in it.'

'Even after last night?' he said. There was anger in his voice and he was struggling to keep it gentle towards her.

'Eli still thinks they wouldn't be so . . . so self-harming,' Zillah said, looking down at her plate, as if she did not want Jacob to see her eyes. 'We are a big part of German society. We have contributed far too much – we still do – for them to do anything more than make a lot of noise and exercise the basest of cruelty now and again. It will be unpleasant, but we've survived unpleasantness before.'

'You sound like Eli,' he said grimly.

'Of course I do. I'm his wife. But I'm glad someone killed Scharnhorst, whoever it was.'

Jacob waited a few moments, eating his slice of bread and sipping at his coffee, still too hot to drink with comfort, his eyes on Elena, watching to see how she would react.

'Have you learned about the un-German books?' he said at last, directing his question to Zillah.

'The what?' She looked at him incredulously.

'The un-German books,' he repeated.

'For goodness' sake, what is an un-German book? If it is printed in German, then it's German, isn't it? So, you mean something translated from another language? It's a big world out there, and some of the best literature, the very best, comes from other languages. English and Greek, for a start. And Russian. And French, and Spanish . . .'

'Un-German thoughts and ideas,' he explained, but there was both fear and intense contempt in his face. 'The works of such French barbarians as Gide, Emile Zola, Marcel Proust; American barbarians such as Jack London and Ernest Hemingway; Englishmen like H. G. Wells; and native traitors to German thought like Marx, Freud and Einstein.'

'Ridiculous,' Zillah said with a mirthless laugh.

'Please don't tell Dr Goebbels that, Zillah,' Jacob said, his voice suddenly grating. 'This is the peak of his achievement, so far. All the works of these people, among hundreds of others – even Helen Keller, for God's sake – are to be collected up and burned, to protect the German soul from their polluting influence.'

Zillah stared at him, as if unable to decide now whether he was joking, exaggerating or just plain wrong, and angry for saying such a thing at all. She was not yet prepared to think that he could be right. 'Nonsense,' she said at last. 'You shouldn't go around saying things like that, even to me. Not everyone understands your rather twisted sense of humour.'

Jacob bent his head, elbows on the table, and ran his fingers through his thick hair. For a moment there was complete silence in the kitchen, except for the ticking of the clock on the mantel above the oven. Finally, he looked up.

'I'm not joking, Zillah. God help us, I'm totally serious. They're going to do it tonight. Fires in every major city in Germany. Here it will be in the Opernplatz, between the opera house and the university. I'm going to watch from the shadows, the darkness at the edge, which is where I imagine a lot of us will be from now on.' He looked across the table at Elena. 'It'll be midnight, so you could come and watch it, with your camera, if you like. It will be a signal moment in history. You should record it for the future. The suicide of the German intellect. It might be quite a spectacle, or it might not. Odd to think that a sudden shower of rain could save the soul of a nation . . . for one more night.' His voice was angry and Elena could hear the edge of despair in it.

Without thinking whether it was appropriate or not, she reached across and touched his hand. 'A temporary insanity,' she said quite clearly. 'Other people have copies. Probably every country in Europe, or America, at the very least. You can't kill an idea by burning a book.'

'You can kill a nation's ability to read it,' he said, searching her face as he spoke. 'And please don't go out alone, and not at all in the daylight. The neighbours here are pretty good, but your description is all over the place, and it takes only one person to report it to get the Gestapo here.'

'I know,' she said very quietly. It hurt to say it. The only thing that would help would be to stay here. 'I can't stay here. I'm endangering everybody.'

'We'll get you out, but not yet.'

'Yes, as soon as I can leave without being seen, and making

216

it worse. They'll be looking for that young man. They mustn't find me, or they'll take you all.'

'I'll find a way. Just stay here and stay inside!' There was an edge to his voice. Was he angry because he had no idea how to help? And because she was right, her presence in Eli and Zillah's house was endangering them all.

'I can't stay,' she repeated. 'If I get caught, it will be hard, but if you are all caught, it will be far worse. I know that, and so do—'

It was Zillah who interrupted her. 'Do you think we have never sheltered anyone before, or that we won't have to do it again? But we do this for ourselves, because it is right. We each have to fight against the darkness in our own way. You will do it with photographs. Jacob does it with words. Eli and I do it by seeing that you have that chance. You have to stay alive to tell the rest of the world what is happening, and what is going to happen.' She gave just the shadow of a smile. 'You are no use to anyone dead in some execution chamber, shot for a crime you did not commit. Empty self-sacrifice may feel like a noble thing, but it is self-indulgent, and we can't afford it. We need weapons that will work. Go with Jacob after dark and watch the books burning. See what Hitler and Goebbels are trying to do, then go home and show people. Not just the facts; make them feel the pain . . . and believe it. Don't let this waste go unseen. Build a fire in the mind that nothing can put out.' As if suddenly exhausted, she stood up and returned to her chopping board, chopping carrots for the pie she was making.

Elena did not argue. She would do what Zillah said. She would build that fire and make it hot enough so no one could deny it, or she would be killed trying.

*

Jacob left and took the film that Elena had already taken of the assassination, and had it developed by a friend with a dark room, but only the negatives. Prints could come later. She would not carry the bulk of prints easily, and they were too easy for anyone to look at, and almost certainly confiscate, with the ensuing questions and difficulties she would face. But if left undeveloped, the film could be exposed and the impressions wiped out.

'You have some good ones,' he told her, handing them back. They were in the sitting room, talking quietly. It was after six, and Eli would be home in minutes. 'There are a couple I'd like to buy from you, to go with my article when I send it back to New York. I might even get it in the *Times*.' He looked at her questioningly.

'Don't be ridiculous!' she said in amazement, and saw him blink, as if she had made to strike him. 'You can have anything you want!' she added. 'You saved my life. You still are doing. Don't you think that's worth something?' She gave a sudden wide smile. 'And I'd rather like to get my photographs into the *New York Times*.'

He relaxed into a smile also, then held out his hand.

She shook it, quite solemnly.

'And I'll come with you to the book-burning tonight,' she added.

Elena and Jacob set out a little before eleven. She wore the dress Zillah had provided, and her few other clothes and personal belongings were in a bag over Jacob's shoulder; she was carrying her camera case. There was no need to cover her hair now that it was blond and short. And she had used Zillah's dark brown mascara to colour and increase her eyebrows. Before leaving the house, both Jacob and Zillah

218

agreed that the change made her almost unrecognisable.

They walked most of the way, stopping now and then as if merely strolling. The evening was fine and the streets were still busy. There was a kind of excitement in the air, the anticipation of some event not to be missed.

Elena looked at the people they passed and wondered what they were thinking. Was this blind excitement or fear of what the future held? Could she not tell the difference in herself? Could any of these young people walking arm in arm, as she was doing with Jacob, whom she had met only yesterday, and yet with whom she felt so comfortable already?

As they walked, he described his home in Chicago, and then the very small apartment he shared with another journalist in New York. He and Elena spoke in German, so as not to stand out if anyone were close enough to catch a word here or there.

'It works quite well,' he said ruefully. 'We're seldom home at the same time. And when we are, he cooks, so that's an advantage. He enjoys it, and I express my appreciation. I'm not sure if I offer any service in return, other than emptying the garbage and doing the occasional errand. Hardly skilled.' It was self-deprecatory, but he said it with such amusement that it felt entirely comfortable.

She told him about her own small flat in London, taken simply in order to be independent of her parents. 'I don't know that I want to be untidy,' she said. 'But I want to have the freedom to do it, if I feel like it. My mother is a perfect housekeeper. Or that's the way it looks to me.'

They talked a little about family. It was easy and seemed a natural thing to do. It kept them from thinking of why they were here, how they had met, and the danger all around them. Above all, it stopped them from remembering last night, and the young man whose name they were safer not knowing. They laughed at memories, and in sharing them suddenly realised how precious family holidays were, minor triumphs and disasters, jokes that were only funny because they had all laughed.

They passed Brownshirts in twos and threes, and they tried to look as if they barely noticed them. They spoke to no one else, except the occasional 'good evening'. There were already a number of people gathered around the open space, paved in granite and covered with sand where the books were to be burned. It was dark, and the buildings were huge shapes blocking the sky. People were almost indistinguishable.

Elena looked around as inconspicuously as she could. When the fire was lit, she would be able to see faces. It was still too early. But from what she could make out of clothes, angles of body, casual attitudes, most of them seemed to be young.

'Students,' she said quietly to Jacob. 'Burning books? Are you sure?'

'Yes. They're going to destroy all the old world of ideas and create a new one.' He was staring ahead of him, and it was too dark for her to read his expression. He kept hold of her, his hand on her arm, as well as linked through hers.

Would this be a solemn occasion? Or a celebration, like the English remembrance of Guy Fawkes and the saving of Parliament from being blown up and everyone inside killed?

Who would bring all the books? Or would it really turn out to be only symbolic? Perhaps half a dozen books, or one edition of each book they disapproved of?

There was a growing tension in the air. Nervous laughter. The odd shout of something lost in the darkness.

Jacob looked around him uneasily. 'I think this isn't such a good idea . . .' he started.

She gripped his arm more tightly. 'We've come this far . . .'

'I mean it. It could get nasty. Let's go back.' He pulled her very slightly.

'No. Nothing's happened yet. I want to see if it really does, or if it's all just talk. I want pictures.'

'Of what? Burning papers and books?'

'No, of people, their faces, what it means to them,' she said quickly. 'They're symbolically getting rid of the past, with its good and bad; starting something again.'

He gripped her arm more tightly. 'Elena, I mean it. It was a mistake to have come. We should leave before it gets nasty . . .'

'It's not nasty, just stupid,' she argued, refusing to be pulled away.

He hesitated. 'Well, if it turns ugly, you'll come . . .'

'Yes, I will. I promise,' she agreed quickly, not looking at him but still watching the thickening crowd.

They had not long to wait. The book burners arrived in a cavalcade of cars and trucks laden with boxes and piles of loose books, and more thrown on top haphazardly.

In the car headlights, Elena saw several trucks with rostrums, each one hung with swastikas, and with speakers to immortalise the event in words that would reach every newspaper by the morning. Who would it be? Hitler himself? Is that why there were so many people? And there were more now than even two or three minutes ago, more all the time, still coming.

Elena moved even closer to Jacob. It was vivid, like a nightmare in primary colours, almost obscene. Squads of students marched beside the slow-moving vehicles. There must have been hundreds of them, with more flooding in to join them. They waved banners and sang Nazi songs, full throated, almost as if they had been hymns.

People beside Jacob and Elena surged forward, shouting as well, carrying them against their will. He tightened his arm around her and she clung on to him, buffeted and even bruised. He was right, this was growing nasty. She clung on to her camera, adjusting the lens by feel, taking picture after picture, with little time to focus before it moved and was lost. She went through the whole roll of twenty-four, rewound the film into the canister, and threaded a new roll.

Many of the crowd wore caps of different colours – red, blue, green, purple – flashing brightly in the headlights for a moment, and then lost again. They were accompanied by a band of officers from the duelling corps wearing immaculate white breeches and blue tunics and looking absurd in the light of the flames. Their high boots had spurs on them! It was nothing like she had imagined, and yet there was undeniably an exhilaration about the event. Elena could not take her eyes away, except once or twice to steady her camera and make sure of the focus.

Someone tipped a pile of books on to the sand and immediately another person poured liquid over them and they caught fire in a quick, hungry blaze. Other people put more books on, and more. The pyre mounted until the glare of it lit more faces than she could count. There was no end to this. Thousands of people were gathered here, all around her, shouting, cheering, cursing the traitors to the nation who had written such filth, such blasphemy against the great German mind and soul.

It was an ecstasy of destruction. The power of it caught

her up, the beauty and the light of the flames. She was barely aware of the rising heat. All around her there was shouting, cheering. She found herself shaking, dry-mouthed, wanting to be part of it, swept up, in spite of herself.

What was happening to her? This was madness! She continued to take pictures, although she wanted to wrap her arms tightly around herself, as if holding herself, in case she should fragment into pieces.

The burning continued. The supply of books seemed endless. The flames never died down. They must have come from shops, libraries, schools, even private houses, perhaps handed down as treasures from the first printing. Some would be silk bound, some leather bound, many gold or deckle edged. They contained the beauty and ideas that had lit the minds of men and women for centuries, civilisation's communication from the past, across the present and into the future, all burned to ashes.

Elena could not pull herself away from the destruction. A few yards distant from her, to her right, she saw people. She saw movement. She could not tell whether they were men or women, but she photographed them as they were capering almost like puppets being jerked by their strings. Their faces were pale, gibbering mouths misshapen as they gaped open, eyes in the reflected flames mere black holes in their heads, red socketed. They were filled with an insane ecstasy as they watched the leather, parchment and paper burn, the passion, intellect and hope of generations destroyed in one single night.

One man let out a squeal of joy, his face bright with the lust for destruction. Another whirled round like a dervish, his pale coattails flying. She caught what could be a perfect picture of the movement, frenzied, hysterical. They seemed, in the red light, to be a distortion of humanity, not insane, but demonic.

They were young: students of thought and belief, of philosophy. How could they have come to this? Was the distance really so short, the skin between sanity and madness so fragile? Is there anything in the imagination so terrible as that which once had been beautiful and, even while you watched, had slipped beyond all reach into ugliness? She could see it through the viewfinder. But had she caught it?

She finally had had enough. She lowered her camera and turned and buried her head on Jacob's shoulder. She wanted to run, but she had no strength and the crowds hemmed her in on every side.

Hatred and jubilation throbbed in the air, like the pulse of music.

She felt Jacob's other arm close around her and for minutes that she could not count, they stood in the bedlam of sound and heat, and held each other, as if they would drown alone.

This, then, was hell, not physical pain – although that might come – but the knowledge of something that had once been human.

And yet she must acknowledge it. This was the face of the future, and she must photograph it now, while it was naked and unmistakable. She pulled away from Jacob and raised her camera again. She frowned, held it steady, and went on taking portrait after portrait of unreason.

Chapter Twenty

Early in the morning following the book-burning, Cordell received an unexpected invitation to take lunch with the Führer. It was not a public function, but apparently a private audience. He held the card in his hand and felt a sudden chill. His first reaction was the certain knowledge that he could not escape it. He had been sent for. However bad it was, to avoid it would make it worse.

The May sunlight filling his room seemed suddenly harsh, almost cutting. He told his secretary to accept, and to express the usual flattering comments that Cordell would be delighted to come. The message should be delivered by hand.

The secretary said of course he would deliver it personally, and then hesitated a moment or two, as awaiting something further. When Cordell added nothing, but remained frozen in the centre of the room, the secretary left, closing the door without sound.

What did Hitler want? They knew Elena's name. Her father had been British Ambassador in Berlin a few years ago, when Cordell had been new to the Embassy. Were they going to ask him if he had seen her? Instinct said to lie; intelligence said that to do so was incredibly stupid, almost suicidal.

And Margot? Did Hitler know she was here too? Almost certainly, but Cordell had not told anyone except his own immediate staff. Did he have anyone careless, loose lipped? Or worse than that, a deliberate betrayer, a double agent? There was always that possibility. He knew that, but perhaps it had retreated to the back of his mind? It was at the front now, sharp, a tightening pain not only of personal danger, but of failure as well. He realised his job was the one area in his life in which he succeeded. It defined him, at least in any part that others saw . . . and believed.

He could not argue that. He could only admit it. It was humiliating to be called to explain himself to Hitler, aware all the time that he knew the answers, and he knew that Cordell knew it too. It was like sticking a pin into a bug and watching it wriggle. There was no point in lying to protect Margot . . . or Elena. The only thing he could do to survive was to tell the truth. To lie, and be instantly caught in it, would render him no use to anyone.

He changed into a clean shirt, put a brush through his hair again, examined his shave to insure it was flawless, and prepared to leave, stomach churning.

He arrived at the hotel early by a quarter of an hour. It would be inexcusable to be late for the Führer. Wasn't it Lord Nelson who said he owed his success in life to always being a quarter of an hour early? And his success had been phenomenal – 'England expects . . .' and all that. Cordell found his 'duty' a good deal less clear than Nelson's had been. The enemy was not arrayed in battleships off Cape Trafalgar. No one knew who the enemy was exactly. It could be appalling ignorance, the crushing reparations demanded of Germany in the Treaty of Versailles. It could be merely a confused, hungry and despairing people pushed too far, for too long.

He forced himself to sit down. He must not pace. It was a clear sign of nervousness that anyone could read. He must be well mannered, but not obsequious. He was a representative of Britain, and not some petitioner coming to ask for something. Britain was an ally, he hoped. It had been an enemy, and might be again, if governments were foolish enough to miss this chance for lasting peace.

An aide had been speaking to him and he had not heard. 'Yes?' he asked.

'If you will come this way, sir, the Führer will see you now,' the man repeated.

'Thank you.' He followed the aide across the foyer and along a short passage. The man knocked on a door, and as soon as he heard the voice from inside, he opened it and ushered Cordell in.

Hitler was sitting in a comfortable chair, padded in leather and with arm rests. He looked exactly like his photographs, except that no camera had caught the luminous blue of his eyes. They were extraordinary, as if the light shone from inside. The rest of his face was perfectly ordinary, and, even sitting down, it was possible to tell he was certainly of no more than average height.

Cordell was not sure whether to salute or not. From an Englishman, it might look like sarcasm. Did Hitler have any sense of the absurd? Impossible. Cordell believed many of Hitler's fears and even some of his ideals. But he was an Englishman – his sense of the absurd was too strong to ignore. He bowed instead, just from the neck. It was a gesture of respect that could not be mistaken.

Hitler waved his hand towards a chair a couple of feet away. 'Sit down, Mr Cordell,' he invited.

Cordell obeyed, instinctively taking both arms of the chair

to steady himself. It was only then that he looked at the third person in the room, and something inside him froze.

Joseph Goebbels was quite a small man, and scrawny, but once you had looked at him, his presence dominated that of Hitler. His nose was straight, his gash of a mouth thin lipped, but his dark eyes would have been beautiful, were it not for their expression of malevolence. He too was sitting. Cordell knew already that he had one leg different from the other: not exactly club-footed, but not normal.

Hitler signalled to the waiter that he might begin serving lunch. Cordell remembered that Hitler was vegetarian and wondered what they would be offered. He would eat it, whatever it was. Years of diplomacy had taught him how to eat almost anything and look as if he enjoyed it. He would remain silent until the Führer gave him leave to speak. He did not even look at Goebbels. He must remember to call him 'Herr Doktor'.

'What is the latest news from London, Mr Cordell?' Hitler enquired politely. 'I hear more and more people are expressing respect for what we have accomplished here in Germany. Is that true?'

'Yes, sir, it is.' Cordell found his mouth dry. How long were they going to dance around? They were playing with him as a cat does with a mouse. When were they going to ask about Elena Standish? 'It was said in Parliament quite recently . . .' He went on to describe some complimentary remarks regarding Hitler's achievements.

Hitler nodded with apparent pleasure.

'And a previous ambassador, Mr Standish?' Goebbels asked softly. He had a beautiful voice, deep for such a slight man, almost seductive. 'Do you hear from him these days?'

Cordell's mind raced. He could feel the sweat break out

on his body. He tried to read Goebbels' expression, and knew he could not. He was cleverer than Hitler, subtler, he understood emotions as an animal does, by instinct, by smell.

'I think perhaps he's one of those who see what they want to see,' Cordell replied. 'Like us, he has no taste for another war. He can see the wisdom of what you are saying.'

Goebbels nodded slowly, but his face was still unreadable. 'It was an Englishwoman who killed Scharnhorst the other day, right here in Berlin,' he observed, then watched Cordell to see his reaction.

Cordell's mind raced. Were they going to ask him if he had known about it? And see if he tried to deny having seen her? How much did they actually know? Better to think they knew everything. He must seem to be sincere, speaking from his own feelings. Hitler might believe flattery, Goebbels would not. Nor must he be seen to hesitate.

'I heard about it,' Cordell admitted. 'It was only rumour then, and I hoped it was not true. I apologise deeply if it is.'

Goebbels leaned forward very slightly. 'You know this young woman, Herr Cordell? This Elena Standish?'

Cordell was cold, in spite of the pleasantness of the day. He was absolutely certain that Goebbels knew the answer to that. He very probably knew that Elena had been to see Cordell the day before the assassination. One lie would be enough to ruin him.

'Yes, Herr Doktor,' he replied without hesitation. 'I knew her reasonably well as a child, when her father was Ambassador here. As well as one knows a girl still in her teenage years! But she came to see me the day she arrived in Berlin, briefly. Of course, I had no idea she intended such a terrible act. But then she would be aware that I would have had her arrested immediately if I had even suspected such a thing. She was in my office a matter of moments. She was tired from a very long train journey, all the way from Naples. And it was the end of the day.' He must not tell too much. That was always a sign of nervousness.

Goebbels sat back in his chair again. 'Of course.'

That could have meant anything and Cordell did not reply.

The silence hung heavily over the table. Both Cordell and Goebbels were waiting for Hitler to speak.

Cordell wished there were wine served. He could use a long glass of a good white wine. But it was known that Hitler rarely ever drank alcohol, and when he did he put sugar with it! Cordell had needed all his diplomatic skills not to let his disgust show in his face when he first heard this.

It was Hitler who spoke. 'We will find her. Not that it matters a great deal. I am sure it was the last thing she intended, but she has done us a service. Is that not so, Herr Doktor?'

Goebbels had a sharper intellect than Hitler, and more instinctive judgement of others. And yet watching him, Cordell was certain that he was afraid of something. Perhaps of his place in Hitler's esteem. There was nothing heroic about him, yet there was some vulnerability, as even a snake has.

Hitler flew into near hysterical rages. But Goebbels' eye could strip a man's soul and read in him what should never be revealed in anyone: The secret hopes and fears, the wounds that still bled, too deep to stanch.

'But Scharnhorst had some good ideas, don't you think?' Goebbels spoke suddenly, and it was a moment before Cordell realised he was addressing him. His mind raced, trying desperately to recall what Scharnhorst had said, specifically. Ideas, not passion or hatred, not worship of Hitler, and of himself.

Goebbels was waiting, watching as if he could see through Cordell's eyes into his brain. Was this what they had invited him for? To startle him into revealing his true ideas, not merely the diplomatically correct, carefully rehearsed ones?

'You need more than ideas, sir,' Cordell began. 'You need to have specific plans as to how you will carry them out. You are efficient, that is beyond question. But you are not blind ideologues. You think, you plan.'

Hitler nodded very slowly, then turned to Goebbels.

Goebbels was smiling, his lips parted. 'Yes, Mein Führer,' he said very softly. 'You were perfectly correct. Too soon. Scharnhorst was right, but too soon.'

Cordell looked from one to the other of them. He was beginning to understand. Could it be that they were quite happy that Scharnhorst was dead? And was it worth the risk to let them perceive that he knew?

The silence prickled with tension. Dare he speak? He had earlier. It was the most dangerous time to chance. He must learn what they were referring to . . . exactly.

'I think we might be wiser to act first,' he said, dropping each word carefully. 'When we are certain exactly what works or what might be better . . . kept . . .'

'Discreet,' Goebbels finished for him. 'Once it is accomplished, then all the arguments are . . . different.' He looked across the table at Hitler.

Hitler nodded very slightly.

Goebbels was looking at Cordell again. 'A final solution,' he said softly. 'We are beginning, but it is a long road yet. I think there are those in England who perceive very well.

231

You understand the need to progress slowly, like a man walking across the ice. You test each step before you put your weight on it.'

'Of course,' Cordell agreed, his heart pounding. Bits and pieces of memory came back to him. Scharnhorst standing in a beer garden with a stein in his hand, singing. He talked a lot, afterwards, his words slurred with excitement. Ideas about getting rid of the Jews entirely.

Some people had looked startled. Others had agreed.

But that had been a while ago. Like testing the water. Scharnhorst had developed it a bit further since then. Trade unionists were a problem. Communists were a growing menace, and most of them were Jews anyway.

Hitler and Goebbels were waiting for him to express an opinion, commit himself. He scrambled for memory from the terrible events of the previous night. What had Goebbels said last night at the book-burning?

Words came back to Cordell now, phrases. 'It is a fight for survival,' he said aloud, conviction not yet in his voice. He must do better. He began more firmly. 'We cannot afford indecision. We have enemies, whether they know it or not. Like . . . like a disease.' He heard his own voice like that of a stranger. 'Strength begets fear in others,' he continued. 'And, of course, envy.' He was drenched in sweat. His clothes were sticking to his body.

Hitler and Goebbels glanced at each other, then back again at Cordell.

'You have an excellent grasp of the situation,' Goebbels said smoothly. 'In fact, perhaps we should be grateful to this young woman from England, whom we don't seem to be able to catch. We do not wish anyone to think we did it ourselves, even if we are relieved that it has happened.' A half-smile flickered on his face, like moonlight on a grave. 'So you know her, this Elena Standish, and your daughter – Cecily, is it? – does she know her as well?'

Cordell drew in his breath sharply. He must answer. They were both staring at him. 'She used to. I don't know if she still does. She hasn't mentioned her.'

Hitler was looking at him. He was outwardly a very ordinary man, except that he put sugar in his wine, and ate too many vegetables, and gave himself indigestion. Only his luminous eyes were unusual, and his pale, sensitive hands. Had they belonged to anyone else, they might have been beautiful.

Then Cordell looked at Goebbels, clever like a serpent, testing the air, smelling fear in others. A mistake could be exactly what they were waiting for. He inclined his head politely and made some innocuous, respectful remark. His mind was racing. One thought crowded out everything else. He must protect Cecily.

What was he going to do about Elena Standish? And what was the price going to be?

He answered automatically, politely, careful not to be sycophantic. Goebbels at least was sensitive to ridicule.

The meal seemed to drag out endlessly. It all tasted like sawdust, and he drank too much water to try to swallow it. Finally, it was over and he thanked them and excused himself.

As he was walking out of the magnificent hotel into the street, he wondered what they had invited him for. Was it to set him on course to find Elena? It seemed likely.

What for? To get rid of her for them out of the country, so they would avoid either killing her, which might not be believed in other countries whose good opinion they still needed? That is, specifically, England? Or the embarrassment

233

of a trial, which might make much of Scharnhorst's appalling ideas? Did they want him to get her out of Germany, and avoid an ugly break with Britain?

It was making him feel as if he were walking into a polar night with no dawn on the horizon. Scharnhorst may have gone but it was Goebbels' vision of a final solution, the extinction of all who did not fit into the mould of Aryan supremacy, that was so terrifying now.

Accommodation, reason, these were impossible. If Goebbels gained more power and influence in Germany, there was no alternative but war, somewhere ahead, not very far.

Chapter Twenty-One

Peter Howard had gone to Cambridgeshire and told Ian Newton's family of his death. It had been even worse than he had anticipated. They had had no idea what Ian was doing for MI6. Like the rest of Britain, they did not even know it existed. Howard could not remember doing anything that had hurt him more deeply.

He got back to London at four in the morning, slept a few hours, then got up again, washed, shaved and dressed. He took only a small case with him.

He did not have to explain his going to Pamela. She stared for a long moment at his face, and understood enough.

He would do it for Lucas. There was no hesitation or question in his mind. Actually, he would have considered anything, for Lucas. But he must do it well.

If he asked questions in Berlin, even if he knew whom he could trust, and who not, he could set the Gestapo on Elena's trail. And not only hers, but those of a population of citizens, all of whom could be hostages to fortune: wives, children, parents who could be arrested if they refused to co-operate. He had seen it all before. Occupied France had been like that during the war. Fear was as thick in the air as a winter fog, choking the breath, distorting sight and sound.

He went out to the airport and caught a plane to Berlin, landing in the early afternoon. He had contemplated checking in with Cordell at the Embassy, or at his home, but decided against either. Cordell was a clever man, long trained to be observant. The assassination of Scharnhorst, apparently by an Englishwoman, was too recent. Cordell would know for certain that Howard's visit had something to do with that. Anyone would.

He went instead to an anonymous-looking hotel and had a meal in a café he knew well . . . and listened.

He heard about the assassination. There was surface outrage, and beneath it he heard also a considerable note of relief.

'Took a bloody Brit to get rid of him,' a man in grey said with feeling.

'Have they got her yet?' his friend asked with a lift in his voice. But no one asked whether he hoped they had, or that she had escaped.

Someone mentioned the attack on the young Jew two nights ago.

'Be quiet!' his neighbour hissed.

'Why?' the speaker demanded. 'Do you want me to approve, or disapprove?' It was a challenge, said with bitterness.

The speaker lifted his head from his mug of beer and glared at him. 'I know nothing about it, and I don't want to hear your opinion.'

'Not until it's you, heh?' someone else sneered. 'Bit late then.'

'It's not going to be me! I'm not a Jew!'

'You're something! It'll be your turn one day!'

That killed the conversation. Howard remained silent, trying to think of where to begin looking for Elena. Who did she know in Berlin that would help her? Who could she trust? Why had she not gone back to Cordell? Or anyone else in the Embassy? Perhaps she had tried and realised that this was the first place they would look for her.

Would she try the American Embassy? Her mother was American. Elena herself was not an American citizen, and they would not have any obligation to protect her. They were neutral. They wanted no part of a quarrel with Germany.

Maybe he had no choice but to go and ask Cordell what he knew? If he was doing anything at all to help?

He stayed, having one more glass of beer. But he heard little else of use, except that the assassin had not been captured yet, and the hunt was getting tighter. Would they even try to take her alive? Or kill her, and claim that she had resisted? Obviously not, as they needed to blame her openly, prove she was English. There was still time.

He spent the afternoon and early evening contacting all the agents he knew working in Berlin, but none of them was able to offer any real help. Elena had not been seen or recognised by any of them. Wherever she was, she must be getting help from someone, because the Gestapo didn't have her. She must have other contacts. Who could be hiding her? Dare he ask Cordell, who possibly could be working for the Nazis himself? Not until he had exhausted every other reasonable avenue. Where would she go? What would she need? She was a photographer. *Film!* New film to shoot, and probably already exposed film developed. There were some people he could ask. He did, but they knew nothing. No one had seen a woman answering her description, or anything like it.

He went back to his lodgings at two in the morning, slept badly. All the years of doing this, and he still could not relax. Some men could. Did they care less or were they just more emotionally disciplined?

He got up early, had a cup of coffee and a pastry, and went out. There was nothing else left to do now but to speak to Cordell. He went to the British Embassy, and loitered across the road, aware that the Embassy would offer Elena her best chance of escape if she were trying to get out of Berlin, which she must be doing.

He saw Cordell arriving, just after eight, and went in after him, catching him at the side door entrance. He would prefer not to identify himself to the guard on the door.

Cordell was surprised. 'Howard?' he asked uncertainly, peering at him. 'It is you . . . isn't it?'

'Yes,' Howard replied with a faint flicker of humour. He was good at blending well into the background, looking anonymous, instantly forgettable.

'What are you doing here?' Cordell asked, leading the way in, up the stairs and along the corridor to his office.

Howard did not reply until they were inside and the door closed.

'Tea?' Cordell asked.

'Yes, please.' His mouth tasted like paper.

'Well? What is it? I assume it's this bloody Scharnhorst business?'

'Did you know about it beforehand?'

Cordell's eyes widened. He barely moved, and yet there was an additional subtle stiffness to his body. 'Yes. Elena Standish told me she had been travelling with Ian Newton, and when he was murdered, before he died, he told her to come here, to tell me, which she did.'

'And you warned the Germans?' Howard made it a question.

'Of course I bloody did!' Cordell snapped. 'Either they didn't believe me, or they took the opportunity to get rid of Scharnhorst. He was becoming a liability, but one they couldn't be rid of and be seen to do it themselves.'

'Is that your opinion?'

'Yes . . .'

Howard wondered if he was making that up, taking shelter in a very believable lie, or if it was the truth.

'And Elena Standish?' Howard asked as unemotionally as he could.

'I don't know!' Cordell snapped. 'I've done all I can think of to find her, without getting the Gestapo on my tail. Which wouldn't help anyone, least of all Elena!' There was anger in his voice, and fear.

'Done what, exactly?'

'Is she working for you?' Cordell demanded.

'No! I've never even met her. But I'd like to get her out of here alive. I think we owe her father that.'

Cordell relaxed a bit. 'Yes. Charles Standish is a good man. Margot, the elder daughter, was here just after the assassination.' He cleared his throat. 'A day or so ago. I got a list from her of all Elena's friends still in Berlin. With last known addresses, of course. I've made discreet enquiries, but no one admits to having seen her.'

'Do you believe them?' Howard asked quickly.

'Yes. On the whole I do.'

Howard looked at Cordell intently for several moments, then decided he was telling the truth, or at least thought he

239

was. It was easy enough to believe. If she had anything of Lucas's intelligence, she would not have gone to any friend that Cordell could know of. She had warned Cordell about the assassination, and he had not prevented it. She would not know whether or not he had tried.

So, would she come anywhere near the Embassy at all? That was the last visible door closing in his face.

'What are you going to do?' Cordell asked. Then he looked more closely at Howard. 'You're not going to tell me. I suppose I wouldn't, in your place.' His voice sounded close to cracking.

Howard's instinct was to deny it, but he understood that it would sound like a lie. 'First of all I've got to find her.'

'I've no idea where she is,' Cordell replied. 'But . . . I doubt she'll go to any of her friends. I destroyed the list that Margot gave me . . .' He stopped.

Howard did not press him. He was not ready yet to push Cordell into a lie. There were far better ways to play this. 'And if she comes here?' he asked.

'They'll be watching. But if she can get this far, I'll have a shot at getting her out of the country.'

'How?'

'Disguise her as much as possible. Get her a new passport. Different name, different age, profession. She used to work at the Foreign Office. She could pass for one of our minor officials easily enough. Even a translator. They're hardly likely to test her. Ticket as far as Paris, at least. Perhaps all the way to London might be suspicious.' A flicker of hope shone in Cordell's eyes for a moment.

'Make it,' Howard decided. 'The passport.' It was the best idea he could think of. To refuse Cordell would betray that he suspected him. Would he tell the Germans her new identity? That would be to betray himself, and destroy his usefulness to either side. Never mind jeopardise his own life. In fact, it would, in a way, bind him to helping her.

'I'll get the photograph,' Howard continued. 'We'll need a new one, preferably one that looks as unlike her own passport as possible. She may still have hers. She'll have to destroy it. One search would find it, and that would be fatal.' He smiled bitterly. 'They'll have every Brownshirt in Berlin looking for her. How the hell am I going to find her?' It was a rhetorical question. He did not expect Cordell to offer him an answer. He had racked his own brain, and not come up with one.

'Where do we go when we're frightened, and as far as I know, alone?' Cordell replied quietly. 'Familiar places. Ones that remind us of happier times, safer. I go to the water's edge. River, not the sea. I like moving water. It's universal, and it plays no favourites.' He stopped himself, as if he had said too much.

'Eat things that I really like.' Howard smiled at memories of the past, of painful moments, long-ago loneliness and anxieties. Sometimes he was so tightly knotted inside that he could barely eat at all. At others, he craved a crisp bacon sandwich, whatever time of day or night did not matter. 'What does she like? Do you know?'

'*Reibekuchen*,' Cordell said with a wry smile. 'With apple sauce. At least she used to. There's a fellow sells them from a stand not far from here. You actually see it from the side door. I stop there rather too often myself.' Then he was very serious. 'She might wait there, if she's trying to make up her mind to come in. She has nowhere else to go . . . to get papers to get out of Germany. She can't use her own name. And she has to be British, or she can't get into England.'

'I'll try,' Howard answered. 'Give me a passport. I'll put the picture in after I see her. She'll have to change her appearance or they'll spot her in a moment. What a bloody mess!'

'Try not to get caught as well,' Cordell said it casually. For a moment Howard wavered. Was he walking straight into a trap of his own making? Was Cordell the perfect actor? Or was that trace of bravado an echo of the old Cordell he used to know, a few years ago when it was closer to the war, and everyone was sure whose side they were on? All the wounds were raw then, and nobody was used to the thought of peace yet. Nobody really thought of accommodating a different kind of world.

'You too,' Howard said, perfectly serious for a moment. 'Now get me that passport. I may need it in a hurry.'

Chapter Twenty-Two

After the book-burning, Jacob took Elena to a cheap rooming house run by an American couple. No explanations were asked for . . . or given. He had paid for one night and advised her not to stay there longer than that.

'I won't,' she promised. 'I'll try to get into the Embassy again. If I can't, I'll . . . find somewhere else for another night and go back next day. That's the only place I can get papers. And . . .' She clenched her teeth, forcing her emotions down. She pictured the books again, the insane faces laughing. Anger overcame fear. 'I don't know why Roger Cordell didn't prevent the assassination after I gave him the message – but if he's a traitor, he still has to help me. Because if he doesn't, he'll give himself away. I'll make sure other people at the Embassy see me this time. Some will know me, even like this!' She shook her loose, shining blond hair, still in its waves. 'If he gets me caught, he'll betray himself to the other diplomats, and then he'll be no use to anybody. I don't know if we Brits kill traitors, but I imagine so. But not in public. Probably don't admit we have them.'

Jacob rolled his eyes. 'Elena . . .'

'Please don't make an issue of this. Isn't it hard enough already?'

He smiled. 'Yes. Very hard, but worth it. More than just a . . . a taste of victory. I'll remember.'

She wanted to kiss him, just once, for all the risks that he'd taken, for being her friend in this crisis and asking nothing in return, even if it was just a kiss goodbye. But it was a bad idea.

Jacob may have thought that too because he looked at her for a long moment, then smiled, turned and walked out of the door.

Elena felt with his departure as if he had switched off all the lights, but she could still see the whole shabby room very clearly. It was tired, and everything in it was old. But it was perfectly clean, it had its own toilet and wash basin, and there was a lock on the door. That was all she needed.

She must sleep. Tomorrow she had to go back to the Embassy. Without papers, she could not leave Germany, no matter how different she looked.

In the morning, it took a moment for memory to clear, then she remembered where she was and, far more urgently than that, she must have papers, very soon. It would only take being stopped once and asked for them, and she would be caught.

At the book-burning, she had seen the face of madness. If she had caught the image in any of the photographs, it would show the world in a way no words could.

Elena ate breakfast of black bread with a little jam, and a hot cup of coffee, then took her bag and left.

She was not far from the Embassy, but it was still a good half-hour's walk. There were no cheap lodgings, the kind that asked no questions, in an area like this. She was hungry. The black bread had not answered her need at all. Was the man who sold the *Reibekuchen* still somewhere around here? Surely, she could smell it? The little grated potato and onion cakes, with apple sauce beside. She could all but taste them now. It couldn't be far away!

She didn't want to ask anybody. Not that there were many people around. It was too early for much business. But not knowing such a thing would mark her as a stranger. These were things you did not forget.

It took her another five minutes and she had bought herself two potato cakes on a cardboard plate, and a good dollop of apple sauce, when she became aware of the man watching her. He was taller than she, but not by much. He was fair-skinned, blue-eyed, but his hair seemed of no particular colour. The only thing noticeable about him was a certain grace in the way he stood. It seemed so natural, he was probably unaware of it himself. He did not fidget at all, as many people do. And he was certainly watching her.

She felt self-conscious, and suddenly afraid again. Why was he watching her? Did he think he recognised her, even though she had changed her appearance?

She should avoid him. Well-brought-up young women did not speak to strangers in the street.

'Are they any good?' he asked, gesturing towards the *Reibekuchen* stand.

'Excellent,' she replied in German, of course. 'And the apple is nicely tart.'

He was still looking at her. 'Did you see the fire last night?' he asked conversationally.

'Yes, for a while. I think it went on almost till morning.'

She took another mouthful of crisp hot potato and a little apple sauce, trying to be casual, but eating it now almost without tasting.

'Who were they?' he asked, taking a step a little closer to her. 'They set fire to the books,' he added.

Should she answer? She might draw attention to herself if she was needlessly rude. She would look afraid, and that was dangerous. The innocent don't run away. 'A lot of them seemed to be students,' she replied, watching as he bought himself two *Reibekuchen* and a good portion of the apple sauce. 'At least, they were that age, early twenties, and dressed as students do,' she went on.

'Students of what, I wonder.' He allowed his feelings of disgust to show through for a moment, then hid them again. 'Philosophy, perhaps?' His eyes were bleak.

'Hardly!' she said too quickly, then she saw the humour in his face and knew she had let slip her opinion of the book burners.

'Perhaps you're a student of philosophy? You watch them and deduce their beliefs,' he suggested.

She wanted to tell him that what she deduced was fear, and a sense of unbelonging. They lashed out at what they did not understand, in the same spirit people will smash what they cannot have. 'Was I wrong?' she said instead.

He put his hands in his pockets. It was a casual gesture, but it made him seem at ease, as if they were friends. Did he do it on purpose? 'I doubt it,' he replied. 'A philosophy spoken of, no matter how elegant and articulate the words, is seldom as powerful as one acted on.'

She was startled. He had spoken in English as naturally as if he had known it as his native tongue. Had she given herself away? Developed an English accent in German since she had left Berlin? That was a mistake! Why had Jacob not told her? Warned her, at least?

As if he had understood, the man spoke again. 'We can continue in German, if you prefer. It would be less conspicuous, and perhaps we should not stand here too long or we will be noticed. I can see the anger and grief in your face, and maybe you can see it in mine.'

She looked at him steadily. It had been said as an invitation, which to ignore would have been a rebuff. But why on earth would she not rebuff him? He was a complete stranger. She did not want to discuss any subject of depth with him. It would be so easy to say something negative, and any criticism of Hitler at all was dangerous. And yet the intelligence in his eyes, the humour, pleased her. In some way it reminded her of good memories, long discussions with Lucas, and with Mike. Laughter that was always comfortable. But now that was dangerous, too. 'Yes, I can, German is fine,' she admitted reluctantly, because she must have raised suspicion in waiting so long to answer. Or was everybody suspicious these days?

A group of young men sauntered past them, arm in arm, laughing. One of them turned back and called something at her over his shoulder. It was in German, naturally, but she did not understand.

She saw the anger in the face of the man beside her. She had not yet learned his name, but she was certain he was English.

'You don't need to know what he called us,' he said bleakly. 'I dare say your German didn't extend to the gutter . . . or the brothels. We should leave. Which way are you going?'

She dared not tell him she was going into the Embassy. The police would have guessed that that was where she would go, in order to get new papers to leave. Unless she intended to remain in Germany? Disappear into the countryside? But now she must answer this man. She started to name the street where the Hubermanns lived, then stopped. How easily she had let her guard down. She should not even go in the opposite direction. That would be too obvious, if they had a suspicion already. But neither could she afford to get lost.

'It doesn't matter,' he dismissed it easily. 'We can go down that way.' He gestured towards the way she had come, and then before she could complain, he took her arm and began to walk at a gentle pace along the footpath.

She was angry. He had no right to do this, but neither could she afford to draw police attention to herself by resisting him.

'Stop looking like that,' he warned with a rueful smile. 'People will think I'm abducting you. Do you want to be rescued by them?' It was as if he had read her thoughts, or perhaps anticipated them. He looked at another group of young men sauntering towards them.

Elena forced herself to smile and held on to his arm a little more tightly.

'Talk to me,' he said quietly. 'We should look natural.'

'What about? I don't know you,' she said angrily.

'You're perfectly capable of talking easily to strangers,' he said. '"Of shoes – and ships – and sealing wax – "' he quoted. '"Of cabbages – and kings". Whatever you like.'

She had loved *Alice*, both *Through the Looking-Glass* and *In Wonderland*. '"And why the sea is boiling hot – And whether pigs have wings",' she said tartly. 'I know most of it. Do you know it all? Perhaps you had better not discuss kings or Führers.'

He was smiling. It softened his face.

Elena regarded him without emotion. He seemed to be in his early forties, his hair a little grey at his temples, not so noticeable because it was not dark. There was nothing remarkable about him at all. Then she noticed shadows in his face. The war had cost him, too.

'What sort of opinions do you want?' He was suddenly completely serious.

'What do you have?' She kept her voice light. It was an old argument, and she had heard all sides too many times. 'Comfortable? No, of course not. We learned the cost of that with the Great War. We won't make all those mistakes again.'

'That's naïve,' he retorted. 'We make the same mistakes all the time. All right, yes, there probably will be another war. Or more accurately, a continuation of the same one, after a decent interval when there's a new generation to sacrifice, and new people in government who think that somehow they will do it differently this time.'

'Isn't that awfully cynical?' she asked. 'Or is that only you saying it? You think that world weariness and wisdom are the same thing?'

'That's harsh,' he observed. They were still walking away from the Embassy, and he was still holding her arm too tightly for her to break away.

'Don't pretend you're hurt,' she replied. 'Did you expect me to swallow that whole?' She was very aware of being younger than he was, and comparatively naïve. Margot thought Elena was waiting for tomorrow to have fun, to do all the dancing and wild things young people should do, except that there was not going to be a tomorrow. The difference between them was that Elena was not pretending.

'I expected you to argue,' the man said quite genuinely. 'If I agreed with you, it would put you in an untenable position of having to contradict yourself. No gentleman should do that to a lady.'

She was not sure whether to laugh or to be angry. Was he deliberately baiting her? Yes. She was quite certain that he was. A wave of anger rose in her. She didn't have to be polite to this man. For once, she could say what she thought.

Then she saw a couple of Brownshirts walking towards them, more or less in the middle of the path. She and this man would have to step aside and let them pass. Would this Englishman have the sense to do that? He was graceful, casual, but there could be the arrogance in him of one used to privilege. He would not be accustomed to the idea of stepping out of the way for bullies, just because they were in uniform. If he had been in Berlin any length of time, he must know their power, surely? Or maybe he was going to hand her over to them? She tensed her whole body in an effort to break free, but he was far too strong for her, and he seemed to be expecting it.

She looked around. There were students coming the other way, a degree of expectation in their faces.

The Brownshirts were only yards from them.

Elena stepped towards the kerb and the Englishman kept his grip on her arm. 'Don't cause trouble!' she said to him sharply, but in so low a voice she hoped not to be overheard. 'We can't afford to annoy them!' Please God, he had no idea how much she could not afford it.

The students, if that was what they were, had stopped and were eagerly awaiting the coming test of strength. There was a sickening excitement in them, eyes glittering, bodies tense. Like a sliver of last night's madness sharply piercing the body.

The Brownshirts stopped, as if Elena and the Englishman

were in their way. One of them put out his hand and closed it roughly on Elena's wrist.

The Englishman stood absolutely still, his eyebrows slightly raised. 'Your name and rank?' he asked the Brownshirt, his voice crisp. He spoke German again now, but with a slightly different accent from the Brownshirt, and he stood very straight, back stiff, chin high.

The Brownshirt was taken by surprise. 'Johann Hartwig. Who are you?'

'Did Herr Doktor Goebbels send you?' the Englishman asked, ignoring the question.

'No . . .'

'Then I have the advantage over you,' the Englishman said, without a shred of humour. The grace had gone from him. 'You have no idea what you are stepping into. This woman is required by Doktor Goebbels. She has knowledge he needs. If you cause a delay or a difficulty in my getting her to him, you will regret it until the day you die, which will probably not be very long from now. Do I make myself clear, Herr Hartwig? I know your name. Unless, of course, you want to murder me here in the street, too?'

Hartwig let go of Elena and retreated.

The Englishman caught hold of her arm and, pulling her sharply, set off at a brisk walk along the centre of the path. Not once did he turn to see if they were following.

'I'm not going with you!' Elena said, pulling away from him again, and failing to break his hold.

'I'm not taking you to Goebbels, for God's sake!' he said, moving so close to her that he did not have to raise his voice.

'How do I know that?' She was still trying to free herself, to no avail.

They were alone on the footpath now, but other people

would come any moment. Fighting like a wilful child would draw people's attention. She could not afford that. Did he know that she was the woman they were hunting for Scharnhorst's assassination? He must do. There was no other reason anyone would look for her, let alone Herr Doktor Goebbels! Even in England, his name was known.

When he did not answer immediately, she asked again. 'How do I know that?'

'I want to get you out of here . . . home to Lucas and Josephine.'

She wanted to believe him, desperately. It sounded wonderful . . . too good to be true. But how could this man even know of her grandparents?

She must get away, but how? He was far stronger than she was, and she had nothing with which to fight. He was English. She was sure of that. With a wave of nausea, she understood that Cordell had betrayed her again! It was all clear now. He had never tried to prevent the assassination, and he knew which hotel she was staying at. He had someone put the rifle there, so she would be blamed. This man must be an ally of Cordell. Another traitor! She had liked him instinctively. Both he and Cordell had drawn on all the old memories, the jokes, the images of childhood that reminded her of happy years and people she had loved . . . and lost. How did he know these things? Of course! Cordell had been a friend of her father. This was worse than her darkest fears. This was something she had not even imagined.

They were close to one of the big trees that lined the avenue.

She had nothing to lose. If he took her to Goebbels she would never escape. They would connect her to the assassination, because blaming an Englishman was the whole purpose of having killed Scharnhorst. A woman could use a rifle as easily as a man. She had simply taken Ian's place.

They were standing next to one of the trees. The faint wind rustled in the leaves overhead. She must escape . . . now.

He started to speak again. She thought for only a moment and then, because she couldn't break from his grip, she did the opposite: she lunged forward, standing as hard as she could with the heel of her shoe on his instep. He gasped and his hand loosened on her arm. She swung the bag carrying her handbag and her camera at his head, and he fell backwards, striking the trunk of the tree. He slid down and did not move.

He might not be dazed for long. She turned and ran, crossing the street as soon as she could, and into a side street, then turned again, then again. Only once did she look behind her, and she did not see him.

Where could she go? Not to the Embassy now! Not back to Zillah's. Not even to the place where she had slept last night. To be caught was terrifying enough, and perhaps in the end it was all that counted. But to be betrayed was a pain that burned in a different way . . . corrosive, as if it could never heal.

The Englishman had seemed so nice. He had made her think of Lucas, even a bit of Mike. She could not let him win – could not let any of them – whatever the cost.

Chapter Twenty-Three

Elena woke with a jolt, staring in the dark, barely making out the lines of the unfamiliar bedroom. Her eyes were wide open and yet she could still see the insane faces of the young people capering around the fires, cheering as the books burned. They were perfectly ordinary humans. She could have met such people in the street every day and not even know them again.

There was one in particular, the man who had been standing near the flames, in whom some remnants of sanity seemed to be left, so that he knew what was happening. She had seen it in his face, had tried to catch it with the camera.

She lay still on the hard bed, huddled up into herself.

There was nobody else in the room, of course! The mad men were in her own mind. Yet they were there because they were real. She saw them, without the masks of daylight and ordinary people passing in the street, talking to each other as if it were any other day.

She was cold now, bolt upright, clasping her arms around her knees, in the second or third strange, bare lodging-house bedroom.

She could not stay here. She must get the pictures developed before someone searched her, either to confiscate the film or expose it to the light and ruin the images.

She got up, washed and dressed, then went downstairs carrying her meagre luggage. She had paid the night before. It was the condition of renting in places like these. She said 'Guten Morgen' politely to the owner, thanked her, and went out into the street. She would have to look for another place to stay tonight. She must find a photographer's shop that would develop her films. A chemist would take too long. And paying extra money for haste would draw attention to her. It was a huge risk that the photographer she found would question her, even betray her if her story was not convincing, but she had no alternative: she had to get the photographs developed.

It was a brisk day, in spite of the sun, and she was glad for the excuse to wear the nondescript scarf she had bought and hide some of her pale blond hair she was so unaccustomed to. She felt self-conscious when people gave her more than a momentary glance, as several people did. She might be noticeable, but not as Elena Standish.

When she got the photographs, what was she going to do? Jacob already had his copies of the assassination. She had hers. But the book-burning pictures were priceless. They were a depiction of utter horror that would haunt the mind for ever. She wished she could forget it herself, and knew she never would, especially not of that one man whose eyes looked out at the camera as if he had seen hell.

Of course, she had yet to see the photograph. It might not be good at all. She might have taken it with insufficient light, or too much, or even had her hands shake at the terrible sight of it.

The negatives would be far too dangerous to carry, and disastrous if she lost them. If the police, or the Gestapo, caught her, they would certainly take them, and almost as certainly destroy them. She must get those negatives developed and the images published. It was the only thing she could do to fight against the darkness coming, a darkness so palpable she could almost feel it settling on her skin, as if it could make her disappear, too. It was a time to choose sides. Later would be too late. It could be some part of her promise to Ian. In a way, to Mike . . . at least to what he had believed of her. Mostly it was a promise to herself.

She asked a passing woman for directions to the nearest post office. There was no time to waste in wandering around looking for one.

The woman pointed and said it was two blocks up, and to the left.

'Thank you,' Elena replied, and hurried on. She must not run, it would draw attention. Be invisible. The sort of person you pass and instantly forget you ever saw.

At the post office, she bought a large envelope, and then enough postage stamps to take it to England, even if it should be the weight of twenty photographs, with negatives and prints.

On the counter, using their pen, she addressed it to Lucas, scribbled an illegible return address on the back. To leave it out might be suspicious. She put the stamps on, then folded it up and put it into her camera case.

Now it was time to go and get the film developed.

She had to ask for a shop that would develop film. There was no help for that. She could waste half a day and never find one. She felt a painful urgency. How long would it take the police to find her? She looked different, but was that enough?

She finally found someone who directed her to a photographer's shop. It was where he told her it would be. She hesitated only a moment, looking in the window. It was small and shabby. But the camera equipment she saw for sale was good quality. What was she waiting for? Some sort of affirmation? There was none. She pushed the door and went in.

The interior was drab, worn linoleum on the floor, one long counter with a bald man behind it, a visor on his forehead to shield his eyes from the light. The light was excellent. The cameras were in locked glass cupboards. She knew it would be glass that did not shatter easily. Two of the cameras were Leicas, older models, very like her own.

'Can I help you?' the man asked.

'Yes, please.' Her mouth was dry. She swallowed. 'I have some rolls of film I would like developed, please. Negatives only will do. I'm not sure if there is time to make prints. I have to travel soon, and if they are opened, to search, or anything, they might be ruined. I'll wait.'

'You want them immediately?' He looked slightly surprised.

Had she made a mistake? What else could she do? If he had time to look at them, he might show them to others, or even burn them. 'Please? If I can get an earlier train, I would like to.'

'Very well. It'll cost you extra.'

'I'll pay twice your regular rate.' Was that too much? 'I realise it takes you from your other work.' Don't be too eager! And she still had to survive, find a room for tonight, perhaps. And pay her train fare. Yes, of course tonight! She didn't have a passport with a name she dared use! She had still to get to the British Embassy! But first, more important than anything else, she had to get the pictures out of Germany.

They would force people to see, before it was too late, the nature of the thing they were fighting.

'Twice?' he asked.

'Do I have to take them elsewhere?' She glanced at the glass case with its cameras. 'I need them well done, and from the look of your cameras to sell, you deal in the best.'

He held out his hand. 'I'll do it.'

She took the film canisters out of her bag and passed them over. Her hand was shaking. He had to pull on them a little to take them from her. Was she making a mistake? There was no other reasonable choice. She could be caught, and if she had them in her bag, they would take them.

The man looked at her. Their eyes met for a moment. He half smiled. 'I will make a good job of them, Fräulein,' he said.

'Of course. I'm sorry . . .'

He took the canisters into the back room, leaving her alone in the shop, pacing the floor.

Eventually she stopped pacing and sat down to wait. There were a lot of photographs and it would all take a long while. The time seemed endless, but finally he emerged. She thought his face had altered. Or perhaps she had never really noticed what he looked like.

'Do you want the prints?' he asked.

'You made prints . . . already?'

'You said you wanted the negatives quickly. But making prints only added a few minutes. I hung them on the line with clips and put the heater on gently. I took the extra water off with cotton. Don't know if they'll be perfect, but that's as fast as I can get.'

'Yes . . .' she agreed. 'Thank you.' Perhaps it had been longer than she thought, almost two hours. 'Thank you,'

258

she said again and walked round the counter, following him into the back passage and then into the darkroom. It felt close, airless, and of course smelled of familiar chemicals, acrid, that always made her eyes sting.

She looked at the pictures.

The instant she saw them, she knew how good they were. The contrast was sharp, the balance was excellent. But when she looked more closely, the real impact struck her. They were laid out in the order in which they were taken. Of the forty-eight exposures altogether, there were ten that he had picked out. She stared, almost mesmerised by the violence of the images. They were at once terrifying and absurd. She knew with sudden insight why some people are terrified of clowns. There was a clown-like look to these people, but it had tipped over from reason to insanity. They were still laughing, but the malice was there, let loose. There was no control to anything. In the silent pictures, she could hear the screaming in her mind, and feel the heat.

She looked for the last one, the one she almost dreaded to see. And yet she wanted to. It would all be an anticlimax if she had not caught that dreadful face as it looked into the abyss.

It was there. Perfectly focused. In the eyes was horror, looking at an endless fall.

She turned away, she could not help it. 'Yes.' Her voice came out sounding almost normal. How could it? 'Thank you. You have made a superb job of them.'

'Who are you?' the man asked. He was standing between her and the door.

'A photographer,' she replied. 'My name doesn't matter.'

'You'd better take the ones you want. And the negatives. I'll burn the rest. Pay me what you owe me and go.'

She began to gather them up.

There was a noise out towards the front.

'The back way!' the man commanded. 'Get out of here!' He did not want to burn the pictures. He put them in acid.

She pulled out all the money she could afford to give him, slipped the pictures and the negatives into the envelope, and sealed it. Clutching it in her hand, she went out the back door, just beyond the darkroom, and into the yard, and then up the steps to an alleyway.

She cared what was going to happen to the man, but she could not save him. In fact, her presence would only make it worse for him, especially if they found the pictures. She must get them out of Berlin, and back to London. Lucas would see them and know what to do with them. Please God, she would be there to tell him! But if not, he would know.

She went down the alley steps and into the street. Better stay away from the front of the shop. She walked as quickly as she could without running. There were little knots of people standing here and there, heads bent in conversation. Some of them stared towards the photographer's shop.

But she must get into the main street, where there would be a post box. She had to get rid of the pictures as soon as possible, not only to save herself, but above all to save them.

She glanced once more towards the camera shop. There was a policeman at the door. Had they worked out that she was a photographer? They knew her name. Perhaps they knew her occupation as well? Not very difficult. She must get away from here. She could only hope the shopkeeper would be all right. She had not asked his name, nor given him hers. She felt as if she were abandoning him as she hurried away, but her presence was damning.

A block further on, she saw a post box and slipped the envelope through the slit. She heard it fall inside with relief but also a sense of loss. She didn't have it any more – it couldn't incriminate her – but neither could she control it.

She walked away. There was nothing left to do now but try to get into the British Embassy and find someone who would give her a passport she could use to get out of Germany.

She was on the right street, she was almost there, just two blocks more to go, when a policeman put his hand on her arm, bringing her to a sudden stop.

'Just a minute, Fräulein. There's been a complaint about you. A woman says that you stole from her. Let me see what you have in your bag.' He wrenched it from her roughly and opened it, saw the camera bag inside, and her few clothes and toiletries. He looked up at her challengingly. 'Come with me!'

Chapter Twenty-Four

'Cherry tree. Now,' Howard had said briefly on the telephone. He had not waited for a reply.

Lucas had heard the tension so tight in Howard's voice that his hand shook as he tried to fasten the lead on Toby's collar. Toby caught his mood and pulled anxiously. Josephine came to the kitchen door. She did not ask what the matter was.

'Just taking Toby for a walk,' Lucas told her. For a moment he resisted the temptation to find a shred of thought to help now, even if it was a reminder of the long past, and all the things they had faced and survived.

'Did he say anything?' she asked.

'Only to be there. I'll be back as soon as I can . . .'

He stood up, smiled bleakly, and turned away before he could read the fear in her eyes, or perhaps it was before she could read it in his?

He took the car. It was marginally faster than walking. He parked it at the entrance and walked quickly through the gate and down the path between the swathes of bluebells.

Howard was already there. Toby saw him first, pulled the

lead out of Lucas's hand, went racing along the outlines of the path and then through the flowers.

Howard bent and took the lead off him, hugging him for a brief, unselfconscious moment. He rose as Lucas reached them and handed him the lead coiled up.

Lucas took it. 'Well?'

'I saw her. Morning after the book-burning . . .'

'Was she all right?' Lucas's voice was hoarse, but he could not help it.

'Very,' Howard said drily.

'Stop it!' Lucas snapped. 'What . . .'

'She was buying *Reibekuchen* at the stall outside the Embassy.'

The mundane absurdity of it was not lost on Lucas, but at the moment he did not care. He was about to snap at Howard again, even though he knew it was unfair, and Howard was hurting nearly as much as he was himself.

Then Howard continued, 'We walked along the street together, quite a distance, before we were accosted by a bunch of Brownshirts, drunk on their own power. I brazened it out and told the one who stopped us that I was getting her for Goebbels.'

Lucas wanted to strike him. 'For God's sake, man, get to the point,' he said between his teeth.

'They let us go, all apologies. We walked a few yards until we were out of sight. Then she hit me, hard, my head struck the trunk of the tree behind me, and the next thing I knew I was sitting up slowly, with a hell of a headache, and Elena was nowhere in sight.'

Lucas looked at Howard's face, pale, except for the definite flush as the blood mounted his cheeks.

'I'm sorry, Lucas. I didn't dare draw attention to her by

making any enquiries. I asked generally. I couldn't afford anything to get back to Cordell. He's still head of the station in Berlin.'

'You are sure it was Elena?' Lucas asked, his voice shaking. He could not imagine her doing such a thing. 'She couldn't have known—'

'Of course I'm sure!' Howard said a little tartly. 'We talked about all sorts of things. She's as English as cucumber sandwiches and tea on the lawn. She quoted from the things you often said she loved, and she no longer looks exactly like her picture, which is good. No one else would recognise her. I told her I knew you and Josephine, but she didn't believe me. She doesn't know me, Lucas. We've never met, and I doubt you've spoken about me to her. I should have thought of that before I went. I should have taken something of yours she'd recognise. And I could hardly draw Cordell into it, damn him!' He swallowed. 'I'm sorry.' He looked for a moment as if he were going to add something, then changed his mind.

Lucas shook his head. 'I suppose I don't know her as well as I thought.'

Howard gave him a twisted smile, but there was real amusement in it. 'Well, she's not nearly as docile as you painted her, which is probably a good thing.'

'Docile?' Lucas was hurt. 'Is that what you thought?'

'Perhaps I misunderstood you. She seemed to agree with you, at least on the surface, at least about pretty much everything.'

'Because I'm right!' Lucas said tartly, with a smile. 'Usually. What can we do, Peter?'

Howard met his eyes. 'Nothing . . . yet. I've told the men I can trust, but there are damn few to trust that much! The only comfort is that the Gestapo haven't got her yet. That I know for certain. And she has allies because she's eluded the Gestapo for days now. Somebody's looking after her, and it isn't us.'

'You sure of that?'

'Yes.'

'Walk back with me?' Lucas requested. He wanted to put off a little longer what he would have to say to Josephine. There were many truths he had not told her, but on the other hand, he had never outright lied. This was not a time to begin.

Charles was another matter. And yet when it came to it, he could not lie to him either. He owed him that. Now he would not want either of them to face the possible loss of a daughter and granddaughter who was so central to their lives, and not be able to give them the grace of honesty.

He parted from Howard without any more unnecessary words and drove home to tell Josephine. There was no avoiding it. To do so would be the first real lie between them.

She waited a moment or two before she answered, then glanced at his hand, twisted in the thick fur around Toby's neck.

'She's got more courage than you think,' she said at last. 'And more fight in her. Poor Howard! Remember how many times in the past you told her not to give up hope? Don't you give up now.'

It was a struggle for her. He could see it in her eyes, in the unnatural firmness of her jaw.

If he replied, the shaking of his voice would give him away. He just took his hand off Toby's neck and put it over hers.

*

Telling Charles was a very different matter. They were alone in Charles's study at his own home. He had papers spread all over the desk, as if he intended to work all evening.

'How the hell do you know this, and not me?' Charles demanded.

'Is that what you care about?' Lucas asked incredulously. 'That I heard before you did? Because I have a friend in Berlin who told me. It . . .' He stopped. Was Charles picking a quarrel because he couldn't bear to face the truth – that Elena was in great danger? They might lose her, as well as Mike. He took a deep breath and let it out slowly. He could not mention Peter Howard. Certainly not that he had gone to Berlin and failed to bring her back. 'There's nothing you can do, Charles.'

'Of course there is!'

'It will only draw attention to her, and that is the last thing she needs. When you've thought about it for a moment or two, you'll realise that.'

Charles turned away, hiding his face. 'You have no idea what it's really like.' He was almost choking over his words. 'Hitler's turning into a monster. He's lost all sense of proportion. The new police force he's created is out of control. God knows what they'll do to her if they catch her. We've got to find her! Get her out of there. They're brutal. Looking for Jews has become an obsession.'

'I know,' Lucas admitted. Perhaps it was unwise, but he couldn't lie to his son. Not now.

'No, you don't,' Charles said bitterly. 'Our man over there, Roger Cordell, tells me the truth now and then. They've built a huge camp outside Munich, at a place called Dachau, to keep suspected dissenters: Communists, gypsies, Jews. The young men who missed the war are spoiling for a fight, to prove themselves, and they've only civilians to pick on!' He swung round to face Lucas. 'God in heaven, what possessed Elena to go there? Do you know that as well?'

Lucas hesitated. He chose the lie. The truth would hurt and do no good at all. 'Not for certain. I haven't spoken to her, Charles, I only know they suspect her of something she can't be guilty of.'

'Can't she? There's a sort of stubbornness in her . . . idealism . . . and she's hopelessly naïve. I . . .' He stopped, unable to go on.

'Taking a sniper rifle and shooting someone?'

'What? What are you talking about?'

'That's what she's suspected of. I told you, it's ridiculous. She couldn't do such a thing, even if she wanted to. I'd bet anything she's a rotten shot.'

'She's not a shot at all! She's never handled a gun!'

Lucas did not know what to do. He could not touch him, although that was his instinct. But they had not bridged that gap in years. It would be unnatural now.

'Margot might!' said Charles. 'She has all the courage in the world, and the temper, but not Elena.'

Lucas did not argue. Charles did not know his younger daughter at all. 'You're quite right. I had to tell you, in case someone else did . . . before . . . before she's safely home.'

Should he warn Charles not to reach out to Cordell? How could he explain that?

'Don't get in touch with Cordell,' he said quickly, his mind racing. 'They'll be watching him. The Embassy is the obvious place to look.'

'Yes, of course. I do realise that, Father. What a bloody mess!'

Lucas wanted to tell him it would be all right, but not

offering platitudes was the one honesty he could afford him. 'Yes, it is,' he agreed.

'Father . . .' Charles hesitated, but the look of urgency was so plain in his face for once Lucas did not evade it.

'Yes?' He knew what Charles was going to say next. It had been inevitable for years.

'Just how do you know this?'

'I still know people in government.'

'I see . . . No, I don't see.' He let out his breath slowly.

Chapter Twenty-Five

The police station was cold and smelled of stale smoke and cleaning fluid. The floor was scratched, its linoleum patchily worn. Elena was taken into a small side room and left standing. When the doors shut behind her, she felt as if deep water were closing over her head. She was so frightened, it was like drowning, except that she was still alive, still breathing, over-breathing, feeling her throat tighten.

Two men entered the room. They faced her, both of them were fair skinned, light haired. No different on the outside from dozens of men she knew at home. Inside, she imagined them as unreachable to her as those students who had capered around the fires that were consuming the dreams and discoveries of an age of mankind.

Neither of them spoke, they just stared at her. She felt as if she were suffocating. Was this the day she would die?

'I did not take anything from a woman,' she said again. 'Anything at all.' Her jaw was so tight, so aching with tension that it was hard to frame the words.

'We know that, miss. What's your name?' One of the men stepped closer to her, too close. His voice was soft, almost purring, but she could feel his breath on her face. She forced herself to look at him, at his eyes. This was it, the moment she had feared. She must not give away Jacob, Eli and Zillah. She thought of Ian, lying bleeding on the floor of the railway carriage. Then Mike, the last time she had seen him, in uniform, going back to the battle line. Had he any idea he would never come home? Perhaps she would never come home either.

And then it struck her: they already knew the answers!

'Name?' the policeman repeated.

There was no point in lying. Her passport was in her bag and they had confiscated it. 'Elena Standish.'

'Is that English?'

'Yes.'

'What are you doing in Berlin?'

'It's a beautiful city.' She took a breath. Any mistake at all and she would end up doing the one thing she dreaded. It was always at the front of her mind. She had already failed Ian. His death was not her fault, but in a way, Scharnhorst's was. Not that his death mattered, only that Britain must not be blamed for it. 'I lived here when I was younger. My family lived here because of my father's work.'

'So, you know the city.' There was triumph in his voice. He was still standing too close to her, crowding her. She refused to step back.

'Yes, some of it.'

He looked her up and down. 'You must have been a child.'

'It was about ten years ago, I was seventeen when I came. Twenty when I left.' So far, this was the exact truth. Always stick to the truth if you can. Easier to remember. Perhaps this was going to be all right.

'What did he do, this father of yours that came to Berlin?'

'He was a diplomat.' No need to tell them how high he was in the service.

'You mean a spy!' The man's eyes gleamed as if he had made her give up valuable information.

'No, a diplomat. Trying to make things better between our two countries.'

He nodded, as if he agreed with her. He even smiled. Then he slapped her across the face, hard. It stung and knocked her off balance, making her fall back a couple of steps. The pain of it made her eyes water. Fury boiled up inside her. She wanted to shout at him, demand he explain himself. She wished to retaliate, but she did not dare to. The humiliation choked her. What was the best reaction? If she showed how afraid she was, he would know his tactics worked. If she didn't, it would look like defiance. Next time, he would hit her harder. She moved her tongue round her mouth, tasting blood.

Was there any point in trying to reason with him? Was he beyond reach, too, like the book burners?

'Is your father here with you?' the other policeman asked.

'No.' Keep it short. Give the bastards nothing else to contradict.

'You're alone?'

'I'm twenty-eight!'

Another slap. This time she was less startled and it seemed to hurt a little less. What had angered him about that? It was only her age. Perhaps he did not need a reason? Was this what madness was like, the pain, the violence out of nowhere? It stung until she felt dizzy with it, and she wanted to strike him back. It was only the conviction that she would lose, and be hurt even more, that stopped her.

'Are you alone?' he said again, the words slow and careful, pushed between his teeth.

To acknowledge being alone meant that there was no one to help her. It made her even more vulnerable. But this was where they would catch her out. She must not betray Jacob, or the Hubermanns.

'Yes.' Don't add anything. Don't give him reason to hit her again.

'Who gave you the gun? Did you bring it with you?' There was a sneer with the last question. 'Nobody noticed a pretty young woman carrying her handbag, and a rifle?' Now he was deeply sarcastic. 'We are not stupid!'

She wanted to say that the very idea proved that they were, but she knew he would hit her again, perhaps a lot harder. 'It would be impossible to walk around with a rifle,' she agreed. 'At least I imagine it would. I've never tried.'

'Liar!' He hit her again, knocking her off balance, sending her sprawling on to the floor. She sat up quickly, and without thinking put her hand to her cheek. Holding it eased the pain a little, or perhaps she just imagined it did. Now there was more blood in her mouth and running down her chin. He saw her as weak, someone too afraid to stand up for herself. She could see it in his eyes. She stood awkwardly, holding on to a chair, and then sitting in it, a little dizzy, forcing herself to look at him.

'I don't have a rifle! Or any other gun,' she said, stumbling a little over her words because her mouth hurt. 'And if I had tried carrying around such a thing, as you said, you would have seen it.'

'We found it in your room!' he said triumphantly.

'In the hotel? Anyone could have put it there. I didn't.'

'Then how did you know it was there?' He was smiling now.

'Because you just told me.' She met his eyes and stared straight at him.

He raised his hand to strike her again, but his companion caught it.

'She's no use to us if she can't speak,' he warned. 'She's not alone in this. Use your brain.'

The first man shook him off angrily, but he conceded the point.

'If you are not guilty, why did you run away?' the second man asked, his voice softer, his temper well in his control. He sounded as if he were merely interested, no more.

But it was a lethal question. There was no completely innocent answer.

'Because I was in the square and I knew someone had shot Herr Scharnhorst. I saw it happen. I saw the panic. I knew you would be looking for anyone who could be connected with it. I was not. I had no idea such a thing could happen. Or who would do it.' That, at least, was close to the truth. But she could hear the tight, high fear in her own voice. They must hear it too.

'You didn't think to hand the gun over to the authorities?' the second man continued, still smiling as if it were a casual conversation.

'No, I told you, I know nothing about a gun, but I was frightened at what I had seen in the square. It was a terrible thing.'

'I believe you. Where did you go, Fräulein . . . Standish? You say you know the city – do you have friends here in Berlin?'

Now she must invent, carefully. One slip and they would have trapped her. She had no doubt that they would hurt her, perhaps badly, if they thought it would help them. When she had arrived, she had just been a British tourist, inconspicuous, noticing and photographing the assault on minorities, particularly Jews. She had seen their faces and humiliation, old men stepping off the pavement into the gutter to let Brownshirt youth strut by. No one retaliated, no one tried to stop them.

She had been part of the 'no one' who passed by, because Jacob had made her see that intervention only made things worse. They had no power. She burned with rage at the offenders, and pity for the victims. Now she was one of the victims, alone, so frightened her stomach churned and she found it difficult to draw in her breath. Her face throbbed where they had struck her, and she swallowed blood.

She could not hide her fear from them. The only good thing left was to make sure she did not bring anyone else down with her.

'Did you go to friends here in Berlin?' the man repeated.

'No. I just ran.'

'Why? Were you afraid they would not believe that you were innocent?'

He was clever. If she said yes, she condemned herself and them. If she said no, then why had she gone to them for help?

'I just ran,' she said again. 'Then I got lost. I got . . . turned around. I couldn't go the way I meant to. I found one house, or I thought I did, but there was no one there that I knew.'

'Were they Jews?' He asked the question without any emotion in his voice at all, nothing to indicate what his reaction would be, whether she said yes or no.

She thought of one friend she had known, in case he asked her. Better to have someone in mind. 'No, they were Catholics.'

'And you thought they would help you? Or did you not

plan to tell them that you were being hunted for murdering Herr Scharnhorst?'

'I didn't murder him! I saw the gun and I was afraid. I just ran, because I couldn't prove to anyone that I knew nothing about it.' She heard the desperation in her own voice. Why did he not believe her? Or was it that he really didn't care? Innocent or guilty, she was the one they were looking for. Or perhaps anyone would do, if they satisfied the crowd. A hideous thought. It filled her with fear, and drove out everything else. Victory was not in getting the right person, it was in getting anyone who could be made to look right. She must get rid of illusions. These people would kill her, and they would kill others, too.

How easy it was to blame someone else when you were sick with fear, the sweat breaking out on your skin, and instantly going cold.

The second man was nodding slowly. 'You panicked, because you realised that the gun had been used to assassinate one of the Führer's best men? You had not the courage to hand the gun over and trust our justice.'

Another trap. 'I didn't think,' she said, as if it were an admission. Did she have to apologise to these arrogant men? 'I should have trusted.'

'Perhaps English police are not so trustworthy as we Germans?'

She looked at his face, his eyes, and had no idea if he was being sarcastic or not. She did not doubt he would do whatever he thought was in his own interest. Perhaps he was too afraid of whoever was higher up the chain of command than he was? Perhaps they were all afraid, of one thing or another?

She said nothing.

'Are English police trustworthy?' he said more loudly.

'I don't know.' She fumbled over the words. Her mouth hurt, her whole face hurt. 'I have friends who say they aren't.'

A tiny victory. It had given him no leverage. Very tiny and lasting only a moment.

'So, when your friends did not answer, where did you sleep? What did you eat? It has been several days. Someone helped you. Who?'

'Different people. I begged.' Did that sound believable?

The first man looked her up and down. 'Don't be stupid,' he said contemptuously. 'She earned it on her back!' His meaning, and his disgust, were both plain.

Elena felt the heat rise up her cheeks. It was humiliating to be taken so easily for a whore, or perhaps just a desperate woman! How many such women might have slept with men for their own survival? Or even, more likely, to feed their children, or save someone else's life. Wouldn't a woman with a child to protect do anything necessary, no matter how repulsive, to save her child? A child alone would die. Or worse.

She nodded her head very slightly. It was believable. Good, if he accepted it.

'Put her in the cells,' the second man ordered and turned away, clearly thinking of the next task.

It was a very ordinary cell: bare stone floor, one small window high up in the wall. Nothing to see out of it but sky. There was a cot along one side, and a bucket. Nothing else. They had searched her handbag and kept it, along with the photographs of the assassination and her passport. At least Jacob had copies of the pictures. They would be safe, as long as Eli and Zillah were. Perhaps Jacob would be safe because he was American? If he kept his activities quiet, wrote for American newspapers only, then his United States citizenship might protect him.

But her British citizenship had not protected her!

Was that because they really thought she had killed Scharnhorst? Would she have been all right, but for that?

Jacob was a Jew. She felt despair well up inside her as she thought of people she had seen beaten and humiliated in the street just because they were Jews. Why?

For the love of heaven, Christ himself had been a Jew! So had the Virgin Mary, and all the Apostles. Hatred was a kind of insanity, and there was no reasoning with it. Any claim of race or religion was an excuse for the inner violence they could no longer control. It was corrosive like acid, burning all it touched, destroying in the cause of, what . . . inadequacy? People who were filled with rage because they had failed, they could not cope with defeat, hunger, or most of all, the consuming darkness.

Wasn't she afraid? Yes. Terrified of failure, of pain, of being alone, helpless, perhaps too injured or ill to survive, but not quite enough to die.

Too much imagination! She was in a police cell, accused of something she had not done. The Nazis were terrible, beyond terrible. There was no word for them. But they were still a minority. She knew the German people. They were as decent as anybody else. She had lived here and been happy. Stop the imagination. Think what to say when they questioned her again.

That time came sooner than she expected. She had gone over and over possibilities in her mind, her head ached from where the man had hit her, and from the turmoil of her own thoughts.

She was taken back to where she had been before, or a room exactly like it. She had been too frightened to take much notice. The same two men were there as before, and both of them looked in ill temper.

'Commandant Beimler wants to see you,' the man who had hit her said angrily. He seemed to resent the fact. Perhaps it was a reflection on his competence that it was taken out of his hands. Elena had no idea whether it would be better or worse for her. Perhaps it made no difference, except that this senior man might be cleverer, far more difficult to mislead.

She did not speak. Nothing could make it better, and a mistake would make it worse.

Elena was marched in silence, her hands manacled behind her back, along several corridors, across an open space almost like a barrack yard, and in through another door. This new building was cleaner and rather better cared for. Definitely, the commandant must be senior.

They stopped and one of the policemen knocked sharply on a door. Neither of the men reached for the handle to open it, until a voice from inside gave them permission.

She was pushed in roughly enough to feel the tweak of a muscle in her shoulder, but she tried to give no sign that it surprised her, or that it hurt.

Beimler, if it was he behind the desk, stood up, looking first at her, then at the two policemen who had brought her. He was tall with fair hair and strong features, the perfect Aryan type. He held out his hand.

'Sir?' the younger policeman gestured.

'Keys,' Beimler said a little impatiently. 'You have her manacled. I want the key.'

'Sir, she could be violent. She already shot Herr Scharnhorst, and from a considerable distance. She's probably trained in unarmed combat, too.'

'I don't see any bruises on your face, and a pretty large one on hers. Looks as if you won that fight,' Beimler responded with a twisted smile, more irritation than humour.

'I've more sense than to let her trick me,' the man replied tartly.

'So have I,' Beimler snapped back. 'Keys!'

He handed them over.

'Thank you. You may go. I'll send for you, if I need you.'

'We can wait outside, sir.'

'No, you cannot. You will go back and continue with your duties.'

Reluctantly, they both saluted, perhaps not quite as smartly as they could have, and went out, closing the door with a sharp snap behind them.

Beimler released Elena from the manacles. 'Sit down,' he invited, relaxing and resuming his own seat. 'Do you prefer to speak in English or German? I'm afraid my English is not very fluent.'

'German is fine, thank you.' She sat down, but well towards the front of the chair, uncomfortably. She did not know if his outward good manners made him better, or worse.

He sat quite still, apparently studying her. She did not stare back at him; it would be bold, and challenging. Instead she looked around the room. It was sunny. Outside, beyond the window, the sky was blue. The office was very tidy. No papers lying around, but lots of books on the pale wooden shelves. Presumably they were all books the Führer approved of. There would be nothing dangerous to the mind, no new ideas, no visions that were uncensored.

She saw on the shelf nearest to his desk, where he could see it every time he looked up, a photograph of a pretty blond woman, smiling and holding a little girl of perhaps two, who was smiling at whoever had been holding the camera, showing white baby teeth.

Elena found herself looking away. She could not think of this man having a wife and a child who looked at him with such trust.

She waited to be interrogated, perhaps hit again. She glanced at the smiling child. Elena was not so close to her father. She had never felt she knew him really well. Margot was his favourite, just as Elena was Lucas's. It might be too late now to mend that. It was a shame, a part of her life that would always be missing now.

She thought of all the things she had shared with Lucas: the laughter, the exploration of ideas, the freedom of being safe and certain of love.

Would Lucas even know what had happened to her? If he did, at least she would not have to say she had betrayed anyone, not even herself.

She looked at Beimler again.

'Why did you come back to Germany, Miss Standish? Why now?' he asked.

What was he looking for? A reason for her to have killed Scharnhorst? 'I had the opportunity,' she replied. 'I was photographing people at an economic conference in Italy. I decided not to go straight home.'

'Ah yes, the photographs.' He gave a bleak smile.

She thought she could see actual humour in it, not something Hitler's followers were known for. If you could laugh, you had a sense of proportion, and of absurdity.

'You've seen them?' she asked. She dared not hope. And yet she did! She felt a lurch of pain inside her as she thought again of what she could lose. And there was a burning anger as well, a rage for everyone who had been terrified and humiliated.

'Yes. You took them?' the man continued.

'Yes.' She stared straight back at him.

'They are excellent. You are professional, yes? It shows in the composition. How many did you take of Scharnhorst's death?'

'Only one of the exact moment. A few around it. If you have seen the photograph I took you must know that I cannot possibly have shot Herr Scharnhorst.'

'Did you know it was going to happen?' He was looking at her very closely. Would he see a lie? This was his job, interrogation.

Should she tell him the truth? That she had warned Cordell, and he had done nothing. Better not to bring MI6 into it at all. It was too hard to explain. And if he questioned Cordell, even graciously, as a foreign diplomat, he would say that he was embarrassed for His Majesty's Government, and yes, she could be guilty.

'No.'

'And yet you very carefully photographed him, just at the right instant. Are you always so . . . fortunate?' His expression was unreadable.

'I took several. I always do. I was lucky enough to have caught the exact moment in one of them. All the rest did not.'

He smiled. It was a warm, easy gesture. Was he actually quite a decent man, in other circumstances? Did most of these men have a side to them that was as human as anyone else?

And did not even the nicest people have a dark, hidden side that their friends had no idea existed? She forced the

281

idea away. She was overthinking it. It was a very bad habit. Mike had teased her about it.

'It takes a lot of work, and luck, to get just the right one, doesn't it?' he said casually.

Had he taken that picture of his wife and child? Without deliberately doing so, she glanced at it, then away again. Was it there precisely to lull whomever he was questioning into thinking of him as a human being, a man gentle with those he loved? What a hideous use of that most beautiful thing.

He saw her eyes. 'Yes. But it's not hard to photograph babies like that.'

'Your wife and daughter?'

'Yes. What do you know of Scharnhorst, Miss Standish? Why did you go to the rally? Is he someone you admire?' There was a shadow in his face as he said that. Was it clever acting, or did the dip in his voice, the instant of harshness, give him away?

How much should she lie? How ugly would it be if she said she admired Scharnhorst, or agreed with anything he said? Could she make herself do that? 'I heard him,' she said simply. 'He wants to exterminate the Jews, the gypsies, the trade unionists and all homosexuals. He said it would cleanse Germany and be the beginning of a new age, a kingdom that would last for ever.' She had intended to keep her voice neutral, but her loathing, and perhaps her fear, too, came through her words all too clearly. The edge of sarcasm was razor sharp.

'It shocked you?' he asked, his own voice carefully neutral.

What should she say? Did her life depend on it? Or was she going to be blamed for killing Scharnhorst regardless of what she said? Would they be any gentler with her? That was an idiotic thought to play with. Mike would be ashamed of her. She thought of him because thinking of Lucas was too much. She would end up weeping in front of the commandant.

'Yes, it shocked me,' she admitted, meeting his clear eyes. They were not blue, as she had thought, but grey. 'He spoke of them as if they were an infestation in the house, termites, or dry rot in the walls.'

'I think that was how he saw them,' Beimler replied. A flush of colour spread up his cheeks. He hesitated, then had the grace not to deny it. 'Where did the rifle come from, Miss Standish?'

'I've no idea. It was there in the room when I got back.'

'How long after Scharnhorst was shot? Be careful what you say. The rifle still smelled of gunpowder.'

'I don't know. The crowds were pretty hysterical. It wasn't easy to get through them. And . . . and I waited long enough to get a pretty good picture of them . . . carrying him away.'

Was that ghoulish? Would he think of that as a terrible intrusion into death?

He appeared not to have heard her. 'Ten minutes? More? Say . . . fifteen?'

'Yes, I think so. Time is different when something shocking happens. You think that it's far longer than it is. Or less.'

'The hotel receptionist doesn't recall anyone else going up to your floor,' he observed.

'Well, he wouldn't, would he!'

'Not if he has any sense, no,' he agreed. He looked at her, and for an instant she saw the bitter humour in him, and the pity; and something deeper, a grief for things that were lost. Did he know what was happening to his country, and hate it? And yet what could he do?

There were a hundred answers to that, all of them terrible.

Was it absurd to sit in this office while he interrogated her about them? The murder of Scharnhorst, whom both of them despised, and both knew she had not killed. Not for any lack of desire to see him dead, but because she knew that the British would be blamed, with all that it meant. Not that she could have shot him anyway, but she might have applauded whoever did.

Beimler asked her more questions about how she had come to Berlin, and she thought of Walter Mann and his help. She told him she had travelled alone. The Commandant asked why she had chosen that hotel. Then, of course, why she had run away and where she had gone. Who had sheltered her, fed her, kept her safe.

Elena lied where necessary about that, too, and felt that he probably knew it, even expected it. But as long as she did not say anything at all that would lead to Jacob or Eli and Zillah, it did not matter.

Oddly enough, he did not suggest that she had prostituted herself to get either money or protection. He assumed she had sought the help of friends from her earlier stay during her father's appointment at the Embassy, and he did not press her for their names. Did he assume she would not tell him? She hoped so. On the other hand, maybe he already knew them?

In between the questions, they spoke of how order had returned to the country. There was work again, and hope. Certainly, there was increased food, even if still not enough. And the despair was gone.

She agreed with him and saw a misery in his eyes that he did not give words to, but neither could he disguise it, although he tried.

Every so often he glanced at the photograph. She did not

ask their names; she did not want to know. In a way, they stood for all the innocents who had no idea what lay ahead, what future guilt or grief.

When he looked across the polished wood desk at her, was that what he was thinking also? Of course, neither of them would ever say.

They mentioned music, briefly. He said his wife played the piano. He wished he could.

'It would be a wonderful thing to recreate such beauty,' he said with a wry, almost dreaming smile. 'To reach back into the past and build such glory, dreams in the air, almost as if the soul of the composer still lived. It is a . . . place to go to . . . to be . . .'

She knew exactly what he meant. There was no need to say so. He saw it in her face. Why use words when silence was better, more fitting both to the understanding, and to the pain of what lay ahead?

Before they could speak further, the other police came for her, the manacles were replaced, and she was returned to her cell. She heard the iron lock shoot home into its place like the weight of a dead thing.

Chapter Twenty-Six

Margot was not going to wait sitting around in her hotel while Cordell, from whom she had heard nothing, looked for Elena. She would at least call on the people she knew best. She had a list of her own, and money for taxis to take her anywhere she wanted. She hailed a cab and set out for the smart Charlottenburg district to the west.

The grand houses looked a little rundown even here. Margot tried first one address and then another. At each, the door was answered by a housekeeper who said she did not know of the former residents Margot sought. At the third place Margot was invited in and offered coffee by Frau Kopleck, who remembered well Charles at the Embassy and had been a friend of Katherine's. When Margot outlined her mission and her fears for Elena, the redoubtable Mitzi Kopleck sympathised. She thought killing Scharnhorst was an excellent thing, but she also thought Elena would not have the courage or the skill to do it.

'Little Elena? Such a big thing to do – a political assassination! I cannot believe the Gestapo really think she did this. They are using her as a scapegoat, I'm afraid, my dear. How did she get caught up in all this anyway?'

'I'm not sure, Frau Kopleck. I . . .'

'Go to the Embassy and see what they can do there, Margot. You are powerless on your own and so many things in Berlin are different now from how they were when your father was here. I'm sorry, I cannot advise you any other way.'

Margot drank her coffee, exchanged news about their families and surreptitiously checked the current whereabouts of other people on her list by asking after them. Mitzi Kopleck knew so many people, and she was no fool.

'Don't waste your time or endanger yourself, Margot,' she advised as she kissed her cheek on the doorstep. 'One question in the wrong place and you never know where it may lead you. You may find Elena but you may also find yourself in deep trouble.'

'Thank you for your advice, Frau Kopleck. I'll be careful,' Margot said, then with a smile and a wave she set out to find the next person on her list.

But each acquaintance she visited said much the same as Mitzi Kopleck had done. They did not know where Elena could be – they certainly didn't think she could have shot Friedrich Scharnhorst – and they expressed sympathy for both the Standish sisters. But they also could not help.

It was after five, too late to do anything really useful, and yet too early to give up, when she decided to make one last effort. She was near where Cordell lived, or used to. Perhaps he still did? It was the time when Cecily was likely to be home. If she were going out for the evening she would be changing for the event. Margot had no qualms about intruding, or being inconvenient.

She gave the taxi driver directions and thanked him when he dropped her there.

It was as she hoped. Cecily was twenty-two now, and she

had always been pretty, friendly and full of life. Winifred was another matter, but Margot was not about to be refused – by anyone.

The butler opened the door and she gave him a ravishing smile.

'Good evening. I am Margot Driscoll – used to be Standish – the daughter of a previous Ambassador. I am in Berlin just for a day or two, but I couldn't leave without calling in. Is Mrs Cordell at home? And Miss Cecily? She was great friends with my sister . . .'

However surprised the butler was at this unexpected visit he would never be rude to a woman so closely related to one of Mr Cordell's previous superiors. He backed away, opening the door for her.

Margot stepped inside. 'So kind of you,' she accepted, still smiling.

He showed her into the elegant drawing room and went to inform Mrs Cordell of her presence.

Margot sat down and forced herself to look casual. She was wearing a pale silk dress, not quite formal enough for this hour in the early evening, but very flattering. It was not like her to be ill at ease in any circumstances. However, this was desperate, dangerous. Intelligence was required, not self-control.

Winifred came into the room and closed the door behind her. She was wearing a greenish blue afternoon dress, very fashionable and, Margot guessed, very expensive. She looked far happier than Margot remembered.

'How pleasant to see you,' Winifred said graciously, holding out both hands, as if to welcome an old friend.

'You are looking so well,' Margot said, meaning it. 'And I adore that dress. The colour is perfect.'

Winifred gave a smile and a slight shrug. 'Thank you. We are entertaining the French this evening and they always set the standard in elegance. I must . . . keep up with things, you know . . .'

'I am sure you are ahead of them,' Margot responded, knowing that Winifred meant fashion and society, the unfortunate shades of competition. 'The French Ambassador's wife will be terribly polite, and green with envy!'

'Oh, it's just a quiet dinner,' Winifred demurred. 'I would invite you to stay and join us, but we are inviting the parents of Cecily's fiancé, Herr and Frau Weissman, and of course Kurt and Cecily. It is the first time they will have been here.' She smiled tentatively. 'Very charming, but . . .'

'You are afraid I will say something . . . incorrect?' Margot said gently.

'Not at all! I am afraid I will,' Winifred confessed. 'They are of the new aristocracy . . .' She stopped, looking at Margot to see if she understood what that meant.

'Connected to the Führer?' Margot said with a sudden catch in her voice.

'Yes. Herr Weissman is something in the new government. I asked Roger to find out exactly what, discreetly. We ought to know. And Kurt is in the police – the Gestapo.' She smiled as she said it. Could she possibly mean it? Perhaps he was a nice young man . . . if any nice young men joined such a body? She must not judge too quickly.

Winifred was waiting for her reaction.

'He must be doing very well,' she said. 'I hear they are a very élite group . . .'

'Yes, they are. And Kurt is already rising.' Winifred clearly did not know what to say next.

'If he loves Cecily, then he has excellent judgement.' The

words sounded hollow even to Margot. 'And if Cecily loves him,' she went on, 'then there must be a lot of good in him.' What a hypocrite she was. 'And perhaps she will sustain even more . . . as time goes by.'

'Yes,' Winifred agreed. 'Yes. I . . . all I want is her happiness.'

'Of course.'

'Roger has only just met him. I am . . . I am hoping this evening will go well . . .'

'I am sure it will,' Margot lied. Now she understood Cordell's silence. She wished profoundly that she had not given him a list of Elena's friends. Some of them were Jewish.

Almost as if hearing her thoughts, Winifred spoke again. 'You are just visiting Berlin for a short time? A pity. We would like to have seen more of you. Are you here with your sister? Elena, isn't it?'

Margot looked at the woman. Was it possible she didn't know of the manhunt for Elena? Of course she knew! But nothing was going to interfere with her daughter's engagement dinner! Before she could respond, Winifred spoke.

'In these uncertain times,' she said with a smile, 'I am so happy to see Cecily settled. And in such a . . . a fortunate family.'

Her voice wavered, and Margot realised in that instant how afraid for her daughter Winifred was. If Cordell were moved, and Cecily wanted to stay here, where her friends were, she would be desperately alone. Winifred would have to go wherever Roger went. But if Cecily married here, she would not be alone . . . lonely.

'Of course,' Margot said quickly. She understood only too well. She could see why Winifred might have done all she could to foster this romance, this apparent safety for her only child. This was not a heroic marriage to a dissenter, or worse, a Jew who would be hunted down, driven out. This was a son of the master race. Cecily would be as safe as anyone could be. 'And you like him?' she asked, hearing the false note in her own voice.

'I like anyone who keeps Cecily safe, and happy, I . . . I don't really know him yet. Perhaps you would like to stay and meet them? They should be here quite soon. And Cecily would be very sorry to think that you were here, and she missed you. Perhaps a cup of tea?'

The last thing Margot wanted was to stay, to be forced to see this young man. She could remember perfectly the night she and Paul were engaged. Her happiness was like a tidal wave, sweeping everything in front of it. 'Of course,' she said, and instantly regretted it. 'And I'd love a good cup of tea.' That at least was true. And perhaps she would see in this young man something of what Cecily saw. She should not prejudge. Just don't mention Elena!

She had not long to wait. She had barely finished her tea and was feeling refreshed when they arrived. She heard them in the hall, and a moment later the drawing-room door opened and Cecily came in, her arms outstretched in greeting. She was all elegance, dark curls untidy but gorgeous, silk skirt brightly coloured.

'Margot! How wonderful to see you. You've made my day perfect.' She hugged Margot warmly, then turned to the young man in stiff, grey uniform behind her. 'This is Kurt. We are going to be married – very soon.'

Margot looked into the just-off handsome face of the young man. 'Congratulations. I hope you will be very happy.' The words were dead on her lips as she met his perfect smile, and eyes as steady and cold as a polar dawn.

'I am sure we shall,' he replied, putting his hand on Cecily and drawing her a little closer to him.

Margot's smile froze on her face. Oh God, Roger! What have you got into? she thought, and tried frantically to think of something to say.

Chapter Twenty-Seven

Elena spent a long, difficult night in the police cell. She was so tired she thought she might sleep, but every time she drifted off into troubled dreams, she was disturbed by footsteps, voices, and now and then the door opening and someone shining a light on her. Then before she could ask whoever it was what they wanted, the door was closed and the iron flanges of the lock slammed into place.

The bed was uncomfortable, a straw-filled palliasse on a wooden frame. The ends of the pieces of straw poked through the canvas ticking. The single blanket was grey and smelled of rancid butter.

Perhaps she did not have much time left? If they found her guilty, they would execute her, surely. How? Shooting? Hanging? Did the Germans hang people, or was it just an English thing to do? The French used a guillotine. Bloody, but quick. Except in the case of Louis XVI, poor soul. They had botched it and had to make three attempts before they succeeded. At least, that's what the history books said.

Was this really it, the end? Was there a heaven? An afterlife? Would she find Mike there? She had not really thought about it very hard. She had accepted it, in the pain of losing him. People did. They were too dazed to question whether all that they said was true, or just to give each other comfort. If you say a thing often enough, at least some of the time you believe it. And who would say to a grieving mother, or widow, that death was the end?

She had never felt so utterly alone. Would anybody ever tell her family, her mother, or Lucas, what had happened to her? Please God – if there was one? – let her do this with courage.

She thought of famous people whose deaths had been witnessed and recorded.

Charles I, who had been executed at the end of January, and asked if he could wear two doublets, so he would not shiver in the cold, and people would think that he was afraid.

How did you keep from being sick when you knew you were going to be shot any minute, absolutely for certain? At having your knees buckle and have you collapse on the ground? How very pathetic, and human. She didn't want to be pitiful. She would look them in the eye and tell them to go to hell!

She drifted in and out of sleep, sometimes dreaming, sometimes falling into a soft, grey oblivion.

When she woke it was light and someone was standing by her cot with a dish of porridge and a wedge of bread. There was something in an enamel mug that looked like tea. It steamed gently, so at least it was hot.

She thanked the guard and took it. Please heaven she was not so clenched up inside that she would throw it up. Was torture better on an empty stomach or a full one? She ate it anyway. It tasted stale, but it was edible, and perhaps she was better for it.

They came for Elena far sooner than she had expected.

She was still sitting with the breakfast dish before her and the dregs of her tea, black and bitter.

'Stand up,' one of the policemen ordered. These three were men she had not seen before. She obeyed. There was no point in causing more trouble than she already had, just for the sake of pride. There was no one to impress.

The thing that hurt perhaps even more deeply than fear was the sense of being so alone. These policemen were all people who looked like most Englishmen. Only their uniforms and their language differentiated them. And yet she had never felt so violated.

Had Mike felt something like this, just before going over the top into the gunfire? She tried to think of him, to imagine he was there in spirit with her. 'Chin up, kiddo,' he would have said, with a slightly twisted smile.

She was walked through the station and out to the back, where a car was waiting for them.

One of the police caught her surprise and smiled. It was amusement, without warmth. 'We're giving you to the Gestapo,' he said with satisfaction. 'You did not know Scharnhorst, did you!' It was a statement.

'No . . . I didn't!' she said fiercely.

'Then it's not a domestic murder, it's assassination. That belongs to the Gestapo. It's an offence against the state, not just a local thing, like you'd killed to steal, or committed some crime against a neighbour.'

'I didn't kill him at all!' she said levelly, almost.

'Bad shot, eh?' he said sarcastically. 'You saying you didn't mean to kill him? Who did you mean to kill?'

She started to deny it again and realised there was no point. They would think whatever they wanted to. Perhaps their own careers depended on catching the assassin. Or at

295

least seeming to. Reality and nightmare blended into each other.

There was a driver sitting at the wheel, on the left-hand side, and for a moment she forgot where she was. It was all unreal. This was not the Germany she knew, the place in her memory where she had been happy, even amid the destruction and loss immediately following the war.

An officer got out of the other side of the car and came around to escort her. Not that she would really have escaped, with her hands manacled together behind her back, and the police on either side of her.

He looked at her curiously, with cold, careful eyes. Then he opened the passenger door at the back and nodded for her to get in. She obeyed rather awkwardly, hands behind you not being the natural way to climb into a car and sit down, unable to straighten your skirt or rearrange yourself.

The door slammed and he walked around to the other side.

They pulled away from the kerb into the traffic. Were the doors locked? She looked. Yes. Of course they were.

It was a clear day, sun shining, and to judge from the movement of people along the pavement, the flutter of summer skirts, the occasional hand to steady a hat, there was quite a breeze.

She saw groups of Brownshirts. You could tell them by the way they stood, not just their uniforms. There was a confidence in them. A sense of power. They could do whatever they wished, and everybody knew it. The only thing worse was the Gestapo, the secret police. Everybody knew that, too.

The questioning at the police station had been no more than a few hard slaps. The Gestapo interrogation would be much worse.

Suddenly, she was drenched in cold sweat. What if they believed that Ian had intended to warn of the assassination, and she had killed him so that she could go ahead and do it? It fitted perfectly with the facts they would know.

And Cordell? What would he say, if they had even questioned him at all? That she had said nothing to him about Scharnhorst? There was no proof. She could have gone to the Embassy for any reason.

She was trapped. Anything she said, true or not, could be twisted to condemn her. And there was no escape from the physical captivity. Both of her guards were armed, and she was manacled and could not run, even if she had anywhere to run to.

They turned a corner into a smaller street.

It was another few minutes at least before they pulled up outside a very ordinary building, just like thousands of others. The man in the front passenger seat got out and opened the door for her.

'Out,' he said, jerking his hand very slightly to make his meaning clearer.

Awkwardly, Elena climbed out, having to balance with difficulty. He took her arm when he thought she might fall. Or did he imagine it would be some kind of chance to run? And be shot in the back? Guilty of attempting to escape?

Reluctantly, trying to walk upright, and stumbling on the step, she went inside. It was small, anonymous-seeming. A narrow-shouldered man with a round belly was waiting for her. He looked ridiculous in his uniform. His rimless glasses were sliding down his nose.

Her manacles were undone, and then relocked with her hands in front of her.

She was forced to sit down in a chair opposite him and

297

the questioning began. He established her name, her nationality, then the facts of her trip to Berlin from Italy. It was all the details that she had already admitted. His voice was higher than one might have expected, and nasal. She could feel the hatred emanating from him the way heat does from a fire.

Neither of the other men had left, but were standing to attention, one at the door, the other at the window.

The questions went on. The man with the glasses lit a cigarette and blew smoke out with an expression of distaste, as if he did not like the flavour of it. She looked at him very steadily. His eyes were neither green nor brown behind the magnification of his lenses.

'You do not agree with Herr Scharnhorst's plans for the destiny of the German people . . .' He made it more of a statement than a question.

How much should she lie? If she said she agreed with Scharnhorst, would that save her life? Or at least, end it without too much pain?

Probably not. And if there was a hereafter, how would she face Mike, and all the others who had died, especially those who had never denied who they were, or what they believed? And if there was nothing? Oblivion? It would hardly matter anyway. Please God, she could do this with some dignity.

'No, I don't. But it's none of my business,' she replied.

He took a deep draw on his cigarette, took it out of his mouth, then stubbed it out, hard, on the back of her hand. The pain made her gag. The room swam around her and she thought she was going to vomit.

'So, you shot him,' he said.

'No . . .' She knew immediately that it was a mistake. Carefully, as if he were preparing for something he was going

298

to enjoy, he took another cigarette out of his case and lit it, pulling the smoke into his lungs, then after barely a moment, letting it out again.

Could she bear it again? The pain was appalling. It shot up her arm as if the red-hot ash were still there on her skin.

The telephone rang, sharp and shrill, like a scream.

Reluctantly, he picked it up. He listened for a moment, and agreed with whomever was on the line, apparently with reluctance.

'Orders,' he said to the man near the door, who was senior of the two. 'They want her right now. You're to take her to Headquarters.'

'Sir?'

'Don't stand there, you fool! Get her into the car and take her!'

The man snapped to attention. 'Yes, sir!'

Dizzy with the pain in her hand, throbbing now, she was led back to the car and pushed into the rear seat. The brush of her hand against the rough serge of the man's uniform was almost unbearable. She felt waves of nausea wash over her as the door slammed and the car lurched forward.

It was a nightmare, and it was not going to stop. From here on it would get worse, until the end. She was not special, she was merely one of hundreds, thousands. She could die with courage, or without it. Did it hurt to die? Or was it just like a darkness that filled you until there was nothing else left?

She was jerked out of such thoughts by a violent collision, hurling her forward, then sideways until she landed on the floor and there seemed to be broken glass everywhere. They were not moving. She tried to get up, but with her hands behind her back it was almost impossible.

She was wedged. The driver's side of the car was stoven in, the doors jammed.

The door on the other side opened and someone reached in for her, clasping her by the upper arms, easing her forward. Her burned hand knocked against the seat and she thought she was going to faint, but after a few desperate moments, she was hauled to her feet and found herself standing in the street, swaying a little, the fresh air reviving her.

The man who helped her was another German officer in uniform. More police! She had not been rescued, just changed captors. He was pulling her forward. There was blood on his arms, and on his face. He must have been driving the other car, the one that had rammed into them. He looked very white, his eyes frightened, as if he had been wounded mortally. And yet there was no visible wound.

'Come on,' he said urgently. 'You've got to run!'

Run? Why?

'Come on! Hurry. We've only got moments.' He fumbled to unlock her manacles. How did he have the keys? 'Come on!' Now that she was free and could come more easily, he dragged her into a shambling run along the street and to a corner.

There was a furious shout behind them. Gunfire! At least one of the two men in her car must have survived the crash.

They made it to the corner and just as they were about to turn into the next street, there was another shot. She felt nothing, except that the man holding her arm let go, almost dragging her with him as he collapsed on to the ground. Beimler! It was Beimler who had questioned her before. The man with the photograph of his wife and daughter on his desk. They had spoken briefly about music.

She stopped and bent down to see if she could help him.

300

Someone pulled at her other arm, ignoring the burn on her hand, now raging as if it were on fire.

'Come on! You can't help him. He's gone!' His voice was choked with grief.

She looked up to argue, and saw Walter Mann, tears on his face.

'Come on!' he shouted at her. Pulling her up by force. 'Don't make it all for nothing!'

'But . . .'

'He's dead, Elena. You can't do anything except turn him over, so it looks as if his men shot him from the front.' He leaned over quickly and heaved the body over. Then he pulled her by the hand, so much it ached all the way through her. She thought that the driver of the car was dead, or too badly wounded to stand, but that the other guard had shot Beimler. If so, he would appear round that corner any minute.

She obeyed, running and stumbling another twenty yards, into an alley, where she banged herself against the wall in clumsiness. Then Walter commanded her to climb into a car that he had left at the kerb, engine still running.

There were more shots in the street behind them. As the car roared away, a bullet shattered the rear window and left a jagged hole in the windscreen.

Chapter Twenty-Eight

'We can't just leave him!' Elena said, as the car swung out of the side street and into the mainstream traffic, an anonymous black car, like any other.

'Yes, we can. He's dead, Elena,' Walter said gently. 'He chose to do the right thing, knowing what it would cost him. They know you didn't have a gun, and neither of the two that had you is going to admit to shooting him, not when they realise who he is.'

'I know he interrogated me . . . Beimler . . . I mean, but who is he?'

'He's pretty high up in the police.' There was a catch in Walter's voice, more emotion than he knew how to mask. 'A good man, caught in a bad part of the system.'

She felt a wave of emotion engulf her, too big for words. She had hardly known him, but she had seen the tenderness in his eyes as he looked at his child, and the trust in the little girl's face. She knew only kindness. Now she would never see her father again. Would she understand, sometime in the years ahead, what he had done, and why?

It takes a great man to make such a choice. Would his

wife understand? Elena was the beneficiary, but it wasn't for her that he had died, it was for what he believed in.

The car swung out of traffic on to a smaller road, and for several minutes neither she nor Walter spoke.

Walter was picking up speed, weaving the car through the traffic with considerable skill. It was late afternoon and the cars were coming from every direction. She wanted to ask where they were going, but there was another question at the forefront of her mind. She had to know, but she was afraid of the answer.

'How did you find me?' She forced the words out.

He glanced at her, and then back at the road. 'Beimler,' he said quietly. 'I've been looking for you for a while. He stood out as . . . a man of conviction. Your coming here had something to do with Scharnhorst, didn't it?'

Should she deny it? She had to supply an answer of some sort, and this was the obvious one. 'How did you know?'

He smiled. 'I didn't, until I saw your picture in the newspaper. That was very clearly you. You look different now, but not so much that anyone who'd met you wouldn't know you. I remember the ring you wear on your right hand. It's still there.'

'It won't come off.' As if it mattered. 'You . . . you took a risk getting me. Why?'

'You can't work that out for yourself?' There was a wisp of humour in his face, there and then gone again. 'And does it matter?'

Her hands were clenched so tightly her nails were digging into her palms. The answer did not matter now, but it might at some time far ahead. 'Where are we going?' she asked instead.

'To pick up a new passport for you, and then to catch the night train to Paris. We should be there in time for the Calais train, and then the ferry to Dover.'

'You make it sound so easy.' It was not criticism, it was gratitude, even admiration.

He glanced sideways at her with a quick smile. 'Not fooling you, am I?'

'Thank you for trying . . .'

It was beginning to feel slightly unreal. She was so tired, she had slipped beyond exhaustion into a strange dreamlike state where only the pain in her hand had any urgency of reality. It was throbbing so she could feel it right up to her shoulder. The rest – the fear, the revulsion, the pity and the debt to a woman she had seen only in a photograph, and a child who might never understand – were all around her, closer than her skin. Perhaps the pain in her hand was preferable.

She glanced out of the window. The light was beginning to fade. She had no idea where they were. It was a part of the city she was unfamiliar with.

Walter suddenly put his foot down hard on the accelerator and the car shot forward, then in a hundred yards he swung to the right, and then right again.

'Is somebody following us?' Elena asked quickly.

'I think so,' Walter replied. 'Hang on. We've got to lose them. If they ram us, we're lost.' As he spoke, he twisted the wheel and the car turned violently to the right, slithered around a corner and then, leaning forward and gripping the wheel, he put his foot down again.

Elena was thrown to one side and then the other, as the car swerved again and picked up speed. Car horns were blaring at them. Walter took no notice. He drove with extreme skill, weaving in and out of lanes, often against the flow. Twice they actually grazed cars coming in the opposite direction. The first blow carried off the wing mirror, the second tore a scar right down the driver's side with a scream of metal and curses from the other driver. Walter ignored it and rammed his foot down even harder, the tyres squealing as the car shot forward.

Elena kept her eyes open, not because she knew where they were, or even where they were headed, but because she was compelled to look at the sheer skill of Walter's driving. It was like being on a racing circuit. They swerved, slid around corners, or even across the road in an instant's gap, and swept the other way, and then went speeding in the opposite direction. She felt her heart pounding so violently it made her whole body shake. But it was victory, not fear.

Walter was smiling, but his teeth were clenched so hard his jaw muscles bulged. All his teeth would ache tomorrow, if they lived until tomorrow. If they were caught now, he would pay as heavy a price as she.

She did not speak. They were probably both thinking the same thing, perhaps even feeling the same. They knew the cost of losing. She had no choice, but why did he do it? What would she do if this were England? Would she stay emotionally safe, and deny the possibility of the evil being anything to do with choice? Would she tell herself it was a temporary necessity, and as soon as survival was assured, it would be cast off? The older order, the old moralities would be restored?

She knew the answer before she found the words for it. You do not need to believe evil, only to use its methods. You will get accustomed to them, until eventually they are not your last choice, but your first. For a while, you can excuse it to yourself, and then eventually you will not bother. Nobody believes it any more. You have forgotten what you are fighting for, it is now only to win! And the more you win, the more you justify it, until the whole idea of right and wrong disappears and only winning matters.

It did not matter now. Walter was helping her, whatever his reason. Right? Wrong? Someone he had loved, and who had died for the same cause?

'Watch the road!' she shouted as a huge car passed them with a black and white swastika fluttering from its hood. 'We can't . . . we can't be stopped for speeding!' Her voice choked. 'He'll not forgive you for being a better driver than he is.'

Walter laughed, but he pulled back a bit all the same. 'That was an officer's car; he won't be driving it himself.'

'Please . . .' Then she realised how frightened she sounded. 'I'm sorry. I should demand to know where the hell they think they're going at that speed!'

Walter swivelled quickly in his seat to look at her with a momentary frown. Then he realised she was not serious, he relaxed. 'Good idea,' he agreed. 'Maybe I can catch up with them so you can ask them.'

'Do you even know where you're going?' She was not sure she wanted the answer.

'Of course I do! We'll get a picture for your passport. We'll take that when we get to Max's. I think you could do with a new dress. Forgive me, but you look like a shop assistant, one who sells groceries or hardware. And we should get that hand seen to, before it gets infected.'

'Of course,' she said tartly. 'I would rather be shot than die of septicaemia!'

'Which is good, because that's the more likely of the two,' he replied drily.

In spite of herself, she laughed, a little bit out of control, but laughter all the same.

'I'll get you a red dress. Nice and brave,' he added.

'We haven't time,' she replied. 'You said the night train.'

'There are still lights in it.'

'What?'

'Lights . . . in the train. They'll see it's red.'

'You want me to be noticed!'

'Yes, of course. Skulking around in the shadows in colourless blue, you'll be suspected . . . of something! Striding out in scarlet as if you owned the place and are perfectly used to people staring at you – in fact, you like it – they will never think you are running away from anything. You know, if you tried, you could be really beautiful.'

For once, she was stumped for words. She was not even sure if he meant any of it, or if he was trying to make her behave in the best way to survive. And that could be as much for his own sake as for hers. If she was caught, then so was he.

She ignored the compliment. It would be ridiculous to take it seriously. But she sat up a little straighter. 'Then you had better get me one that fits properly,' she said with a smile. 'I should look as if I always wore such things, not as if I've borrowed it.'

'I will,' he promised. 'We're nearly there. Have something to eat, wash and put some decent makeup on. Quite a lot. A woman who wears red dresses doesn't look like a terrified rabbit!'

'Have you ever been bitten by an angry rabbit,' she retorted.

'Do rabbits get angry?' He began to laugh, and she joined in, because the whole thing was so ridiculous, and dangerous, and maybe they were going to escape after all!

They were going much more slowly now. It seemed to be a residential area. He pulled up outside a fairly small house.

'We're here,' he announced. 'We must be quick.' He opened the car door and climbed out, then came around and opened her door, but she had done it already and was halfway out. He held the door and offered his hand.

'Please hurry. We don't have a lot of time, and we need to catch the night train.' He locked the car and led the way up to the front door. He knocked three times and it was opened immediately.

The man who answered almost pulled them inside, and then slammed the door. He barely looked at Walter, but stared at Elena as if studying her face. He was a little shorter than she, instantly forgettable in appearance, except for the intelligence in his pale green eyes, and she noticed that his fingers were stained with ink.

Walter introduced him only as 'Max'.

'Come back in an hour,' he told Walter. He shook his head. 'You didn't say she was going to be this much of a mess.'

Elena was stung. She thought of what anyone wearing a red dress would say. She raised her eyebrows. 'Is it beyond you, do you think?'

He was startled for a moment, and then he smiled, a curious, crooked expression. 'Nothing is beyond me, young woman. I can make you look as if you were born brave and beautiful; I can't make you behave like it. Perhaps Walter can do that?' There was more than a touch of sarcasm in his voice.

'I'll be back,' Walter said from the doorway. Then he

opened it again and went out, leaving Elena alone with the man.

For a moment, she would have given anything to be able to follow Walter, but she thought Max was expecting that, so she stood a little straighter. 'My shoes are fine. I'm comfortable in them, and I don't want to be any taller.'

'No, you don't,' he agreed. 'Not that it would matter if you did. I don't have any women's shoes big enough to fit you! A pity. It would be better if people looked at your feet, rather than your face!'

'Well, maybe you could paint a rude verse on them?' she suggested waspishly. 'That would draw their attention, long enough at least to read it!'

He looked at her, eyes wide. 'You have a sense of the absurd. That's good. I will try to save you. We need somebody left alive to laugh at us as we sink beneath the slime. Sense of humour isn't enough, you need to have a real deep awareness of the ridiculous. Come with me. We'll see what we can do with you. First wash, for goodness' sake! Where the hell have you been? No! I don't want to know.' He led the way toward a downstairs bathroom and showed her soap and a small, rather thin towel, but it appeared to be clean. 'You'll have to keep your underwear. Haven't anything that'll fit you. But we'll get rid of that dress. You look like a fugitive housemaid! The art of disappearing is to look like something else, so people can stare right at you, and not see a fugitive, but someone who has a right to be here, and is afraid of no one. Well, get on with it! And wash your hair. Clean, it's probably quite good. And don't use all the hot water! Not that there is that much.'

Twenty minutes later, Elena was sitting in her underwear

with a blanket around her, while Max did her hair and made her face up, then put an old blouse on her to get a passport photograph. By the time Walter returned with the dress, and a light coat to go with it, she was ready to put it on.

She watched while he lifted it out of its box and held it up. He waited for her to speak.

It was breathtaking. Scarlet silk, in the small room it seemed to radiate its own light. It was impossible to tell its cut without a body inside it, to make it hang exactly right. A dress hanger would not do it, not even a padded one.

'Well?' Walter asked. There seemed to be a look of anticipation in his face, even of hope.

She put out her hand and touched it softly. She looked up and met his eyes. 'It's gorgeous!' She was praying silently that it fitted her. 'Wearing that, I should be able to slay . . .' She wouldn't be predictable and say 'dragons', as she had intended to. '. . . rabbits,' she finished. 'Really angry ones.'

Walter burst into laughter. Perhaps it was relief.

Max looked totally lost. He shook his head. 'Not German rabbits,' was all he said.

Elena took off the blanket and slipped into the dress. For a horrible instant she was afraid it was going to be too small, but then she fastened it and found it was perfect. She looked at Walter and saw the same delight reflected in his face.

'Superb!' he said, breathing out slowly. 'You look fit to take on anyone.' He put his head to one side a little. 'Are you ready to?'

'Of course,' she lied. 'Even furious German rabbits.' It was going to take a mighty effort to make that true. But too many people had risked their lives for her not to succeed. She had every hope of getting out – of going home – to be free of the hunger and the fear. How dare she not be grateful for it? She turned to Max. 'Thank you. You've done the outside very well. I'll do the inside.' She touched the red silk with her fingertips.

Walter picked up Elena's camera bag, and her handbag, and put them all into one larger bag. Commandant Beimler must have made sure her vital belongings were in the getaway car for her! 'Come on. We've got to get to the station.'

'Papers?' she asked, squashing a moment's panic, while Max handed her a jacket and some light gloves to cover her injured hand.

Walter patted his pocket. 'I've got them. I need to buy only tickets to Paris. From there we'll go to Calais. Different terminal. Not far.'

'I know!' Then cold reality gripped her again, just for a moment. 'What's my name, please? I think I ought to know . . .' She tried to make it light.

He looked for a moment at the ceiling, and then down again. 'Anna Hermann,' he replied.

'Thank you.' She thanked Max again and followed Walter out to the darkening street.

Walter took her arm a little sharply. 'Don't be so . . . innocent!' he said. 'Don't look like a fugitive, but you've got to damned well think like one! Max doesn't need to know your new name.'

'Oh . . .' She realised her mistake. She had relaxed completely. How stupid. Walter had seemed to trust Max, so she had also, and let her guard down.

He pulled her more gently. 'It's Marta Lindt, like the chocolate. You ought to be able to remember that, and spell it. Martha, but without the "h", and then L.I.N.D.T. Remember Lindt chocolate.' He smiled as if he meant it. 'I

311

don't suppose you've had much really good chocolate lately. We'll buy some when we get to London, to celebrate.'

She was surprised. 'Are you coming all the way to London?'

'Yes. I'm going to take you right to the door. You're not fit to be alone.' Then he gave a sudden smile that lit his whole face.

'Thank you,' she replied. It was the only thing she could say, in the circumstances.

Chapter Twenty-Nine

'Come on, Toby,' Lucas said at last. He had been standing in the bluebell woods, looking at the light slanting through the high branches of the wild pear trees. They were small flowers, like drifting snowflakes, high up, catching the sun. It was time to go. He had accepted the decision that perhaps he should have made earlier, even years earlier. He would tell Charles as much of the truth as he wanted to know.

Toby arrived and sat at his feet, looking up expectantly.

'Time to go home,' Lucas told him. 'Stand still a minute.' He always said that to him, although Toby very rarely fidgeted while his lead was being clipped on to his collar again. 'Come on.' Lucas set out to walk back to the car.

It would be difficult talking to Charles now, but he would understand. His own work was highly confidential. The difference was that his family had always known what he did in principle, if not in detail. With Lucas, everything was hidden, secretive.

No, that was only an excuse, though it hardly mattered now. What Lucas was really thinking, and what drove him to tell Charles now, was the very real fear gnawing, like an ulcer in the soul, that Elena might not come home. No wonder they called some of them 'rodent ulcers'; he could feel the pain of it inside him.

Charles might believe that the political climate in Germany was a spring storm that would pass, and that better times would come. Lucas knew, or thought he knew, that it was the beginning of a long winter that would kill much of the landscape, including the dearest of their own. They would need each other. There was no room for quarrels. The real wounds would be deep enough; all others needed to be dealt with first. That meant now . . . today.

When he got home he telephoned Charles at the Foreign Office and made an appointment for them to have lunch together.

'Today?' Charles sounded doubtful and suspicious. It was not something Lucas had ever done before. 'How about Friday? I'm free then.'

'Today, Charles,' Lucas replied. 'If you have a lunch appointment you can't change, I'll see you in your office. But I would prefer it's where we will not be interrupted.'

'What's wrong? Is Mother ill? Or is it Elena?'

'No, your mother is fine. I'll be there at noon.'

'Father . . .'

'Noon.' Lucas hung up the phone. It was not something to be told in bits and pieces, and while he could not see Charles's face to read his reactions he could picture them perfectly in his mind. It was going to be hard enough now, after all the years of concealment, no matter how necessary they had been. Complete discretion, even from your own family, was not a suggestion, it was a command.

He did not drive into the city. There was nowhere near the Foreign Office to park, and traffic was always bad. The city was two thousand years old, and not designed for horse traffic, let alone automobiles. Now it was the biggest city in the world, and a nightmare to navigate. The Underground, then on foot, was the only way to do it. The trick was to prevent the time between now and then pulling his nerves raw. Rodent ulcers! He could feel the rat's teeth inside him.

He arrived at Charles's office at five minutes to twelve, and Charles was waiting for him. He looked relaxed, as if he were receiving some foreign dignitary, but underneath it Lucas could see that he was frightened. He still governed the desire to move his weight from one foot to the other, an obvious sign of tension, but he was too stiff. There was no ease inside him at all. If he was not careful, sooner or later he would knock something over.

Lucas felt guilty doing this to him. He should have found some way to tell him the truth when he retired. No matter how difficult their relationship, it was up to him to have tried. No one was supposed to know about the existence of MI6, but Charles understood necessary secrets. He would not repeat any of it.

'I've booked a table,' Charles said, looking steadily at Lucas. 'I'm not sure how long I can spare for you.' He came round from behind his desk and walked towards the door. 'Are you ready? I'd rather go before the phone rings or somebody wants something.'

Lucas turned back to the door and opened it. 'Right,' he agreed.

They walked in silence, neither of them wishing to make the pretence of normality. The restaurant was only a couple of blocks away, and Charles had reserved a quiet corner table, slightly apart from other diners. They took their seats and ordered, then the moment the waiter left, Charles spoke.

'Well, what is so urgent? It can't be good, or you would simply have told me.' He cleared his throat. 'Has Elena got herself into more trouble? Why would you know that, and not me? What was she afraid to tell me? Does she need money?'

Lucas saw that Charles was talking too quickly, naming the problems he could bear to think of, the ones he could deal with, blocking out the ones that were unbearable. The constant thought of Mike's death was in his eyes, and Lucas could see it. It was at the back of his own mind also. It took him into the past, whatever he did to try to prevent it. 'No,' he said quietly. 'I don't have any news of her, except that she was alive and well a couple of days ago, but unable to leave Germany.'

'What the hell do you mean, "unable"?' Charles snapped. 'Is she injured? Ill?'

'No . . .'

'For God's sake, Father! Stop playing the fool and tell me. I'm fed up with your oblique games. You've played secrets for years, and I don't know why! I—'

'I know you don't,' Lucas cut across him. 'I couldn't tell you at the time, any more than you can tell me the secret parts of your job.'

'What the hell is so very secret about the civil service? You shuffled papers for some minister of this or that . . .'

'No, Charles, I had one of the jobs that even one's own family doesn't know about,' Lucas said sharply. 'I could have told you when I retired, and I think now that I should have done, and for that I apologise. Secrecy became a habit. I never discussed it with anyone, not even your mother.'

The little remaining colour drained from Charles's face. 'What were you? A hangman, or something?' It was half a joke, and probably the worst thing he could think of, and yet the fear was real in his eyes.

'MI6. A department no one knows of. Military Intelligence,' Lucas said quietly. 'We were not allowed to tell anyone, even family. I suppose a single careless word could jeopardise so much – lives . . .'

Charles was incredulous. 'You? MI6?' Then he stopped abruptly as it dawned on him that Lucas was perfectly serious. 'What the hell could you do for them? You're an academic . . . aren't you?'

'Not really,' Lucas breathed in and out slowly. 'Actually, I was head of it.'

'You . . .?' Charles still could not grasp it. 'Does Mother know?'

'Yes, she does know. At least she guessed some of it.'

Lucas was not sure if that was a greater blow to Charles than the fact that he had not known. Should Lucas tell him the truth, that Josephine had done her own secret work in the war? If they did not get Elena back . . . He wanted to block out the thought, but his mind refused. If she did not come back, they would need each other more than ever before. It would be too late then to mend untruths. There was no time for lies at all, of any sort.

'I didn't tell her,' he said very quietly. 'But I found out in the last few days that she knew. She did her own work during the war, decoding work. Secret stuff as well.'

'You knew.' It sounded almost like an accusation.

'I had to. We used much of her decoding work in our own.' He looked at the hurt in Charles's face, a sudden knowledge of the exclusion he had imagined for so long.

But his loneliness was from the things of his own life that he could not share! Lucas reached a hand towards Charles, who ignored it. 'It is for everyone's protection. No one should have to bear the weight of another person's secrets, of the decisions that go wrong, the deaths you can't prevent, and also be protected from ever having the suspicion of a careless word having come from you.' He leaned a little further forward. 'Do you tell Katherine every secret grief or betrayal you know about? Every suspicion you have of incompetence? Would you tell Margot, or Elena?'

'No, of course not,' Charles said hotly. 'But you could have told me after you left.'

'I know. And I'm sorry.' Lucas meant it. He regretted it deeply. Perhaps they were so different, they had grown apart so far, that they could not now be reconciled.

'Or have you really left?' Charles asked. That was a challenge. There was accusation in his voice, and hurt at discovering Lucas had held more power and more secrets than he ever would. 'Have you left?' he repeated.

'Yes, I have. I get bits of news now and then, but no action. I mean it, I miss it, but I don't have the ability any more, or the trust of any but a very few of the people I used to work with who are still there.' It hurt, putting it like that, it was so final in its loss. He could not tell Charles about Peter Howard. That knowledge was not his to share.

Charles was silent for a few moments. When he spoke at last, his voice was tight, as if his whole chest hurt. 'Is this because Elena hasn't come back yet? You're telling me . . . in case . . . in case she doesn't?' His face was too full of fear for there to be any room in it for anger.

Lucas's mind raced. One second, two . . . it was already too long. An honest denial would have been instant. If he had to wonder how to phrase it, then it was not the truth.

'I tried to find her,' Lucas said quietly. 'Sent a man out. But it seems your daughter is very resourceful, and apparently violent, when needs must.'

'That's ridiculous!' Charles burst out. He had to deny it somehow. 'If you had said Margot, I'd have believed you, but not Elena! She hasn't the—'

'It seems they are less different than you think . . . than we all thought.'

Charles leaned his elbows on the table and put his head in his hands.

Lucas did not say anything. Words would only make it look as if he did not understand.

The waiter came and he waved him away.

'I've got to be able to do something!' Charles said desperately. 'I've got contacts, favours I can draw on.'

'We both have,' Lucas said gently. 'But things have changed since you or I knew Berlin. She's got someone helping her. We could make it worse.' He hesitated. He had to tell Charles the whole truth now. 'And loyalties change. We have at least one traitor in the ranks. Telling the people we used to trust could put her in more danger.'

'Not the people I would ask!' Charles said angrily.

'Charles! People change, pressures change. We all have hostages to fortune. Let it be!'

Charles stared at Lucas long and steadily, as if searching for honesty in his face. 'You're sure?'

'As sure as I can be.'

At last Charles seemed satisfied. 'Finally, the truth. It makes sense of so many things. I can't even argue with it. Katherine never asks me about the sensitive stuff. She knows

I can't tell her. Wish I could. Sometimes it's lonely, especially if you don't know if you've made the right decision – or the wrong one. Far more often . . . I don't know. Were you always sure you were right?'

'No.'

'How do you live with it?' It was an honest question.

'One day at a time. Talk to the dog a lot,' Lucas replied with a half-smile. 'Dogs are endlessly patient, and they never repeat anything.'

At last Charles smiled, but there were tears in his eyes. 'I think I'll get a dog,' he said quietly. 'God knows, I need one.'

Chapter Thirty

It was already early dusk when Elena and Walter reached the railway station in Berlin. It was crowded, but it did not take Elena more than moments to pick out the police at all gates into or out of every entrance, and at platform ticket collection points. There were also Brownshirts, even more easily recognisable, all heavily armed.

She felt Walter's hand tightening on her arm. It was surprisingly comforting, given that she had known him just a short time.

'Chin up, eyes straight ahead,' he said, leaning a little towards her so no one in the crowd pressing around them would hear his words. 'You have nothing to fear. Remember, you are one of the winners! You are fair-haired, blue-eyed, you speak German. You are one of the master race!'

She smiled in spite of herself. It sounded so ridiculous.

'That's better,' he said softly. 'Remember it.' He hesitated a moment, then added, 'If it makes you laugh, so much the better. You look lovely when you laugh. And far more important than that, you look confident, innocent.'

She felt a wave of gratitude for his help, both practical and emotional. It banished the present fear, and the dark memories of those she had left behind: Ian, the man in the hotel cupboard she had never seen alive, Jacob, Zillah, who were still in danger, Beimler, who had knowingly sacrificed his life so she could get the photographs out of Germany, a truth that could last for ever, as long as there was a single copy in existence. All working together to make possible her escape to freedom.

'Thank you,' she said quickly, and walked past a group of Brownshirts with a smile, a woman wearing a scarlet dress, and with no cause to fear anyone. She smiled even more widely, conscious of the absurdity of it.

They went to the counter and Walter bought two round trip tickets for Paris.

Elena drew breath to speak. It was an extravagance. Money was precious.

'Return, you say?' the clerk asked.

'Of course!' Walter said in surprise. 'It is fun to travel, but who wishes to live anywhere else these days?' He glanced at Elena for confirmation.

She smiled at him, trying to make it real. Quickly, think of something anyway! The clerk is waiting for your reaction. She deliberately conjured up a memory of Mike looking ridiculous, riding her infant tricycle, and smiled, blinking away tears. 'You leave all your adventures, but you always return.'

Walter put an arm around her.

The clerk smiled back. 'Enjoy yourselves,' he said cheerfully. 'Next, please!'

The Brownshirts at the entrance to the ticket counter did not stop them.

'Well done,' Walter said almost inaudibly.

They walked past a stand selling *Reibekuchen*, and the delicious aroma snared her with a hundred memories. The

322

chief among them at the moment was the man who had so nearly caught her only a couple of days ago. She must make no mistakes. Even one was enough, not only to catch her, but to catch Walter as well. He was risking his life to help her escape, and he did not even know about the pictures of the book-burning. He might guess, knowing her passion for photography, but he had not seen them. And they were gone now, on their way to Lucas.

She forced her mind to the present. She must look as if she knew where she was going. She did not want to meet anyone's eyes, yet she must not appear to avoid them either. She had never even thought of such things before, but this is what it was like to be a fugitive, or one of an inferior station, inferior race, inferior anything! No wonder those so labelled were angry and frightened.

It was getting darker. The station was still crowded and getting more so. She realised she had no idea what day of the week it was. Perhaps it did not matter anyway.

They were twenty yards from the right platform. One more set of guards to pass. There were people ahead of them showing papers. She felt her stomach knot painfully. This was it. The first test for her false passport.

It was their turn.

'Name?' the guard asked her. He was a middle-aged man. He had missed a little bit of grey stubble on his neck when he was shaving. She had to force herself not to stare at it. 'Name?' he snapped again.

'Marta . . .' Her mind was a blank! She had no idea what Walter had told her. She had the passport in her hand. The guard snatched it away from her.

'Marta Lindt,' Walter said, handing over his passport as well.

The guard looked at Walter's passport, then at hers. 'Not Mann?' he said with a smile, glancing at the red dress.

'Not yet,' Walter said with a conspiratorial half-smirk at the guard.

'We're just going for a couple of days in Paris.' Elena smiled directly at the guard.

The guard gave them back their passports and looked at Walter with understanding. 'Have a nice trip,' he said, his look lending the words a world of meaning.

Walter nodded and put his arm around Elena again. 'Thank you.'

They walked quickly on to the platform and climbed the steps into one of the first-class carriages. Elena had not bothered to look at the tickets before. Anything was good enough, just to be out of Germany. Even out of Berlin was a good start. Although, in the countryside, in this dress, she would be as conspicuous as a black fly on a white ceiling.

There was too much to say, and no words were strong enough to convey the gratitude she felt. A weak 'thank you' was almost worse than none at all. It reduced the enormity of the emotion.

They searched for a compartment where there was room for them. The third one along the corridor was empty. They went in and sat opposite each other, next to the window. It was exactly as she had done in the train from Milan to Rome, only a few days ago. So much had happened, it seemed to be part of another lifetime.

Elena had never known Walter before this, and yet he had always been there in the most desperate times and helped without question. Perhaps he was MI6 too? He wouldn't tell her if he was. Ian had only told her when he was dying, and he had had to, so she would finish his mission in Berlin.

Except that she had fallen into the trap set for him and made a complete mess of it.

But even if she did not get out of Germany, the pictures had already gone, and Lucas would know how best to use them. They did not need any explanations. The faces spoke more than any words could. They were fixed in history for ever, the time and the place: the book-burning, the insanity of the attempt to obliterate the spiritual light of an entire culture.

Perhaps that was what Walter cared about?

The train started to move and she relaxed into the seat. It was comfortable, and even quite warm. She might go to sleep, she was certainly tired enough, and as the speed of the train increased, the rhythmic passage of the wheels over the tracks and the gentle sway of it was comforting. They were alone in the compartment, which was pleasant.

She woke up with a jolt, feeling her hands held by the wrists, quite hard. She gasped and pulled away.

'Elena!' It was Walter's voice.

She opened her eyes and saw his face a couple of feet away, filled with concern.

'Were you dreaming? We're on the train to Paris. We're coming towards the border. They'll stop here for a little while. You can stretch your legs if you want.'

'No.' She did not know why she refused. It was a good idea, but she was filled with fear at the train somehow going without her. 'I'm sorry,' she said. 'I was . . . dreaming.'

His face tightened. 'I'm sorry,' he said very gently. 'If there had been any other way of leaving except by train, I'd have taken it. But this is the last hurdle. Once we're in France, we'll be all right.'

'Will we? I know the German authorities can't get us, but they could follow us, couldn't they?'

'They've no authority to arrest us . . .' he began. Then, understanding flashed in his eyes. 'They don't know it's you,' he said more gently. 'If they did, they'd have stopped you in Berlin, not followed you on to the train. Think about it. I know Newton was killed on the train to Paris, but that was . . .'

'Yes?'

'I was going to say ages ago, but I suppose it was barely a week. It seems like longer. I sometimes think counting time is ridiculous. It's totally elastic. When you're exhausted, an hour of sleep is nothing. It's here and gone. But if you're in pain, in a dentist's chair, it's eternity.'

She laughed in spite of herself. 'And if you're waiting for someone, and they're late, then in your mind a hundred different things have happened to them. It only takes once that it really has, and all waiting after that is—'

'Endless. I know.' His voice caught with emotion and he stopped speaking.

She searched his face, perhaps seeing him for the first time as a person with his own life, his own griefs and fears that had nothing to do with her, or Scharnhorst, or any of this. She touched his cheek gently. 'I'm sorry. You must think me terribly self-centred, and you're right. I have been.'

The train was already slowing down. The rhythm was different. She could feel the drag of the brakes on the wheels. Walter sat back in his own seat. She wondered if perhaps, by taking her mind off her own fear and thinking of him, she had made him afraid she would intrude. She would have to be careful not to. There was something elusive in him, perhaps badly hurt. And he had helped her twice now, even at the risk of his own life. She owed him far more than just the sensitivity not to intrude.

They were rolling into the station now. Would they be asked to get off, maybe one coach at a time, to go through the Customs and Passport Control? Or would the officers come on to the train?

She sat back and realised that her hands were clenched. Deliberately, she relaxed them. A diligent border guard would notice that and see it as fear. If she were innocent, she should not be afraid!

The train slowed even further, and a few moments later it stopped altogether. She heard doors slam as people came aboard. They were ordered to stay in their seats. They could get up after they were cleared by Passport and Customs.

It seemed like for ever before their compartment door opened and a uniformed officer came in. He looked at them both carefully. Elena's heart seemed to be beating so violently, he must be able to see her body shake.

'Passports, please,' he asked.

She wanted to look at Walter, but she dared not. The guard would wonder why. The instruction was clear enough. She fumbled in her bag for it. While the guard was waiting, he took Walter's passport, glanced at it briefly, then turned back to Elena. Why was he more interested in her? Was the reason that they were looking for a woman? An ordinary-looking Englishwoman with long, mousy fair hair and dressed in something conservative. She was not that woman. She was Marta Lindt, with short, fashionable pale blond hair, and wearing a stunning scarlet dress!

She found the passport and handed it to the guard with a charming, friendly smile. She was beautiful. All men at least took notice of her, if not more than that. She felt as if she were sweating. Did it show? She was hot one moment and cold the next.

Walter drew in his breath as if to speak, and then changed his mind.

The man closed the passport and handed it back to her. 'Thank you, Fräulein. Is that your luggage? Have you not any more?' There was suspicion in his eyes. A woman dressed as she was must have more luggage than one overstuffed bag.

She smiled at him charmingly. 'Yes, it is. Why do you think I'm going to Paris? I promise you I shall come back with more . . . far more!'

Walter's expression was impossible to read. Elena knew he was trying to look chagrined, and at the same time not to laugh.

The guard did not bother. He laughed outright. 'Get your money's worth, friend,' he said to Walter. And then he left, clanging the door shut behind him.

'Sorry,' Elena murmured.

'Don't be, it was brilliant!' he commented. 'We're free to go now. Do you want to stretch your legs, get out of here for a few minutes?'

She could sense that he wanted to. 'Yes, by all means. A little fresh air.'

She did not realise how close the air was inside the train until she took Walter's hand to steady herself down the steep drop to the platform. It was dark and windy, gusts pulling at her hair and skirt, and far colder than she expected. For the first moment or two, it was even refreshing, and then it was just cold. She was glad of Walter standing to windward of her, shielding her.

'There's a coffee stand over there. Would you like some? It's probably pretty rough, but it'll be hot.'

'Yes, please,' she said, certain that he would, too, especially if it really was hot.

He walked beside her and she kept up with him. There were already at least twenty other people standing uncomfortably, uncertain how to use the brief time before they continued their journey. Some groups talked to each other. Some stood silently, every few moments glancing at the train. She wondered if any of the other people standing in little huddles on the platform were escaping something. Police? Gestapo? Were any of them Jews, going while they could? Leaving behind the people they loved.

She could not read their faces in the yellow artificial glow. Could they read hers?

The train was higher than the platform, its metal sides slightly curved, catching the lights with brilliant sheen. Drifts of steam blew from the train, briefly obscuring the stars.

Walter returned with the coffee.

'Thank you.' She took it gratefully.

'I don't know if you like sugar, but there wasn't any anyway,' he apologised.

She smiled. 'I don't. I grew up unused to it, and now I don't really like it very much.' She sipped the coffee. It wasn't bad. Then looked yet again at the train. People were still getting off further up the platform. That must mean the passport officers were not finished.

There were groups of men in work clothes moving around. Perhaps the steam engine would need coal, more water? They all seemed bent on some purpose or other. She was so nearly safe! The last few moments seemed to drag out with all this activity.

The engine belched steam again, startling her. It was difficult to remain outwardly calm when she was minutes from safety, and yet not quite there. She took several more mouthfuls of coffee. It seemed the border crossing formalities were taking ages, but it could not be so long: the coffee was still hot, even in the cardboard cup.

The passport officers came off the train at the last carriage and she turned to Walter. She did not even need to speak.

'Yes,' he said quietly. 'It's time, for goodness' sake. We are going shopping in Paris, remember?' He looked at her directly and smiled.

She deliberately put on a brave, eager face and took his arm back across the cold platform and up the steep steps, back into the carriage. They found their seats again and within a few minutes there was a piercing whistle, a belch of steam, the cloud drifting around them as they lurched forward once, twice, then settled into increasing speed as they crossed the German border into France.

Walter looked at her. He looked happy, relaxed, as if he, too, had passed a dangerous crossing and was safe on the other side.

'Thank you,' she said quietly.

Elena waited until the train had gathered full speed and was roaring through the night before she stood up. 'I'm going to the cloakroom.'

'Three carriages that way.' Walter indicated the direction.

She nodded her thanks, then set out. They were moving very rapidly now, and it was not easy to keep her balance in the corridor, where there was nothing to grasp. All the compartment doors were closed, and blinds drawn across the windows. People were probably trying to sleep. Her watch said it was half past one in the morning.

The corridor lights were dim. The outer windows were mirrors reflecting only her own face and the scarlet dress. There were no lights outside, no signs of human life at all.

She could see no towns or villages. They could have been anywhere. For that matter, nowhere.

The speed had settled steadily and the rattle and sway of the train were rhythmic, soothing, like the life signs of some medieval beast.

She reached the toilets and was there only a few minutes. When she washed her hands – so careful with the burned one – she glanced at her face in the mirror. She stared at the stranger reflected back at her. She saw a striking woman with high cheekbones and soft, pale hair. For a moment she admired it. It was who she would like to be. Daring, reckless, brave, positive about everything. Then the moment after, she felt ridiculous. Did it really reflect any part of her?

She dried her hands on the towel, then opened the door and went out. It was dark in the connecting corridor, especially after the light in the toilet. She almost bumped into the guard standing there. 'Sorry,' she said in German. She did not dare use English yet.

As if to steady her, he put his hands up and grasped her shoulders.

'Thank you, I'm fine. Just . . . the darkness.'

His hands tightened a little. He was middle-aged, overweight. His face was too close to hers. She tried to pull away, but it was impossible. With a wave of fear, she realised his intention. Her eyes were becoming used to the dim light now and she could see the smirk on his face, on his lips.

'You're very pretty, Fräulein. You must be used to this. You want it? Yes? That is why you wear such a dress. It is an invitation. I accept!' He pulled her a little closer.

What could she say? She did not dare earn his enmity, and yet the thought was revolting! There were empty compartments. He would know which ones they were. At least in the corridor there was the possibility of someone else coming along to use the toilets. She must stay outside, at all costs.

'The second compartment,' he said.

Her mind raced. 'Don't be so predictable,' she said. This was absurd. She was repulsed by the idea, and yet she managed to make her voice seductive. 'A little danger . . . adds spice.'

'A little danger, hey? And do you like to be hurt, just a little, perhaps?' He gripped her arms so tightly it hurt.

She refused to cry out. It might be just what he wanted. 'Only if it goes both ways,' she said, looking straight at him. Was there enough fabric in her skirt to allow her to lift her knee and catch him where he was most vulnerable? Maybe not. She would have to lift it, so as not to tear the silk and expose herself, or worse, find she could not complete the action.

'Both ways?' he repeated, as if the idea puzzled and intrigued him.

'Yes.' She put her hands to her sides, lifted the skirt, then her right knee as hard as she could.

He doubled forward, almost knocking her off her feet. She lost her balance and fell against the wall of the compartment, but she was free. She must escape before he could get hold of her again. There was no one to turn to, and she could scream her heart out in the roar and clatter of the train, and no one would hear. It would be just one more sound in the whine of the wind, and of metal on metal.

At first, she stumbled, losing her balance as a lurch in direction tilted the train, but she regained it quickly and ran in the opposite direction to where the guard was blocking her way to her own compartment, not caring if she bruised herself against either wall. She reached the end of the carriage and fumbled with the doorway to the next one. She could hear the guard cursing behind her. She dreaded the touch of his hand on her shoulder any second.

Nothing moved! She was pulling the handle the wrong way. She pushed it the other way and heaved the door open. It was the guard's van! Full of luggage, but it was the last one on the train. There were no passenger carriages beyond this. No one she could ask for help. No one to even see what happened to her! He could say she jumped, and no one would contradict him.

It could not all end like this! She must hide if she could. There were piles of luggage in here. He could not spend all the rest of the journey looking for her. He must have some kind of duties. And if he found her, she would have to fight! He was coarse, brutish, but he wouldn't kill her . . . would he?

She searched for the easiest place to hide that was not a blind alley. She must have a way of escape. She looked at the piles of luggage and boxes. There were several piled high. *Behind one of those. Not the nearest. But be quick.* There was no lock on the door. Why would there be? It would be on the outside, if there was one at all.

She heard the handle turn and a strip of light appeared on the ceiling as the door opened. He was less than three yards away from her. She could hear him breathing heavily, like an animal panting.

He moved one of the boxes, then another. 'I'll find you,' he said quietly. 'This is the last car. There's nothing beyond here but the night . . . and the empty track! You've nowhere to go, proud lady in the red dress. Think yourself so good? Take that red dress off, and you're just like anybody else.'

333

And without his uniform, he'd be just like any ordinary fat man! But he would not trick her into saying so.

He was closer now, maybe two yards away, and still moving luggage. He was wheezing and grunting from the effort. Once he got hold of her, she would be lost. And in the guard's van, he could do anything he wanted. There was nowhere to run to, and no one to help. She looked around for something small enough to use as a weapon. But people kept their small pieces of luggage with them. Only boxes and valises too big to put in the overhead rack were loaded here.

Where was the tallest pile? Could she knock it over to land on him? She dared not move much. A sound would hardly matter. She could drop a lead weight and no one could hear it above the roar of the train.

She saw the right pile. He would see her movement, but she could stand on the first box, if she was quick, and push the top one over on to him. That might give her enough time to run for the door. She had nothing to lose; he would find her in moments. She climbed on to the nearest box.

He saw the movement. 'Ah! Got you!' He lunged forward.

She waited until he was close enough, then pushed the top box over on to him. It crashed down, catching him on one side and sending him sprawling.

She did not wait to see how badly he was hurt. She bolted for the door and was almost through it when she heard his scream of outrage. At least he was not dead. She certainly did not want to kill him! But she did not want him merely enraged, either. No time to look. She got through the door and slammed it shut, and ran as fast as she dared up the corridor, thrown from side to side by the train careening through the night.

She was almost at the door at the far end, when she felt his hand like a claw on her shoulder. It spun her round, slamming her back against the wall, knocking the breath out of her. His face was less than twelve inches from hers. She could smell his breath, and the sweat on his body. This time, he pressed his belly on hers, and his legs made it impossible for her to kick him. Could she butt him with her head? Bite? She stared into his eyes with all the hatred she felt, for everything vile and tragic that had happened since she first got on any train since Naples. Before that . . . since the body of the man had tumbled out of the hotel linen cupboard.

He hesitated, as if startled by the passion in her.

Next to him, the connecting door to the next carriage burst open, knocking him hard, but only his arm. He swung round, his face surprised and angry.

For two seconds, no one moved. Walter stood frozen, horrified.

The guard was the first to move. He pushed Elena even harder against the wall with his right hand, then threw all his weight behind a charge at Walter, carrying him back through the doorway into the connecting platform between the two carriages. Walter stepped backwards, reaching for the exit doorway and touching the handle.

The guard followed after him, missing a step and staggering. He was far bigger and heavier than Walter. If he caught him, it would be over in seconds. He had the uniform, the authority. What he said would be believed.

He reached Walter and drew back his arm to lash out at him. He could break his neck with a blow that was just right.

Walter staggered against the door, caught hold of it and threw it open, then dived on to the floor. The guard stumbled.

Walter rolled over and used both feet to kick out at him as hard as he could. The guard swayed, arms flailing, reaching for the door handle and missed it. His mouth opened wide as he slipped out of the doorway into the darkness, his scream lost in the night.

Walter climbed to his feet slowly, his face slack with shock. Then the instant passed and he reached for Elena's hand to steady himself.

'Hang on!' She gripped his hand and leaned backwards as Walter grasped the door, still swinging, and slammed it shut. Then he fell back against the wall.

A hundred things flooded through Elena's mind, but none of them contained words that were enough.

Walter straightened up. 'Are you all right?' he said loudly enough to be heard, even above the roar of the train.

'Yes.'

'He didn't hurt you?'

'No, not . . .' Elena took a deep breath. 'No! He made me bloody angry!'

Walter started to laugh, almost as if he wouldn't be able to stop. He pulled her towards him and put his arms round her, still laughing, and buried his head in her shoulder.

She wanted to say thank you, but it seemed wildly inadequate. Instead, she hung on to him with infinite relief.

Chapter Thirty-One

The train slowed down and came to a stop, but they were far short of the platform.

'What's wrong?' Elena asked.

'Probably nothing,' Walter replied, but there was uncertainty in his voice, and he looked around to find the reason for stopping where they could not reasonably get off.

There were a few moments of silence when neither of them spoke. Then the compartment door opened and a guard with an anxious expression regarded them. 'One of our guards is missing,' he said grimly. 'Totally missing! It is a very serious matter.'

'Are you sure he got back on the train at the border?' Walter asked helpfully.

'Why would he get off at the border?' the guard said irritably. 'This is no joke. He has a good job! One a man would want to keep!' He turned to Elena. 'He said he was coming to . . . question you? Is that so?'

Her mind raced over all the possibilities. What could she say that would demand no further response from them? They were so nearly there! They were actually in Paris!

Silence.

Walter leaned forward. 'I saw him, towards the back of the train. He had a bottle of Schnapps. Are you sure he is not asleep somewhere in a baggage car? He was . . . staggering a bit . . .' He left the suggestion in the air.

Elena forced a smile. 'Maybe when you have off-loaded everything . . .?'

The guard shrugged. 'Drunk again! Serve the fool right. If . . . if we found him . . .'

He went out, and after what seemed like ten minutes, but was perhaps only two or three, the train lurched forward again, and then stopped. This time they were beside the platform.

Elena was weak with relief when at last she stepped out of the carriage on to the platform and heard the sound of French voices around her. The few police she could see were gendarmes in French uniforms. Even the air smelled different. It was like a familiar embrace. Paris!

She turned and smiled as Walter stepped down on to the platform behind her.

He took her arm. 'We're almost there. Last leg. You'll be home tonight. Now we'd better get out of here, so they don't connect us with the Berlin train. A cup of coffee, perhaps. It'll be French coffee!'

'Are you still coming with me . . . all the way?' she asked. She wanted him to, too much to dare show it. After the terrible night, she was still more afraid than she wished him to know, or even to acknowledge to herself. There was a search under way for the guard. Word would come soon enough that they had found his body on the tracks. She had no idea where they had been, but definitely in France. It was after they had crossed the border.

'Of course I am!' Walter said, pushing her forward and then walking beside her towards the way out.

She caught his urgency. Once they were out in the street, no one would know they had come in on that particular train. Unintentionally, she increased speed.

'Hold on!' Walter said, a momentary sharpness in his tone. 'Don't go so fast. We look as if we are running away!' His hand tightened on her arm and reluctantly she slowed.

They were nearly there. She must not look back. Head high, she walked out of the station. She had no idea if anyone was watching her or not. The street was already crowded with the early rush-hour traffic. They would be invisible in moments.

Elena tried not to think of the people she had left behind. She could not feel guilty. She was no use to anyone in Berlin, especially dead. But she was still aware with a grinding pain deep inside her that Jacob was there, in Berlin, with Eli and Zillah, helping where they could, a terrible risk. There were people like the man in the camera shop, prepared to lie to save a stranger with pictures of a reality that scorched the mind. And God knew how many now, and yet to be, like Beimler, who would give their lives to fight the darkness she knew now was coming.

They found a little bistro and took a table near the back. There was nothing to say that had not been said already. Their silence continued as they drank dark, aromatic French coffee and ate croissants . . . hot, flaky, delicious.

Elena and Walter returned to the Gare du Nord and went to the platform for the Calais train. They bought tickets and stood waiting, Elena too tired, too emotionally exhausted, for conversation. They still had three more legs of the journey: the train to Calais, the cross-Channel ferry, and then the journey from Dover to London.

Walter did not speak either, but when she glanced at him

she saw the concern in his expression. She forced herself to smile. 'We're free,' she said quietly. 'It's just travelling from now on.'

He hesitated a moment, and she saw a flicker of doubt in his expression.

'Probably,' he agreed. 'But we must still be careful. I'm not leaving you until I hand you over to someone who will take care of you. From what you've said, that's your grandfather. Safer than your father. It would be easy enough for them to find out who he is. In fact, they will certainly know already, and where he lives. For my safety, as well as yours . . .'

'Yes. I'll go to my grandfather's, please. He's anonymous, as far as they're concerned. There are lots of Standishes in London. Probably most of them in the telephone directory. Thank you.'

'Did you think I was going to leave you on a railway platform in London?' He raised his eyebrows. 'In that red dress? I've seen enough of what can happen to you.'

She meant not to let her fear show, but she knew it did – in her face, the clenched hands, the shivering of her body she could not control, no matter how hard she tried.

He reached over as if to touch her hand, and then pulled his hand back again. No words were necessary.

The journey from Paris to Calais was easy, and they had a while to wait for the next ferry, but they would still be in Dover before dark. Once or twice Elena thought she recognised a face in the crowd, gestures, attitudes she had seen before, but she said nothing, even when she caught a look on Walter's face, as if he, too, had noticed.

She was tense going through Customs and Immigration,

and apologised to the officer when she dropped her passport out of nervous fingers. 'Not much sleep,' she added.

He made no comment, and she passed through the barrier drenched in sweat and shivering with relief.

'Is that all your luggage?' the Customs officer asked her incredulously. The red dress did not fit the image of a woman who travelled with nothing extra, hardly even a change of underclothes.

Her mind raced. 'It was mislaid,' she said quickly. 'I'm sure they'll find it, and then send it on after me. I'm going home, so I shall be all right.'

He opened her bag and searched it. 'Nice camera,' was all he said. He closed the bag and handed it back to her, shaking his head.

She had no idea whether he believed her or not. It did not matter any more.

Walter had arranged to hire a car. He told Elena he had wired from the Paris railway station. It was waiting for them, and they took charge of it and set out on the road inland. The last leg home.

There was traffic out of Dover, but soon they were clear of it, and the wide, pale evening sky was fading, shadows lengthening across the road. The air through the open window smelled sweet.

Neither of them spoke. Perhaps Walter was as emotionally drained as she was and, like her, might find it hard to believe that the adventure was nearly over . . . at least for them. Germany was behind them.

She directed him when he asked, but most of the road was plainly signed, and she had told him the general area. It was comfortable to be silent. The night darkened, but outside the air was still warm.

341

She was wondering how much she could tell Lucas. Had the photographs arrived yet? What did he think of them? Would he know how they could best be used? In fact, were they as good as she thought? Would he berate her for being stupid? Not if he knew what the stakes really were. Not if he had seen the violence, the fear, the hatred. Sitting at home, safe in England, he couldn't even imagine it, though everyone knew the loss of war, the carnage, the crippling of mind and body that went on and on . . . all life long, for some.

But did they really know the alternative? The humiliation, the terror and the shame? The corruption of all you thought you believed in, when the gun was pointed at your head? Or at the head of someone you loved more than your own life? Was there nothing so precious you would not pay the final price, rather than betray it? Most of us live and die without ever having to find out. But Elena had seen it too closely to plead ignorance any more. How could she tell Lucas that?

Walter swung the car round the corner. 'Somewhere along here?'

Her attention snapped back to the present. 'Yes . . . yes, we're home, next house.'

Walter drew the car up against the kerb, familiar to Elena even in the near dark. The curtains were closed, and there was no light visible from the windows, but the lamp was lit over the front door.

She turned in the seat and smiled at Walter, overwhelmed with gratitude and, at last, peace. 'Please come in and have something to eat. Stretch your legs. I expect you want to get to wherever you're going, but if you don't, you'll be welcome to stay the night, and then go on in the morning.'

'I don't think so, not now. But thank you, I do need to straighten my back. I don't know if my driving scared you, but it certainly scared me.' Without waiting to see her acknowledge it, he opened the driver's door and climbed out, moving a little awkwardly for a moment, and then easing himself to stretch. 'I'll get your bag.'

She climbed out of her side before he came round to open it. It was a relief to stand. She turned to make sure he was following her, and saw him close the boot, her bag in his hand. She walked slowly up the front path, intending to push the doorbell, but the door opened before she reached it and Lucas stood on the step under the light.

She had never seen anything more welcome in her life. He represented everything that was bright and good and safe, everything that was worth fighting for, and being the best you possibly could. She could not recall his ever saying 'I love you', yet it was the one thing she had never doubted in her whole life.

'Hello, Grandpa,' she said almost steadily. She gave a brief glance over her shoulder, then back again at Lucas. 'This is Walter Mann.' She would tell him all the rest later – maybe.

Lucas smiled, and for a moment his face filled with intense emotion, then looked beyond her to Walter. 'How do you do, Walter?' He gave a slow, charming smile. 'We're very grateful. Would you like to come in and have a cup of tea, or even a meal? If you're in a hurry, we understand, but it would be nice if we had a chance to express our gratitude.'

Walter stepped forward to be just behind Elena. 'Thank you, sir. That would be very kind. A cup of tea that wasn't made by the railway would be wonderful. I don't want to put you to any trouble.'

'Not at all, come in.' Lucas stood back, pulling the door wide open, and Elena and Walter followed him into the hall, Walter still carrying the bag.

Josephine was coming forward from the drawing room, arms wide. She hugged Elena so hard that, for a moment, it actually hurt.

'Lavatory is at the top of the stairs, straight ahead,' Lucas continued to Walter. 'How about a decent sandwich? We've got cold roast beef? A little French mustard, or the hot English stuff, if you prefer?'

'French mustard is excellent, sir,' Walter replied, showing the deference due a man two generations older than himself.

Elena stepped back, now overwhelmed with relief, and turned to Walter. She wanted to show him something of the gratitude she felt, and to make sure he was comfortable, that indeed he felt welcome. He was standing in the hallway looking a little confused, almost as if some deep emotion stirred him. She realised that she had told him that this was her grandparents' house, but she had not mentioned his full name. How thoughtless of her.

'Walter, I'm sorry. This is my grandfather, Lucas Standish, and my grandmother, Josephine.' She turned to Lucas again. She would tell him the whole story later: how it mattered so deeply that it had changed who she was, and who she must be from now on. But she should acknowledge at least some of it, so he knew now how much she owed Walter. 'Walter rescued me from one or two unpleasant situations. And then he drove me here from Dover. He's an economic journalist.'

Lucas regarded Walter with considerable warmth. 'Then we are doubly grateful to you.'

Josephine's face was alight with pleasure. 'And we are happy to offer you anything you care for,' she said warmly. 'After roast beef sandwiches, I have an apple pie and cream. They're last year's apples, of course, but they store very well.'

Walter smiled, colour rising up in his face. He looked tense, as if his shoulders were stiff, but he had driven a long way, and sometimes at dangerously high speeds. Elena saw that he was exhausted.

'Thank you,' he said a little awkwardly. 'It sounds perfect.'

Josephine smiled back at him. 'Then I'll get started. Would you like the apple pie warmed? I do.'

'Yes, please,' he accepted. But he did not look as if she had put him at ease. Rather the contrary.

'Top of the stairs,' Elena reminded him, smiling also. 'We'll be in the drawing room.' She pointed to the nearest door.

Walter put down Elena's bag and went up the stairs.

Lucas led the way to the long-familiar drawing room with its blue curtains and the arch where the dividing wall had been removed, so the room ran the full length of the house. At the far end, there was a second fireplace and French windows opening on to the garden. This was the house where Elena had been born, and she still felt bone-deep that this was home. There was the copy of a Delft painting over the fireplace, all in deep blues and greens, shadows and light on water, the outlines of ships resting in the harbour, the ghosts of buildings behind them. No one pretended it was the original, and she had seen many among the world's great paintings, but none she loved as she did this one.

There was a small fire in the hearth. Even in May, the weather growing warm, there was still a coolness in the air after sunset.

Now that they were alone, Lucas looked at Elena more closely. If he even noticed the scarlet dress, he made no comment on it.

'Are you all right?' he said gravely.

'I will be,' she replied to the far deeper question. 'I've got a burn on the back of my hand and a few bruises, but otherwise I'm not hurt, just tired . . .' She left all the rest of the fear and pain unsaid. She would tell him about it later. 'It's . . . bad in Berlin. The books . . .' She gave a little shrug. 'Later.'

'I know about the books,' he said. 'And I got your photographs. We'll talk after Walter's gone.'

When Walter returned, Elena went upstairs to find the ointment to put on her hand, and a clean bandage. The burn looked angry and sore, as indeed it was. Tomorrow, she might see the doctor, but for tonight anything was bearable. She was home. Safe.

At least the photographs were here, and in a way that was all that mattered.

Downstairs again, she went into the kitchen and began to take cutlery out of the drawer.

'You don't need to do that, my dear,' Josephine said briskly. 'It'll be a little while yet. I have to heat the pie slowly or it will burn. Go and be pleasant to Mr Mann. I dare say it's your gratitude he would rather have than Lucas's.' She frowned. 'And you look exhausted. It's good to know you're home. You've been rather a long time and we've been concerned. You should telephone your parents and let them know you're back. Margot sent a telegram to your parents to say she's on her way back to London, too, with interesting news.' She looked at the bread, butter, beef and mustard sitting on the kitchen table. 'I think I'll start the sandwiches now.'

Elena went into the hall and telephoned her parents, assuring them she was well. She would decide how much to tell them later, perhaps tomorrow. Her father had asked her several questions, but she had pleaded exhaustion, and promised to tell him the details when she saw him. That was a promise she did not intend to keep. It would worry him far more than necessary, and she did not want to relive it.

In the drawing room, she found Lucas and Walter deep in conversation. They were talking about something during the war. She had been nine when it started. She could quite clearly recall the golden summer just before. *The end of history and the beginning of modern times*, Josephine had called it. Walter was about her own age. His memory must be like hers, all the emotions of war, the fear and the loss, but he was too young to have fought. Mike, five years older than Elena, was only just old enough for it to be required of him, although she knew there had been boys as young as twelve who had lied about their age and volunteered by 1918.

Both men looked around as she came in, closing the door behind her. Walter stood up. He moved awkwardly, as if his body was so tight that he was almost locked into position, and his face was flushed with some kind of emotion that he could barely control. He kept his right hand by his side.

Lucas watched, his face tense also. 'Perhaps you should go and help your grandmother in the kitchen?' he suggested to Elena, looking very directly at her, his eyes clear blue, light as the sky.

What was wrong?

'Grandpa . . .' she began.

Then Walter was half behind her, and suddenly his left arm was around her, just above the waist. 'No, I think you should stay here,' he said quietly, his voice utterly changed. 'It's been many years in coming – since 1917, in fact – but now it is time.'

Lucas started to rise to his feet.

Walter's arm tightened around Elena, and his right hand was near her neck.

She felt the very slight prick of a knife blade at her throat. She fought against believing it, but now her body was drenched with fear. 'Who are you?' she asked, her voice cracking. He had changed utterly! The friend who had helped her in the worst times had vanished, leaving a stranger behind.

'Walter Mann! I told you! Well, Walter Mannheim, actually. Ask your grandfather. See if he remembers Richard Mannheim, my father!' He said the last words so choked with emotion they were almost indistinguishable.

Silence filled the room. One second, two seconds.

'Better still,' Walter continued, 'ask your grandfather who *he* is! If he doesn't tell you, I will!'

'Walter . . .' Lucas started, then stopped as Walter's hand tightened on the knife handle, and Elena winced as the blade pricked her again, and a slight trickle of warm blood slid down her neck.

'Be quiet!' Walter snapped. 'I'll tell her. Your grandfather was head of MI6 during the last part of the war. Spymaster general. A man whose power was secret, complete and unanswerable to anyone. He could order a man executed, and it was done.' His voice was growing thicker with emotion, and higher in pitch. 'Someone made a mistake and my father, Richard Mannheim, one of your grandfather's men who risked his life over and over again, on Lucas Standish's orders, was blamed for that mistake. And Lucas Standish accused him of being a traitor and had him hanged! Hanged . . . by the neck . . . jerking and twitching on the end of a rope . . . until he was dead. Because he could! He didn't have to justify himself to anyone.'

Elena could feel Walter's hand shaking, the knife moving fractionally, cutting a little deeper, the blood running.

Walter was so knotted with fury and grief that his whole body was rigid. His voice was unnaturally thin and high. 'Do you know what that's like? Do you? Have you any idea at all what he suffered? The betrayal by the one man he trusted?'

'Walter,' Lucas began. 'Let Elena go. It's not her fault.'

'Shut up! Was it my fault? You killed my father in the most hideous disgrace imaginable. A traitor! You hanged him like a criminal! My father! Do you know what that was like for me? It's not Elena's fault . . . of course it isn't! She didn't even know. You committed all your acts anonymously, where no one could find you. You didn't care what you did to my father's family, to my mother, to me! Yet you expect me to care what this does to Elena, or your wife? Why?'

'Kill me, if you think it will make you feel better, but leave Elena—' Lucas began.

Walter laughed, a harsh, raucous sound, ugly in its pain. 'Idiot! I'm going to kill all of you! Elena first, so you can watch her fear, watch all that beautiful, passionate life slip out of her . . . watch her struggle . . . and lose it . . . knowing it was you who took it. And you will be blamed. I prefer to see you suffer for it, see you try to explain how it wasn't you, and be condemned anyway, and then hanged. But that isn't possible, because you might talk your way out of it. I expect you've still got friends. You could still be part of MI6, for all I know, although they didn't rescue Elena in Germany! I did! I did – after I killed Newton.'

Elena was stunned. That was one thing she had not even thought of, but now that she heard it, the pieces all came together in her mind with a sharp, cutting reality.

'I sent him on a wild-goose chase, all the way from Amalfi to Berlin, to stop them from killing Scharnhorst. He thought it was your orders. I killed his contact there, so he couldn't check. But then I met Elena – sweet, trusting Elena – at the hotel, and I heard she was your granddaughter. So, I killed Newton, because I knew she'd be all quixotic and take over his task – and she did.'

Elena tensed, trying to struggle, but he held her too tightly.

Lucas's eyes darted round the room, as if trying to see any way of distracting Walter.

'Don't!' Walter said between his teeth. 'It will take one movement to cut her throat.'

Elena froze.

'She went to the British Embassy in Berlin,' Walter continued, 'to tell them there would be an attempt on Scharnhorst's life, but they did nothing about it. Did you know that?' He was talking rapidly now, almost stumbling over his own words. 'They betrayed you! Your own man in Berlin betrayed you. I killed Scharnhorst and put the rifle in Elena's hotel room. She went along like a good little English girl and did all I wanted her to.'

He tightened his grip until she flinched. 'Pity. I quite like her, but she's your granddaughter, the one you love the most. Perhaps you love her as much as I loved my father? What do you think, eh?' His hand tightened. 'There's a symmetry to it, you know. She was an obedient little puppet, except that I lost her for a while, after the assassination. She went to ground in Berlin, but I found her again. She couldn't resist coming out for the book-burning, with her Jewish friend.'

Elena tried again to alter her weight so he would have to change his grip. He yanked her hard, closer to him. 'Enough talking! I needed you to know, because there's no justice if you don't know why your family's going to be killed before your very eyes, and you are going to be blamed for it.' He moved the knife a little higher and cut across Elena's cheek.

Lucas's face was ashen. 'Do anything you want with me . . .' he began.

Elena had always loved Lucas more than anyone else. No reason that she knew of, it was simply so, and she would protect him at any cost. Without giving it any thought, she put her right hand forward, then jerked her elbow back as hard as she could, straight into the soft spot beneath Walter's ribs. As his grip on her eased for an instant, she pulled away and swung around, lifting her knee into his groin. She lost her balance and fell to the floor on her hands and knees, as Walter lifted his foot to kick her. It could have landed in her face. Except that there was a crack of gunfire from somewhere near the door and Walter fell on top of her, with blood gushing everywhere.

Lucas lunged forward, dropped to his knees and grasped her, pulling her free.

She wiped her hands across her face and they came away covered in blood. She stared towards the doorway where her grandmother was standing, very still and very pale, with a heavy Luger pistol in her hands, now pointing at the floor. Elena looked at Walter. His head was almost unrecognisable. It was hideous, a mass of blood and bone.

Lucas's arms tightened around her. 'Don't look,' he said quietly. 'He's not there any more. That's just what's left of who he used to be.' He turned towards Josephine.

She was beginning to tremble, and very slowly she let the gun slide to the floor.

'How did you know?' Lucas asked.

'I came to see if you'd like tea straight away,' she replied, 'and I heard him talking. I knew where your gun was.'

'Did you? I never told you I even had it!' His voice dropped. 'Are you all right?'

She was shaking visibly now. 'Lucas, I don't need to be spoon-fed. I fought in the war, too, and some of it was nasty.' She left the gun where it had fallen and walked over towards Elena. She looked at her anxiously. 'I'm proud of you, sweetheart,' she said quietly. 'We've got to bandage that cheek and clear all this up. I don't think any of this is something we want to report to the police.' She held out her hand.

Elena took it and got to her feet rather clumsily. She looked at the red silk dress that she had been so proud of. She wasn't ever going to be able to wear it again, nor would she want to anyway. She felt a little dizzy. Her whole world, the safety she trusted so long as she could remember, was changed. Her grandmother had just shot Walter, who had intended to kill them all. She turned to face Lucas. He looked exactly the same as he always had, but how could he be?

'I'm sorry, my dear,' he said quietly. 'Very sorry indeed. Now come upstairs and get that dress off. We'll get you into something clean and attend to those cuts. Come on.'

She was battling tears and losing. She felt them slide down her cheeks. 'It's just . . .' She looked at him and shook her head. He seemed exactly the same, the blue eyes, the grey hair thinning now, the gentleness that went back to her very first memories. 'Nothing is what I thought it was.' She could barely form the words. 'In Germany, or anywhere, not . . . not even here.'

The grief was intense in his face, and what, she realised with amazement, was the fear that she would reject him. She stepped over Walter and put her arms around her grandfather.

He had square shoulders, but he was always thinner than she expected. She held on to him as tightly as she could and felt his arms go completely around her.

It was Josephine who broke the moment. 'What are we going to do about this, Lucas? Shall I call that nice young man you speak to so often?'

'What?' Lucas was startled.

'We need help,' Josephine said more clearly. 'Shall I call Peter Howard?'

'Do you—'

'I know where his number is,' Josephine reminded him. 'He gave it to me if ever I were in real trouble and you were not here. And I think this is about to become real trouble.'

'Yes, please.' Lucas pulled away from Elena. 'You need to change out of that dress.'

'Get rid of it,' Josephine interrupted from the door. 'Go upstairs and change into something of your own, now! We aren't expecting anyone, but don't waste time. I'm going to tell Mr Howard what happened and request that he come over immediately, with whatever equipment is necessary. I hope we can save the Turkish carpet.' She went out of the room after picking up the gun from where it lay on the floor.

Lucas took Elena upstairs to the bathroom and very gently, and surprisingly efficiently, cleaned the slight mark on her throat and the deeper one on her cheek. She could not see what he was doing, but it eased the pain quite a lot and it stopped bleeding. Then she went into her bedroom and took off the red dress and put on a far less glamourous one of her own.

When she came down Lucas was waiting. 'Are you up to this?' he asked grimly. 'Would you rather stay in your room while we deal with Walter Mann?'

'Yes, of course I am! I'll help. I was interrogated by the Gestapo, and I escaped from them, and I didn't tell them anything about who helped me in Berlin. Of course I'm up to it!'

Lucas looked at her steadily for a moment, then accepted what she said.

She looked down at Walter. He seemed smaller, now that he was lying crumpled up, and there was no one inside his body any more. 'The people in the photographs I sent, they look half human, half something unreachable. They were dancing and laughing. What can you say to people like that?' She looked up at Lucas intently, needing to hear his answer.

Lucas jerked her back to the things that mattered. 'Your photographs are superb . . . and terrible,' he said softly. 'I wish I could tell you it's going to get better, and there won't be another war, but I don't think that's true. I also can't tell you that I won't fight against this new madness in every way I can. That wouldn't be true either.'

She nodded very slightly. 'I know. I'm going to fight, too. I'm scared stiff of them. But I know it's real. I'll tell you about Jacob, the Jewish friend Walter referred to. He's still in Berlin.' She looked at him steadily, searching his face, his eyes. 'I can do something, can't I?'

'Yes,' he said simply. 'You already are.' He moved towards the door. 'Now come on, we can't leave all of this to your grandmother. Right now, we need to start clearing this up. See how bad the damage is to the carpet.'

'People are being murdered in Berlin!' Her voice was suddenly out of control. 'Old people, women and children! What the hell does one bloody carpet matter?'

'It matters that we remove all trace of what happened here,' Lucas said firmly. 'Spies operate in secret, Elena. Once everybody knows who they are, they're useless. We'd better be busy doing what we can until Peter gets here. He'll remove the body and probably my gun. No one should be able to find it here. I'll have to get a different one.'

She said nothing, but drew a long, shaky breath, crushing down her feelings until she was in control again.

Josephine came back with a bucket of water. First, they rolled Walter's body in an old picnic blanket, and then they worked for a hard twenty minutes to wash all the blood they could out of the Turkish carpet, which was fortunately a dark red and blue pattern.

Josephine took the bucket away to empty and brought back a tray of tea and insisted they each have a cup. 'We'll eat later,' she told them. 'Need to keep our strength up,' she said calmly. 'And you do know that you will tell your parents nothing of this, don't you?'

Elena stared at her.

'They know now of your grandfather's position during the war, but less of mine. But it is totally necessary that we keep this from them, do you understand? It's not fair or sensible to bother them with it. We each have our own load to carry, and our own secrets.' She reached across and pushed a stray strand of hair off Elena's forehead. 'You are now one of us, my dear, no longer one of them.'

Elena knew it was true. Perhaps she had known it since the night of the book-burning, but it was different hearing someone else say it, someone who had known her all her life. But she was prevented from replying to this immense statement by a ring on the front doorbell.

She froze.

Lucas climbed to his feet and went out into the hall to answer it. Nothing in his demeanour betrayed that there was a dead man lying in a blanket on the drawing-room floor, and his granddaughter had a plaster on her cheek and on her throat where that someone had intended to cut it.

Josephine sat motionless, her body strained with tension.

There were voices in the hall, Lucas's and another man's. Then the drawing-room door opened and the man came in, fair haired, his face unremarkable. He moved with a certain grace.

Elena felt a wave of horror engulf her. It was the man from the *Reibekuchen* stall outside the Embassy in Berlin. The man she had left slumped unconscious at the base of the tree. She tried to speak, but the words stuck in her throat.

'Elena,' Lucas said, 'this is Peter Howard. I sent him to Berlin to get you out, but you rather got the better of him.'

The man looked at her with faint, rueful humour. 'How do you do, Miss Standish?' he said, extending his hand.

Slowly, still shaking, Elena put her hand out and took his. It was firm and strong. 'How do you do, Mr Howard?'

FOR MORE FROM ANNE PERRY, TRY

THE THOMAS PITT SERIES

_____

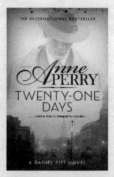

AND THE DANIEL PITT SERIES

_____

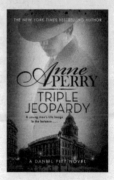

_____

GO TO WWW.ANNEPERRY.CO.UK

TO FIND OUT MORE

DISCOVER THE
WILLIAM MONK SERIES

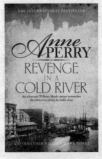

THE FACE OF A STRANGER

A DANGEROUS MOURNING

DEFEND AND BETRAY

A SUDDEN, FEARFUL DEATH

THE SINS OF THE WOLF

CAIN HIS BROTHER

WEIGHED IN THE BALANCE

THE SILENT CRY

THE WHITED SEPULCHRES

THE TWISTED ROOT

SLAVES AND OBSESSION

A FUNERAL IN BLUE

DEATH OF A STRANGER

THE SHIFTING TIDE

DARK ASSASSIN

EXECUTION DOCK

ACCEPTABLE LOSS

A SUNLESS SEA

BLIND JUSTICE

BLOOD ON THE WATER

CORRIDORS OF THE NIGHT

REVENGE IN A COLD RIVER

AN ECHO OF MURDER

DARK TIDE RISING

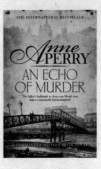

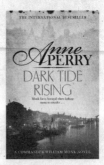

GO TO WWW.ANNEPERRY.CO.UK
TO FIND OUT MORE

DISCOVER FESTIVE MYSTERIES
FROM THE INIMITABLE
ANNE PERRY

THRILLINGLY GOOD BOOKS FROM CRIMINALLY GOOD WRITERS

CRIME FILES BRINGS YOU THE LATEST RELEASES FROM TOP CRIME AND THRILLER AUTHORS.

SIGN UP ONLINE FOR OUR MONTHLY NEWSLETTER AND BE THE FIRST TO KNOW ABOUT OUR COMPETITIONS, NEW BOOKS AND MORE.